I0822765

MATT LEGEND: Veil of Lies

D. W. Mills

DEDICATIONS

To Debbie, Matt, Scott and Stephen, my inspiration.

Special thanks to Susan K. Varesko for your encouragement, moral support, brainstorming, wisdom, advice and faith but most of all for getting the whole *The World Needs Dreamers And The World Needs Doers But Above All The World Needs Dreamers Who Do* thing.

To my good friends Ben and Sue Uribe.

To Abeba, the messenger.

To the totally awesome high school, middle and elementary school students, faculty and staff of the Modoc Joint Unified School District, Alturas, California, and the fabulous staff of the Modoc County Library in Alturas.

To the memory of F-16 driver 1st Lieutenant Scott Trapp, United States Air Force, who did it right.

To the memory of James V. Forrestal, the first United States Secretary of Defense and former Secretary of the Navy. A good man.

To the memory of Wu Yongning. Some people risk a little, some people risk a lot. A brave few risk it all.

And last and least, to those the Outer Barrier is for – your time is nigh. Good riddance.

No animals were harmed in the writing of this book although a great many trees met an untimely end.

ISBN: 978-84-09-03703-2 (Paperback)
ISBN: 978-84-09-03809-1 (Hardcover)
ISBN: 978-84-09-03808-4 (eBook)
ASIN: B07KPDRZX7 (audioBook)
ISBN: 978-17-99-76137-2 (CD-ROM)

Editor: Shelby Villnow

Front cover photography by:
Paul Nicklen/National Geographic Creative

Book design by: Matt Legend LLC

Audiobook Narrator: Vivien Swain

Printed and bound in the United States of America
First printing edition 2018

Matt Legend LLC
California USA
www.mattlegend.com

En-Dor
[a dire warning]

THE ROAD to En-dor is easy to tread
For Mother or yearning Wife.
There, it is sure, we shall meet our Dead
As they were even in life.
Earth has not dreamed of the blessing in store
For desolate hearts on the road to En-dor.

Whispers shall comfort us out of the dark –
Hands—ah God!—that we knew!
Visions and voices – look and hark! –
Shall prove that the tale is true,
And that those who have passed to the further shore
May' be hailed – at a price – on the road to Endor.

But they are so deep in their new eclipse
Nothing they say can reach,
Unless it be uttered by alien lips
And framed in a stranger's speech.
The son must send word to the mother that bore,
'Through an hirelings mouth. 'Tis the rule of En-dor.

And not for nothing these gifts are shown
By such as delight our dead.
They must twitch and stiffen and slaver and groan

Ere the eyes are set in the head,
And the voice from the belly begins. Therefore,
We pay them a wage where they ply at En-dor.

Even so, we have need of faith
And patience to follow the clue.
Often, at first, what the dear one saith

Is babble, or jest, or untrue.
(Lying spirits perplex us sore
Till our loves—and their lives—are well-known at En-dor).

Oh the road to En-dor is the oldest road
And the craziest road of all!
Straight it runs to the Witch's abode,
As it did in the days of Saul,
And nothing has changed of the sorrow in store
For such as go down on the road to En-dor!

— Rudyard Kipling

TABLE OF CONTENTS

FACT AND FICTION

This book is based on actual historical and archaeological events no matter how strange they may seem, though it uses fictional events, places and characters.

Chapter 1 – BANISHED

MATT LEGEND didn't choose a life of fighting demons. It chose him. Before that he was just a normal everyday teen if there is such a thing which is doubtful.

We live in a strange and mysterious world. We think we know so much about it but we know so little. For instance, did you know there is a barrier around our solar system? That's right, a barrier — an energy barrier through which nothing is allowed to pass – nothing living that is, apart from the beings that put it there. First encountered by Voyager 1, it isn't something your science teacher will know anything about. Only a few deep inside the blackest, scariest, super-secret government agency you've never heard of and never will. It sounds like science fiction only it's real. The barrier was put there for a reason. A reason four kids are about to discover, but not in a good way . . . in a kick you in your gut, drag your body down the street and stuff it in the dumpster kind of way. A barrier is to keep something bad out . . . . or in this case, in.

The beings who put it there are immensely powerful and immensely old – billions of years in fact, and are watching us this very moment and know everything about us down to the actions of one boy. Sometimes they intervene in the lives of those they have a reason to.

Trouble is the entities the barrier was put into place to keep in are watching too. They too are very old and very powerful. And very, very evil. Most parents tell their children monsters aren't real. They're wrong.

Before the world became a place of battling caspers, ripleys and pennywises there was Thousand Oaks, a suburb of Los Angeles named for its many oaks – an idyllic, peaceful place with few cares and fewer worries. A place where a kid could be a kid and wile away the endless summer days any way he or she chose; a place where your room was your castle and where every night the moon and stars put on their shows for free. A place where your only cares were friends, school, relationships, surfing, bikini and swim trunk season, never enough spending money, what the future holds, and parents. It was a carefree place where your friends were your friends – and be they real friends – life was good. Then everything changed.

Matt backed his candy apple purple stunt bike to the schoolyard steps and waited for the signal to begin his run through The Gauntlet, a simulated dry run through zombies, something cooked up by The Valley Boys, a clique of skateboarders from wealthy families with far too much time on their hands.

Lost, angry and alone he adjusted his earbuds and clicked his helmet strap. He pressed his phone's play button, adjusted the volume to pain minus one, gave his friend Venn a nervous nod and steeled himself for the danger lying ahead.

There was something in the air. Truth be told there was coming a series of curious events that would thrust him into the hidden world of the supernatural; one foot in each of three worlds when most people know only one, blissfully ignorant of the others. Those worlds would soon collide ultimately forcing him to choose sides and in doing make nightmarishly powerful enemies.

It was a time of firsts – first kiss, first heartbreak, first seriously bad decision –

Everyone called it Bone Buster. Lying at the end of The Gauntlet, it was a stainless steel handrail which ran down the center of a marble stairwell outside a busy downtown hi-rise on North Oak Boulevard. Matt Legend had been doing some big talking and the day had arrived to back it up – or try at least.

Not being a jock meant having to find another way out of high school invisibility. But in twenty minutes he would more likely than not be lying broken and dazed on its cold hard steps or even paralyzed like Charlie — another victim of Bone Buster. Or he could be a coward and just walk away. But then he would never know. He would have to spend his life wondering. Boys are supposed to be brave. Girls are supposed to be pretty. That's just how it is.

The whole crazy idea was to hop your bike onto it and grind down it on its stunt pegs. Mr. Toad's Wild Ride had nothing on Bone Buster. Its 90-degree bend at the bottom where it turned under the street into the pedestrian tunnel that led to the metro rail was the killer, a maneuver considered by everyone to be impossible. But the scariest part was the nasty business which came three blocks before.

A dozen boarders and BMXers had broken thirty-seven bones on Bone Buster and it wasn't even summer yet. The worst off – Charlie – number twelve, the best of them, paralyzed from the waist down, in a coma at New Mercy. She would emerge two months later wiggling her big toe, a good sign, begging her nurses for a Pink's hot dog.

Inseparable since the day they first met at the bike cage when Matt had righted someone's fallen bike to its kickstand. It turned out to be Charlie's. It was a pain having to constantly explain she was only a friend but she was the only one of them who knew all the Starfleet General Orders by heart.

His parent's divorce had left him feeling quite distressed and his mom was constantly threatening to send him to Tennessee to live with his aunt and uncle if he got into trouble again, a place where kids' idea of fun was hanging out on the benches at the local A&W. He could ill afford another school suspension. Except for the fireflies and some legend about a swamp monster the flyspeck of a town was an utter wasteland. And when the wind was blowing a certain direction the Hormel plant made the whole town smell like bacon. And there was that obnoxious brat of a girl next door there who'd had the nerve to challenge him to a foot race. He was still smarting from that defeat.

He studied Venn for the signal.

Three … two … one …

With a drop of Venn's outstretched arm Matt blasted past the veiled tennis courts, dropping through the sloped planter strip's wood chips and scattered Spartina grasses that swayed gently in the waxing afternoon breeze. Behind him Tiffany Zimbalist's desperate cry went unheard – drowned out by *Crack Babies Don't Cry,* 160 beats per minute coursing through his ear buds, a diversion from the agonies of life, a drug that heightened his senses while dulling thoughts of his troubles.

"STOP HIM! That creepoid . . . Hotas," she gasped . . . "He did something to Matt's bike!"

Tiffany was walking past the bike cage after school with a girlfriend when they observed Hotas Clutterbuck bent over Matt's stunt bike with a wrench in his hand looking like the cat that swallowed the canary.

The feud had begun simply enough, with a question. But as with most questions, it's how it's put . . . "So what nationality are you anyway," Hotas had hissed loudly for everyone in the cafeteria to hear, for Matt was a delightful mix of races and nationalities – African-American, Caucasian, Chilean and part Native-American with honey golden skin, light brown eyes and wavy, curly dark brown hair. Matt took in turn to calling the bullying Clutterbuck twins "cluster schmucks" and "garbage trucks" which Hotas and Otis didn't like at all, which led to a slap fight outside the cafeteria and suspensions for all. But that was in the third grade.

"DON'T JUST STAND THERE! DO SOMETHING!"

Venn's call went to Matt's voice mail . . . "Hi, if this is my parents I need money . . If this is a friend I'll get you your money . . If this is a hot girl don't listen to what I said, I've got plenty of money". . . (BEEP) . . .

Matt weaved his way through the startled "zombies" on the busy sidewalk along a block of stores, zipping past an LAPD officer outside a Willy Nilly talking to a skateboarder. "HEY!" the officer shouted as he raced after him. Matt pedaled faster. The monotonous hum of the busy four-lane intersection ahead joined the whir of the drone trailing behind him. Green light or red the point was to make it across without stopping. The foolhardy stunt was undoubtedly what *The Valley Herald* had meant by. . . "before someone is killed." Warily he approached. His heart beat faster.

Sometimes we do stupid things only to stop and ask later – What was I thinking? In the days of fire alarm call boxes when firefighters asked kids why they pulled false alarms the answer was always – " 'cause it's there." Good idea or bad, we each have our own ways of exploring our world. It's what makes us unique, like our fingerprints or our DNA or our biofrequency.

The light was red. Matt shot off the curb. A tired blue Ford pickup piled high with reeking abandoned mattresses screeched to a stop. The acrid stench of burnt rubber galled his lungs. Moments later a sickening dull thud sent the mattresses flying . . .

"1 . . . 2 . . . . . .3 . . 4 . . . . . 5 . . .," the crash counter counted, a plump girl in a yellow hoodie standing on the corner tallying the crashes . . .

Meanwhile the driver of a speeding big rig transporting storefront windows bound for Newberry's department store, behind schedule, distracted, looked down swearing at the *thirsty-four ounces* of ice-cold Mr. Pibb soaking her lap. A terrible screeching was followed by a monstrous crash and the horrible grinding, crunching and rattling of metal and tinkling of glass. Two grungy mattresses dropped out of the sky sandwiching Matt like cheese on toast a blink of an eye before a tsunami of broken glass slammed him to the blacktop.

"Wow . . . bonus points for the glass truck," the crash counter squealed . . . "New record! . . ."

Lying on his back on something soft the stomach-wrenching smell of stale pee shocked him back to his senses. Hefting a mattress filled with broken glass aside he staggered to his feet. He drew in a dazed deep breath. His eyes widened. All around him shattered glass glittered like diamonds amongst a menagerie of mangled vehicles that formed a wrecking yard of twisted metal serenaded by the angry blare of a stuck horn.

In the adrenaline rush it's easy to overlook a little thing like two mattresses falling out of the sky in the nick of time to prevent you from becoming mincemeat. A strange coincidence? Something warm ran down his cheek. Blood.

Like a dead bug the upended jackknifed big rig's eighteen wheels faced skyward tying up traffic in all directions. He mounted his bike and hopped the curb as an LAPD cruiser screeched sideways as muddled drivers emerged like spectral phantoms through clouds of hissing Prestone and the nauseating smell of transmission fluid. His left rear stunt peg fell off skittering along the sidewalk, its ringing drowned out by the stuck horn. Captured by a traffic cam the scene went viral.

"He's crazy," said one girl.

"He's either really brave or really . . . " spouted another.

He had rehearsed it in his mind a hundred times – *line-up, speed, balance. Line-up, speed, balance.*

But there was something he hadn't planned on – sabotage. His phone rang. He ignored it.

He was close enough to Bone Buster to see kids waiting. Nadia would be there with her pink camera . . . line up, speed, balance . . . line up, speed, balance . . .

Adrenaline fueling him he blasted through the sun-filled plaza. To his right the cooling spray from a fountain's thundering wall of water tingled his skin. To his left it was business as usual at a tiny but busy Bank of America branch. Zipping past the fountain through workers heading for home early his bike left the ground as he launched onto the handrail. Time seemed to stand still as he jockeyed the death slide. Balancing like a trapeze artist he disappeared in the shower of sparks created by the ferro rods he had clamped to his stunt pegs, his own brand of special effects. He screeched down the rail which seemed to go forever. Voila! He even managed the impossible turn which led into the pedestrian undercrossing tunnel. The rest was a cakewalk. Move over star quarterback. Suddenly the sun, sky, stairs and handrail all began to rotate. His body armor pressed hard into his back. His body went one way his bike another as he tumbled down the stairs like a rag doll, head bobbing and arms and legs flailing with each bruising step, his bike clattering behind him. With a loud crack his wrist went numb. His crumpled form came to rest on the steps, his bike landing atop him, the loosened stunt peg at his side, the drone hovering over his motionless body.

"Is he dead?" a little girl asked her mother.

Bone Buster had claimed victim thirteen. Nadia Patel had captured it all and posted it on social media. The same Nadia who twenty minutes earlier he had looked up from his locker to see heading for him with her trademark graceful back and forth swaying motion, clutching her books firmly to her top.

For better or for worse there are times when the braver amongst us sometimes venture outside ourselves, who we normally are that is, to temporarily at least, be someone we're normally not. The next day bruised, battered and sore, Matt made a pained beeline for the courtyard lunch table where he knew Hotas and his friends would be sitting. Somebody must have seen him coming because Hotas started to rise. "Lights out loser!" A many autographed fiberglass day-glo green blur swept Hotas' temple leaving him sprawled among the wind-strewn hot tamale and corn dog wrappers. As Matt walked away applauding kids opened a path. A smile creased his lips.

The end of the path revealed Principal Marshall in his wheelchair, arms folded. The smile disappeared.

"Let's go young man." The principal took him by his day-glo cast and wheeled him back across the yard to where Hotas was coming back to life. After paramedics arrived Matt was escorted to the principal's office. The principal's secretary told him to be seated, that his mother was on the way.

He agonized over how she would take it … and her punishment. She was already threatening to pack him off to his aunt and uncle's in Chickasaw . . . a real goose egg. As far from the likes of Southern California as one can get. The whistle stop only had one stoplight. One. It didn't even have a McDonald's.

Wearing robin's egg blue heels and a pleated navy blue skirt and blazer with white silk blouse and golden earrings, Lena Legend was the spitting image of professionalism and wasted no time in getting right to the point. "Matt, what's going on! I get a call at the office about you being in another fight. And some kid's going to the hospital? And a police officer came to my office today. I'm sure you know what that was about. Did you think there wouldn't be consequences?" Her accusing blue eyes blazed as she brushed away a dangling stray blonde curl.

Truth be told he hadn't.

○ ○ ○

Principal 'Hanging Judge' Marshall opened his office door and invited Matt Legend and his mother in. The principal withdrew a thick manila folder from the center drawer of his worn desk. Matt's life of school crime passed before his eyes. There was the time he flew a drone into assembly causing Mrs. Beecher to run swatting and screaming from the stage much to the delight of the student body, ratted out by the girl two seats away. And the time he tried to impress juvenile delinquent cheerleader Vangel Creech. Gorgeous. Fearless. Dangerous. The kind of girl who inspires boys to do crazy things like turning the school's cinder track into a motorcycle track during the All-State track meet to get her attention. Lesson learned – don't crash into the high hurdles.

Twelve weeks of Saturday all-day detention was the cost of that misadventure. It was there he met Rain, the dreamy social media star with a heart of gold – fool's gold. Lots of girls had given him their numbers but he never called any until she came along, that is. It was love at first sight. There is no love like the first love. It is all endorphins, adrenalin and dopamine. It is forever. It was over a week later. The pain was just as crazy. And there was the time he caused the entire school to be evacuated – a tinkerer, he was the kid whose science project burned the hole through Mrs. Bacon's classroom. It would not have been so bad had the pie-size hole not burned clean through the entire school and through the showers of the girls locker room, the cafeteria, the teachers lunch room and the freezer of the Dairy Queen down the street. The device focused sound into a concentrated beam of energy – a saser, a sound laser. The Defense Department promptly dispatched someone to look into its military applications then whisked it away.

"Your incident involving Hotas Clutterbuck is a blatant violation of the school district's new zero-tolerance policy. It calls for mandatory expulsion," the principal began.

Expulsion! Matt gulped.

"You're in deep yogurt son. Your timing's not the best. Last month you'da gotten off with a ten-day suspension. A woman died because of that darn fool stunt of yours, Matt." Matt's face went blank. He swallowed hard. He hadn't heard.

"You've got a monkey on your back," said the principal.

Most monkeys you can shake. Others dig in like an Alabama tick. The principal fixed his eyes on Matt. Matt's eyes welled.

"I can see you feel bad about it. Stuff happens. This doesn't have to ruin your life too. Don't let it. The lady's dead. Nothing's going to bring her back. Certainly not you pining over it the rest of your life. You have to let it go, son. LET .. IT .. GO."

His mother's eyes stayed fixed on her son, never turning them away as she thanked the principal for his kindness.

Blinking back tears Matt sensed the man knew what he was talking about.

"So, your mother tells me you're going to Tennessee . . ."

Chapter 2 – TROUBLE IN PARADISE

Grimm's fairy tales were once considered too terrible for children. What changed?

"WELCOME Y'ALL to Memphis," the pilot drawled over the PA. "Have a pleasant stay and come fly with us again soon."

Fat chance thought Matt as the plane rumbled down the tarmac. His thoughts were on the poor lady his bike stunt had caused an unfortunate demise. They had shown her and her new scrunched-up Mini Cooper on TV. She was twenty-eight. A day care worker whose kids doted on her. They had shown her and her husband and three little children smiling in their matching Christmas sweaters in front of their Christmas tree unaware of the catastrophe to come.

The thought of being away the whole summer in some backwoods crawdad hole was terrifying. It was after all the South – not Southern California — the South. A place where, to a Southern California kid anyhow, they talk in strange dialects and eat strange foods and where people have two first names and listen to strange music. A place where people of color have a history of being treated badly. A place where they had slavery and murdered Dr. Martin Luther King and a whole bunch of other people and where he learned in American History basic liberties most people take for granted had to be fought and died for in something called The Civil Rights Movement. Hadn't he read somewhere about Emmett Till, a black teen from Chicago, murdered while visiting relatives in Mississippi. And George Stinney, a black fourteen-year-old executed by electric chair no less for a crime he didn't even commit.

Matt's father had always told him black peoples' affinity for God had its start in slavery. The wicked slavemasters had allowed the slaves Christianity hoping its non-violent message would discourage revolt. The gift of knowing God was an unintentioned consequence.

His thoughts drifted to the week past . . .

Clucking filled the seventh period hallway. It was Hotas Rapfmussen and his fellow miscreants. It had been a month since he had accepted Hotas' dare – first a dare, then a double dog dare, then a triple dog dare, then a quadruple dog dare that he was too chicken to grind Bone Buster. He had bragged he would be the first to grind the full 256-foot handrail of death. It would have meant equal status with the star quarterback, getting in *Guinness World Records,* maybe even a TV or movie role if he was lucky. *YouTube* fame at least.

"Ignore him. He's just jealous," school heartthrob Nadia Patel had said admiringly. "I heard you barfed all over Mr. Little fifth period. I can't stand him. Can you do it again? *The Invisible War; What Every Believer Needs to Know About Satan, Demons, and Spiritual Warfare.* Good book," she said, stooping low, plucking it from the floor, passing it to Matt. "Nobody's ever made it to the bottom of Bone Buster. If you do, you'll be the first. Here's my number in case you do. If you don't, don't call me." Then with a perfect 9.7-level-of-difficulty hair-flip-with-backward-twist-and-glance at Matt, she turned and walked away. Their eyes had locked. All eyes had followed her as she rounded the corner.

Matt took a deep breath. "I need a girlfriend."

"She's out of your league, man," Venn had said. "Dude, that's *all* you had to say? … nothin' to the smokin'est hot megababe ever? Dude, she's a tenth degree drop-dead-gorgeous trophy babe. No meet me after *Bone Buster*? No whatcha doin' for the rest of your life?' Dude … I'd read that book if I were you. At least next time you'd have somethin' to say to her."

Replaying the scene, Matt had studied the thin book that had tumbled from Venn's locker – *The Invisible War; What Every Believer Needs to Know About Satan, Demons, and Spiritual Warfare.* Venn's monologue on trophy megababeness faded into the din of slamming lockers. Matt's thoughts were on Bone Buster. His stomach was turning back flips but having hurled his Fiesta Chicken Burrito Cafeteria Special lunch all over his world history teacher no chunks were left to spew. Mr. Little had just finished telling the class about World War II and the brave men and women of the Resistance. Members of the Greatest Generation, and how they had risen to the challenge to force the surrender of the Axis powers by which time unfortunately Matt's stomach had already surrendered.

He spoke of brave resistance fighters like 14-year-old Marthe Cohn who spied for the French Resistance against the Nazis; sisters Freddie and Truus Oversteegen who at 14 and 16 took up arms; and of 17-year-old Sonia Butt who became a spy and a specialist in using explosives. From the Philippines to Scandinavia civilian fighters made a stand for everything they held dear so future generations could enjoy what they fought for. Mr. Little told the class never to forget them and be thankful that such people lived to stand up against evil.

With pain Matt's thoughts turned to the photo in the school paper of him and his dirt bike being extracted from the hurdles by the coaching staff. How embarrassing. The student body wasn't impressed either, most notably Vangel's. Done in by love. The things we do for love. Boys wear their scars on their bodies. Girls wear theirs on their hearts. This was his chance at redemption.

His parents had come home from work early one day only to quietly gather him into the family room to break the bad news. There were no raised voices, no yelling, no screaming, no dirty looks – just the plain simple announcement they were getting a divorce. They had seemed the perfect family which made it all the more incomprehensible. Music blared day and night from his three thousand-watt sound system which his friends swore must have been stolen from aliens at Area 51. Anything more powerful would have been weapons-grade. It was an endless source of friction between him and his mother and the neighbors kept awake by its pressure waves. Staying up until two a.m. and getting up at two on weekends had become a routine.

Three days later his mother delivered still worse news.

"Matt, I don't know how to tell you this . .. I know how much you loved your father." *Loved?* Matt held his breath. "*Your father was killed today . . . a convenience store holdup.*" No. It couldn't be. His mind refused to process it. His body went slack as she related something about the shooter and where it happened and being at the wrong place at the wrong time. But he didn't hear any of it. His mind was stuck on the word *killed.* After denial, anger set in.

"This is your fault. I hate you! Dad would still be alive if it wasn't for *YOU!*" He had always suspected she must have done something to drive him away. "I wish *you* were the one dead. I hate you ... *I HATE YOU!*"

His mom started crying. "That's not fair, it's not fair," she cried as she pounded her son's chest with open palms, each weaker than the last. Distressed over her own uncertain fate, she resolved to see Mad Marie the very next day to have her fortune read.

Sitting across the table from Mad Marie in her dark parlor at 15 Spyglass Hill Road, Lena Legend had come to ask questions about her future and most certainly not to waste time answering any. But that's how it was going to be. The irritable old witch was insistent. She would ask the questions that day. She had glimpsed something in her crystal ball. Something which terrified her. A fifteen-year old boy wreaking havoc against the spirit world. The hireling was desperate to know things about Matt. "Why on earth would you want to know about *him?*" Lena had asked. "I came to know about *me*."

"He interests us," was the hoarse reply from the haggard, overweight red-haired medium as she leaned forward to extinguish the butt between her clicking six-inch, scythe-like blood-red-painted nails.

Us? *L*ena worried.

With labored breath the witch exhaled a noxious nicotine cloud at Lena with a vicious stare that sent an icy chill through her DNA. Then the psychic began a conversation – but not with Lena. And not with anyone Lena could see.

Lena desperately wanted to get up and leave but dared not alienate the old witch. So she answered the hireling's questions one by one – all six, even the last, which for reasons she couldn't completely fathom triggered the alarm bells of a mother's protective instinct – "*What does he fear?*"

"What does he fear?" the witch screeched. Frightened, Lena told her – being buried alive in a coffin – a consequence of one too many late-night horror movies. She had betrayed her son to a medium. An agent of the spirit world. A world she feared. A world she did not understand. There was no taking it back.

"Ahhh," the medium smiled.

Us? … "Exactly who is *us*?" Lena had asked trembling. There was only silence.

Chapter 3 – WHISTLE STOP

THE UN-CALIFORNIA-LIKE hot muggy Southern air smothered him like a wet towel as Matt strolled through the jetway into the cool terminal. In a sea of strange faces one stood out sprouting a ginormous pair of metallic blue headphones, a red Pokémon ball cap cocked to one side, a distressed yellow Adidas athletic shirt whose armpits dangled to his waist, crimson cargo pants that stopped just below the knees and a pair of blinding white high-top boats whose tongues hung out like winded bulldogs, his face glued to a phone. The Chase of two summers past had worn only polo shirts with a little elephant on them tucked neatly into his pants and loved singing along to *Little Red Riding Hood* by Sam The Sham and The Pharoahs. He had always gotten a kick out of the howls. Little Red Riding Hood had become *Werewolves of London.*

"Yo cuz, NTSYBA."

"What!?"

"Jus' checkin' if you're one of us dude."

"He's into that text stuff don't ya know... " said his aunt, and he does the tweeter. Honestly, nobody knows what he's saying 'ceptin' his friends."

"*Nice to See You, Been Awhile*," said Chase. And it's Twitter, mom."

"You'll never get a decent job talking that trash," snarled his father, wiping a bit of airport pizza from his chin.

"Heard you got kicked out the crib, man . . . banished from La La Land. Like Romeo and Juliet … 'O, swear not by the moon, the ever-changing moon, that monthly changes in her circled orb, lest thy love prove likewise variable,' " Chase swooned.

"It's inconstant moon, not ever-changing moon," Matt pointed out.

"Whatever, dude."

Uncle Ned worked for a company that made oil well drill pipe. Aunt Nell liked being a housewife. Far different from Matt's friends' mothers and his own, all of whom worked.

Matt and Chase hit it off right away. They found they were interested in much the same stuff – Star Trek, fast-action flicks, cars, massively multiplayer online role-playing games, beats, Bigfoot, and girls or so it seemed at least. Chase was always talking about his friends. Strangely they didn't seem any different from Matt's friends in Southern California. Besides, he was bored. So when Aunt Nell suggested he go with Chase the next day he quickly agreed.

Two pops sounded. "… 106 . . . 107 . . ."

"You ready?" asked Chase.

Matt lowered the pellet gun. "I think that should about do it for the pidgeottos. You're a no-fly zone now . . . flying rats." He cast a final look at the body-littered barn roof.

"Yeah, ready."

A mid-morning breeze ruffled rows of corn beneath wispy cirrus clouds that feathered an azure sky as Matt mounted his uncle's candy apple blue retro Schwinn Stingray and nervously followed Chase onto the shady tree-lined street of towering purple ash trees that ran past the water tank along the railroad tracks. Lush green crops stretched endlessly on both sides in the hot muggy air, a delightful reminder nonetheless of being in a new world. A handful of fields bore stately mansions. A few bore weather-beaten clapboard houses, little more than shacks really which time seemed to have forgotten. Matt wondered if anybody lived in them. Chase swung into the drive of a palatial estate. Had he misjudged the whistle stop?

Through an electric gate they pedaled past the watchful eye of a closed-circuit tv camera and up a brick paver driveway lined with pencil-like Italian Cypress trees which wound to a five-car carriage house. Avocado finials topped towering block granite piers of violet-hued bricks that matched the mansion's whose six-foot-tall lattice windows formed circles and parallelograms that glimmered in the late morning sun. Exotic cars dotted the drive – a black Bentley, a yellow Ferrari, a red Lamborghini, an SUV and a sleek white model the likes of which he had never seen before. Engines, tires and tall rolling black tool chests stood beside a Formula 3 racecar.

It was a hangout house. Kids were playing video arcades, billiards and darts. A girl wearing military fatigues and combat boots sat astride a red Honda dirt bike, cords dangling from her ears. Her light golden blonde sun-flecked pony-tail swished back and forth through the back of her black broad-billed ball cap as she sang *Let's Get Physical* at the top of her lungs like nobody's business and she just didn't care. Even in her orthodontic neck gear she was the kind of girl Matt's mother called a "knockout."

It was love at first sight. Boys are looking for a princess to save. It's in their DNA. Girls are looking for a prince. It's in theirs. She looked like a princess. There was just one problem. She looked like she needed saving like Superman needs an airplane.

Nervously Matt searched for anything he might have in common with this small-town girl. He consoled himself with the thought he was a man of the world, from Southern California no less, a sophisticated megalopolis of twenty-two million, a place where everybody wants to be as he saw it.

Truth be told Chickasaw was a sleepy little one stoplight town with sidewalks only on Main Street and deer that strolled through town whenever they wanted and a movie theater open only on Friday and Saturday nights that never showed anything stronger than PG-13. The quaint town was as far from the likes of Southern California as one could get. There was no dressing to impress. And nobody was running.

The twang of an electric guitar followed a random snare drum roll. Chase dropped his bike and picked up a mike. The garage band rehearsed a hot track with its own unique style of cutting back and forth between English, Spanish and Reggae in a tune entitled *Go Girlfriend,* something they called flip-hop.

"WHO LIVES — " Matt screamed just as the band stopped playing –

" — here?" he gulped.

"The family that owns that field," said the girl in the military fatigues giggling, gesturing to a crop that stretched to a distant windbreak of white pines. A barren mound stood in the distance, a blight on the verdant landscape. It looked out of place. It made him unsettled for a reason he couldn't put his finger on. A puzzling thin beam of dark light rose from it disappearing into a thin gray layer of clouds. The locals had their explanations for it none of which made any sense. In the end it was thought like rainbows. You can't really explain them either. Only the local Tenamuc tribe knew what it was and they weren't talking – not yet anyhow. The tribal elders were still arguing over having been told by The Star People it is no longer forbidden to tell the white man of things they have been forbidden to speak of for more than two thousand years. They were scared that if they got the message wrong a harsh punishment would be meted out by The Star People who they also called "the witches of the world of the dead."

"They're rehearsing for the state fair . . . Hello!"

"Huh, oh . . . Guess there's not much else to do around here," he replied, staring still at the mound.

"Excuse me!"

"Who's your friend Cathy?" asked an elegant lady in a pastel green sun dress.

"Who cares," she said sliding from her Honda casting Matt a nasty look.

"Hi. I'm Matt, Chase's cousin," he said, tearing his gaze from the distant slowly fading beam.

"Welcome to our little corner of the world, Matt," the lady said as she offered a glass of pink lemonade. His taste buds screamed for joy. Southern accents were anything but distasteful too. Perhaps the South wasn't so bad after all.

“Salt tablet?” she offered. Chase gulped one of the pink tablets. Matt did the same wondering what it was for.

“Why don’t you join the other kids out back.”

Matt and Chase trailed Mrs. Kozacky through rooms like the ones in his mom’s *Architectural Digests* until they came to a large balustraded patio surrounded by a golf course. Mr. Kozacky and his portly son, Zak, elbow-deep in a bag of Fritos, stood surrounded by a small group of girls and boys. Reggae blared from speakers made to like boulders.

Mr. Kozacky, a sturdy forty-something former Navy no-nonsense Southern gent with a pencil thin mustache and full head of graying hair, had made his first fortune in tobacco. He had also created the first ever real-life Madden gameplay computerized indoor football field with droids that block, tackle and defend that could be programmed to match the performance profile of any player. After he added soccer, soccer moms and dads began using the centers to instill field vision in their little monsters hoping for the next David Beckham or Mia Hamm. It was said he was busy inventing a wearable drone. Out in the distance on the manicured lawn Matt observed a small jerking triangular red flag.

“Zak, tell Cathy to turn off the music . . . Okay, to call in an airstrike,” Mr. Kozacky began, “the FAC, the forward air controller, must provide certain information to the pilot – call sign, type of target, in this case tank, target coordinates, target elevation, altitude expressed in mean sea level, its 906 feet MSL here, and the location of friendlies. The latter is especially important if you don’t want to get bombed. Any volunteers?”

Matt’s hand shot up.

“Ah, a brave soul. What do they call you?”

"Matt … from California," he proclaimed proudly.

"California!" he sneered. "We'll try not to hold that against you. Okay, Matt from California, guide my aircraft to target."

Matt cleared his throat. "Ah, call sign Matt to pilot … your target's a tank … 906 feet MSL … target in Kozacky backyard" Matt gazed expectantly at Mr. Kozacky.

"Ah, say again Matt, you're breaking up."

Breaking up? I'm standing right next to you!

Matt studied him. He wasn't joking. He wasn't.

He struggled to remember what he'd said . . . "Call sign Matt, target's a tank, 906 feet MSL, target behind Kozacky house." He held his breath . . .

"Ah, roger that, Matt, commencing run. Keep your heads down."

Matt breathed a sigh of relief as Kozacky thumbed his joysticks. A B-52 bomber roared into view. Matt dropped to the patio as the bomber roared low over their heads before turning to make a low sweeping pass across the golf course. As the others laughed at him a bright flash and explosion sent tank parts sailing. A hot flash warmed Matt's skin as the hang glider-size model roared away.

"D'y'all feel that? . . . infrared energy . . . IR," Kozacky beamed, turning to Matt, "You forgot to give the location of the friendlies – us. You bombed us too. We're dead."

"California," someone huffed. Matt's heart sank. Kozacky handed his controller to his son and disappeared into the house.

On their way to the garage Matt and Chase encountered Mrs. Kozacky. "See you boys at the airport? . . ."

“Yeah, sure,” Chase replied, seeming to know what she meant. Matt looked at him quizzically.

“Mr. Kozacky has a World War II fighter plane,” Chase explained. “Forgot to ask what time. Be right back.”

Matt’s eyes drank in the car’s dreamy profile. He raised his phone pondering how a car can be sexy.

“What’s up?” It was GI Jane without her orthodontic neck gear.

“Jus snappin’ a pic for my friends in SoCal.”

“Socal?”

“Southern California.”

“Why the long face?”

“I bombed everybody. We’re crispy critters.” Matt forced a weak smile.

‘Don’t worry. Like hardly anybody gets it right the first time,” the girl giggled. “You like NSXs?”

“I’m not anybody. *NSX? Acura*? It looks European . . . I thought farmers were supposed to be poor.”

“Do we look poor?” she huffed.

Great, that’s twice I’ve insulted her.

We? “You live here?” asked Matt.

“Don’t look so shocked.”

“You said ‘the family that owns that field’ . . . ”

“I was messing with you. I’m Cathy Kozacky. “Wanna see my trophies?”

Trophies? Matt followed the girl along a winding flagstone path bordered with glistening pink wet rose bushes.

“So are you in the army or something?” he asked, eyeing her crimson and gold shoulder patch.

“Young Marines,” she said to his blank stare , , . “It’s like Girl Scouts or Boy Scouts . . . on steroids. ‘Course, I’m prejudiced.”

Prejudiced? Oh no. She seemed so nice. He decided to give her the benefit of the doubt.

“You mean biased?”

“Yeah, biased. Prejudiced means something else. I was a girl scout, too.” He sighed with relief.

They came to an equestrian jumping course dotted with scattered trot poles surrounded by a perfect white fence . . . “It’s not military. It’s a youth organization. Some former Marines started it.” A chiseled palomino sauntered over, its sinewy golden frame rippling with strength. With a nicker the beast nuzzled her hand. She lovingly stroked its neck as she launched into a well-memorized spiel, playfully rocking her head back and forth as she spoke . . . “Its role and purpose is to promote the moral, mental and physical development of its members, to instill in its members the ideals of honesty, fairness, courage, respect, loyalty, dependability, attention to duty, love of God, and fidelity to the United States and its institutions; to stimulate an interest in, and respect for academic achievement and the history and traditions of the United States and the United States Marine Corps; to promote physical fitness through the conduct of physical activities, including athletic events and close order drill; and to advocate a healthy drug-free lifestyle by continual drug prevention education programs,” she said feigning boredom. “I had to memorize that.”

“I’m impressed,” Matt said.

“You should be,” she smiled. “You like horses?”

“Yeah,” Matt replied, hoping she’d ask nothing more to expose his lack of knowledge about them. “What’s his name?” seemed a safe enough question.

“Judge . . . You ride?”

“Ummm, a little.” (translation: No)

The girl gave Judge’s coarse golden mane a final loving stroke.

“So do you get to blow stuff up?” asked Matt over the vociferous barking of a golden Standard Poodle. He bent forward and patted the big pooch’s head.

“Hmmm, Cody likes you. That’s strange. It always takes a while before he likes anybody,” she said eyeing Matt strangely.

“So do you get to blow stuff up?”

“It’s not like that, silly. There’re like rules. No guns, no grenade launchers, no flamethrowers, no blowing stuff up,” she giggled. “Seriously, we do cool stuff like camp, raft, hike, rappel, go on field trips, do community service, learn military history . . . stuff like that. Why? Want to join?”

“Nah, I’d want to blow stuff up. How come you don’t get to blow stuff up? Don’t the Girl Scouts get to blow stuff up for their plastic explosives merit badge?”

“No silly,” Cathy giggled. “Anyway, you just have to be between eight and eighteen. Check it out.”

“Is your brother a Young Marine?”

“Zak? You kidding? Someday he’s going to hack the wrong computer. The FBI’s been here twice already.” They came to a barn. Inside she stopped at a large glass case. The aroma of horses, fresh manure and hay filled the hot sticky air. A sticker read, “It’s my world, you’re just in it.” There were trophies for karate, basketball, soccer, fast-pitch softball, shooting, karting, tennis, fencing, swimming and motocross. There were trophies for archery, equestrian events and a big silver loving cup from a science fair. Every trophy was first place; no seconds, no thirds, no fourths. Oddly every ribbon was blue; no whites, no yellows, no reds. In a back corner of the case sat a small trophy with a broken handle. Matt opened the door and picked it up. He studied it. There was something familiar about it. A drowsy smile played across his face.

“I wondered when you’d remember,” Cathy said. “That was the first trophy I ever won and you broke it. What’s the matter, Alzheimer setting in early?”

“So it’s you,” Matt muttered. “Maybe you weren’t that memorable.”

“I doubt that.”

“I want another race,” Matt spouted.

“I’ll bet you do.”

Zak had a special talent, too – one for which there is no trophy – computer hacking. Something he was very good at.

Matt had one too. He could hold his breath longer than anybody. Years earlier at a Chickasaw pool party in a contest to see who could hold their breath the longest when he didn’t come up after the other kids had popped to the surface his dad dove in fully clothed after him only to find him sitting comfortably on the bottom, cheeks puffed out like a puffer fish's. He had read somewhere the record is twenty minutes and was going for it.

"Those are mommy's," she said, gesturing to a smaller case.

"Your mom has trophies?" he asked, still reeling from her last bombshell.

"Daddy calls her his trophy babe with trophies," she laughed. A trophy with a golden pistol atop caught his eye.

"Don't look so shocked. Girl's rule! How many do you have?"

"A few," Matt said, unconvincingly, unaware he was expected to have any. Where had he been when they were passed out?

"I'm underwhelmed. And the winner ISN'T! . . ."

Matt's eyes narrowed. "What's your problem. Why do you have to be so nasty? You haven't changed."

"Maybe I'm a nasty girl."

"I doubt it. I have you figured for the goody two shoes daddy's little girl type."

"Really! Bless your heart! I have you figured too – ***FOR A MAMA'S BOY***!"

"You don't know me!" Matt snorted. "Bless my heart?"

"And you don't know *me*," Cathy snorted back.

"You were obnoxious when I met you and you're even more obnoxious now," Matt shot back.

There was a dangerous pause.

"So what's your sport then?" she asked.

"Football."

Knockout Rambo Girl turned real quiet-like then said, “Follow me. Let’s she what you got.”

Chapter 4 – FIELD OF BAD DREAMS

BANKS OF OVERHEAD LIGHTS lit, their electrical relays thunking loudly. An indoor football field stood bathed under the lights of the aluminum-sided building. A John Deere green tractor, combine and other farm equipment sat in a corner.

Knockout Rambo Girl plucked a football from a ball cart. The way she juggled it with one hand portended trouble. "You said football's your sport so show me."

This should be interesting, thought Matt.

Walking to a nearby laptop still juggling she punched in a command. A bright X appeared on the synthetic turf.

"Line up. On the X. Flag route. My call."

Three big blue padded dummies wearing smiley faces sat dormant on the sidelines, each on a pair of wide triangular rubber tractor treads. The goal post was two short posts covered in thick red vinyl padding.

"SET . . . ONE, TWO, THREE . . . *HUT!*" Cathy boomed. Matt streaked ten yards, cut to the outside corner of the end zone and looked for the ball

A high-velocity spiral was bearing straight for him. He grabbed for it. It slid through his fingers. Frustrated he retrieved it and threw back a wobbly pass.

"This time go long."

Breathing hard he lined up on the X.

"SET, ONE, TWO, THREE, *HUT!*"

Streaking for the end zone he watched for the ball. He stretched. There it was! It hit his hand and tumbled to the turf. He strode frustrated back to the line of scrimmage.

Post route. On three. This time with the smilodons. Here, put this on." A helmet skidded across the turf.

. . . *Smilo whats?*

The dummies jostled menacingly as their servo motors whirred. A six-foot-six-inch bot whirred across the field and towered over him. *How bad can this be?* he fretted. *It has a smiley face.*

After the count the girl faded back to pass. Streaking for the goal post something big shifted out of the corner of his eye ... *BLUE* . . . then *BALL!* A foot from his nose! In a panic he threw up his hands. It was an amazing catch. And the crowd goes wild he imagined. *She's good. Pro ball material.* He imagined her in a Los Angeles Rams uniform.

He awakened to find Mr. Kozacky kneeling over him speaking a strange language – English. His daughter was standing beside him, beside her a big blue smiley face.

"What happened?" asked Matt.

"You got hit dummy . . . I mean you got hit by a dummy," Cathy giggled.

"What day is it?" her father asked.

"Oc . .to . . ber? . . ." Matt replied frowning to Cathy's unabashed giggling.

"We'd best get you looked at," said her father.

After the MRI scan seemed a good time to call a truce.

"Can we start over? Hi, my name's Matt," he said, extending his hand from his wheelchair in his hospital gown.

"Cathy," she tittered.

"Will you be at the airport?" he asked.

"Been there a hundred times. Next time watch out for smileys," she giggled. "And remember . . . girls rule!"

Had he missed the football trophy?

"Chase, her trophies are all firsts!"

"She uses the others for target practice, dude. She can shoot the leg off a fly from three hundred yards."

What kind of girl shoots up her trophies? Matt asked himself. He knew the answer – his kind.

• • •

At the small wooded airfield the WWII fighter stood tall and proud in the pink rays of the dusk sun. Standing on the wing, Mr. Kozacky cut a dashing figure in his dark green fire-resistant Nomex flight suit hands on hips.

"This is a P-51 Mustang, designed and built in 1940 to win The War – World War Two, that is."

The sleek fighter's polished aluminum skin reflected the dusk sky like a pink mirror. Everything on it looked brand new from its tires to its four-blade propeller the size of the hands on Big Ben. It loomed over the other aircraft like a saber-tooth tiger over kittens. Matt scanned the airport looking for someone.

There were many questions.

"How fast does it fly?"

"How high can it fly?"

"Do the machine guns work?"

"They don't work," a boy proclaimed.

"Actually they do," was all Kozacky had to say about that.

"Isn't that illegal?" Matt whispered. Chase shrugged.

"For those wondering if it's legal or not," Kozacky boomed, "this isn't California."

"Man he's got good hearing!" Chase whispered.

Kozacky patiently answered the questions one by one. Matt proudly proclaimed how his grandfather had been a Tuskegee Airman, one of the famed African-American fighter and bomber pilots during World War II and how he'd flown a P-51 too, except painted with a distinctive red tail and how he'd been awarded the Silver Star for bravery. He told how the pilots, who were called 'colored' back then, won the U.S. Army Air Corps' first ever annual aerial gunnery competition known as Top Gun at the end of the war and how the Air Corps, now the U.S. Air Force, purposely 'lost' the trophy until it was discovered in a dusty warehouse sixty years later by a determined research lady with a cool sounding name, Zellie Rainey Orr, who went searching for it and wrote a book on it and how the trophy is now in a museum. "Interesting," Kozacky beamed. "Anybody who's flown Mustangs is alright with me."

Matt's father had also told him his grandfather, an Army Air Corps captain, had married a pretty Polish girl and how after the war he and his bride had settled down in California. Being a mixed race couple had been a big deal in the States due to its history of slavery though people couldn't have cared less about such things in Poland and most everyplace else with the exception of the Germans, but they had all been brainwashed by Hitler so it figured. They were madly in love and viewed it as just another barrier to be broken. Matt's father, coincidence or not, had also married a white girl which was how boy genius came by his honey golden skin and wavy brown hair.

Matt also told how at war's end his grandfather had applied to the airlines but it being 1945 and because of what Matt called "that Martin Luther King stuff" there were no commercial pilot jobs open to colored pilots despite a wartime service record so exemplary some white bomber crews specifically requested the colored fighter pilots and only the colored fighter pilots fly fighter escort for them because of the way they always stuck with the bombers, never leaving them to take off after enemy fighters ensuring they would get home, not that they didn't want to chase after glory mind you, but they had orders. Strict orders from their colored commanding general, Gen. Benjamin O. Davis, Jr., to stick with the bombers no matter what. Grief stricken, Matt's grandfather became a lawyer working at a law firm which he likened to working at a morgue, the only difference being the customers were still breathing.

A white Tahoe pulled alongside the hanger. Matt's heart skipped a beat as out stepped Mrs. Kozacky, Zak, and Cathy, who had changed to a pair of pink shorts, a matching white short-sleeve crop top and flip flops with a girlfriend in tow.

A belch of black smoke appeared from each exhaust stack as the powerful twelve-cylinder Merlin's heavy melodic rhythm rumbled across the small non-towered airfield like six unruly Harley-Davidsons. It took off and flew a tight circle around the field ending with a thundering fly-by low enough to see every passing rivet.

“He’s never done *that be*fore . . . Can you guys come over after supper? Twenty hundred hours,” Cathy said.

“What’s up?” asked Chase.

“Just a lil’ larkin.”

There was much to learn about this strange place where dinner is “supper,” where people “make a wash” instead of doing the laundry and where larkin’ isn’t bird watching.

“Is he looking?” Cathy whispered to her friend as they were walking away.

“Yes,” her friend replied.

“ ’Larkin?’ ” Matt asked. “Twenty what?”

“It means to play a joke on somebody,” said Chase, “and that’s military time for eight o’clock. Don’t you know anything?”

Matt wondered on who.

Chapter 5 – 29 MESSAGES FROM ET

Conspiracy theories are only theories until the truth becomes known.

MATT'S UNCLE OLIVER had come for a visit. Uncle Ned's kinder gentler term for his older brother was "conspiracy theorist" but otherwise called the stocky, tousled-haired medical EKG machines repairman a nut. That was because it seldom took much to launch Oliver into one of his conspiracy tirades – in this case the six o'clock news.

The tired but sporty balding KALS newscaster/weatherperson/ cameraman/janitor wearing a bad toupee and ill-fitting orange and brown plaid jacket and equally hideous tie, had just finished reporting the weather in his usual monotone. Tiny Chickasaw with its little population of 2,032 had its own TV station only because, Stanley Bogg, the owner of Bogg's Feed and Ranch Supply, the biggest store in town, had figured how to get money out of the federal government. One of the nice things about the little station, being accountable to no one but its advertising customers, was it could air pretty much whatever it wanted. It had to do something after all to get people to watch. It reported the news stories the major networks couldn't or wouldn't air ever since two wealthy families quietly bought up all the world's news agencies and control all the news, something which disturbed Mr. Boggs no end. The newsman was in the midst of a story about a mysterious missile launch off Catalina Island.

“Matt, you live in California. Remember that unsolved missile launch ‘round Catalina ‘round 2010? Remember? Nobody ever found out who launched it?”

Matt stared blankly. He didn’t keep up with the news.

“The military said it wasn’t theirs. Everybody saw it. Heck, there was video of it streakin’ ‘cross the sky. Veterans even said it was a missile. I saw the video. I’ll tell you what it was. There’s underwater UFO activity around there. Tons. Ever hear of the Battle of Los Angeles?[1] LA was invaded that night by a UFO. Google it. You’ll see. And there’re deep submarine canyons there. Only the military has missiles like that. One of our subs shot at a UFO and missed. Missed! It looks like they missed again. You think they’re gonna say, ‘oh yeah, we shot at a UFO and missed’ – heck no. So they just say it wasn’t one of ours. Denial. Like who else’s missile is it gonna be? And did you hear? – somebody sued the NSA, the National Security Agency. They’re even secreter than the CIA . . . secreter, is that a word?”

“Ollie, I don’t think Matt wants to hear about that,” said Nell. “And don’t get so excited. Remember what the doctor said.”

“It’s okay,” Matt said.

“Somebody sued ‘em for documents in 2011. The NSA lost the suit. The judge made ‘em turn over the docs. They had to admit they’ve been in contact with *ET* and received twenty-nine messages.[2] Twenty-nine! Don’t take my word for it. Google it. You’ll see. It’s a fact. Google it – ‘NSA ET Contact.’ The NSA isn’t even disputing it. The media ignored it. If that doesn’t make people sit up and take note nothing will. Ignored it!”

Ollie, finding no audience with his brother and his wife as usual, turned to Chase and Matt. "Google it and you'll see. How come we don't hear about *that*? *That's* what's important. Not suzie starlet slipping on the sidewalk or her tenth divorce. Who needs to know that crap? But you wait, we'll be hearing everything soon. The government's just waitin.' I tell you, they're waitin.' They're gonna come clean. You'll see. The question is when and why. That's what worries me. It's been lies, lies, lies ever since 1947. Now they're leaking gun camera footage suddenly? They're prepping us for the coming big disclosure."

Chase's phone audibled 8:00 pm. Ollie glanced at his watch, a rose gold Rolex Day-Date II President, a gift from a Tongan princess he had guarded on a security detail while working for an executive protection firm in Studio City with a very exclusive clientele. When the job became too stressful it was off to crisscrossing the country fixing ailing EKG machines.

"Gotta run unck."

"You'll see. Won't be long now. That's a fact," Ollie replied. "And while you're at it google 'Malibu Underwater UFO Base.'[3] "

As the screen door slammed Ollie could be heard telling them to read the official NASA Apollo mission control moon landing radio transcripts. "Get 'em. Read 'em. You'll see why we never went back. We were kicked off the moon. Kicked off I tell you. ET's up there, too. Read 'em. You'll see. It's all in the transcripts. Nobody reads the transcripts. We were kicked off the moon. We'll *never* go back. And if the Chinese are fool enough to go, they'll get kicked off off – or worse. And Mars . . .

and Jupiter. And the other planets. Just wait'll you get a load of what's up there.

And ancient aliens weren't aliens."

"You believe that crap?" asked Chase.

"Naw. Only in what I can see," Matt replied.

"What about air? You believe in that?"

" 'Course . . . I'm from Southern California . . . some days you can see it."

Chapter 6 – WHERE'S THE THUNDER?

There is nothing wrong with your television set. Do not attempt to adjust the picture. We are controlling transmission. If we wish to make it louder, we will bring up the volume. If we wish to make it softer, we will tune it to a whisper. We will control the horizontal. We will control the vertical. We can roll the image, make it flutter. We can change the focus to a soft blur or sharpen it to crystal clarity. For the next hour, sit quietly and we will control all that you see and hear. We repeat: there is nothing wrong with your television set. You are about to participate in a great adventure. You are about to experience the awe and mystery which reaches from the inner mind to – The Outer Limits.

The Outer Limits Control Voice

CHASE AND MATT rolled into the Kozacky's driveway.

"Waz up?" asked Chase.

"A witch lives on the other side of town," Cathy said. "We pay her a visit now and then. The last time with toilet paper."

Matt wondered what the Young Marines would think of that.

"Yeah, you up California?" said Zak stuffing a fistful of orange chips into his plump face.

"I'm in. Do you ever go *anywhere* without a bag of Fritos?" Matt shot.

"It's not the same without Bubba," someone complained.

"What happened to Bubba?" Matt asked.

"Oh, something," Cathy replied. "He was in some secret government program or something. He was never the same after that."

"What happened?"

"We don't know."

In the heat of the night six riders swung out onto the dark farm road, their shirts clinging to their bodies in the humid air heavy with the sickly sweet scent of fresh-cut alfalfa and the musty odor of water ions mingled with fresh-turned earth. Lightning shattered the night sky casting crooked branches like celestial fishing nets.

"Look," Matt said, "the Big Dipper. Can't see *that* in LA. Only a star here and there . . . I saw The Rock on Sunset once."

Chickasaw was unlike anyplace he had ever been – every sight, every sound, every smell was new. There is something about nature and the harmony of damp earth and fallen decaying leaves that makes you feel alive. It was sweet, sour and bitter all at once, the most glorious of perfumes. He drew in a deep breath. Being accountable to no one for the first time in his life was intoxicating. Master of his destiny. He was completely on his own. No parent telling him what to do. *I'm free! he thought.* The twinkle of fireflies flittered among the brambles.

A shrill high-pitched whine filled the air.

"Cicadas. They're like locusts," said Chase. "They come out of the ground every thirteen years."

"They're freakin' me out, cuz," Matt said, batting at one of the giant grasshoppers as it buzzed loudly into the side of his head. The air was full of them. It seemed millions of the bulging red-eyeballed arthropods had taken flight. They covered the road, their shells cracking and popping as their tires squashed them by the thousands creating a gooey paste of vanilla-colored bug innards, clear orange-veined wings and shells that clung to their tires and spun into their clothing and their hair.

Past dark fields they pedaled. A crooked flash overhead illuminated the dreamscape. Matt started counting but there came no thunder, only a constant train of jagged streaks of Zeus' rage that transformed the sky into a flickering celestial lightbulb. He stopped counting. Something was wrong. Since the dawn of time lightning has always been accompanied by thunder yet it was discharging its terawatts without as much as a peep. Slowly it moved on.

The cool air from an irrigated field offered a brief respite from the heat. Matt marveled at the soft green flying LEDs. He reached for one forgetting the silent thunder.

"They don't have *those* in California." The voice was Miss Young Marine's over the monotonous brush of brake pads against a rim in need of truing.

"I think I'll take some back with me."

"I'm sure TSA will love that," Cathy laughed.

"Are you in 4-H?" asked Matt, expecting to impress her with his awareness of the rural youth organization few city kids have ever heard of.

"No! What, Mister Big City Pretty Boy thinks everybody in small towns is in 4-H? Besides, we can google it."

"4H?"

"Lightning bugs, silly," she said, slapping her neck. Slowing to a halt she pulled out her Razr as the others rode on leaving them behind, "Lightning bugs . . . California," she uttered. The display softly illuminating her powder blue eyes and pouty lips, the mechanical voice of the digital assistant replied, 'There are about two thousand firefly species. There have been unconfirmed reports of fireflies in California, Arizona,

Idaho and the Pacific Northwest. They prefer humid climates. The come in light red, green, yellow and orange. Each species has a specific flash pattern. Males use a specific pattern to let females know they are interested. If a lady notices him she flashes back with her own specific pattern to say yes.' "

"I guess no flash means 'no'," Matt laughed.

"So what's *your* pattern?"

"I'm not a firefly. So there you are . . . Oh, and lightning bugs are our state insect. Any more questions?" she giggled.

"You're pretty good with that."

"Naturally curious I guess."

"Curiosity killed the cat," Matt said.

"Satisfaction brought her back," she replied.

Looking at the bejeweled night sky Matt marveled at the billions of twinkling prisms set against the Milky Way stardust.

"I never knew you could see so many."

An eerie shimmering iridescent curtain of red, blue, orange, green and violet lights fanned down from the heavens.

"The Northern Lights," Cathy said. "Pretty southern tonight. This never happens here. This is a first. This is so weird. What are you doing?"

"Wishing on a star," Matt replied.

"Aren't we the romantic," Cathy said, fearing suddenly which meaning of the word he might have taken her to mean. "Funny, I got the impression you weren't that thrilled to be here," she added quickly. "After all, this isn't L.A." *Romantic?* "On the contrary … it is more deeply stirring to my blood than any imagining could possibly have been." Matt returned his gaze starward.

"Last of the Mohicans . . . So you're a reader, too," she said in a way that for once didn't sound like a slight. "Why is it some people look at the sky and see a thousand wonders when others see only sky?"

Too? "The same can be said for a lot of things. Now who's the romantic," he said, knowing exactly which meaning *he* meant. Cathy blushed.

Then something quite amazing happened. Thousands of fireflies began blinking in unison like traffic lights gone haywire. Cathy had heard of the phenomena but had never believed it. Almost as soon as it started it stopped –

"Okay, that was weird," Cathy said.

– What's *that*?" Matt blurted.

Cathy followed his gaze. A dull orange light like the glow from a jack-o-lantern was drifting slowly above the tree canopy, "DON'T LOOK!" she blurted.

Heavy branches snapping caused them to break into goosebumps.

"What is it?"

"Some say it's the kid who was playing chicken with the Red Ball Express. Some say it's the devil. It lures people. They're never found . . ." Cathy groaned, who had grown unnaturally still.

Matt gulped. Wringing his grips, his eyes stayed on the orb, "Dyatlov," he muttered. Suddenly all they wanted to do was hightail it out of there.

"What – ?"

"Dyatlov Pass. . . the Urals . . . Russia. There was an orb there too . . . orange . . . red, I can't remember . . . nine hikers . . . they cut through their tent in the middle of the night . . . ran into the snow barefoot still in their underwear to try to escape it. . . . it was 24 below . . . body parts were missing . . . bodies drained of – "

"**SHUT UP!**" Cathy screamed. "If you're trying to act brave I'm not impressed."

. . . "the only footprints in the snow were theirs . . ."

"**SHUT UP!**"

"It's probably somebody's drone . . . or swamp gas," he added nervously.

The crickets stopped chirping. The trees glowed with a dark light. Their eyes turned slowly upward with a tingling sense the thing was watching them. As it darted at them they dove. The will-o'-the-wisp split into three fiery balls which reformed behind them. Sweat poured down their backs. The opaque balls of fuzzy light exuded an intelligence. They alternated between red, orange, white and yellow before turning a pulsating brilliant blue-green. Cathy closed her eyes. Her lips were moving. Her pulse pounded in her ears. Silently the ghostly balls reformed into an orange orb then rose and flickered from view. A lone cricket timidly chirped joined soon by a brave frog.

A hysterical laugh passed Matt's lips . . . then a whimper, "That was no swamp gas."

"**G-GO-GO-GO-GO!**" Cathy screamed.

“Light your phone. I can’t see you,” Matt blurted. The sound of her phone striking the ground was followed by a swear word. Nervously she began to sing the same refrain over and over . . .

♫ *I am bound for the promised land ...*

I am bound for the promised land ...

Oh who will come and go with me?...

I am bound for the promised land ...

Up the road the others were waiting. “That was close,” Cathy gasped. Strangely, nothing was said about the apparition. She didn’t go back for her Razr. Matt would learn later there are many ghost lights throughout the South.

The witch’s house was an old two-story farmhouse framed by two lone weeping willows whose crooked branches drooped to the weed garden like a Portuguese man o’ war waiting to sting the unwary.

In the eerie luminance of the bug-swarmed sodium vapor lamp mounted to a wood pole in the front yard, the house sat on regularly-spaced concrete trapezoidal piers and sagged in places. Its shabby roof was a checkerboard of missing pea-green and black-speckled asphalt shingles.

“Ready *California*?” Zak wheedled.

“For what?”

“Here’s how it works California. You go to the window, look in, come back and tell us what you saw . . . unless you’re scared. Oh, and she has a shotgun.”

"No sweat," Matt replied. "B'right back wacko, I mean Zacko." A conspiratorial grin spread across Zak's fat face. Matt gulped as he started for the house, burrs pricking his ankles determined to find who had set him up. At least it didn't involve the Red Ball Express. The crickets stopped chirping. The only sound was the crunch of dry weeds underfoot and his ragged labored breathing. An eerie quiet descended. He slapped his neck praying the witch hadn't heard the mosquitoes die. He desperately wanted to turn back but what would the others think? He was scared but scared more of letting them know how scared he was.

The top half of a window looked as if it hadn't been windexed in years. The lower half was open with no screen. Odd given the mosquitos. He tried to rid from mind the image of the shotgun trained on him. He had seen what they do to pig carcasses, turning them into something that looks like Alpo. Slowly he crept on. An owl fluttered past. His phone chimed – I SEE YOU, the display read. It showed no sender. He looked behind him for who could have sent it. Confused he looked for something to stand on. Spying a rotten wheelbarrow whose wood had long ago turned gray he dragged it scratching through the weeds. He stepped onto the teetering perch. Hesitantly he grabbed the windowsill and began to pull himself up . . .

muscle clamped down hard on his wrist . . . "*LET GO! LET GO!*" he screamed. He struggled to get free but the harder he pulled the faster it held. He began to feel lightheaded. As his energy began to drain a dark barren panoramic wind-swept plain ringed with snow-capped peaks stretched before him. Black clouds heavy with rain roiled. A city stood nestled against a mountain range – not a modern city but the kind in books on ancient civilizations — with battlements, towers and ramparts. A line of interlocking H-shaped stone blocks stood nearby in a line like giant Legos waiting to be assembled. A stone gateway stood nearby; the lone arch-like structure a seeming doorway to a hostile uninviting plain. He watched in fascinated horror as giants chased down humans, slinging them over their shoulders, tearing off limbs and eating them as they strode the way a person might casually tear off a fried chicken wing. A young woman with flowing long black hair made eye contact before being devoured, her desperate eyes pleading for help, a look that would haunt him forever. Stitched animal hides girded the monster's loins. Was what he was seeing real? The colossus turned to face him. It wiped its filthy matted red hair littered with twigs from its wild eyes. The ground trembled. The monster bounded forward grabbing him around his abdomen with six giant fingers, staring him in the face with its grotesque countenance, its breath stinking like rotten eggs, its body like a garbage dump. The monster let out a terrifying roar unlike any animal's.

A sharp blow left Matt gasping for air. Nettles pricked his back like a bed of nails. He looked around. He was back at the witch's house.

"HE'S THE ONE, KILL HIM," screeched a woman's voice inside his head. The others had fled leaving him all alone. He staggered to his feet and ran. A shotgun blast shattered the stillness. His thigh felt on fire. Reaching his bike he started to pedal. Another blast pierced the silence. In the road lay a sprawled form — Chase. The sound of snarling shocked Matt back to his senses. Gripping his cousin by his collar he jerked him to his feet.

"***GO! GO! GO! GO!!*** . . ." Cathy screamed from out of nowhere.

Chase scrambled awkwardly onto his bike. He had just started to pedal when one of three angry Rottweilers sank its teeth into his pant cuff shaking its head from side to side to rip him from his bike. Matt kicked it. With a yelp it let go. Pedaling like mad inches slowly became feet until the beasts finally abandoned the chase. What had lasted a minute had seemed hours. The black and brown devil dogs stood panting evil-eyeing the intruders in the sodium vapor.

As Chase licked his bleeding forearm Matt turned and faced the growling dogs. "IS THAT ALL YOU GOT!"

"I know you didn't just trash talk those dogs," Cathy laughed. "We'll have to do this again soon," she quipped as she picked the nettles from his back.

"You kidding me?" Chase blurted.

"Not anytime soon I hope," Matt breathlessly grinned.

That was when he noticed Cathy eyeing him strangely. She looked away awkwardly at first then back and said, "You just might could be Young Marines material."

"You think?" replied Matt, kicking himself for responding too enthusiastically.

"I said *might*."

"Actually you said *might could*."

"Just something we say in The South," Cathy giggled, "like calling everything Coke. That's The South."

○ ○ ○

You have enemies? Good. That means you've stood for something at some time even if it was only you.

.

Matt tossed his *Introduction to Calculus* textbook aside.

"Chase, you 'sleep? At the witch's house . . . ." he held out his wrist.

"Whoa, dude, that's like Monster Energy drink scratches. I'd put something on that before you get that flesh-eating thing!"

"There was a voice. It said "He's the one. Kill him. *Kill me? . . . Seriously?* And she shot me! Look!"

"It's just rock salt. But whoa, like what'd you see dude?" .

"When the witch grabbed me . . . I had a . . . a . . . a vision."

"*D*oo-doo, doo-doo, doo-doo, doo-doo," Chase trilled *The Twilight Zone*.

". . . btw, dude, when the witch grabbed you, you screamed . . . sorry. Thought you should know."

Horror of horrors. Boys don't scream. It's in the Boys' Manual on Page One.

"Zak said you screamed like a girl. '*Let go, let go.*' Chase screeched in a high-pitched voice. "I never liked that dude." Matt's heart sank. Then he became angry. With himself.

"Then he goes ... '*Big California Man ... screams like a girl.*' You got a hater, dude."

"I've got more than one," Matt confessed.

"*THAT's* what I'm talkin'! Anybody who doesn't have 'em needs 'em. People hate when they feel inferior or insecure or just have to have somebody to hate to feel better about themselves. Or are envious or feel threatened or are just plain evil. But let's face it, if you've gone your whole life without any haters, you're probably pretty boring."

Matt laughed.

"A thousand Facebook friends means squat. I've got a website, *HateMe.life*. I've got forty-two haters so far. That kid who killed himself last year should've been glad kids were hatin.' Who wants to be invisible? Being hated is so validating! Don't hate the player. Hate the game."

"Never thought about it like that." It was true. He *had* screamed like a girl. He shuddered at the thought.

Chase had another bombshell.

"I'm gay."

"You can't be. You're my cousin."

"Somehow I don't think that matters, cuz. I dreaded telling you."

In the days to follow they would have many heart-to-hearts about what it means to be gay and what it means to be straight. They agreed everyone is who they are and life is about how you live it.

Cathy announced she was going into town.

"Anyone want to come with?" she asked.

"I'll come," Matt said.

As they biked they met with many hostile stares. They stopped their bikes in front of McNary's Drugs, went inside and took seats at the counter. There they were met by an unfriendly soda jerk. The term "soda jerk" had become obsolete by the '70s except at McNary's where it was still used to describe the kid who squirted Coke syrup from a dispenser into a glass of soda water and vanilla ice cream under the watchful eyes of

Old Man McNary watching the lunch counter from behind the swinging doors to the kitchen.

"What's wrong with people around here?" asked Matt.

"That's just how they are."

A pretty African-American girl spouted, "Oh, excuse me . . . is there a white boy shortage?"

"Leave some brothas for us," the girl's companion tittered. Cathy giggled. She knew them both well – both fellow cheerleaders.

"Like that was interesting," Cathy drawled.

"That kid looked at you like he hated you," Matt said of the soda jerk.

"I know him. He's a creep. I know I'm cute and blonde but I've never gotten this much attention. We'll have to go places more often," they laughed.

Chapter 7 – THE MOUND

The universe does not exist as we think it exists.
John Keel

MATT WOKE to the beeping of the jumbo numbers alarm clock. Groggily he tapped it. It kept beeping. He tapped it harder but the beeping persisted. He stumbled to the window and peeled back the curtain. A dump truck was backing. A knock sounded at the door.

"Get up boys. Ned's going to need your help."

After their Cheerios Matt overheard his uncle talking with a deep-tanned Native American man with a long ponytail peppered with gray strands, the etching of years on his face.

"We won't touch a burial mound," the Indian said.

"Why not?" asked Ned.

The spirits would be angered."

"It's my land. I'll do as I please. The spirits ain't payin' the mortgage."

"This mound was here long before my people. My ancestors say they were built by the Cloud Eaters with hair like red flames. They ran alongside the buffalo and slung them over their shoulders. They roasted and ate my people. They called us 'long pig.' The Cloud Eaters did not respect the Great Spirit. They committed crimes against man and animals so great the Great Spirit heard the cries of my people and sent a flood to destroy them. All nations tell – our brothers the Hopi, Sioux, Cherokee,

Iroquois, Apache, Arapaho, Lakota, all . . . This ground is sick. Powell missed this one."

"Who?" Ned asked, scratching his head.

"Powell. The director of the Smithsonian. It was created to hide the Cloud Eaters. He ordered burial mounds destroyed. What is inside goes against their science. He did what the white man does with everything he touches – he destroys it."

"I won't argue that," said Ned. "I still want it gone."

"Get someone else," the Indian said. Turning to Matt, "Wherever you go take this." He pressed a knife into Matt's palm, closed Matt's fingers tightly around it and left.

"What was inside?" Ned shouted.

Matt looked down at the two-toned dark brown and cream imitation elk horn-handle clasp-knife. He pressed his thumb to its blade. A thin red line formed.

The next day two men with a bulldozer, a backhoe and a dump truck arrived. The boys planted themselves under a wizened old hickory and watched as boys do, the backhoe operator push and pull his long yellow rods with shiny black plastic balls on the ends, biting into the earth, swinging the backhoe's hydraulic arm back and forth making a marvelous noise. Matt noticed around him what appeared many graves, each fifteen to twenty-five feet long, each oriented precisely east to west on the compass, each overlaid with a careful buildup of rock rubble mixed with topsoil. By dusk the men had departed. The backhoe had left a small opening. Matt peered inside. His gaze met only darkness.

○ ○ ○

That night Matt looked up from his web browsing to find his aunt leaning against the doorpost.

"We had no internet when I was your age. We had to go to the library. There was no www-ing anything."

"Nobody says *www* anymore Aunt Nell," Matt laughed.

"No cell phones ... no GPS ... no email ... no texting. If you wanted to communicate with somebody you had to talk. A lost art. And the only way you could get your money was to go to the bank. No ATMs."

"Were there dinosaurs?" asked Matt. Nell laughed. Then her voice changed to low and forbidding. "About that mound . . . nothing grows on it . . . birds don't fly anywhere near it. One of our farmhands put a bird feeder on it eight years ago. Three days later he was dead. The birds still haven't touched it . . . and my cats . . . what happened to my cats?" Her lip trembled as she thought of Puddy and Mister Pickles, her four-years-straight county fair prize-winning Persians found on the mound stiff as boards. '*Two More Half-Cats Found*,' the *Chickasaw Clarion* article had read.

She fiddled with her button, "You stay away from it, hear? There's somethin' not right about that mound. Don't go messin' with things you don't understand." The house line rang. She went to answer it. "Promise," she shouted as she hurried down the hall.

The next night after everyone had gone to bed Matt grabbed a shovel, a length of rope and with thoughts of buried treasure dancing in his head pushed an ATV out of earshot and stole away to the mound.

The Tannenhook's land occupied one hundred forty acres, half spindly pines and a swamp, the other half a dying moringa tree orchard. A tree expert found too much aluminum in the soil.

Early settlers spoke of strange lights, frightful howls and shadow people. And of a sense of dread and despair that only grew more unbearable the longer one stayed. And bad things always happened to those that did. Children mostly who were told never to wander from the camp. An entire wagon train vanished once on its way to the Santa Fe Trail leaving only its wheel ruts behind. As with the disappearance of the Roanoke Colony in 1587, the first English settlement in America. It was said to be a place of giant birds that could swoop down and carry off a full-grown man. All tribes steered clear of "The Devil's Hunting Ground" as it was known. It is interesting how so many places where terrible strange things occur have the word "devil" in them.

The air hung heavy with sweet pine resin. Angry clouds drifted past a luminous moon through trees draped with moss. It was no place to be alone. The Dogman and Mothman seemed behind every tree. The occasional cry of a bird could be heard deep in the swamp. Matt's veins ran cold. A chill went through him as he approached the mound. It was too quiet. Not a hoot, not a chirp, not a croak. A twig snapped.

Scared he started to dig. He reminded himself to look up the punishment for digging into an Indian burial mound. Silent lightning began to strike. Something was pelting the ground. Hail the size of golfballs was falling but only on the mound. It suddenly turned cold and windy. *There's something not right about that mound.* Quickly he anchored the rope to the ATV, grabbed up the slack and tossed it in.

He entered feet first, his phone clenched in his teeth. Immediately he began to feel unwell. The light gave out. Most would agree there are places one should never be at night. A graveyard is one, a giant's graveyard especially. He lowered himself until his feet touched a hard surface. What am I doing here? he asked himself. To find the gold he reminded himself.

He began to snap pictures. Each flash only magnified the terror. He thought he heard whispering.

His phone buzzed. It was a text message.

WE ARE WATCHING YOU. It gave no sender. Goosebumps stood on his arms and neck. He lit a match. In its flare were petroglyphs of human sacrifices, blood-drinking rituals and the worship of standing-up alligators. He ran his fingers over a bison with two pairs of legs, a well-defined and a lesser-defined pair with two like tails and four arrows sticking out of its back. A fine orange mist surrounded the animal. It looked sprayed. Through the tangle of cobwebs the petroglyph gave off a strange three-dimensional appearance. With each flicker the creature walked, switching between its pairs of legs! So much for animation being a modern invention. Another depicted beings arriving from the sky in balls of light.

The match singed his fingers. He dropped it. Fire raced around the chamber inside a stone trough. In the dim light he was standing on a ledge.

Through the flickering light sat a horrible sight – a human skeleton of gigantic proportion. Sitting upright it was frightening, terrifying and exhilarating. Eyes bugged he slid further down the rope. Under the slab roof supported by regularly spaced rock columns he stepped off the giant's size.

Legs — thirteen feet; torso — the same — altogether twenty-six feet!

He stood gaping at the bushel basket-size skull with its deep wide jaw and scattered strands of scarlet, almost orange hair. In its jaws sat double rows of teeth with molars large enough to crack a coconut. Cavernous eye sockets stared back from under a bulging brow ridge. A tarantula crawled from a jagged hole in the side of its skull.

Around the monster's neck a necklace of copper and stones woven together with thin strips of leather formed a gorget, a mat that would have protected its throat from being cut. Beside it sat a clay pot filled with freshwater pearls. There was no gold. As the pearls cascaded through Matt's fingers a silver ring fit for a king caught his eye. He stuffed it into his pocket.

At the giant's side lay a beam, at one end a double-edged copper battle-axe, its blades almost as big as the flag outside the town's post office. At its other side sat an enormous book of hammered copper pages. Straining he lifted its cover.

Through the dust appeared a hologram. Above the copper pages reflected in Matt's wide eyes an epic story began – the explosion of the fifth planet from the sun into cinders much like the planet in *Star Wars* and the destruction of the fourth planet (Mars?). It showed the Earth's moon being moved out of Earth's orbit, sent into space and deposited at the edge of the solar system.[4] It then showed a moon three times bigger being transported to Earth and replacing it in orbit, all common knowledge to Australian Aborigines but not to a Southern California kid. He watched as thousands of spheres of light descended from the moon, landing atop a mountain on Earth. Seeing it from space he recognized a land mass. It was the Middle East. He had done a report on the Suez Canal once. The hologram zoomed into a region of city-states comprised of advanced stone buildings, complexes, walls, fortresses, and temples, each built for a specific pagan god. He watched their destruction as fire rained from the sky and covered a thousand kilometers and burned so intensely it melted stone. Baffled archaeologists would call it the Bronze Age Collapse in which the entire region was mysteriously and suddenly destroyed. He saw the same destruction wrought elsewhere, particularly in Scotland, Ireland and India. A war between heavenly angels and fallen angels laid waste.

The sound of an exhale emerged from the darkness. He tried to rationalize it as the outside wind then tried to convince himself it was his own but knew it wasn't. He dashed for the rope clawing his way to the top until he reached the ATV. Out of breath he pushed the starter button. The knobbies spat rooster tails as the two-cycle yinged.

It is a strange thing with lines and cords and ropes and things. They always go out of their way to snag things. As he sped away with a loud crack the rope snared the monster's clavicle ripping it from the giant. It wedged in the entrance cavity. Spitting a mouthful of dirt and pine needles Matt fought to right the ATV. As he rummaged for the rope an orange glow turned the dark green foliage a frightful brown and the light green foliage a ghoulish beige. He suddenly remembered the clasp-knife. Pulling it from his pocket a dozen thrusts and it was through. Three fuzzy balls of orange ionized gas swirled around him. The balls planted themselves in his path as the engine cranked. The two-stroke yinged as he twisted the throttle. The ATV reared onto its rear wheels with Matt hanging on for dear life as he made a mad dash for it veering around the fireballs into the shallow swamp sending a bow wave through the stagnant orange waters, the balls chasing him all the way.

Chapter 8 – GIANTS, GIANTS EVERYWHERE

The eyes of that species of extinct giants, whose bones fill the mounds of America, have gazed on Niagara as ours do now.
Abraham Lincoln, 1848

MATT burst through the back door filthy and dripping swamp water. It was after midnight. The lights were on. Someone was up.

"You went to the mound, didn't you. After you promised!" Matt's aunt blurted mad as Hades. "And you stirred something up! I can feel it. What happened to your face?" His skin was reddish and hot to the touch and he was experiencing the mild form of dizziness that often accompanies a bad sunburn.

"This is bad … this is really, really bad," Nell kept repeating over and over as Matt kept watch through the kitchen window curtains.

No one slept a wink that night. It began as scratching inside the walls. Then thumping on the roof, noises in the ceiling, cabinet doors banging, window blinds fluttering, dishes crashing in the sink, things pushed over, pounding on the house, shaking beds and worst of all, something breathing and moving around inside their mattresses. And a big gray fuzzy cat walked through the house and disappeared after it turned the corner to the kitchen which would have been perfectly fine except the Tannenhooks didn't own a cat.

The next day between Nell's worrying over whether they would all be dead in three days and Ned's dismissal of the event, it was decided to report the incident. But to whom? The county sheriff? The FBI? The Smithsonian? No, definitely not the Smithsonian. The pope? She called her minister who promptly came over and blessed the house and those in it. The strange things stopped for a while.

"I need you to call the school too," said Nell. Ned searched through his mountain of business cards. Forty minutes later he had found it.

Father Brin W. Brainard, Ph.D.

St. Francis Skyfell Academy
The future of world leadership passes through these doors

10 Soggy Bottom Road, Chickasaw, Tennessee USA
Tel. +1 01 555.439.1761

It so happened the priest was away visiting The Lucifer Telescope in Arizona (yes that's really its name, which causes one to worry about what they are looking for) but a professor in the Anthropology Department was only too happy to inform him all mounds were built by Native Americans and the bones were Native American. Matt told him the skeleton was twenty-six feet. There was a long silence. The professor asked for the address. Matt gave it. "Those are mastodon bones," the man said then hanged up.

"That's the trouble with kids nowadays," Ned huffed. "You don't know how to measure. In my day we had wood shop and metal shop in school."

"Twenty-six feet!" he scoffed. "Why do you know how big that is? That's the length of one of our stands of drill pipe! How tall are *you*?"

“Five-six,” Matt said angrily.

“That would mean that supposed giant you found would have to be” . . . Uncle Ned who wasn’t very good at figuring big numbers in his head fell silent as he figured . . .

“Five *mes*. And they weren’t mastodon bones,” Matt fumed.

Where had the giant come from? Was it the only one ever found? He had to find out.

His bedroom became his library where every day he sat at a computer by a window with a tall glass of lemonade playing Sherlock Holmes. It was a great adventure. Old newspapers took him to the Old World, to the New World and to the Orient. They took him to the Old West, to the Near East and to the Americas. They took him to the South Pacific. They took him by horseback, by covered wagon, by tall-masted sailing ship. They took him by Chinese junk and by chariot. Incredibly everywhere they took him there were giants.

There was a lot of dodgy information but with persistence he was able to sort the real from the fake.

Matt showed Chase a photograph he found in the December 1895 issue of the British magazine *Strand*. It showed a twelve-foot giant in a wooden shipping crate propped against a railcar, a time long before any photo manipulation. And the magazine was still in business:

> ***Strand* (Dec. 1895)** -- Pre-eminent among the most extraordinary articles ever held by a railway company is the fossilized Irish giant, which is at this moment lying at the London and North-Western Railway Company’s Broad street goods depot, and a photograph of which is reproduced here. . . This monstrous figure is reputed to have been dug up by a Mr. Dyer whilst prospecting for iron ore in County Antrim. The principal measurements

are: entire length, 12 ft. 2, in.; girth of chest, 6 ft. 6 in.; and length of arms, 4 ft. 6 in. There are six toes on the right foot. The gross weight is 2 tons 15 cwt.; so it took half a dozen men and a powerful crane to place this article of lost property in position for the Strand magazine artist. Dyer, after showing the giant in Dublin, came to England with his queer find and exhibited it in Liverpool and Manchester at sixpence, sixpence a head, attracting scientific men as well as gaping sightseers.

All in all Matt found nearly a thousand newspaper stories on giants. In the *Oil City Times*, Pennsylvania, Dec. 31, 1869 he found this:

18 Foot Human Giant and Enormous Helmet of Iron Found --

In an excavation made by Mr. William Thompson and Robert Smith, they exhumed an enormous helmet of iron which was corroded with rust. Further digging brought to light a sword which measured nine feet in length, and after some little time they discovered the bones of two very large feet. Following up the lead, in a few hours time the unearthed a well-preserved skeleton of an enormous giant, belong to a species of the human family which probably inhabited this part of the world at the time of which the Bible speaks, when it says, 'and there were giants in those days.' The helmet is said to be of the shape of those found among the ruins of Nineveh. The bones are remarkably white, the teeth are all in their places, and all of them are double, and of extraordinary size. These relics have been taken to Tionesta, where they are visited by large numbers of persons daily. The giant must have stood eighteen feet in his stockings."

In the *Niles' National Register* he found this:

Volume 69, Oct. 4, 1846; *A Giant Exhumed"* – "We are informed on the most reliable authority, that a person in Franklin County, Tenn., while digging a well, a few weeks since, found a human skeleton, at the depth of fifty feet, which measures eighteen feet in length. The immense frame was entire with an unimportant exception in one of the extremities. It has been visited by several of the principal members of the medical facility in Nashville, and pronounced unequivocally, by all, that of a huge man. The bone of the thigh, measured five feet; and it was computed that the height of the living man, making the proper allowance for muscles, must have been at least twenty feet. The finder had been offered eight thousand dollars for it, but had determined not to sell it at any price, until first exhibiting it for twelve months. He is now having the different parts wired together for this purpose. These unwritten records of the men and animals of other ages that are from time to time dug out of the bowels of the earth, put conjecture into confusion, and almost surpass imagination itself.

And in the *New York Times* he found a great many including this:

April 9, 1885*, St. Louis, Mo., --* The city of Moberly, Mo. is stirred up over the discovery of a wonderful buried city, which was discovered at the bottom of a coal shaft, 360 feet deep, which was being sunk near the city. A hard and thick stratum of lava arches in the buried city, the streets of which are regularly laid out and enclosed by walls of stone, which is cut and dressed in a fairly good, although rude, style of masonry. A hall 30 by 160 feet was discovered, wherein were stone benches and tools of all descriptions for mechanical service. Further search disclose statues and images made of a composition closely resembling bronze, lacking luster. A stone fountain was found, situated in a wide court or street, and from it a stream of perfectly pure water was flowing, which was found to be strongly impregnated with lime. Lying beside the foundation were portions of the skeleton of a human being. The bones of the leg measured, the femur four and one-half feet, the tibia four feet and three inches, showing that when alive the figure was three times the size of an ordinary man, and possessed of a wonderful muscular power and quickness. The head bones had separated in two places, the sagittal and the caronal sutures having been destroyed. The implements found embrace bronze and flint knives, stone and granite hammers, metallic saws of crude workmanship, but proved metal, and others of similar character; they are not so highly polished, nor so accurately made as those

> now finished by our best mechanics, but they show skill and an evidence of an advanced civilization that are very wonderful. The facts above given are vouched for by Mr. David Coates, the Recorder for the city of Moberly and Mr. George Keating, city Marshal who were of the exploring party. A further search will be made in a day or two.

Matt marveled at the endless newspaper stories on giantsm which were considered normal at the time. In Valencia, Spain a 22' skeleton was found in 1705. By the time he came to the report of the well-regarded French anthropologist Georges Vacher de Lapouge who in 1890 discovered the bones of an 11'6" human in a Bronze Age cemetery which were verified by University of Montpellier professors as being a human who would have weighed a thousand pounds, it was clear there was no end to the reports from all over the world. It was all quite disturbing. Giants roamed the earth where gas stations and shopping centers now stand. Even Abraham Lincoln had something to say about them.

Why today has not a single news media ever mentioned a single thing about giants? Matt wondered. He set out to find out.

"Chase . . . how would you feel if something you learned in school was a big fat lie?"

"You mean like the *Glomar Explorer*?" Chase sat up in bed and flicked on a lamp.

"Gramps said when he was in fifth grade there was a news story in the *Weekly Reader* about a ship they were building to pick up manganese nodules off the ocean floor. He said he thought it was a cool idea. It said there was a fortune in manganese nodules waitin' for somebody to come along and scoop 'em up. So they built the Glomar Explorer. He said of all the stories in the *Weekly Reader* it's the only one he still remembers. He never heard anything else. He said he'd always wondered what happened with the Glomar Explorer. One day he was watching History Channel. It said the Glomar Explorer story was a lie and that the CIA really built it for a secret mission. It had robotic arms and super long cables to reach down and grab a sunken Russian sub off the bottom. They lied to everybody – even kids! My dad said he felt betrayed. He said after he thought about it, it was okay though 'cause it was for national security and stuff. Like that, dude?"

"Yeah," Matt replied. "Like that. So are there manganese nodules or not?"

Chase shrugged. "Who knows, dude, who knows."

"What we're learning in archaeology's like that Glomar Explorer," Matt said. "They even have a name for it – forbidden archaeology."

"Is there forbidden algebra," Chase tittered.

They amused themselves by adding "forbidden" to every science they could think of until they drifted off to sleep.

Chapter 9 – JAIL BIRDS

"WANT TO RACE?" asked Matt.

"I haven't met the boy who can keep up with me or have you forgotten that too?"

"That was then. This is now."

"It's my world. You're just in it," Cathy crowed as she kick started her dirt bike. With a grin he swore to wipe off her face she roared off leaving him choking in her dust.

"Okay, Young Marine babe, fight's on."

Out of the corral he chased her on Zak's Honda to a nearby moto-cross course. Up and down hills, over jumps, through switchbacks and across bone-rattling whoops they raced, trading the lead back and forth. The only reason Matt never entered any of the American Motorcycle Association sanctioned races his friends did was because there were four rules at his house – no running with scissors, no ball playing inside, be home before the street lights come on, and no motorcycle racing. Truth be told his mother hated hospitals. Who could blame her? She had read somewhere nine hundred people die every day in the U.S. alone from mistakes by incompetent doctors. Educated witch doctors, quacks she called them.

Matt trailed her into a turn where she roosted him. The tiny rocks stung like wasps. He pinned the throttle and managed to slip past. Ahead was his favorite, a right-hander. Time for a brake check. She slowed to avoid rear-ending him and fell back as he pinned the throttle. Whoops, a series of moguls, were ahead. The quickest way through is to skip across like a pebble across water. It takes practice. Lots. He nailed each one. Cathy hit the face of the second ruining her momentum. He pinned the throttle. The final turn was coming, his last chance to roost her. He slowed to let her catch up but she was coming in too fast. She slammed into him and fell off.

With a grin from ear to ear he followed her onto the street to an alley where a moving van, its ramp lowered, blocked their way. There was space enough for only one of them to pass. Cathy grabbed a handful of throttle. Matt grabbed a handful.

"I SEE IT!" he shouted over his screaming motor. His focus zig-zagged between Cathy and the truck … Cathy . . truck . . Cathy . . truck . . truck . . *TRUCK!* He swooped, his rear tire missing her front by inches and the rear of the truck by little more.

"YOU'RE CRAZY!" she screamed.

An electronic *CHIRP* sounded. Startled he looked back into the angry red lights of a police car.

He gunned it.

Chapter 10 – LIARS and THIEVES

It takes more effort to disbelieve in something than to believe in it.

MATT SAT ON THE front porch swing flipping through the pages of The Wall Street Journal.

"Trying to impress somebody?" Cathy blurted from her bike.

"You should read it. Might learn something . . ."

"Like what?"

"Like the Atlantic Current is dying like in that movie *The Day After Tomorrow*. And the Magnetic North Pole's moving. It's moving to Russia. It's really haulin.' It's never done that before. Airports are having to change their runway numbers. And the magnetic field's getting weak. It says birds and other migratory animals, whales, butterflies, turtles, salmon and stuff, they're losing their way. It says erratic migration behavior is being reported everywhere. No more swallows in Capistrano. And the ozone layer's almost gone. And the forests are dying. And the marine life's dying. And the birds and insects are dying. The bears are skin and bones. The bees are almost extinct. The Pacific Ocean is radioactive. Everything's dying. The biosphere's collapsing. We're facing extinction."

"Is Santa bugging out?" Cathy giggled.

"Very funny." Putting the matter of the end of the world aside, while she was giggling seemed a good time to bring up giants. "Will you help me research them?"

"Don't be stupid. I don't believe in giants and I don't eat Twinkies."

"What's wrong with Twinkies?" asked Chase.

"Why not?"

"Chase said you got kicked out of school."

Chase pulled out his phone and pretended to text.

"What for?"

"Fighting."

"Over what? Let me guess. A *girl*."

"Let's just say he had it coming."

"What! You're gay?"

"NO!"

Matt shot a look at Chase. Cathy looked at Matt, then looked at Chase wondering what she had missed. Chase gave a lopsided grin.

"Is that how you got that scar?"

Matt ran his finger across his cheek pondering the glass blizzard and the mattresses.

"No."

"It starts off with the little things. Next thing you know you're on the slippery slope to prison."

"What would *you* know about prison goody two shoes?"

"Just sayin' home boy."

"You're not so perfect, *Cat*," Matt said, figuring she wouldn't like her new nickname. So you've never told a white lie?"

“A liar thinks everybody’s a liar. A thief thinks everybody’s a thief. You need to join Young Marines. It has an honor code. ‘I will not lie, cheat or steal or tolerate those who do.’ What’s yours? Anything goes? Get the job done no matter what? Being sincere and honest means doing the right thing because it’s the right thing. Qualities that build trust. If we can’t trust each other, we can’t help each other. You’re an arrogant *twaat*!” It was a term she had picked up in the U.K.

“*Twaat*? What’s a twaat? You sound like some stupid tv commercial,” Matt sneered. “*Come bank with us . . . we build trust.*”

“Cathy rolled her eyes. There was an awkward silence.

. . . “Okay, if you join Young Marines,” she said finally. “Do it. You can’t lose. And call me *Cat* one more time and I’ll break your other arm.”

“Do and I’ll slap you into tomorrow,” Matt replied. There are times you have to stand up for yourself black belt or no black belt.

“You can’t. I’m a girl.”

Matt laughed, “Oh, so you’re a girl when it suits you. Don’t call me homeboy then. Got a nickname home girl?”

Cathy laughed. “*Too Cute.* But only my friends can call me that.”

“You’re kidding, right?

“ . . . Okay. I’ll join.

“What about you Zak?” Cathy giggled.

“I’m not joining any Young Marines. Are you high on Mountain Dew?”

“Not *that* silly . . .Giants!”

“Count me O-U-T out,” Zak replied.

A Chickasaw County Sheriff cruiser rolled up.

"Run! It's the feds," Chase laughed. Zak scowled, reminded of his past troubles with the Feds – the real ones as did Matt and Cathy, reminded of the day before, sitting on the rock-hard mustard-colored fiberglass back seat of a Dodge Charger police cruiser, charged with reckless driving, driving without a license, driving an unregistered motorcycle on a city street and evading an officer of the law, each offense carrying a three hundred dollar fine, and in Cathy's case – sassing an officer, which added forty hours of community service cleaning the precinct's mounted stables, shoveling horse manure to put it less delicately.

"Now who's on the slippery slope?" Matt twanged.

Ned was overheard explaining to the deputy that someone had trespassed onto his property during the night.

Chase and Matt grabbed two ATVs and sped for the mound Cathy and Zak in tow. When they arrived they could scarcely believe their eyes. The bulldozer and backhoe were lying scattered in pieces. A length of rubber hose hung from a tree dripping red fluid on Matt's shirt. Inside the mound he picked up a solitary pearl, all that remained. The mound was picked clean. The stone channel was still afire. Matt patted his pocket. The ring was still there.

"Is that thing moving?" asked Cathy, staring at the bison.

"The giant was right there."

"Sorry. No can believe. Is that thing moving? . . . is that thing moving? You kidding me?"

Matt slid the ring onto his finger. When Cathy noticed him staring stupidly at his hand he fumbled for words.

"It . . . it shrank . . . it shrank to fit my finger."

In the days to follow Matt began to wonder if the archaeological community cannot stand the idea of having to rewrite the history books or if there was some other reason. “Isn’t science about finding the truth?” Instead he found archaeologist after archaeologist tarred and feathered and run out of town on a rail for discovering something new and exciting that revealed what was previously thought was wrong, then banned from working in archaeology ever again.

It seemed *The Emperor's New Clothes* is the story of modern archaeology. Once upon a time there was an emperor who walked around in public with no clothes. His subjects dared not say anything lest they lose their heads and even remarked how splendid the emperor’s non-existent clothes were until one day a boy cried out, “But he isn’t wearing anything at all!” A dead baby plesiosaur washed up on a beach in Georgia in the United States on March 16 of 2018. No scientist dared say anything that might smack of a departure from the textbook tale that plesiosaurs went extinct 65 million years ago. Someone forgot to tell the plesiosaur. In the past there have been a few brave archaeologists willing to out the emperor but their voices were quickly silenced. Now hardly anyone dares it seems.

It is the same with being human. We have lost our roots, lost our origin. Have you never stopped to think what it means to be human, especially considering all the other things you might have been? Have you ever wondered how your dog or cat views you? Texts of ancient cultures tell what an amazing privilege it is to be born into these precious human bodies – today a great lost secret, something we never ever stop to think about. Like being born royal, thin, rich, good-looking, famous, smart and athletic all in one; you take it for granted just as we take being human for granted, yet it is something all the wealth in the universe cannot buy. Matt found more accounts of giants.

Amazingly there were even references to giants in the Bible of all places. Matt found the Book of Genesis spoke of "giants in the earth in those days." *Giants in the earth?* It told that the giants are the offspring of fallen angel trash and the daughters of men.

Matt discovered that after the fallen angels were cast out of heaven two hundred chose to do something so terrible they made a pact knowing there would be a terrible price to pay. They abducted girls and women from their families, their boyfriends, their fiancés, their husbands; all powerless against them. That didn't stop brave men and boys from trying, theirs the greatest stories of love never known, stories of broken hearts and rivers of tears. The two hundred's punishment – bound in chains in Tartarus; a place so terrible the mention of it makes demons cringe.

Cathy ran across a story in the Book of Numbers about a walled fortress city named Jericho in a land called Canaan which she learned is modern day Israel, Lebanon and the western parts of Jordan and Syria. It had been promised by God to the descendants of Abraham, which Satan, as the story goes, had taken and caused to be populated by vicious depraved, human-eating giants called Rephaim or Nephilim as some call them. According to the account, God ordered Moses to wipe them all out – every depraved giant man, giant woman and giant child. The walls of the fortress were destroyed by blowing trumpets. Matt thought of his science project confiscated by the Army. Moses first sent spies into the land to scope things out. Cathy found a verse which read, '*We saw the giants there ... We were as grasshoppers in their sight.*

The Spanish conquistador Francisco Pizarro reported encountering giants in Patagonia. A scholar brought along to keep a journal wrote in it, "And he was so tall that the tallest of us only came up to his waist."

Bernal Díaz del Castillo, a swordsman in the army of Hernán Cortés wrote what the Mayans told the Spaniards:

They said their ancestors had told them that very tall men and women with huge bones had dwelt among them. But because they were a very bad people with wicked customs they had fought against them and killed them, and those of them who remained had died off. And to show us how big these giants had been they brought us the leg-bone of one, which was very thick and the height of an ordinary-sized man, and that was the leg-bone from the hip to the knee. I measured myself against it, and it was as tall as I am, though I am of reasonable height.

Cathy learned Goliath stood six cubits and a span, making him around twelve feet tall, the same height as the *Strand* giant.

In English class Chase had just finished Homer's *The Illiad.* He learned Philostratus, a Greek philosopher reported that Ajax, the real life main character of *The Iliad*, was fifteen feet tall, and Achilles, the greatest warrior of the Trojan War, stood thirty-three feet tall, a common height for full-grown giants. Chase learned a forty-six foot body was found inside a tomb belonging to the Ethiopian Ariadnes – a commonplace finding in his day. But most bizarre of all was a report of the seventeenth century Jesuit scholar Kircher of a skeleton found near Palermo on the Italian island of

Sicily of a giant four hundred feet tall. It could only have been Polyphemus, one of the Cyclops described in Homer's *The Odyssey*.

Impossible thought Chase. Then he happened upon a second report dated 1342 confirming just such a skeleton had been found. Its thigh bone measured one hundred twenty feet. Chase pulled out his calculator to disprove the nonsense. Would a thigh bone that long be anywhere in proportion with a four hundred foot human? He did the math.

He began by looking up the thigh length of the average human male (23.2 inches) and the height of an average human male (68 inches). He found that a thigh bone of one hundred twenty feet is in exact proportion with a four hundred foot human!

Cathy also learned that Philostratus referred to a skeleton so large it was "horrible to behold."

"Next thing you'll be eating Twinkies," said Matt.

Zak remained a holdout until he hacked a top secret Pentagon report that reported an encounter between a U.S. Special Forces team and a giant that occurred in the Kandahar province of Afghanistan in the summer of 2001. A team sent to locate a missing squad was jumped by a 15-foot giant that came charging out of a cave along a goat trail. It moved with supernatural speed spearing one of the soldiers before being killed. It had scarlet hair, six fingers, six toes, double rows of teeth and a stench beyond belief. The locals all knew it was a place of terror where a man-eating giant lived. A helicopter airlifted it out. The soldiers were ordered to rewrite their after-action reports to remove all mention of the giant. The remains of the missing squad were found inside the cave. Word of the incident leaked. Zak's hacking had uncovered one of the most controlled subjects in the world — the subject of giants.

○ ○ ○

"Matt, want to go to the Trace Adkins concert? Daddy said I can bring some friends."

"Country music? No thanks. Not into that stuff," Matt said, having heard somewhere girls like boys who don't fall over themselves trying to get their attention.

"*That stuff?* I bet you ten bucks if you go you'll start likin' country music."

"Make it twenty," Matt said.

So Cathy's dad flew Zak and Cathy, Chase, Matt and a couple of Cathy's girlfriends who were allowed to call her *Too Cute* to Nashville.

Maybe it was the lyrics, maybe it was the melody, maybe it was the screaming fans and the gyrating red, blue, green, orange and purple laser lights that pulsed through the dry ice fog as Atkins sang his *Songs About Me*. Whatever it was Matt found himself loving country music. He exchanged a panicked glance with Cathy who sat wearing a bemused grin. After the concert they went to a teen dance club where they spent hours in a state of trance, lost on the dance floor, lost in the laser lights, lost in the music, remixes and the world of 132 bpm.

During the flight back Matt was enjoying *Jamaica Mistaica* on the inflight sound system. Tucking his fingers into the fold of the slightly-cracked gray leather seat he pulled out a crumpled dollar bill and a handful of crumbs.

"Daddy wants to see you. I think he's out to make a pilot out of you. Chase and Zak didn't work out."

"Here, I owe you nineteen," Matt said, passing her the bill.

He made his way to the glow of the flight gauges. Mr. Kozacky motioned him into the right seat.

"So, you and Cathy seem to be getting close ... you seem like a smart kid. Where're you from? L.A?" It was a rhetorical question.

"Keep your big city ways away from my little angel. We understand each other amigo?" Matt gulped.

"Not exactly, sir," Matt replied meekly, having noticed people around Chickasaw seemed to use 'sir' and 'ma'am' a lot.

"Leave them in the big city otherwise there'll be trouble. Catch my drift amigo?"

"Yes sir, I think so." Matt swallowed hard again, offended by the way Kozacky was assuming things about him in the way *he* had been assuming things about small-towners.

"Let me make it simple," he said. Matt gulped.

"Steer clear of my daughter." There was an awkward silence.

Kozacky burst out laughing. "You should see your face. You look like a deer in headlights. Relax. I'm messing with you. Seriously . . . I'm just not ready for my daughter to start dating boys . . . maybe when she's thirty." Matt breathed.

"Now, how about a flight lesson."

Chapter 11 – SKYFELL

RISING FROM THE LANDSCAPE like a medieval castle, St. Francis Skyfell was *the* independent Catholic college preparatory boarding school destination for students who found themselves sharing the campus now and then with the occasional skunk or meandering cougar. On one occasion a copperhead slithered its way into second period chem lab creating quite a stir. Not that the school was backwoods mind you, anything but.

Matt and Chase were biking to the campus at Aunt Nell's urging to meet with Father Brainard with Cathy tagging along.

Lymon E. Penning III, the *E* stood for Elvis, which is how he preferred to be addressed, was the billionaire founder of a killer tech start-up and to be perfectly honest it was either lose money to taxes or give it away. So Lymon, er Elvis gave – every year – millions, to Skyfell. Campus rumor had it he was old – thirty-one, thirty-two, and the socially awkward type who can't get a date.

The campus had its own observatory, airport, planes, yacht and even a mini-sub. In the great dining hall mail was delivered by drones, androids did the work of staff and teaching assistants, and the dorm rooms had crazy fast broadband.

The majestic hills, big sky and crystal lake were a welcome respite from the sirens of the city. Unexplored hinterlands beckoned like the mythological sirens, those beautiful but dangerous man-eating creatures who lured sailors to their doom causing ships to crash and sink on the dangerous reefs near their island, reefs which sailors said at times seemed to rise up out of the waters. We are far too quick to dismiss the tales of our early seafarers, the astronauts of their day. There seemed fewer dragons in the wilderness waiting to swoop down and scorch one, such as bad memory dragons, where the only thing you can do to ditch them is to think of something else.

Dragons torment adults mostly — dragons of loneliness and despair, of regret, of things that should have been done that weren't, of things that should have been done differently, and things that never should have been done at all. But some dragons hunt kids — dragons of fear, of insecurity, of not feeling good enough. Dragons of divorce, dragons of illness, and dragons of death. And dragons of other things too.

The sun shone a luminous orb its soft edges melding gently into the thin haze. Ivy crept up the clock tower overlooking the quad which chimed two as if to announce their arrival, its copper weathercock searching for the breeze. Each hall bore a name, Yeshua Hall, Covenant Hall, Eden Hall . . . They parked their bikes and strolled through the quadrangle passing a fountain crowded with students dressed in impeccable blue blazers, white blouses and shirts, ties and khaki pleated skirts and trousers.

A group of boys zoomed through the quad on hover boards cutting in and out amongst the students, snatching and pushing as they went. One bumped into Matt sending him sprawling.

"Hey, watch where you're going."

"You got somethin' to say?" Matt ignored him.

"Hey, I'm talkin' to you."

"Relax," Matt told him.

The boy advanced threateningly.

"I'm not looking for trouble," Matt said, fists clenched ready for a fight.

"Well you found it," the boy shot back.

Matt sidestepped the punch and delivered a right uppercut of his own followed by an elbow to the face sending the boy to the pavers. The metallic taste of blood filled the bully's mouth.

"Get flying and don't look back."

"I'll get you," he threatened. "Let's go," he said to the others as they sped off.

"Making friends and influencing people, I see," Cathy joked.

They found Father Brainard in a darkened richly-appointed lecture hall of deeply-beveled recessed dark wood panel squares where his students were sitting in rapt attention staring at images from an overhead projector whilst taking notes. They took seats in the top row.

" . . . and every legend is rooted in fact. In the Western world we've lost touch with our roots and with things taken for granted in other countries," the priest coursed. "Things that happened long ago we dismiss as legend. Based on that, if we were to wait long enough, someday we'd all be legends."

"I *am* a legend," Matt blurted.

The class burst into laughter.

"I'm sure you are," replied the priest. "Can anyone provide us an example?" he asked the priest from his lectern far below.

"Genies?" ventured one student.

"Okay, firmly rooted in Middle Eastern lore."

"Mermaids?" ventured another.

"Good, now let's have a look at the famous U. K. Coast Guard video." The class watched an official government video taken by a U. K. Coast Guard crew during a training exercise in 2003 that had caught a merman surfacing mere feet from their fastboat. The authenticity of the footage was attested to by the head of Her Majesty's Coast Guard himself, who humorously called the slowed, crystal-clear footage of a scaly human-like skull with a pronounced sagittal crest popping out of the water beside their rescue boat a seal. It was followed by an undersea video from an offshore oil rig showing the same sort of creature observed in another part of the world. A cellphone video captured a flowing-haired mermaid sunning herself on some rocks at Kiryat Yam in Israel until aware she had been spotted wriggled back into the sea like a seal.[5]

"Anyone else?"

"Giants," Matt shouted excitedly.

"Ah yes, giants. Folklore is filled with them." The priest adjusted his glasses and peered down at his seating chart . . . "I'm sorry, I don't seem to have your name . . "

"Legend . . . Matt Legend."

"Ah, yes. Of course. So it seems you really are a legend" (to more laughter).

"Fire-breathing dragons?" ventured a shy frail girl wearing horn-rimmed glasses and pigtails sitting a row ahead to a chorus of jeers as she hung her head.

"Yeah. Fire-breathing dragons. Big honkin' ones," Matt shouted (to more laughter.) The girl turned and smiled sweetly.

"You laugh. Yet who's to say fire-breathing dragons didn't exist," said the priest. "There has to be a reason why the folklore of so many countries so distant from each other is so full of them, each describing them exactly the same way." The chuckles stopped. "Bombardier beetles are known to defend themselves by spraying a boiling-hot pulse jet of hydrogen peroxide mixed with a catalytic enzyme formed in a reaction chamber inside their bodies, a form of chemical warfare that persuades frogs to look elsewhere for their meals. Who's to say a flying lizard didn't do the same using a flammable liquid concoction. A flying flamethrower if you will. We all know what happens when water comes into contact with magnesium."

The priest dropped a magnesium strip into a beaker of water. It flared into a white-hot lantern. "Is it possible? Of course. How do you explain electric eels and octopuses that become invisible against their backgrounds like that car in the James Bond movie? Eight hundred fifty volts anyone? Remember, if you can imagine it, it's possible. If you can't, it's just as possible" (laughter). Don't forget . . . final exam Friday, fifty questions, multiple choice. And don't forget your research papers on chemtrails due tomorrow. I want original research. What they are, what they do, who's behind them and why."

The trio descended through the student exodus.

"Thank you" the girl with the pigtails mouthed.

"Looks like somebody's made a friend," Cathy huffed.

"I've been expecting you," said the priest. "Care to see the campus?"

The priest led his guests past a huge borehole in the hallway floor encircled by a waist-high glass partition. A large spongiform of pitted iron and nickel sat at its bottom . . . "It's a meteorite. It's how the school got its name. We left it where it fell. Our scientists have analyzed it. It came from Mars. We know that because of all the meteorites only Mars meteorites are loaded with crazy amounts of Xenon 129 from a past nuclear catastrophe."

Father Brainard seldom missed an opportunity to wind guests around the campus in a golf cart ending with a "fam dive" as he called them. He found the submarine a great ice breaker with visiting VIPs and derived a peculiar satisfaction from making them puke. Harris, the sub tender, held the unpleasant task of wiping it up.

The tour continued. "We have a thousand students," said the priest pointing out an astronomical observatory. "Our educators are the finest anywhere. One of our tenth graders, the son of a Chinese rocket scientist, went aboard a Russian spacecraft for a visit to the ISS. Maybe you'll meet him," he said, straining to be heard above the roar of a vertical takeoff and landing aircraft rising above the treeline.

"Shut up dude!" said Chase.

"What'd you say?" the priest snapped.

"S-s-sorry Doctor … I w-w-wasn't saying shut up. I meant the other kind . . . you know … like means you're kidding but you're not … so …ah … oh well … never mind …"

"Relax, I know what it means," the priest laughed. "Just pokin' fun. What's life without a little fun, eh?" he said with a friendly jab.

“What’s that? . . .” asked Cathy, pointing to a circle of stone slabs set in the grass beside the forest-girded lake. . .“a cemetery?”

“Hardly!” the father cringed. “Ever hear of prayer war?”

“Is that a joke?” Cathy said.

“No joke,” said the priest. “Prayer’s the most powerful weapon there is. It’s a tactical nuke to spirits. They hate it. Most people think it’s just something you do before going to sleep. There was a worldwide study proving how powerful it is. Most people’ve never heard of it though. It’s not the kind of thing you find in the news.”

They traveled across a causeway at the water’s edge which stretched to a round concrete blockhouse offshore.

Bathed in halogens the sub resembled a jet fighter except with stubby wings and a propeller.

“Meet *Nemo III.* She can dive a thousand feet and has a top speed of ten knots. She has a carbon fiber hull, can descend at two hundred fifty feet per minute, ascend at four hundred fifty and has a range of fifty nautical miles. With her lithium-ion battery she can stay down five hours. *Nemo IV* when we get her will be able to dive the deep sea. Did you know more men have been to the moon than to the deepest parts of the ocean?”

“Why only men?” Cathy drawled. “And why are ships called *she* anyway*?*”

“Oh … well … The last time we went to the moon was back in 1972. Things were different back then,” said the priest. “As far as ships are concerned, that’s a good question. Why’s Mother Earth called Mother? Maybe it’s because all the early seafarers were men.”

“My uncle says we got kicked off the moon,” said Chase.

“Kicked off? By whom?” the priest asked.

“Aliens.”

“Oh. Well, I’m sure he must have a very good reason for believing that,” the priest replied diplomatically.

“Father Kubriak says the Wright Brothers made their first flight in 1903,” Cathy added. “It was only seventy years from the invention of the airplane to landing on the moon. So how come it’s been almost fifty, a thousand in tech years, and we haven’t been back? Our science book says we were supposed to have had bases on the moon long ago. Instead moon visits stopped suddenly for reasons that were never adequately explained and we never left low-Earth orbit again. What happened?”

“I don’t know,” said the priest. “Never thought about it.

Cathy was right. Not much more than a hundred years ago in the first true motor race a Panhard et Levassor crossed the finish line after a grueling 48 hour race with a blistering average speed of 15 mph. Twenty years earlier the theoretical limit of travel was thought 30 mph. Any faster and a person wouldn’t be able to breathe it was thought.

Humans have been dying to have bases on the moon. It was the whole purpose of the moon program. Then it was suddenly abandoned. Abandoned with the trillions of dollars in gold and precious rare metals badly needed for cellphones, stealth bombers and flat screens, not to mention the military advantage, the real purpose of moon bases. All of the spacecraft under construction for the planned future missions were sold as scrap metal.

“But as I was saying, there needs to be more women in oceanography. We live on a planet that’s seventy percent water but we’ve mapped less than three. And explored virtually none of its deepest parts. Our oceans are one great mystery. You should do something about it," said the priest.

"Maybe I will," Cathy replied flatly.

"And ninety percent of the planet's animal life lives in the oceans and most of it's unknown to us. Un…be … liev …able. Who says space is the final frontier. And don't get me started on what we know or don't rather about what's under our very feet. It's 4,000 miles to the center of the earth. We've penetrated only seven with a metal tube, the Kola Superdeep Borehole in Russia. Truth is we have no clue what's under our feet. Don't believe what you read. Fancy passed off as fact."

A young Jamaican technician in a lab coat, his black thick coarse hair pulled into a braided ponytail, wearing Coke bottle lenses scurried about in the hot sticky air taking readings from banks of instruments. His round spectacles made him look like a comic book figure with boiled eggs for eyes, magnifying and accenting every blink. He seemed hardly to notice his visitors.

"Soon we'll retrofit her with robotic arms," said Father Brainard. "There're all kinds of things on the ocean floor waiting to be found."

"Like manganese nodules?" said Chase.

"What do you know about those?" asked Father Brainard.

"Long story," replied Chase.

The Jamaican dropped his clipboard and moved to another bank of instruments.

"N fadder, do bringer bok deez time w'out nee damages and wit evy' ting working, kay?"

With a thumbs up Father Brainard slid behind the controls. Matt took the seat beside him.

"Why do *I* have to sit in the back," Cathy fumed.

"BDGOI," Matt responded.

"What!"

"Big deal get over it."

"Oh great, not another Chase. No offense Chase," she quickly added.

"None taken," said Chase. "I'm surprised you don't want to drive."

"Can I?" Cathy asked.

"Some other time little lady," the priest chuckled.

"She's a pilot. Her dad too," Chase added.

"Why didn't you say so," the priest replied. "Here, you two switch places." Cathy beamed. Matt frowned.

"Fasten your belts," said the priest.

After a few minutes explaining the dual controls Father Brainard donned a headset and handed one to Cathy.

Water gurgled across the canopy as the sub entered a portal to the lake. The electric motors whirred as the sub's lights bathed the mouth of a submarine canyon.

"She handles like a jet ski as you can see," the priest announced. "You have control."

With a yank of the stick Cathy rammed the thruster control to its stop, laying the craft on its side like flying aerobatics in her father's P-51. She did a tight counterclockwise circle outside the canyon then whipped hard in the opposite direction. Bubbles engulfed the sub like a dropped fizzy drink.

“No need to be afraid to put it through its paces,” Father Brainard grunted.

“I wouldn’t have said that,” said Chase.

Cathy looped and rolled until they were all quite sick, including the priest who doubled over and with a great ‘ARRGGHHH’ disgorged the meatball and mayo sandwich he’d had for lunch all over the instruments. Nostrils dripping he retarded the thrusters. “ENOUGH!” Matt directed a quivering finger at a fish twice as big as the sub. “*LOOK!*” he gasped as a wall of bony armored plates wriggled past. Then with a lazy wag of its tail the giant sturgeon was gone. The priest grabbed Matt’s outstretched arm.

“Where’d you get that?” A ring worthy of a king graced Matt’s finger, a silver signet ring used to stamp important documents that bore the Star of David and the real name of God in Hebrew.

“I have control,” Father Brainard muttered as he took the stick and hurried back to base.

Chapter 12 – THE CROWN JEWELS

All things are possible.

THE GOOD FATHER reached across his desk to his pipe rack knocking over an ornate carved wood plaque, on it *When in Doubt Kill Everyone, God Will Sort Them Out – United States Army.* Plucking it from the carpet he lit his pipe.

"What brings you kids here?" he asked.

Chase, Cathy and Matt all began talking at once. They told him what they had learned about giants.

The priest studied the ring. "If that's what I think it is. . . I know this sounds crazy . . . I want you to do something. It's just a hunch . . . Say queen's crown jewels appear on Father Brainard's desk."

Matt peered at the crazy man.

"Humor me," said the priest.

"Crown Jewels of England – appear on Father Brainard's desk," Matt obliged. The priest leaned back in his chair and took a slow drag of his pipe.

"Well, it was worth a ..." The priest's jaw dropped. His eyes bulged from their sockets. Spilling over the desk were the most splendid purple robes and breathtaking bejeweled crowns, gold orbs, rings, priceless jeweled scepters, dazzling bracelets and gold daggers. Reaching down he plucked the Sovereign's Orb made for Charles II's coronation in 1661 from the floor, a gold orb inlaid with precious stones and pearls. Thinking it a delusion he picked up his desk phone.

"Sister Cherry, would you step in here a moment please."

The door popped open. In stepped a perky young sister wearing a pink habit.

"Sister Cherry, what do you see?"

"Ummm ....you mean the robes and costume jewels and crowns and stuff?" Her confused eyes darted back and forth. Where had she been when they were carted in? She had been at her desk all day.

"Thank you, Sister Cherry . . . thank you, sister . . . you can go now sister," said the befuddled priest as a no less befuddled Sister Cherry backed her way to the door, her eyes fixated on the priest's desk. She stumbled against a table sending a lamp crashing. Father Brainard stared at his phone and counted down for the red LED to light, the one that told him Sister Cherry was on her phone. Sure enough in the time it took her to reach her desk it lit.

"You'd better put those things back before somebody misses 'em."

Too late. Somebody had already missed them. A Yeoman Warder of Her Majesty's Royal Palace and Fortress the Tower of London, and Member of the Sovereign's Body Guard of the Yeoman Guard Extraordinary, commonly known as the Beefeaters, who had been guarding The Crown Jewels scratched his head. The first time he had looked The Crown Jewels were there. The next they were gone. The next they reappeared before his eyes. The poor man would require years of therapy. "I knew it! That's the lost ring of King Solomon," the priest proclaimed. "The Nazis looked everywhere for that. If they find it we're all dead. Where on earth did you find it?"

A knock sounded. It was Sister Cherry again.

"I'm ah . . . going on break," she said as her eyes scoured the room.

"Where are the Crown Jewels?" she gasped.

"Hypnotic suggestion," the father replied.

"Oh," said the poor Sister Cherry unable to resist one last perplexed look. Her LED lit.

The reverend father went to his bookshelf. He slid a book across the desk. "The two hundred worst human monsters in history," he announced. Matt noted it was also the title. "Can you imagine what any of these psychos would have done with that ring? It must never fall into the wrong hands."

"No women, right?" Cathy smugged.

"I wouldn't say that . . . and Hitler, the great *corporal*," Father Brainard sneered, "was obsessed with finding that ring … *and* the Ark of the Covenant … *and* the DNA of fallen angels . . . *and* the Holy Grail. All part of the failed artist's plan to create technology and a super race to rule the world. He sent his occult Thule Society agents to the four corners of the earth to find them."

The priest shook his head, "We should have lost that war you know. They had jets before us, rockets, superior tanks, better submarines, better torpedoes, more-ferocious machine guns. And I dare say they almost got the atomic bomb first. During the war the famous medium Edgar Cayce said unless there's 'divine interference' the Axis will win. He didn't call it intervention. He called it 'interference.' That tells you which side he and the other mediums were working for. Thank God the Allies got their 'interference.' "

Matt's brain struggled to comprehend the deaths of so many kind, loving people like Anne Frank whose diary he had read in English class, all attributed to one lowly failed artist/psycho corporal turned führer acting with help from other monsters, all evil beyond human capacity.

During a field trip to the Holocaust Museum he had seen the steel cups with the yellow Star of David on them. The ones the children carried to their deaths thinking they were going to get soup. He became angry. Then he cried. Some kids can view the past as the past. Others are condemned to live it. Matt *became* the little boy carrying his cup to the gas chamber in his new shoes. He couldn't bear to finish the field trip. A terrible evil had been committed. He had to do something. But what? How?

"Why are some people good and some bad?" asked Cathy.

"Good question," said Father Brainard. "That's what Congress needs to spend its money on instead of wasting $592,000 to study why chimpanzees throw feces at passersby!"

"They do that in prisons too," said Chase.

"What that is …" said Father Brainard gesturing to the ring, "…is death. Who else knows about it? Think."

"Just us," Matt said.

"Are you sure? *Absolutely* sure?"

"I think so."

"We have to keep it that way. Tell no one. Not your mothers, your fathers, your sisters, your brothers, your best friend, your dog, your goldfish – no one!"

The door swung open. In walked a priest chewing on a piece of straw.

The cowboy priest took one look at Matt and Chase then turned to Father Brainard, "I hope I'm not interrupting."

"Actually you are. What happened to knocking?"

"Aren't you going to introduce me to your fine guests?" pointed the dangerous-looking stranger.

"Matt, Chase, Cathy . . . Father Malvic. The father heads our archaeology department." The name sounded familiar, Matt thought.

"I'm sorry. I didn't catch your last name," said the cowboy priest.

"Legend."

"Ah," he uttered. A disturbing glimmer shone in the stranger's eyes.

The priest turned to Cathy. "Don't I know you?"

"I was in your Anthro class," she sneered. "You gave me a C. It should've been an A. You ruined my gpa."

"Hmmm. Interesting ring," he said turning back to Matt. "May I see it?"

"You wanted to see me?" Father Brainard interrupted.

"Ah, yes. Nothing that can't wait. Sorry for barging in." Father Malvic stole another look at the ring before heading for the door. Before reaching it he stopped.

“By the way, there’s a rumor going ‘round . . . something about some crown jewels,” the dangerous-looking priest said, his eyes scanning the room.

“Surely you jest,” the priest laughed. “Are you going on the field trip?” he asked, changing the subject.

“Wouldn’t miss it,” said Father Malvic closing the door behind him.

“I’d sleep with that on if I were you,” said Chase.

“I agree,” said Father Brainard. “It may have to be destroyed. But think of the good we could do with it. We have thinking to do. Matt, you’re a smart kid. I don’t have to tell you what would happen if that ring were to fall into the wrong hands. I’d sleep a lot better if you’d let me put it in our safe.”

Another kid might have said yes.

“No thanks,” said Matt.

“Be careful then,” said Father Brainard.

The father doubted Matt would be careful enough. Matt wondered why the Father had a kill everyone plaque.

“By the way,” said the priest, “the parapsychology department’s going on a field trip to the haunted penitentiary tomorrow. Care to come?”

“I’ll go,” said Cathy.

As the good father handed out permission forms Sister Cherry returned to find Father Malvic’s ear pressed to the priest’s door. He quickly departed. Sister Cherry pressed her intercom and told the father of Father Malvic’s strange behavior. Father Brainard began to worry.

“Kids, come with me. You need to meet someone.”

Chapter 13 – INVISIBLE WAR

The dark forces will not win.
a Zuni elder

MATT, CATHY AND CHASE followed the priest across campus to where another was winding up a conversation with a student . . . "There're demonic elements to UFOs.[6] People encountering them report the same exact elements as in demon encounters."

"Come in. Come in," invited the bubbly, forties-something, slightly scruffy, ruddy-complected father. He kicked off his penny loafers and hastened across an expensive antique Bezalel rug that depicted King Solomon, Queen Sheba and great Israeli historic figures. "Please, sit down, sit down." The father seated his guests around a badly-gouged oak coffee table, a piece of furniture out of place with the office's fine décor. As it turned out the father was something of an expert on everything biblical – especially giants.

"Fascinating . . . fascinating. The biblical record speaks of them. Every civilization has stories. Granted there's some hoaxery embedded in the archaeology by those trying to suppress the truth but there're enough genuine archaeological finds. Did you know the Great Wall of China was a defense against giants? It was a wall to match the threat. Same with the Himalayan Towers, fifteen-story stone skyscrapers in the Himalayas, some a thousand years old, baffling engineering enigmas, impenetrable fortresses against giants. Built with no windows, only a few tall narrow portals from which arrows could be fired. The reason too for the seventy-foot-high stone wall around the Mayan city of El Mirador and the Great Wall of India, sister wall to the Great Wall of China, all ignored by the quackademics.

And ancient underground cities. Giants are only part of the story. There's an invisible war being fought." Matt remembered the book that had tumbled from Venn's locker, *The Invisible War; What Every Believer Needs to Know About Satan, Demons, and Spiritual Warfare.*

"Matt's mad at God," Cathy said. "Either that or he thinks he doesn't exist." Matt exchanged a dark look with Cathy.

"He let my parents get divorced and my dad die. If there was a God he wouldn't've let that happen."

The father went to a shelf and returned with a river rock. Extending his arm it dropped onto the table –

BANG! !!

His startled guests jumped out of their seats, the reaction he expected.

"There's your proof of God."

"Excuse me?" Matt said, trembling.

"You're right to be mad. Just not at God," said the father. "I was a missionary in Africa. A place where UNICEF says witchcraft is rampant. Ever wonder why Africa's known as The Dark Continent? Despite its beauty it's a continent of juju spells, voodoo and where otherworldly animals and spirits roam when they're summoned. Darkness is its heritage. You grow up in Africa knowing there's black magic and that it's dangerous. There was a young girl training to be a witch doctor. Her training was to spend three days underwater learning from a demon. A water spirit. A mermaid. A Mami Wata. Demons do things in threes to mock the Holy Trinity. One day she went down to the river where a great many swimmers had disappeared, weighted herself down with a bag of rocks and waded in. Three days underwater! No scuba. No snorkel. Dayo . . . Dayo was her name. I had to see for myself. I sat on the bank for three days with the rest of the village until she came up. I'll never forget the dead look in her eyes. Her clothes weren't even wet! She was lucky. The people they abduct are held for three weeks, three months, many for three years even, most are never released. It took two months to get my head straight after that. That rock came from her bag. I keep it as a reminder of what we're up against. I have to get rid of it though. Strange things happen when it's around. I sleep with the lights on. Demons operate in the open in the Third World. It's there you catch them red-handed. The devils are easy to find there. It's here that he wants you to think he doesn't exist. The Devil's the one to be mad at, Matt. He's the source of every bad thing. Evil spirits are most everywhere."

Matt's mind was made up. The demons' extreme wickedness demanded extreme measures. But what could one mortal boy do?

"How come he's only easy to find in the Third World?" asked Chase.

"That's because in many villages evil spirits and demons are all they've ever known. Here people know about the Bible. They may not read it but they know about it. It speaks of demons. If they saw that demons are real even the most doubting Thomases would know the Devil's real, and if the Devil's real God's real. The Devil's working overtime to keep us ignorant about that."

"What about ghosts?" asked Matt.

"Not dead people. Evil spirits. About that giant of yours … the Dead Sea Scrolls say the giants' fallen angel halves become evil spirits upon the death of their human halves. We estimate their current number at just under a million."

"I don't believe in ghosts," Matt said. But if they do exist they're dead people trying to find their way to the other side. Everybody knows that."

"I keep hearing that," said the father.

"No way they're evil spirits," Cathy said. "My grandma leaves a white feather every time she visits. She did that when she was alive too. That's how I know it's her."

"Cathy, they know about her white feathers. And they know much more than that about her too. All used to make you think it's her."

"I'm not buying. How could they know?"

"Evil spirits are everywhere, watching, listening. Not omnipresent thankfully. Sometimes you can feel or see their presence. Other times you can't.

"You heard the father. Why does it have to be grandma?" asked Chase.

"Shut up. Who asked you."

"I used to think they were dead people too," said the father. "The Bible changed my mind. It has over a thousand prophesies. Every one has come true exactly as foretold! There're none in the other so-called holy books. It's proof of The One True God. Because it accurately told of things before they happened it can be counted on to have accurately reported history – and things to come. It says ghosts aren't dead people.

It says the dead are silent in their graves and know NOTHING . . . NOTHING. And it says people have one life to live then they're judged. That rules out reincarnation."

"He's got a point," said Chase. "Why does it have to be grandma?"

"Shut up!" said Cathy.

Chapter 14 – THE RING

"BEN, LOOK AT THIS." Father Brainard gestured to the ring.

Father Herzl leaned forward. "Where'd you get this?" Without waiting for a reply he hustled everyone to an upstairs room where he excitedly waved page after page of tattered golden-yellow Hebrew manuscripts across a big flat screen.

"The Dead Sea Scrolls . . . as the story goes, in 1946 the Dead Sea Scrolls were discovered in a cave on a cliff face within view of the Dead Sea. A Bedouin teen, Jum'a Muhammed, was responsible with two of his cousins for tending goats when some of the goats climbed too high on the cliff and he began to grow concerned. He climbed the face of the cliff when he came across an opening to one of thousands of caves, many unexplored. He threw a rock in and heard a clicking sound. He called excitedly for his cousins who climbed up to view the find. As it was getting late and they had to gather the goats, they would return the next day to find the gold they hoped was inside.

"Muhammed edh-Dhib, the youngest at fifteen, got up the next morning before his cousins and went to the cave. Inside he found tall clay jars along a wall. He frantically searched each but found no gold – only scrolls of papyrus, some of leather and one of copper. Only the greatest archaeological find in history.

"In all nine hundred scrolls were found. They comprise the Bible in its entirety written in Hebrew, Greek and Aramaic, and some books that never made it into the Bible, such as the Book of Enoch and the Book of Giants.

"The Book of Enoch tells of a race of giants that overran the Earth," said the father. "Evil forces have been tampering with our genetics and animals.' The DNA of chimps is ninety-eight percent similar to ours but chimps have less than two hundred genetic disorders. We have six thousand. Six thousand! Mixing between humans and fallen angels is responsible. It created the giants. Archaeologists are passing off juvenile giants as 'neanderthals.' The Book of Giants tells us at least one of them grew to three hundred cubits."

"That's four hundred fifty feet," Cathy spouted.

"I see you're good with numbers. I find that hard to believe myself," said the father, "but it's in the scrolls.

"Genetic engineering," Father Brainard grumbled.

"I'd hate to see *his* grocery bill," Chase snickered. "The Greeks mentioned a giant that big too, your holiness!" The father studied Chase curiously.

"And there're the ruins of Sodom and Gomorrah and at least three other sites around the Dead Sea. The ground's strewn with sulfur balls of a unique composition unlike any sulfur naturally occurring on earth, which is yellow. "Here's one." The father picked up a mason jar bearing a whitish lump.

"It looks like dirt," Matt said.

"*Dirt!*" This made the father very angry because he had gone to great lengths to obtain the priceless relic. Without a word he unscrewed the lid and removed the lump. He placed it on a saucer and held a match to it.

With the stench of rotten eggs and an intense blue flame the lump bubbled into a slowly spreading volcanic black mass of destruction.

"When's the last time you saw dirt do *that*? It's 98% pure monoclinic sulfur mixed with magnesium my young friend. A mixture hot enough to melt anything. Don't worry, I have more.

"And we've been cataloguing disappearances. Look," he added, waving pages, "900-1200 AD – the Mayans disappear … 900-1200 AD – the Anasazi cliff dwellers, who were into using corpse powder of all things, disappear overnight ... 1150-1250 AD. It's still one of the most haunted places on earth – Angkor Thom abandoned … 900-1200 AD – Nan Midol in the South Pacific abandoned … Cahokia on Mississippi River abandoned around 1200 AD and the list goes on and on. All haunted. Tiahuanacu, Machu Picchu, Great Zimbabwe, the Senowa cliff dwellers, the Olmecs … all disappeared around the same time. One pagan civilization after another disappeared off the face of the Earth. The Inca tell some of them fled to Machu Picchu to escape the giants. The same giants who sent the Anasazi and Senowans high into the cliffs where the giants couldn't reach them. God cleaned house."

Desperate to escape the giants many humans also sought refuge below ground, burrowing like moles to avoid their depravities and being torn limb from limb and eaten. Archaeologists are still finding underground cities like Derinkuyu in Turkey, able to house 30,000 people extending thirteen stories down with thousand pound stone doors that can only be rolled opened and closed from the inside, an underground skyscraper. Giants built underground too.

The giants' bottomless hunger exhausted the world's food supply, each eating fifty times what a human eats. They kept humans as livestock. When their supply of humans ran low they ate each other. Indian mythology says giants called Rakshasas reigned over the forests. They ruled a country named Lanka and challenged the authority of the gods. Medieval knights reported encountering giants. Native Americans tell of walled fortress cities in America like Jericho where savage human-eating giants with red hair lived and of those cities being destroyed by "burning pieces of falling moon and stars."

Giants overran The Americas, China, Europe, Africa, the Mediterranean, Australia," the father added. "They dominated most every continent. We're finding some of their cities now and their skeletons and tools and weapons and footprints in stone belonging to giants up to thirty-six feet tall. A legion of Celtic giants, the Senones, even defeated the mighty Roman Army in 390 B.C. at the Allia River and forced the evacuation of Rome – 800,000 people. The largest city in the world. I'll bet they didn't tell you that in school," said the father. "Now *that* kids is history. The Romans' swords were two feet long and weighed three pounds. The giants' swords were eight feet long and weighed forty pounds. The Roman Army, the greatest army in the world. Ran. Routed and massacred. The giants brought an end to Rome. The Greek biographer and essayist Plutarch reported on it."

"How come they don't teach real history in school," asked Matt.

"Maybe they think you'd run screaming from the classroom," said the father. "Seriously a lot of archaeologists built their reputations on what you've been taught in school. If they were to admit there were giants they'd be admitting the Bible's truth. They're atheists mostly. That's why demonic forces are hiding the truth about giants. They don't want people knowing the truth so that they'll keep on believing in lies rather than Jesus Christ. They want everyone thinking giants are nothing but fairytales."

Matt had found the truth he had been seeking.

The Testament of Solomon tells of this ring," he continued. "Many other strange things have been found. Mayan settlements in Georgia, Egyptian artifacts in the Grand Canyon. That's why so many places in the canyon have Egyptian names. There's an ancient underground city of giants there. Big enough for fifty thousand. It's forty-two miles upriver from El Tovar Crystal Creek two thousand feet above the river bed on the east wall. It's 1,486 feet down from the rim just above a shelf that hides it from view from the river. I know. I rappelled it. Almost broke my darn fool neck. It's scary inside. Even the Park Service rangers aren't allowed. A forbidden zone. Look at this . . ." The screen filled with a feature front page six-page article from the Arizona Gazette newspaper dated April 5, 1909. "The paper's still around. It tells the whole story. The Smithsonian can't deny it. It's an embarrassment to it. Someday they're gonna lock those Smithsonian criminals up." The headline read *Explorations in Grand Canyon, Mysteries of Immense High Cavern Being Brought To Light*.

"And the scrolls say this ring of yours gave King Solomon powers."

"Like x-ray vision?" asked Matt.

"Get real," said the father.

"The Testament of Solomon says God gave it to him. He used it to seal letters and decrees. But most of all it gave him absolute power over the seventy-two demon kings of the underworld. He forced them to build his temple with it against their will. He made them cut and levitate its massive blocks. He could even talk to animals with it." As the father summoned another image Matt wondered what good it would be having absolute power over the demon kings. Besides it sounded dangerous.

"This is the *Ars Goetia*. A seventeenth century medieval book. It lists the seventy-two demon kings by name. But never speak their names. Their names must never be spoken unless you want to end up on a freeway sign like that poor kid in L.A. Sacrificing a goat to ward off the demon didn't save him. The demon made an example out of him."

"Huh?" Cathy said.

"That's another story," said the father.

A frayed old worn-out leather volume enclosed by two locking iron hasps appeared. It must surely be an important book to have locks, thought Matt.

And look at this . . ." On the screen was a woman sitting on a thin platform above a crowd of gazing onlookers. "We found this in Iraq."

"You gotta be kidding," said Father Brainard. "A flying carpet?"

"Want to see something that'll really blow your minds? Look closely . . . what do you see?"

"Looks like a wheel," Matt said.

"Not *like* a wheel. It is a wheel."

An underwater photograph showed a four spoke wheel striking in its fine detail and craftsmanship.

"Anyone care to tell me what a chariot wheel's doing on the bottom of the Red Sea?"

“The parting of the Red Sea,” Cathy gasped.

“That’s right Goldilocks. And it never so much as made the six o’clock news.”

“An amateur archaeologist found it. A line of chariot wheels, cabs, axles, human skeletons and horse skeletons along a compressed path on the sixteen kilometer-long sea floor that runs between a beachhead at Nuweiba, Egypt and one on the other side in Saudi Arabia where the evading Hebrews are said to have crossed the Red Sea before the weight of the sea waters held back by God collapsed back in on the pursuing Egyptian army. This is a gold-veneered four spoke chariot wheel lying on the sea floor. One of many. King Solomon commemorated the parting of the Red Sea with a tall inscribed marble marker at each beachhead. The one on the Egypt side is still there, for now anyway.”

Scenes from *The Ten Commandments* danced through Matt’s head. The impact couldn’t have been greater had God himself come down from Heaven.

The good father hustled everyone back to his office to an aquarium.

“Talk to it!” The father’s eyes danced wildly.

“Say what! . . . ” Matt said, thinking another father to have lost his mind.

“Try it,” Cathy said.

He touched the glass and thought the word “Hi.” His eyes grew big as saucers as he stood straight.

“It said something, didn’t it?”

“Somebody said hello. Who said that?” asked Matt.

“Yes!” The father pumped his fist in the air and spun an awkward dance.

“Try again,” said Father Brainard.

“It says it’s hungry … and … and it wants more fish food and that it would be nice if there were other fish for him to talk to ... and … he says Mrs. Ogilvy doesn’t like him. He wants somebody else to feed him.”

“We’ll make a fortune in the fish business,” Chase murmured.

“So what are you going to do, Matt?” Father Herzl prodded as he hustled his visitors down the hall, “You know something the rest of the world doesn’t. That ghosts are evil spirits. The human race is sleep-walking. You have to warn it.”

“Why me?

“You have the ring that makes demons do things against their will.”

“My father died . . . nobody’s helping me . . .”

“This is all new to him,” offered Cathy.

“So what are you going to do son?” the father asked.

“Tell me about your father, Matt,” said Father Brainard.

“Nobody understands.” As he stopped a lump filled his throat. His chest tightened. Some dragons last forever . . . “we were gonna do things . . . when I was nine he bought me a suit . . he took me to his meetings. He told everybody I was his son and that I was the future of the company,” Matt smiled, picturing himself seated at the massive boardroom conference table, his feet dangling over the edge of the chair, barely able to see over the table. “There was this one meeting . . . I was asking lots of questions but I was excited about being there,” his voice cracked. “After my second question he said I should hold my questions until after the meeting. I felt like my questions weren't important. I felt like *I* wasn't important. I felt like I'd let him down. All I wanted was for him to be proud of me." Matt grimaced. Tears filled his eyes.

"They always say that at meetings. You didn't let him down," said the father. "He was proud of you. The best way you can honor him is to use what he gave you."

"My advice is don't look back. You're not going that way. You want to do something about it or not?"

Matt nodded.

"I like this kid," said Father Herzl.

"I guess we'll find out soon enough whether you have the heart for it or not," said Father Brainard.

"There's a light coming from you," said the father. "I saw it when you came through the door. You're going to do something great for God someday."

A light? Matt pondered.

"I didn't see that coming," said Cathy.

Chapter 15 – LYING SPIRITS

It is said two percent of people think. Three percent of people think they think and ninety-five percent of people never think at all. Sit alone in a room for a day without phone, TV or internet. If you're still sane, you might be a thinker.

A TEN-FOOT-THICK WALL encircled the dark brooding penitentiary. Built of the same rough-hewn dark brown stone as its sorrowful buildings it was comprised of a central guardhouse with six cellblocks that radiated from it like the spokes of a wheel.

"Six blocks. Choose your block," said the guide.

"Stay out of six," she warned.

"Why? What's in six," asked Zak.

"Just stay out."

The air was electric. As the lights dimmed the guide flicked on a lamp attached to her ample waist, its beam casting an eerie shadow across her sagging jowls. A hush fell over the boisterous crowd as she explained it was built like a wheel so its guards could look down the length of each block.

"This is a place where criminals could be made penitent for their crimes it was thought, hence the term 'penitentiary,' said another docent, an old man who you could still see the boy in wanting to get home to his train set. "It didn't work. Most are still here."

"There's an energy," voiced the ample guide. "Feel it? It's the prisoners and the dead guards. The poor souls. They don't know they're dead. They're still trying to find their way to the other side."

"I can see dead people," Zak laughed.

"Laugh now fuzz ball," the docent scowled. "You'll be screaming for your mama before the night's out." Zak gulped.

Two students stood outside Cellblock Three and four outside Cellblock One. Cathy stood alone outside Five. Matt opened the door to forbidden Cellblock Six and stepped inside. With a bang the steel door slammed.

"It closed by itself! I saw it! It closed by itself!" Chase cried.

The tour guide struggled with the locking arm. "It won't budge. Nothing like this has ever happened before. I said not to go in there. Y'all heard me!"

"It's part of the frightfest," Zak proclaimed. "This place must be dope on Halloween!"

"Is there another way in?" asked Father Brainard.

"A utility tunnel runs beneath the cell block," the guide replied frantically.

"Show me. Don't move, Matt," Father Brainard shouted. "I'm coming Matt."

Matt inched forward, his eyes straining to adjust to the dark. A sliver of moonlight glimmered through a line of evenly spaced rectangular ports overhead. Plaster crackled underfoot.

The cellblock reeked of two hundred years of blood, sweat, fear, feces and urine – things no amount of Clorox will ever make clean. Mold, mildew, standing water, rat droppings, vomit, sputum, fermented fruit used to make illicit hooch, cigarette smoke, teargas, tears, greasy clothes and the rotting sheets and mattresses left behind by its last inmates made for a stench a thousand times worse than the boys locker room at school.

He came to the end of the cellblock. The air grew icy suddenly. A cell door creaked open. A figure in a flowing white nightgown stood watching him. He cleared his eyes. It was gone. He hastened shuddering back the way he had come, away from the cold spot passing a cell, its shelf coated with a thick layer of dust, cobwebs and dusty glass jars that bore peeling decaying labels. Behind him a cell door slammed. His heart pounded. He heard a faint weeping, whispering and giggling.

"Father Brainard?" . . . there was no answer.

Two small red lights appeared. Matt pressed his face against the cold steel bars.

"THE RING!" thundered. He exploded back striking his head on the concrete wall. The lights in his head flashed. Holding his throbbing skull he stared in horror as a wispy fog-like form wafted through the bars. His eyes couldn't look away no matter how much they tried. The thing's red glowing eyes were like embers in a fire making their own light. Matt's muscles stiffened. He tried to run but couldn't.

"Give it to us," many voices cried.

"The boy knows the ring's power," a female voice screeched. "Do not tarry with him." It was the voice from the witch's house!

The wispy form transfigured into an array of brilliant alternating strands of ruby and white lights in the shape of a human before assuming the form of a man in a black suit with an open-collared black silk shirt. Sweat poured from Matt's brow.

"In return for the ring we will grant you three wishes."

"W-w-w--what are you?" Matt squeaked.

"The vast and ancient multiverse holds mysteries and powers of which you know nothing."

"Three wishes?" Matt whimpered his breathing short and ragged.

" -- and the wisdom of the ages – *for* the ring. Imagine — the lost knowledge of the Library at Alexandria. Where to find diamonds, gold, oil, lost treasure, King Solomon's mines – anything your heart desires. Power and riches beyond your imaginings. Yours for the taking." A once in a thousand lifetimes opportunity beckoned but Matt was nobody's fool.

"I don't need that. We have the internet."

"Do not be stupid. It is no match for celestial knowledge."

"He's been here before," his grandmother used to say. Not that she believed in reincarnation for she was a church-going woman. It just rolled off the tongue easily.

Matt knew with the wishes would come a terrible price. The devil is in the details they say.

"We will grant you powers beyond your imaginings. These our gifts to you."

"Gifts?" asked Matt shaking, remembering *Something Wicked This Way Comes*, a story about the devil going around collecting souls in exchange for so-called gifts – the desire of one's heart – beauty, health, wealth, fame – only to trick the desperate, rendering the grant useless and the person far worse off than before, less their soul.

A blood-curdling laugh bore through the cellblock. Matt's stomach contracted. "There is no good. There is no bad, my boy. There is only life. Notions of good and bad are but an illusion."

"… and heaven? What about heaven?" asked Matt timidly.

"Everyone is there. Those you call good, those you call bad … everyone goes to heaven. As the creature spoke the cells filled with all the dead prisoners they had ever held as if to underscore his point. The anguished souls vanished just as quickly. You should make the most of the time you have. Life is what you make it my boy. Grab life by the horns, er . . . why *shouldn't* you have everything you want? Life is yours for the taking. There are no rules. It's survival of the fittest. It always has and always will be. A smart boy like you knows that surely.

"Do what you will. There are no penalties. Penalties are a lie. Everyone goes to the afterlife. Join us."

"Will Hitler be there? . . . and you," asked Matt.

"Everyone," the devil replied. "Don't you want to go having done everything you have ever wanted to do in this life first? If you don't, you'll have regrets. Regrets for eternity. It's not the things you do you regret most. It's the things you didn't. You only come this way once my boy. Do you like cars? money? girls? Do you have a girlfriend? . . . boyfriend?"

"Girlfriend. No," Matt replied.

Three of the prettiest girls he had ever seen appeared, beside them a cart piled high with precious gems and bars of gold. From a red leather attaché case spilled banded bundles of thousand dollar bills. A red Ferrari F355 (his favorite car) and a red Honda superbike stood nearby their engines revving furiously surrounded by other earthly treasures – the latest laptops, expensive sports shoes, cell phones, jewelry and other needful things.

"I don't have a driver's license."

"Yes you do my boy." A driver's license floated before him. He grabbed it. It looked real. It even bore his photo, a photo he had never seen before of himself and a strange address — 666 Headless Lane, Broken Dreams City. A shiver ran through him.

"I never would have believed it." Matt spun on his heels relieved to see Father Brainard.

"I heard it all. They're things I must know. I have questions . . ." .

"After me," Matt ventured, feeling a might bolder. With this ring I command you. Answer my questions truthfully. Are ghosts dead people?" he asked, turning back to the demon.

Snapping back to Father Brainard, "Is there anyone with you?" he asked anxiously.

"No," said Father Brainard.

Matt turned disappointed back to the demon. "Answer," he ordered.

"Ghosts are the spirits of the children of the Fallen Ones."

"Who are the Fallen Ones?"

"We are the Fallen Ones who lost our place in the First Estate," the demon snarled.

"First Estate?"

"You mortals call it Heaven."

“How m-many are you?” Matt gulped.

“We are legion.”

“Who are the offspring of you fallen?”

“Giants. We are their fathers. Human women are their mothers.”

Matt’s research had told him the offspring were giants but still he was confused.

“How can giants be ghosts?”

“Giants become spirits when they die.”

“How many are there?”

“Millions.”

“Are there giants living today?”

“Yes.”

The demon’s words were cold and exact, revealing no more than necessary.

“Where?”

“Inside the earth.”

“Is there life after death? . . . for humans.”

“Only through The One Born of a Virgin. None inherit eternal life but through him.”

“What’s the purpose of ghosts?”

“To deceive.”

“How? Why?”

“To steer mankind away from The One Born of a Virgin. We deceive you into believing there is life after death for everyone.”

“But you said there’s life after death for everyone.”

“I lied. That was before I was commanded to tell the truth.”

"Explain."

The demon revealed how he and the other Old Ones have been tampering in the affairs of mankind since the dawn of time and how being ever-present and knowing much about the lives of most people who have lived are able to impersonate the dead for the purpose of steering mankind away from God. He spoke of the Old Ones, having been transformed by "The Creator" into creatures to match their ugliness inside, creatures so hideous as to cause nausea. The reason demons hate mirrors. It taxes their energy to maintain other forms, including their long lost heavenly angelic forms. He revealed how they lie about still possessing them to recruit what he called "stupid apostate cattle" such as celebrities willing to sell their souls thinking Hades will be party time at a country club grateful for their service, not having read the fine print in their contracts, never knowing the unspeakable tortures awaiting them when they die. Fresh meat in a world that knows no sleep, where their begging and screaming is the entertainment, the price of ill-gotten fame from creatures who know their worst fears and will inflict them 24/7/365, most unaware they can cancel the contract by turning to God. The demon went on to explain how they can even transform themselves into animals, even a mosquito or other insect, even the illusion of distant inanimate objects such as an airplane though the image taxes their energy which is why they can only maintain it for brief periods and why it is often seen to falter.

"Is there a Hell?" asked Matt.

"Yes."

"What's the main thing keeping people from finding this God you fear so much?"

"Television and our false religion."

"Television?" Matt laughed until he saw the demon wasn't joking.

"False religion?" asked Brainard.

"We war against the sons of Israel and Christians and we distract," the demon roared.

"Why do you hate us? We've done nothing to you," said Father Brainard.

"Answer him," Matt ordered.

"In you we see our enemy, The Great I Am. You, made in his image. He who banished us from our First Estate. He who destroyed our Second Estate, now the asteroid belt. He who destroyed our abode on Mars – once a garden planet, now a wasteland, and the other planets." The demon's rage over being forced to answer questions was causing Matt and Father Brainard no inconsiderable fear.

"We hate you – your bodies, your creativity, your arts, culture, music, emotions, although I do like your Ferraris And your love, the strongest force in the universe. It is even stronger than our hate. We want to be you. You see what we want you to see. Think what we want you to think. Do what we want you to do. We will not tolerate you thinking for yourselves. We were once proud with high positions. We looked down on man. Now there is not one among us who would not exchange places with the lowliest of you. I want to be worshipped.

"Stupid humans. You propagate like locusts even as you drown in your filth and destroy your planet. We have pulled the wool over your eyes so completely you do not know what you are or where you come from.

"This world is not yours. We hunger but cannot eat, thirst but cannot drink." Red orbs swirled as the creature ranted swirling faster and faster as he grew angrier. "And when The One Born Of A Virgin returns, I and the other gods will be destroyed . . . **DESTROYED!"** . . . Plaster rained as a fissure opened in the floor. The cell doors opened and slammed making a terrible racket . . . Matt covered his ears . . ."with the sheep who follow us . . .that is why we hate you so. Why we gave you forbidden knowledge – how to smelt bronze and iron for swords" – *the Bronze Age and the Iron Age thought Father Brainard* … "and the formula for gunpowder" – *he had puzzled his entire life over that too – the intricate mix of diverse chemicals in specific amounts that no one in a million years would have thought to look for let alone to combine to form something unheard of — an explosion, let alone Man in the Stone Age. It had never made sense before* . . . "has anything worked so well at leading you pathetic puppets down the paths we send you." The hair on Matt's body stood up.

"Show your true self," he demanded. The gargoyle let out a fearful howl. It had the head of a bull and the torso of a man. From the waist down it was a goat. Two red forked tongues flicked between pointed teeth.

Between its red horns sat . . . a vegetable? . . . a cauliflower? The strange growth bore a resemblance to the cordyceps fungus — a fungus that grows on the heads of ants and transforms them into zombies. Matt had seen it in National Geographic. It seizes control of their brains, makes them climb to a high spot, clamp down on a leaf and as it liquefies their organs makes them wait for a signal, like a human suicide bomber, to explode a cloud of spores to infect their colony. Genetic engineering by devils.

"Have you tampered with our genetics?" Father Brainard asked.

"Yes," the demon arrogantly replied.

Starfleet Prime Directive General Order 1 prohibits interfering with other cultures and civilizations. The demon's contempt for mankind was like the Borg's contempt for all things living, thought Matt.

Demons have ranks. There are nine levels just as there are nine levels to the underworld. The lower ranking have loose lips. Those higher guard their secrets well. This one appeared of high rank. "We have polluted your DNA and that of animals. We have created hybrids that have infiltrated your militaries, your governments, your societies, your churches."

"Tell me more about your false religion," asked Father Brainard. As the demon went on Matt was shocked by a familiar voice.

"How's my Kid CEO?" Matt spun on his heels.

"Dad! . . I thought you were . . ." he couldn't bring himself to say it – *dead.* His thoughts flashed to his father's funeral. Unable to say goodbye he had run crying from his mother's side,"Wake up Daddy! Daddy wake up please! Don't leave me daddy," he had cried climbing into his father's casket, tugging on his body. "Wake up Daddy! Daddy wake up." Laying his head on his father's rock-hard chest, "Daddy please, please don't leave me," he wailed. "Ah, the love of a boy for his father," pronounced the astonished minister whose eyes filled with tears even as he struggled to continue his eulogy on love as he rushed over to pry the boy from his dead father. He scooped him up into his arms a moment before the casket crashed to the floor breaking apart spilling his father onto the church floor.

The horrified preacher plopped beside the distraught boy, took him into his arms and rocking him gently said, "Listen to me, listen Matt, it's going to be okay … your father was a good man …. I'm sorry … it's okay to cry …. he loved you very much. But we have to say goodbye now. You have to say goodbye. You have to be strong."

There wasn't a dry eye in the congregation.

"I missed you son."

Matt rushed to his dead father's waiting arms. He wasn't dead after all. His was the rush of relief only those getting a second chance at life can know. But the blur between what is real and what is imagination made it easy to forget where he was.

"I love you Daddy. I never got to say goodbye . . . then –

– Straighten up little soldier. Go 'head. Give 'em that dumb old ring if that's what they want . . ."

He had forgotten about the ring. If surrendering it was the price of getting his father back he would gladly give it a million times.

"Go for it Matt," said the red-haired girl.

"Come with us," said the chestnut-haired girl. "You can't lose."

Can't lose? … Where had he heard those words? He remembered. Cathy, on the front porch swing. Her demand he join Young Marines — her price for helping him.

"Don't move," Matt ordered. The teens froze.

"So this ring works on you too . . . and you," he said, turning to his father . . . "*Are* you my father?" he asked, fighting back tears, praying his dad was not some devilish imposter.

"My father knows something about me nobody else does," Matt said.

"There's no need for this son . . . It's me."

"Sorry father. You taught me too well. If you answer this right I'll give them the ring."

"There's no need s–"

– When I was five, you promised me something for Christmas. Something I really, really wanted. We even went to Toys "R" Us to pick one out. On Christmas morning I ran downstairs. It wasn't there. I was heartbroken. You found out years later from mom. It's haunted you ever since. What was it?"

"Heck, son. How do you expect me to remember that? That was such a long time ago."

Tears filled Matt's eyes.

"It was a battery-powered ride-on. A Jeep. You're not my father," he sobbed. The entity transfigured.

Deep inside half of him desperately wanted his father back no matter if he was an imposter. He could always pretend the thing wasn't couldn't he?

"Matt!" Father Brainard snapped, wrenching Matt from his daydream. He drew back from the dark thought.

"Matt . . . Houdini, the greatest escape artist of all time said his greatest escape act ever would be to escape from the grave. Just before he died he gave his wife a password so she would know it was him. She never heard back from –

"GIVE ME THE RING," the demon screeched.

Summoning his courage Matt faced the creature. "If you could take this ring, you would," he said. "Because you haven't means you can't. And if you can't, there's only one reason – someone's keeping you from it. Someone more powerful than you I'm guessing. The only way you can get it is if I give it to you. You're right, I *do* know the ring's power and I know there's nothing you can give me I don't already have with it."

Matt held his breath. The demon was about to say more when with a wave of his hand Matt cut him off. "All of you. Go. Not you. You stay," said Matt to the devil. The teen monsters and imposter vanished.

"No one's going to believe this," said Father Brainard."

"Where'd this ring come from?" Matt said.

"A gift from The God of Gods to King Solomon."

"Is there anything I can't do with it?"

"You cannot harm anyone, you cannot bend anyone's will to yours except ours, you cannot make anyone fall in love with you, you cannot travel across time."

"Near-death experiences . . . are they real?" asked Matt.

"The King of Kings gives them. So do I. Mine are lies."

"Who are you?" asked Matt.

"I have many names . . . "Lucifer . . .The Evil One . . . Destroyer of Worlds . . . Satan . . . The Count of Saint Germain . . . The Father of Lies . . . The Old One . . . Djinn . . . The Serpent . . . The Exalted Snake . . . Prometheus . . . Enki . . . Azazel . . . The Morning Star . . . The Giver of

Knowledge . . . The Lord of Er . . . The Lawless One . . . Lord of the Flies . . .

"Okay, I get it — "

Matt and Father Brainard cringed. They were face to face with The Devil himself. The rattled priest struggled to collect his thoughts.

"W-w-what about reincarnation?" he stammered.

"A deception."

Matt turned to Father Brainard . . . "Anything else?"

"Not now," said the priest terrified but chomping at the bit to ask questions having to do with technology. Trillions stood to be made. He had just learned from The Devil himself that man did not arise from primordial ooze, nor did any plant or animal for that matter, a theory he had always found laughable were it not so preposterous given the fantastically complex biological software coding found in every living thing and the mind-boggling array of millions of fantastically-engineered plant and animal life forms, not to mention only complete fully-formed plants and animals have ever been found, glad for the confirmation nevertheless. He hated that science confirmed the Bible but the more he learned about computers and engineering the more he marveled at their similarities to living things. Living things didn't create, code or build themselves either he reasoned, having found never a shred of valid evidence supporting the evolutionist lemmings' beliefs that one species can turn into another and that their relatives are monkeys.

"Wait, where do we come from?" asked Father Brainard. It was the question for the ages.

"The Great I Am is the creator and ruler of all the universe."

"The Great I Am? God? Why are we here? . . . What's man's purpose?"

"The purpose of man" . . . the devil began . . . the priest held his breath . . . "is to respect and honor the Name Above All Names, and to fulfill His individual purpose for you, his children, benefitting yourselves, The Creator, all mankind and every living thing in the universe through living life abiding by the Commandments," echoed through the cellblock.

"The Ten Commandments?"

The priest pondered how different the world would be.

"Are you able to harm us?"

"Not so ever as you hold the ring," the devil replied.

"Don't let anything happen to that ring, Matt," Father Brainard blurted.

"In that case let's have some fun," said Matt.

"Devil, jump up and down on one hoof."

Obediantly The Devil began to jump up and down.

"Faster! And moo like a cow."

The devil jumped up and down and mooed like a perfect fool . . . "What a wuss. No wonder you got kicked out of heaven. I'm done," Matt laughed.

"Yes, master," the devil replied angrily.

"Make him do the Funky Chicken," said Father Brainard.

"What's that?" asked Matt.

"He'll know."

"Do it," Matt ordered. The ruler of the underworld began walking around in circles flapping his arms and jerking his neck on an unseen dance floor. Rufus Thomas' *Do the Funky Chicken* played.. Matt and Father Brainard laughed until their sides hurt and they remembered where they were.

"And bounce a basketball on your head at the same time," Matt ordered. "And dress like a court fool, fool."

"He's got skills, I'll say that," he laughed at the jingling bells of the fool's red and green hat.

"From now on you'll be known as 'Devil Trash.' You're stupid and you'll be extinct soon. You're a joke . . . What?"

"Yes, master. I am."

"Stop," Matt ordered. "Anything else?" he asked the priest.

"One more question … do the Sumerian tablets tell the truth?" asked the priest of the thousands upon thousands of ancient clay tablets found which tell the story of the fallen angels and their dealings with humans.

"Lies sprinkled with fragments of truth to make the lies believable," the devil trash replied. "Our answer to the Dead Sea Scrolls."

"Leave us," Matt ordered. The jingle bells, the court fool, the gold, money, car, needful things, the superbike vanished.

"You'd have to be an even bigger fool than him to follow him. And he wants to be worshipped!" Matt laughed. "Give me a break!"

The consequences for the future seemed dreadful with devils skulking about causing wars, murders, suicides, pestilence, disease, famine and every form of mayhem with their needy leader and those stupid enough to follow him foolishly trying to win a war they've already lost. Demonic spoiled brats obsessed with burning down the candy store after being refused candy by their parents.

Cathy was waiting with the others in the guardhouse when Matt and Father Brainard appeared.

"Did you find Casper?" asked Chase. Strangely, those in the guardhouse appeared to know nothing of the raucous goings on in Cellblock Six.

"Yeah ... and he's not friendly," said Matt.

"What'd he look like?

"A big L."

Cathy was having a full on panic attack.

"Something pushed me, something in there pushed me, and scratched me," she blurted, with fear in her voice staring at the raised welt on her forearm just before a big chunk of plaster fell on her.

Matt began to research ghosts and found some interesting and disturbing stuff. He went as far back as 10,000 B.C. when woolly mammoths lived, the time of Jericho, the first civilization, and found there was no transition between it and the Stone Age. The Jericho-Sumerian civilization, an advanced brutal sadistic society that lied in the region of the fertile valley between the Tigris and Euphrates rivers, modern day Iraq, suddenly appeared out of nowhere. The Sumerians possessed advanced farming and agriculture, metallurgy, writing systems, mathematics, astronomy, construction and more. The Sumerians made many references to ghosts and they all without exception had to do with the underworld. The Sumerian afterlife always involved a descent into a gloomy netherworld to spend eternity in a wretched existence as a ghost. Therefore ghosts and the underworld were linked! The Sumerians claimed they landed on Earth from somewhere else and there was no mistaking they were the fallen angels. Matt had found the missing link connecting ghosts with fallen angels. It was the underworld. He would have to tell the world.

Chapter 16 – "WE ARE ALL IN DANGER"

We're living in Jurassic Park and
99% of us don't know it . . yet.

IN CELLBLOCK SIX, Father Malvic stood rehashing everything he had heard from the shadows.

"The boy knows our secrets," cried many voices.

"Kill him. Kill him now. If you cannot kill him, kill the girl. If you cannot kill them, kill their parents.

"They're in the light," Father Malvic warned.

"Use the suitcase nuclear bomb."

The priest gulped. "As you wish my lord."

"Recover the enslaver at any cost," the many voices cried.

"The enslaver?" Father Malvic asked.

"The ring you fool."

"When I deliver this . . . enslaver . . . "what gift will I receive?"

"You dare to ask? You who have been given so much!"

It was true. Father Quintus Malvic's star had risen in academia overnight due to his ability to translate dead writings. Prestigious institutions had been vying for him for years. He had chosen the Skyfell order because it was far from prying eyes. Little could his colleagues know his understanding came from the underworld.

All Quintus had to do to receive the meaning of any pictograph, hieroglyph or other writing was to ask. For the asking a demon would even reenact any important speech or conversation through the ages – even ones before recorded history – by any person word for word in the speakers' own voices. Any conversation – even privileged ones – reenacted by the very demon who had been present, which meant having to locate that particular demon.

Malvic knew the identity of Jack the Ripper and who killed JFK and Secretary Forrestal. According to the Navy, U.S. Navy Secretary James Forrestal died of "suicide" of having jumped from the sixteenth floor window of the Bethesda Naval Hospital where he had been forcibly hospitalized and prevented from seeing or talking to anyone, including his wife. The reenactment told a different story – he was thrown.

Almost a year after WWII ended a top secret joint Russian, U.S., British, Norwegian, Australian and Canadian battle group led by U.S. Navy Admiral Richard Byd steamed to Antarctica to destroy a secret Nazi stronghold. World War II wasn't over it seemed. Codenamed Operation Highjump, on arrival the fleet was attacked by flying disks defending the base. The destroyer USS Murdoch and many men and planes were lost. The Murdoch's records were later changed to make it appear it was lost otherwise elsewhere. The humiliated battle group limped home. The Nazi base is a city state, Neuschwabenland, New Berlin, a warm world two miles below the Antarctic ice sheet with a population of two million in solid land cavernous regions so large they have their own weather systems.

A man of great honor, Forrestal had demanded the public be told. General MacArthur dared warn only there would someday be an intergalactic war. Admiral Byrd went so far as to warn through a Chilean newspaper *El Mercurio* and a news conference that it was imperative the

United States initiate immediate defensive measures against hostile regions, stating that though he didn't want to frighten anyone unduly, it was a bitter reality that in case of a new war the continental United States would be attacked by flying objects which could fly from pole to pole at incredible speeds. When he returned to the United States, he too, was forcibly "hospitalized" and prevented from holding any more news conferences and ordered to keep quiet. As for Secretary Forrestal, the Navy would later name an aircraft carrier class in his honor.

Admiral Byrd, another man unwilling to sell out his honor, kept a secret diary. He gave it to his son with instructions to publish it after his death. When his son did he was threatened with death. He published it anyway. He was found dead under strange circumstances. The diary told of the hollow earth and of an advanced civilization the admiral encountered there during his arctic expedition of 1926, an expedition for which he became a national hero, a hero under strict orders to keep quiet about the discovery. He went looking for the North Pole and found The Land Beyond The Poles.

Brave astronaut Buzz Aldrin tweeted from Antarctica in 2016, "We are all in danger. It is evil itself." He was forcibly hospitalized and told to stop tweeting or else.

Chapter 17 - STONEHENGE

Hell is empty and all the devils are here
—William Shakespeare

WE LIVE IN A VIOLENT world. One need only turn on the six o'clock news to know that.

And there was Stonehenge. Known by The Old Ones as 'The Ruin.' While the archaeological world bumbles over its purpose thinking it an observatory or cemetery or such, Father Malvic knew its purpose. On the winter and summer solstices it was a place of Druid terror — a witches' disneyland. One of many stonehenges. A place where innocent men, women and children, especially children, the demons' favorite victims, were subjected to every form of demented torture, mayhem and death. Made sport of before being burned alive, made to bob for apples in boiling water, beheaded and disfigured, their faces smashed in with clubs, their beating hearts cut out for the pleasure of the demons summoned through its portal. Into the circle of one hundred fifteen "Aubrey Holes" surrounding the henge were sunk pine posts onto which human sacrifices taken from the surrounding countryside were impaled and set aflame, a grisly circle of living torches to light the abomination.

And there was Burning Man, the towering seventy-foot wicker basket in the shape of a human into which victims were imprisoned before being burned alive. Archaeologists are finding upwards of four thousand human remains and may find more. As with every single of the world's megalithic sites from the great pyramids down the ground is soaked in human blood compliments of the fallen angels (aka "The Gods").

They ate children. Hooded Druids went about the countryside amid hovering orbs after dark banging on doors demanding a "trick or treat." Lest the household give up a child or other inhabitant if there were no children, the door was marked for visitation later that night by demons thirsting for the blood of the entire household. The true meaning of Halloween.

Demonic-faced Jack-o-lanterns were fueled with the body fat of their victims. At the end of the festivities the bodies were buried and the witches flew home before the dawn. Stonehenge; a far cry from the sanitized well-scrubbed world of Harry Potter.

In the Encyclopedia of Witches, Witchcraft & Wicca a witches Sabbat is described thus:

> *In 1659 a French shepherdess gave this description of a sabbat that occurred on the summer solstice, observed by her and some companions: They heard a noise and a very dreadful uproar, and, looking on all sides to see whence could come these frightful howlings and these cries of all sorts of animals, they saw at the foot of the mountain the figures of cats, goats, serpents, dragons, and every kind of cruel, impure and unclean animal, who were keeping their Sabbath and making horrible confusion, who were uttering words that were most filthy and sacrilegious that can be imagined and filling the air with the most abominable blasphemies.*

So was Stonehenge.

In 1692 in the colonies there were the Salem Witch Trials. As Malvic learned, a great many nasty witches were done away with. Unfortunately, along with them, many people who weren't witches, victims of old grudges that could be settled by simply declaring someone a witch. The Devil had planted his witches in the emerging nation to try to prevent it from becoming the nation under God it was destined to become. The witch trials caused the Devil's plan to fail and the nation under God was born.

Chapter 18 – FATHER MALVIC

PROFESSOR OF ARCHAEOLOGY, Father Quintus Arelius Malvic, the only child of Walter J. and Doris P., the New York construction magnate Malvics, never had the slightest interest in archaeology. He had to major in something in college so he chose archaeology because that was where the dart had landed.

To be honest the twisted way Quintus turned out wasn't entirely his fault. Little would that have mattered to the West African village he wiped off the face of the earth. Forty-seven men, women and children slaughtered by mercenaries called in to rake the village with machine gun fire because its chief had refused him permission to dig, their deaths blamed on rebels.

Father Malvic's father's construction cronies thought themselves like the Spartan warrior class fathers of ancient Greece, who placed their twelve-year-old firstborn sons alone in the wild. As a rite of passage the boy had to kill a wolf to prove his bravery and skill. That was where the similarity ended. The self-styled wannabes gave their sons a big hunting knife, a pep talk and put them inside a chain-link ring with an angry pit bull. Fathers spent weeks, months, years prepping their sons for the big day. When Quintus' turn came he climbed the chain-link to get out. His embarrassed father never forgave him. Quintus never forgave himself. Only after another unfortunate boy didn't make it home did his grieving mother put two and two together and the ring was shut down.

There is no money in archaeology so he peddled stolen archaeological treasures. Cut off from the family fortune, his ill-gotten gains eased his pain. He owned a modest bungalow in Chickasaw and a palatial estate, Lavisham Cottage, secreted three counties over, defended by cassowaries, vicious attack birds. Cassowaries are rare three-toed emu-like terror birds, five-feet tall weighing around 125 pounds with a 5-inch-long dagger claw on the middle toe that can slice a person open with a single kick. One of the birds killed his gardening crew. And his shady dealings led him into something even shadier – arms dealing, for which his archaeology professor day job and turned-around collar was the perfect cover for passing through Customs on the way to peddling nerve gas to terror groups. And he was spiritual. But not the way one might expect.

At an archaeological dig on an Indian reservation Quintus had witnessed a shape-shifter, a medicine man, a skinwalker, change into a half-human, half-wolf-like creature that shifted into a cat, then a crow, then fire, then a whirlwind – a "dust devil." The Navajo Rangers were called in to investigate the death of a woman ripped apart by an "unidentified animal" which it declined to identify. From hiding he had watched the creature slip into and out of invisibility. Should you ever run across such a creature, I suggest you follow the Native Americans' advice. Don't look at it, stay far away and lock your doors. Shotgun blasts fired point blank don't faze them. It was a short leap from not believing in any higher power to believing in the wrong one. Though it meant he was making God his enemy in his personal misery none of that mattered. And there were dues to be paid – vile ones.

○ ○ ○

The nosey Mrs. Kravitz thought nothing out of the ordinary when a light blue Ford Econoline van bearing the graphics of the You Dirty Rat Pest Control Company pulled to the front of Chase's house. Nor did she think twice about the men in the blue jumpsuits who got out and strode to the rear pesticide sprayers in hand though their swaggers belied military training. When they finished they swaggered back to their van as casually as when they had arrived whereupon one of them placed a call.

"You have ears," he said.

Chapter 19 – DEMON ON A FIELD TRIP

THE NEXT DAY Father Brainard delivered the news. For all his and Father Herzl's talk of revealing that ghosts are really demons, the Academy's board of trustees would hear none of it.

"We have the school's reputation to think of," they were told.

"What planet are you people from? This is more important," Father Brainard argued.

There was some advice however for the young ghost and giant busters. "You're placing yourselves in great danger," Father Brainard warned. "You're dealing with an evil a million years old. They'll do everything in their power to protect their secrets. First they'll try to recruit you, then they'll try to kill you."

Their families weren't much help either. At least not the way they wanted.

"I don't want you anywhere near that stuff," Cathy's father warned. "It follows you home."

There was good reason to be alarmed. He had read that TV ghost hunters are followed home by the ghosts they hunt and often are possessed by them, something the shows forgot to mention along with the fact the Vatican is reporting an exorcism pandemic. What had always been a couple thousand exorcisms a year worldwide has become a half million a year in Italy alone and is growing out of control. According to the church, séances, visits to mediums, tarot card reading, ouija boards, hypnosis,

Eastern meditation and remote viewing were among the causes, and visits to magicians (the demonic kind). Oh yes, and ghost hunting. Public officials were quick to dismiss the face-eating and feats of superhuman strength as people being on drugs even when no drugs were found in their systems. To call it attacks by demons would be politically incorrect. Remember, in the First World they aren't supposed to exist.

"I have to go with your father on this one," said her mother. "We don't want any ghosts here."

Uncle Ned told Matt, "It's great you want to help the world by showing it ghosts aren't dead people but what did the world ever do for you? This thing'll blow up in your faces. I'd get as far away from that mess as I could."

"It's too dangerous," warned Aunt Nell. But to Nell everything was dangerous – flying, driving, going to the ATM, leaving the house, eating anything out of the Pacific, though she was right about the Pacific.

"What if they're wrong," said Chase.

"That would be Kid Rule Number One."

Matt rattled off *The Kid Rules* posted in his room:

Rule One

Question everything

Rule Two

Get help from someone who can give it when things aren't going the way you need them to. The magic words are "I need help. Will you help me?"

Rule Three

Follow your dream. Tell that little voice inside your head that says you can't do it to take a hike.

Rule Four

Question everything again

Rule Five

Read, read, read.

Rule Six

Take that good advice you didn't listen to

Rule Seven

Be yourself. Everyone else is already taken.

Rule Eight

Never, never, never give up

Rule Nine

Say no to drugs

Rule Ten

Don't worry about what people think.
They don't do it very often.

Rule Eleven

Remember you are your successes, not your failures.

Duck Dodgers in the 24½ Century signed off. Zak went in search of more Fritos. A CNN reporter was in the midst of reporting on something called the "God Gene," a gene that makes it easier for people to believe in things they can't see. Then a researcher who refused to give her name spoke of her role in the discovery of the "Satan Gene," a cause of extremely evil behavior in people, though not the only cause.

A ring tone drifted through the room. Chase fumbled for his phone. Twisting and snapping her fingers Cathy threw out her arms playfully.

"Come on," she begged.

Matt sat petrified.

"Can't dance?"

"Don't feel like it."

"I thought all you pretty city boys knew how to dance."

Pretty city boys? Matt wondered if she meant black.

The music stopped. "How'd *you* learn?" he asked sheepishly.

"Dance shows."

Her moves were smooth. His were always jerky like a marionette with a broken string. Had anyone been selling camouflage he would have gladly bought some to blend into the sofa.

CNN news anchor Katie Loveland and her co-anchor Bill Tufoy were doing the headline news.

"Television!" Matt blurted. "We can take the story to CNN . . ." Cathy stopped dancing. It was decided Mr. Big City would place the call.

"S-sir, I'd like to speak with Katie Loveland."

"The phone's not a snake. It won't bite you," his father had said.

Cybertas was his father's company that Matt was being groomed to take over someday. By nine he could read a balance sheet. By ten talk business. At eleven he had made up his mind to be a billionaire, or a fighter pilot, or President of the United States, or a football star, or a motorcycle mechanic. Business was fun. He even read The Wall Street

Journal every day. It meant A-list friends, a fat monthly allowance, his own American Express Platinum card and weekends at the galleria. Now there was no allowance, no platinum and the C-list was the new A-list.

He had learned business is one problem after another and it's how good you are at solving them that determines whether you stay in business or not. Matt loved solving problems. Like David Stuart, the teen who cracked the lost Ancient Mayan hieroglyph code. Like Lewis Hamilton, the go-karter who became Formula 1 champ. Like Nadia Comaneci, the gymnast who at fourteen achieved in her sport what no Olympian had ever achieved before; perfection. Like Joan of Arc who at thirteen led France to victory over the English in the Hundred Years War. Like Jack Cornwall who at sixteen was awarded a posthumous Victoria Cross for gallantry at the Battle of Jutland. Like Steve Jobs who at nineteen began collaborating with electronics wiz Steve Wozniak which led to the personal computer. Like David who slew Goliath at fourteen. Just a handful of the achievements in art, science, business, technology, military, culture and sports by other teens who refused to play small and subordinate their thinking to what others considered appropriate for their age.

His father had taken to calling him *Kid CEO*. The future had been bright. No more. Like that – gone! Vanisho.

"I'm sorry, Ms. Loveland doesn't take calls," said the gatekeeper.

"But sir, it's important!"

"You don't need to sir me. Just a moment." Someone in public relations answered.

"I could only get her email address," Matt lamented.

"We heard big shot," Cathy grumped.

Matt set about composing an email.

> To: Katie Loveland
> From: Matt Legend
> Subject: Ghosts
>
> Dear Ms. Loveland:
>
> This summer I found a giant and a ring with powers. The Devil on a field trip told me ghosts aren't dead people. Please call meat 555-534-5804.
>
> Very Truly Yours, Matt Legend

"What kind of stupid email was that!" Cathy snapped. "The Devil? *Really?* And I didn't know the Devil went on field trips! And there's a typo. Please call *meat*?"

The next day came a response.

> To: Matt Legend
> From: Katie Loveland - CNN
> Subject: Re: Ghosts
>
> Dear Matt,
>
> Thank you for contacting CNN. We always enjoy hearing from our younger viewers. May I suggest contacting your local TV news station to determine if it might be interested in airing your story. That is always the best place to start. Please feel free to follow up with me after your story has aired. Thank you again for contacting CNN.

"She blew us off! It was that stupid devil on the field trip," Cathy fumed. "I'm not doing this on our rinky dink tv station. It's all or nothing."

“The way you do everything?” Matt snarked.

“Yeah,” Cathy giggled, thinking back to the time she taught herself to walk in high heels. Most little girls start off in their mother’s high heels. Not Cathy. Being a tomboy she had no need for them – until she became interested in boys, that is. She loved the feel of the leather as it caressed her feet. Gone was the girl willing to let her mother be the only girl in the house. Thrilled with her newest discovery she spent a wobbly weekend with her toes and the balls of her feet on fire. *How come these things don’t come with instructions? Where are the training wheels? Are they supposed to hurt?* A sight she was teetering in her four-inch heels holding ski poles. By Tuesday she had mastered the art of making the boys look. By Wednesday it was the pivot and strut and twist and turn, which left only how to run in them. Good luck with that. Two weeks later the fire had died and she wore them nervously in public for the first time, sure everyone was watching. It seemed fine for tomboys to be girly when they want. How come boys can’t be tom*girls* if *they* wanted she wondered? Life is full of questions and contradictions. It is a journey. Little could she know she would soon learn how dangerous that journey can be.

“Loveland’s not taking us seriously,” Matt grumbled.

“Atlanta . . . that’s too far for our bikes . . . hundreds of miles,” said Chase.

“No problema,” Cathy blurted.

“I thought your parents said steer to clear of this,” Matt said.

“They did. I’m not even supposed to be around you. You’re radioactive. When I told them about the magic ring –

– It’s not magic,” Matt blurted. “Magic’s evil.”

Chase rolled his eyes. “Oh please!”

“I’m not talking sleight of hand. I’m talkin’ that guy who levitated himself across the English Channel and those Chinese face changers.”

“Anyway, they didn’t believe me,” Cathy replied. “They think I’m getting real life mixed up with a video game. So, I thought … maybe we might . . . well . . . borrow it – the RV . . . Daddy always said someday I’d find something I believe in. This is it.”

“You don’t have a driver’s license,” Matt said, “do you?” he asked the girl who seemed to be able to do anything.

“Not exactly.”

“Big House here we come,” Chase moaned.

“You sure about this?” asked Chase . . . “Stealing your parents’ motor home? . . .”

For a moment Cathy’s face reflected doubt. “It’s not stealing . . . it’s my parents.’ Zak returned with a fresh bag of Fritos.

“What’d I miss?”

Chapter 20 – ROAD TRIP

WHEN YOU'RE FIFTEEN the fate of the world hangs on everything you do. Sometimes it really does.

Matt and Chase's phones vibrated.

> Text Message
> *meet my house. 1 hour.*
>
> ---
>
> *Mon, Jul 21 8:12 am*
> *From: Cathy*

"Don't tell Zak. He can't keep a secret," Cathy said. Paper lunch sacks filled with tuna sandwiches, tangerines, oatmeal cookies and orange Gatorade sat in a box. An approaching summer squall line carried the metallic scent of rain.

"Are you sure about this?" she asked.

"I guess," Matt said.

"You guess! You'd better know! I'm putting it all on the line here homeboy!"

Zak appeared out of nowhere, a backpack strapped to his back, in his arms two bottles of Coke Zero and four bags of Frito Lays.

"You didn't think you were going without me did you?" The Fritos dropped to the RV floor.

"I should've known," Cathy drawled."

"You can't go," Matt said.

"Or what *California?* I'm in or I blow the whistle on this op. I'm sure mom and dad would love to know about your little road trip. Here, let me call 'em right now," he said flipping open his new Motorola Razr.

"*NO!*" sounded through the RV.

"You don't want to go," Cathy said. "We're gonna be in big trouble when we get back."

"You can forget the Jedi mind trick crap," Zak replied, plopping into the nearest seat as he slipped on his VR headset.

"I haven't been in this much trouble since I set fire to the vacant lot across the street from my house – accidentally, of course," Matt said.

"Of course," Cathy teased.

Matt glanced around – kitchen, bath, computer workstation, satellite internet, 40-inch plasma tv, GPS, dishwasher, washer/dryer . . .

"1.2," Cathy said. "Million," she added.

"I thought farmers were supposed to be poor," Matt laughed.

Cathy giggled as she reached under the steering wheel to adjust the pedal extensions she used when flying her father's King Air. "It costs a thousand to fill up."

"Dollars? Is it full?" asked Matt.

"No. But the gas card's in there," she said gesturing to a compartment. A worried look crossed her face. She was feeling a bit lightheaded. It's one thing to talk about stealing, er –borrowing your parents' RV. Quite another to do it.

Maybe it's not such a bad thing having Zak along, thought Matt. Trouble divided by four is less per person than divided by three. There was logic in there somewhere. He tried not to think of the trouble they were in.

Cathy pressed an overhead button and waited for the gate to open. It began to pour. With an ear-splitting boom and a flash the instrument cluster swung to zeros.

"What was that! I have a bad feeling about this," Zak grimaced, ripping his headset off. "We haven't even left the driveway and bad stuff's happening already. I want to go back."

No one noticed the black SUV with black windows parked at the side of the road.

"It's too late," Cathy said, reaching for the radio as she rummaged through stations finally stopping at a Van Halen song, *Welcome To The Jungle*. She cranked it.

"I'm going to the bathroom," Matt shouted, having spied Zak's Coke bottles in the kitchen sink.

Forty minutes later the red and blue lights of a state trooper appeared. Cathy turned white. It screamed past. They breathed. A line of stopped cars was ahead. Zak gulped a handful of antacids, a consequence of GERD, a digestive disorder.

"*TURN! TURN! TURN!*" Matt shouted. The RV leaned dangerously as Cathy swerved onto a dirt road taking out a sign which read 'Smokey the Bear Says Only You Can Prevent Forest Fires – Fire Danger Today – HIGH,' leaving it in splinters. HIGH was in big red letters.

"Recalculating… Recalculating," the GPS babbled. There was no way of knowing the roadblock was just motorists stopping to watch a trooper tussle with a drunken female motorist.

"I still can't believe we're doing this," Cathy panted.

"Stay focused," Matt said.

"I'm always focused."

"How did I know you were going to say that," Matt said nervously.

"How did I let you talk me into this Matt Legend?"

There were no cars along the new route except a dark SUV with blacked-out windows following behind.

■ ■ ■ ■

When Ted Kozacky received the frantic call from his wife he rushed home. Trembling she handed him the note.

Dear Mom and Dad – Chase, Matt and I borrowed the motor home to drive to CNN. We have to tell the world ghosts aren't dead people. I'm sorry. We couldn't think of any other way. I hope someday you'll understand. Don't worry. I can drive it fine. We'll be on Route 75.

Love, Cathy

"**BORROW THE MOTOR HOME!**" he roared. "Is she crazy? This stinks to high heaven. What would possess her to do such a thing! It's that Legend kid. He's behind this. Just wait until I get my hands on his scrawny neck!"

It would take them five hours to reach Atlanta. On *Craziest Police Videos* Cathy had seen an M&Ms-munching nine-year-old and his partner in crime, a Dalmatian puppy named Hot Stuff sitting in the passenger seat, commandeer the family Pinto. The little rascals led police on a merry chase until done in by a dead-end.

Maybe they'd all look back someday on this and laugh but in the meantime things were going terribly wrong. Could things get any worse? Oh yes, Mabel.

"Where are we?" Cathy demanded.

Matt pulled out a Rand McNally. "This way'll take us two or three extra hours," he said measuring out three inches.

"What have you gotten me into Matt Legend!"

The radio blared reggae… ♫*The whole world is troubled*♫ . . . "That song fits your top," Matt said.

"You checkin' my top out or me?"

Matt blushed and changed the subject . . . "So you're going be a Marine someday."

"Yep, I'm flyin' Super Cobras."

"She's not flying any military helicopters. She has OCD," Zak blurted.

We should've left him behind, thought Cathy. A poster of a Cobra attack helicopter had graced her bedroom wall since fourth grade, given her one day by a snappy Marine recruiter in his sharp-creased uniform outside the Green Hills Mall. "We can use more bright young women like you in Marine Aviation," the snappy gunnery sergeant had told her.

It happened a veteran Womens Airforce Service Pilot was with him that day. The elegant elderly lady shouted a quiet dignity. Her demeanor bespoke having reached a certain station in life. The woman was only too glad to share that during "The War Years" as she called them she had been a WASP, one of the women aviators who ferried military aircraft with the purpose of freeing the men for combat.

"I would've given anything to be where you are. Women weren't allowed to fly combat in those days. It was the Forties. What we were doing was so important. I loved flying more than life itself." The lady's eyes grew misty as she spoke. "It was a calling. When the war ended the airlines wouldn't hire us or Jews or blacks. It was so unfair. Honey, find something you love. If you do you'll never work a day in your life," her voice cracked. Then she said something Cathy would remember for the rest of hers – "It was the time I felt most like me . . . the only time in my life when I knew exactly who I was."

There are jobs and there are careers. There are careers and there are callings. To be called is a gift. To be able to answer it a gift greater still. Cathy had heard the call.

"She's one tough lady," said the gunny. "Eighty-two and drives a 'vette with a kickin' sound system. That's it there," he said, pointing to a little yellow number taking up two parking spots. It chirped and its lights flashed once.

"What's OCD?" asked Matt.

"I don't want to talk about it."

"So you think we're doing the right thing?"

"Are you kidding? We are *so* dead. When my parents find –

"No, CNN. Do you think it's the right thing?"

"A bit late for second thoughts don't you think?"

"I'm not. I was just thinking," Matt said. "Why was I the one to find that giant?"

"Everything happens for a reason," Cathy said.

"Now my whole life's changed. It was nice not knowing what's out there."

"You mean like an ostrich?" Cathy said. "What if the Marines don't let me fly Cobras 'cause of this? You'd better hope that doesn't happen Legend."

"Ostriches don't really bury their heads. So why are you doing this again?"

"I guess I don't want to spend my life asking what if I'd given everything," Cathy sighed. "If I only do one thing just for me I want it to be something that counts, like flying Super Cobras. This counts," Cathy replied.

A rebel without a cause is like a vacuum. Nature abhors a vacuum. It will always try to fill it. The bigger the vacuum the bigger the need to fill it. Cathy's was big.

"It's called osteosarcoma . . ." she sighed.

"Is that what 'OCD' stands for?" asked Matt.

"No. That's something else."

Fighting back tears she told of the cold cap that froze her scalp to keep her hair from falling out. And of the chemotherapy. And the fear. Fearing every day how many she had left. Always fearing. Fearing with every ache, every pain, every cold symptom if it was the beginning of the end. But she had pulled out a giant can of whup and spanked the Big C's behind.

"What do *you* care about?" she asked.

Matt pondered . . . "Payback . . . for the kids in the Nazi death camps. Their guards told them they were walking somewhere to get soup." *Cancer?*

He was the kid who had balled his eyes out at the Holocaust Museum. It was so embarrassing. Survivor's guilt. And hatred for the Nazis. He hadn't been there for the poor kids. He needed to do something for them. But what? It had happened long ago.

"I thought gentlemen are supposed to carry a handkerchief for a lady," Cathy sniffled.

"Sorry, fresh out."

"Daddy's never even complimented me once on anything. I'm sixteen. You'd think in all these years he would've complimented me on something. Instead I have all this pressure. It's complicated."

"Sounds like somebody has daddy issues," Matt chuckled.

"You think that's funny?"

He reached his hand to her shoulder. She batted it.

"For once I want to do something that's my idea," she said – "something that makes a difference. There're two kinds of people. Those who do and those who watch. I'm one who does," she said, glancing into the rear view.

"News flash. This isn't going to make any difference," said Zak, peeling off his VR headset after two hours of staving off falling Tetrominoes. "People don't care. They're too busy living their lives."

“What’d you learn in business?” she asked, swerving to avoid a whitetail.

“Take no prisoners. Business is war. Eat the other guy’s lunch before he eats yours.” He looked at Miss Young Marines who would surely appreciate the battle mentality. She wasn’t smiling.

“Daddy would like you,” she said. “You’re a miniature version of him.” It wasn’t a compliment.

“So it’s win no matter the cost?”

“Of course!”

“Do you know what an unlawful order is?” Cathy asked . . . “It’s a military order you shouldn’t follow because it’s wrongful,” she replied, answering her own question. “What else did you learn?”

“Take all the time you have before making an important decision to be sure it’s the right one.”

“And . . . ?”

“Act like you’re powerful and people assume you are. Attitude is everything.”

“Is that why you’re such a butt hole? Matt raised an eyebrow.
She studied the rear view again. Her smile dimmed. It was getting dark.

“What is it?” asked Matt.

“Nothing.”

“So why do you live in dueling banjos country again?” he asked.

“Dueling banjos!” Cathy snapped. “That’s what you think? We’re dumb redneck hillbillies? Is that it?”

“But, ah, I didn’t mean it that way . . . Just wondering why you live here instead of California,” Matt gulped.

"BECAUSE YOU COULDN'T PAY ME TO LIVE IN CALIFORNIA!" Cathy said, stressing each syllable.

"What's wrong with California!"

"Nothing if you like liberal political correctness, another name for cowardice and stupidity. California's the world capitol of PC."

"Nobody's perfect, ♫ I wish they all could be California girls . . ♫ "

"Do us a favor. Don't try out for American Idol . . . there're nice things here too," Cathy laughed.

"Like what?"

"Like people are real for one."

Matt's world was a world of things, not people . . . the growl of a muscle car . . . the magic of a VR headset . . . internet speed in terabits per second . . . they were what mattered most. He didn't give a flying fig newton for the stick figure families on the backs of minivans. Not that he had anything against people mind you. He just hadn't discovered them yet.

"Nothing's even open twenty-four," he snapped. "And those stupid Blue Laws." It had been a shock to enter a store one Sunday to buy batteries only to discover the hardware aisle roped off with a thick blue rope. The clerk told him he couldn't buy anything in hardware because something called "blue laws" prohibits the sale of hardware on Sundays. It was very un-California to say the least. And two men in the supermarket were talking about their cows! The only cow talk in supermarkets in L.A. is in the butcher section.

"Things like being able to leave your door unlocked and knowing everybody in town. That's what I love . . . and . . . come to think . . . hate

. . . Mark Twain said a small town's the place to know someone. He said you know people inside and out there and all you know about people in the city is their outside and it's usually a lie. Small towns are better. Everybody in small towns doesn't think small." Then her voice changed to low and dangerous like before his football tryout.

"Do you think *I* think small?" she asked innocently.

DANGER, DANGER WILL ROBINSON!

"No," Matt replied smartly. *Minefield crossed. What's Mark Twain got to do with it?*

"Have you been to Paris?" she asked coyly.

"No. Have *you*?" he replied, taking the bait.

"Twice," she replied.

"Have you been to Athens?" she added.

Athens? "No."

"I have," she said . . ."Bonn? … Zurich? ... Brussels … Cairo … Nairobi? … Prague? . . . Madrid? . . . London? . . .

"Okay. I get it."

Zak put in his two cents worth, "You're a snob. You think you're all that."

"It's called confidence," snapped Matt.

"Arrogance you mean," Cathy said softly.

Arrogance not conceit, makes a man complete [Sister Sledge].

"You should talk Chatty Cathy Who Only Keeps the First Place Trophies."

"Oh oh!" Chase breathed.

Cathy bore a shocked look, "Bless your heart, I call it being competitive. I'm descended from Cossacks . . .
Kozacky? . . . *Cossack-y?* So watch it!"

Bless your heart? It seemed an odd thing to say, but in The South "Bless Your Heart" is the meanest thing you can say to someone without actually swearing. There was much to learn about the South.

"No wonder ***y'all*** lost the Civil War."

"It wasn't the Civil War," Zak bellowed. "It was The War of Northern Aggression. And what's up with that stupid polo shirt? You don't even play polo."

"You don't know what I play. You're just jealous 'cause you don't live in California. Slave owners . . . you were the first American terrorists."

"Are you smokin' something? We never owned any slaves! . . . *did* we, Cathy?" asked Zak.

"Cathy, you thirsty?" asked Matt.

"A little," she replied.

"Cathy wants a Coke or Pepsi . . . or whatever you call it," Matt said.

"Got it dude," said Chase.

"Sit down. Let Zak get it," Matt insisted. Chase sat back down.

Zak disappeared into the galley returning with a Coke bottle and two cups. Gripping the bottle between his knees he twisted the cap. With a hiss the Coke bomb exploded sending a geyser of frothy brown liquid to the ceiling. Dripping with the sticky syrup Zak looked confused until Matt burst out laughing. They fell struggling to the floor.

"Yankee scum. . . . chowderhead. . . troglodyte . . . rebel trash . . .pork pie," the name-calling waged back and forth.

"You're just a big fat roly poly bug," Matt snarled.

Zak held Matt in a chokehold. Who knew roly poly was a black belt.

Caught in the moment, Matt delivered the coup de grâce . . . "You're not even a real Kozacky. You're adopted."

Zak's grip slackened as he looked at his slender step-sister with numbed horror.

"That's enough, Matt," Cathy said, softly. "He's as much a Kozacky as – "

A green glow filled the cabin. A brilliant green dot was dancing around Matt's shirt like a crazed firefly.

"***LOOK OUT!***" Chase screamed.

A helicopter hovered in the roadway, its searchlight turning the night into day. A man sat aside the co-pilot's seat, his feet on the skid, his eye glued to the scope of a high-powered rifle.

"The police!" Chase screeched.

The motor home lumbered to a stop.

The RV stood face to face with the chopper. "That's not the police," Cathy blurted. She mashed the gas pedal.

"*SHE'S NOT STOPPING*," the gunman shouted.

"She's bluffing," the pilot huffed.

"*SHE'S NUTS*," he yelled as the motor home filled his bubble. He applied power and yanked up on the collective. The helo pitched sharply up as the RV cleared its skids but not its searchlight, showering the ground with sparks.

As the RV dodged in and out of tree cover Matt texted three letters – **SOS**. "Forces will try to stop you," the priest had warned.

Father Brainard was at home talking on the phone with an astronomer at the Lucifer Telescope when he received the text. On receiving Matt's prearranged code he hurriedly dialed Sister Cherry.

"Sister Cherry. Assemble The Seven."

Sister Cherry texted the prayer group which hastened to the site Cathy had mistaken for a cemetery. They took their places at the water's edge with Father Brainard, kneeled and began to pray. An unseen angelic force formed above the seven to the harmonious drone of discordant voices then suddenly burst eastward 40,000 times faster than light.

"Did we lose 'em," asked Zak.

"Don't think so," Cathy replied worriedly.

Again the green glow filled the cabin. A hole appeared in the windshield.

"They're shooting!" Cathy screeched.

A wheel dropped off the road as she fumbled for her phone. "No signal . . . signal anybody? Signal?" she screamed.

"Turn! Turn! Turn!" Matt shouted pointing to a dirt road.

"Recalculating . . . recalculating . . .make a U-turn on Buzzard Roost Road," the GPS protested.

"Where's this go?" Cathy spouted. After ten minutes she stopped beneath a stand of Virginia pines. In the warm night air the rising and falling of beating rotor blades drowned the night call of a Northern Mockingbird.

Few terrors can match being hunted by a helicopter at night. As one brave soldier once put it, it's like playing hide and seek and keep-away all at once. You're *it* except when you're tagged, you're dead. The soldier didn't make it.

Cathy pulled out the road atlas. "There's a reservoir or a dam a mile ahead. A phone maybe too." Disappearing behind the RV with a hunted look in her eyes she hastily unscrewed the red plastic lens covers over the taillights and removed the bulbs.

"Now we won't light up like Las Vegas every time I hit the brakes," she said dropping the bulbs to the ground.

Zak wove the pliable branches of black cherry trees into the roof rack as the moon-lit crystal waters of the lake shimmered through the trees.

"Try your phones," Matt said.

"Nothing," said Chase.

"Dead," said Zak.

Cathy pulled out her phone again.

"There're no signal bars," she cried. "There's a red line through the phone symbol." She pressed a speed-dial button . . it was ringing . . . the call was going through! . . . how was that possible? . . . "CATHY, WHERE ARE YOU?" the voice blared.

"Daddy we're by a lake on Buzzard Roost Road . . . some men in a helicopter . . . they're shooting at us . . . I can't— . . ."

"Is Zak with you?"

"Yes."

"I know the place. I'll be there in forty-five. Do anything you need to to survive. Call me or signal with the flashlight when you hear the Mustang . . . okay, baby?"

"Okay, daddy. Hurry."

If his years in naval aviation had taught him anything it was to always expect the unexpected. *The Breaks of Naval Air* it's called — when things go from great to horrible in half a heartbeat.

"He's on the way," Cathy cried. "There're still no bars. There's still a red line through the phone symbol!"

"How can a call go through without bars!" Chase mumbled. Cathy stopped beneath a stand of yellow poplars and twisted toward Matt – "Did you know this was going to happen?"

"Of course not."

"Get the flashlight," she said wiping her eyes.

As Matt rose something thudded to the floor.

"What's this?" asked Cathy . . ."It's a bullet . . . but . . . that's . . . that's what they look like after they hit metal," she stuttered. She studied the hole in the windshield, then the hole in his polo shirt, then the hole in the windshield again.

"Pull your shirt up."

"What!"

"Just do it."

Matt lifted his shirt.

She pressed the mushroomed bullet to the purple welt above his heart.

"It matches!" she gasped. "This is nuts. That means . . ." Cathy's eyes darted wildly, looking for an explanation – any explanation.

Without lifting her head she raised her eyes to his. “This means the bullet flattened against your skin, but that’s –”

“Impossible?” Matt said.

“This bullet should have killed you instantly. It’s a .308 round. Very powerful. It should’ve gone through you and out the back of the RV. I don’t get it,” she gulped, her eyes darting manically as they searched for an answer. “What just happened? Who *are* you? . . . *What* are you?”

Headlights swept the motorhome. “Somebody’s coming,” Matt shouted. Cathy flashed to something her father had said once: “There’re times to think and times to do. Don’t think when you need to do. MBAs make lousy fighter pilots. They think too much. It gets them killed. You have to act instinctively.” She started the RV and drove to a concrete block pumping station at the water’s edge. Its dirty coarse gray concrete looked a hundred years old. Two pipelines ran from the building up the side of a hill. A ratty old trailer was parked in front of the building. She rammed it, shoving it against the building.

A disheveled man burst out. “Killers are after us. They’ll kill you too. Will you help us?”

“Aw, waa, yeah,” the little man replied, holding his limp arm.

From inside Cathy dashed the trailer’s side window with the flashlight as an SUV with blacked-out windows pulled into the clearing. Two men got out.

Quickly she smashed the building’s small metal-framed window. An infrared motion detector winked blue as they climbed through. One of the men spoke something into his radio.

Meanwhile Ted Kozacky turned to his wife, "The kids are in trouble. Gotta go."

Jumping into his NSX he pressed its metallic red start button. The 573 horsepower engine revved to life. The tach needle flirted with its redline as he raced the snaking backroad through the storm.

Skidding to a stop he dashed through the howling rain, rolled open the hangar door, flicked on the lights and sprinted to his plane. Sliding under its wing he removed two heavy metal olive drab ammo boxes from a padlocked locker, climbed onto the wing and popped open the access door to its three machine guns. Ignoring the razor-sharp magnolia leaves whipping through the hangar slicing his exposed skin, he popped open the airtight box and fed a belt of the WW-II armor-piercing incendiary tracer bullets into the feeder slots. Was he wasting his time? Would the bygone era ammo even fire? He shut the wing's access door, fastened it and repeated the procedure on the the guns on the other wing. Jumping into the cockpit, he started the engine and taxied to the end of the runway. Keying his mic button he activated the runway lights. Pushing the throttle to its stop, the engine straining he released the brakes. The torque of fifteen hundred horses fought his leg as he pressed hard on the right rudder pedal to keep the aircraft centered as it hurtled down the runway. With a flash of light a tree fell across the runway. It was V1 — commit speed. Abort was no longer an option. The left wheel struck the tree, snapping off. It tumbled down the runway as the other retracted slowly into its well as the Mustang roared off into the night.

Chapter 21 – LAKE OF NO RETURN

You only live twice. Once when you are born
and once when you look death in the face.
Ian Fleming

THE TWO MEN RETURNED to their SUV. In the glare of its xenon headlamps they appeared to be waiting.

"I knew I shouldn't have come. This is your fault," Zak whined. Everything was fine 'til *you* came. Go back to California."

"You okay?" asked Matt.

"Yes … no," Zak fretted.

"Get it together, Zak," said Chase.

"What do they want?" asked Zak, popping a handful of antacids. The answer arrived in a high-pitched whine as the copter, its broken sparking searchlight dangling, landed beside the SUV. Its engine spooled down as four men stood gesturing as if arguing over what to do next.

"Got any gasoline?" asked Matt.

The scruffy man pointed to a can in the corner. "It's almost empty."

"I don't need much," Matt replied. He grabbed the can, reached it through the window and poured the contents into the trailer.

"HEY! What the heck. That's my trailer!"

"Got a match?"

"NO!" the man replied, a vein popping out in his neck.

Matt plucked the cigarette from the man's lips and tossed it into the trailer.

“Those are bad for you,” Matt declared as the trailer burst into flames.

“What part of they’re shooting as us do you not understand, dude,” Chase pointed out.

“Maybe they thought you were deer,” the man said.

The copter took off only to return minutes later.

“You may think you’re smart barricading yourselves in,” the loudspeaker blared. “Just give me the ring . . . that fire won’t keep us out forever.”

“How’d they find us?” Chase gulped.

“Does it matter?” Zak cried. “Give ‘em the stupid ring.”

“No,” Matt said.

“They wouldn’t kill kids,” asked Chase, “would they?” he added worriedly.

The man rushed over with a fire extinguisher.

“In here,” the scruffy man yelled as he scrambled into one of the pipelines. When they were all safely inside Zak slammed the hatch.

“I can’t see anything,” Matt said worriedly.

Rummaging through his pack Zak produced a glowstick. He snapped it and gave it a shake casting the malodorous dank humid cylinder into a yellow pall.

Red and green lasers combed the pumping station. “Nobody touch Legend. He’s mine,” Malvic hissed. He removed a straw from a thin 24-karat gold Fabergé cigarette case and inserted it delicately between his teeth. “They’re in the pipe,” he smirked. “Let’s see how they like this,” he said snapping the case shut. Studying a control panel he pressed three green buttons, pumped a large circuit breaker primer handle labeled HIGH

VOLTAGE several times, pressed the green ON button and waited as a yellow warning beacon flashed and a klaxon blared.

"This'll flush those rats out," Malvic sneered, his face flashing yellow.

With a distant roar and the rush of wind the pipeline began to rumble.

"What's that?" Cathy said.

"Oh no, hurry. They've turned the pumps on," the worker gasped as he fumbled with the hatch.

"Faster!" Cathy screamed. Matt helped him turn the wheel.

The hatch flew open. The cool night air filled their lungs. One by one they scrambled out until only Zak remained. The rumble grew louder as Zak struggled to free his stuck backpack. A geyser blasted him high into the air dumping him onto the forest floor. Cathy listened for her father's plane.

"Daddy where are you? Where are you daddy? Where are you?"

A bird soared at the center of the lake as a distant train horn echoed through the valley. Cathy's ears perked at a familiar sound – could it be? It was the faint mellow roar of the twelve-cylinder Merlin!

Dots and dashes! ••• •••• ——— ——— — •••• • •—•• •—•• ——— punctuated the dark.

Cathy was using the Morse code she had learned in Young Marines – *SHOOT HELLO DADDY.* His little girl was alive! *HELLO? "Some men in a helicopter are shooting at us,"* she had said. Hello? Must be a typo, he thought.

The turbulence from the Mustang's wingtips caught the helo crew unawares.

"What the . . . " the shooter snarked.

"It's sweetpea's father," said the pilot. "Relax. He can't do anything."

"But it's a mustang."

"It's not armed. All he can do is watch," he snickered. "Let's wrap this up."

Kozacky switched off his nav lights and swung around for another pass. With the helo at twelve o'clock he rammed his power control lever forward to full military power. Tiny flashes appeared. The plexiglass exploded. A blow like a sledge walloped his left shoulder. In disbelief he stared down at his bloody shirt, yanked on the stick with his good arm and banked hard. Through the moonlight he glimpsed his target. No uniforms, no law enforcement markings.

His finger over the red protective Bakelite cover protecting the master arm switch, he flicked it up and the switch to ARMED. He yanked hard on the stick and pulled a 360°. As the synchronous white flashes continued he took careful aim and squeezed the trigger. With a perceptible deceleration from the recoil of all six guns firing at once, a bright red stream of illuminating tracer rounds streaked to the target. Parts began to fly off the copter as it pitched down and began a downward spiral. It exploded in a fireball, sending its tail rotor whizzing through the forest into a tree trunk inches from Cathy's head.

A lightheaded Kozacky maneuvered for a final pass. He rocked his wings to signal victory but something was wrong. As the plane commenced a climbing turn its engine sputtered. He checked the gauges – no oil pressure. Cathy watched in horror as the plane disappeared trailing a thick white plume. A crash sounded in the distance.

"You killed daddy!" Cathy screamed. "You killed him! You killed him!"

"What?" Matt responded in a daze.

"Zak's right. You never should've come. Get away." Cathy pushed him away.

With a frustrated kick Matt sent a piece of smoldering helicopter wreckage flying.

"I t-think I saw a p-parachute."

"What?" Cathy said softly.

"A parachute. I think I saw one," Matt repeated.

"You *think*?"

"Did. I mean . . . I did."

"You think or you did! Which is it?"

"I did . . . I think."

"Are you sure?"

"Pretty sure."

"Pretty sure isn't good enough. Did you see one or not?"

"I did! I did! Okay?"

"Now what?" Zak moaned.

"I hate to break the news but it's game over dude," Chase sighed.

"I didn't plan on this," Cathy moaned.

"Me either," said Zak.

"We can't give up," Matt said.

"Give it up dude, said Chase.

"If we give up now, people'll think ghosts are dead people."

"Who cares, dude! Dad crashed and all you can think about is ghosts?"

"I think they killed my father," Matt said.

"Who?" Zak asked.

"*Them!*" replied Matt angrily, "Alright? . . . *THEM!*"

After a minute, "He's right," Cathy finally said. "We can't go back. It's personal now. They've messed with the wrong Young Marine."

"You sound like dad. Everybody in favor of going back raise your hand," said Zak, his the only hand raised.

"If I know daddy, he got out. We'll never find him in the dark.

"Boy, are we in trouble," Chase declared.

"We can't get into any more trouble than we're already in. We're up to our necks. I've never given up on anything in my life. I'm not about to start now. Let's go," she added. She dialed 911. Nothing.

The only way down the hill was to slide down the pipeline. One by one they slid. Zak fell off, rolling to the bottom, a screaming rolling burrito of mud and pine needles.

A figure emerged through the smoke and scattered fires.

"Devil Trash, grab . . ." Matt fumbled for the name.

"Father Malvic …" Cathy whispered.

The professor snapped ramrod straight, arms pressed against his sides as he hung helpless mid-air yelling for his henchmen.

"Clever boy. Not so clever. The boy who knew too much. Do you really think my master is going to write off three thousand years of manufacturing ghosts on a scale that boggles the mind just to let some stupid kids come along and ruin it. Do you have any idea how much work goes into manufacturing a single ghost? … how many facts have to be gathered over a person's lifetime to make it convincing? . . . how much time and effort goes into watching people day and night? You haven't the slightest idea what you're up against. You'll never make it to Atlanta . . . they're waiting. They're going to kill you a million times over for what you're doing."

"Who?" Zak gulped.

"Not who fat boy . . . what."

"How did you know we're going to Atlanta?" asked Cathy, her body tense to the point of shaking.

"By the way . . .your dog's dead. What was it's name . . . Cody?

"Your parents are next. Oops, looks like daddy saved us the trouble."

Cathy really began to worry.

"What's waiting?" Chase asked nervously.

"Devil Trash, tie him up," Matt ordered. Nervously he searched the priest's pockets. He found a ring of keys, a wallet, six .38 caliber bullets and a USB thumb drive.

Chapter 22 - AMBUSH

A FAMILY OF WHITETAIL DEER was enjoying a meal of sumac shrub on the side of the road when their blood flash froze suddenly inside their veins. The spirits of the air had decreed. Four enemy combatant kids would advance no further. Cathy gripped the wheel. A freak hailstorm engulfed the RV.

"Grab something," she screamed. The road turned white as the RV slid and rolled onto its side.

As Matt fidgeted with his seat belt it unbuckled sending him onto the steering wheel sending searing pain through his side. His eyes followed Cathy's . . .

On the other side of the shattered windshield stood a wild boar, its bloodshot yellow eyes drilling theirs, its head hung low as when stalking prey. Blood-specked saliva poured from the diseased animal's black lips and slowly spreading jaws. It was joined by another, then another and still another as the shadowy figures emerged from the brush.

"Are you kidding me," she breathed.

The ground was heaving — alive, the way it is in the underworld, a living spongy black mass of only God knows what.

"H-h-how strong's that windshield?" Matt whispered, his lips barely moving.

"Not strong enough," Cathy whispered. They crawled their way to the rear of the motorhome trying hard not to look up at the snakes which covered the wall of spidery cracked glass above them.

With a terrible racket the ravens and their cousins the crows arrived. It is with good reason a flock of crows is called a 'murder' and a flock of ravens an 'unkindness.' The ravens stood on the backs of the boars as the crows rode the snakes.

"We're done for," Chase mumbled.

"Where're they all coming from? I've never heard of animals of different species coming together like this," Cathy said.

"Matt . . . the ring. What are they thinking?" Zak sputtered.

"Concentrate," Cathy said.

Matt remembered what Father Herzl had said about talking to animals.

In the dying flickering headlamps stood a boar bigger than the rest covered with coarse red bristles watching.

"Don't do this. You'll be sorry," Matt thought to it.

"You'll be dead," the boar thought back.

"They're getting ready to attack," Matt yelled.

"The snakes!" Cathy screamed. "Do something!"

He wasn't sure exactly what the ring would and wouldn't do. It was like learning a martial art. The first time you need it you don't think to use it.

"Devil Trash, lift us!" Matt yelled. The motor home began to rise through the same supernatural force which lifted the great blocks of Solomon's Temple.

The eight hundred pound hog crashed through the windshield foaming at the mouth followed by another as the murderous crows and unkind ravens streamed in.

A large rattlesnake stared Chase in the face with its beady black eyes, its fearsome rattle rattling as it uncoiled. With an ear-shattering blast it thudded to the floor.

A bloodcurdling scream rent the cabin as a crow affixed itself to Cathy's scalp inserting its talons like fish hooks. Blood streamed down her face, her screams unheeded as the others struggled with their own flapping denizens.

Blast after blast tore through the cabin as Cathy in a panic emptied her mother's .357 in the direction of the snorting. The ravens and crows scattered. The demon-possessed hog skidded to a stop, its head a red mist.

"You can stop now," Matt said, gently prying the clicking revolver from her hand.

Outside animals of every kind were rushing past – all in the same direction, all in an awful hurry, coyotes, bears, raccoons, deer, wolves, field mice. A raptor swooped in and snatched up a flaming bunny.

"OMG! OMG!" Chase cried. A wall of flame was approaching. It appeared the entire forest was on fire.

"Devil Trash, rise us, tilt us," Matt screamed. The motorhome began to rise.

"*THE OTHER WAY*!" he screamed.

It see-sawed first one way then the other as the boars tumbled through the windshield frame disappearing into the dense smoke.

"Devil Trash, rotate us 90° counterclockwise," Matt coughed. Soon they were safely above the raging inferno. They searched for Mr. Kozacky but to no avail.

People become paralyzed when they come up against something so strange they cannot believe it exists. To escape the reality Zak slipped on his virtual reality headset and returned to launching Angry Birds at Bad Piggies while Chase stared in horror at the bullet hole in his ballcap. When signal bars returned to her phone Cathy called the state police to launch a search for her father.

○ ○ ○

Matt inserted Malvic's USB flash drive into the still-working Mac.

From: pMalvic@amanmu.org
Date: Thursday, August 26, 7:36 PM
To: Distribution
Subject: GHR Confidential
Attachment: Discredit strategy

Colleagues,

Our online hoaxes are working better than planned making serious study of GHRs more difficult. Our Cardiff Giant, India Giant and Saudi Giant hoaxes misled millions into dismissing the existence of GHRs outright, especially the Saudi Giant. As some of you know, an ARAMCO geological team discovered giant human remains in the desert of Saudi Arabia during the summer of 2000. The skull size corresponded to a skeletal height of 20 feet. I was alerted by our contact at the Saudi Commission for Tourism and Antiquities. At my direction he arranged for the Saudi police to

seize control of the site, confiscate all cameras, interrogate and intimidate all witnesses and confiscate the remains. Then the religion police, the Mutawwa'in, moved in and put a lid on it. Within days of the discovery, I announced the find online with an amateurishly altered photo featuring a grossly exaggerated 100' giant. Viewers associated the "Saudi Giant" with a hoax and never learned of the real one.
Q

Matt opened the attachment. It was instructions on how to handle giant human remains – labeling them fakes, dismissing them as animal bones, discrediting the discoverers and refusing to discuss them.

It stated that as far back as the 1700's scientific papers on the human body were more than sophisticated enough to distinguish between mastodon bones and giant human ones. With the internet making it too easy to compare them, the email suggested dispensing with that ruse.

From: dh1771@alsenuss.ru
Date: Wednesday, July 14, 5:23 AM
To: pMalvic@amaru9.net
Subject: Giant Human Remains

Arriving Aeroflot Flt 562 into Anchorage, Saturday, July 16, 6:55 AM AKST.

Have femur ready for DNA extraction. 100 million euros ready for wire transfer. Meet Dimitri outside baggage claim.

From: QianruKe @wanglab33.hk
Date: Wednesday, June 2, 3:13 PM
To: pMalvic@amaru9.net
Subject: meeting

MEET MR. CHAOXIANG AT WANG LABORATORIES, 0700 LOCAL TIME. 24938 E. ASH STREET, NEW YORK, MONDAY JUNE 7 FOR DNA TEST. BRING SAMPLE. AFTER CONFIRMATION 100 MILLION US TO TRANSFER.

From: ben.j.rossi@usda.gov
Date: Friday, April 30, 11:07 AM
To: pMalvic@amaru9.net
Subject: Operation SS

Confirming $100M US wire transfer after validation. No foreign third-party transactions.

What would a priest teacher have worth three hundred million dollars? They were in way over their heads.

Chapter 23 – CNN

KATIE LOVELAND SAT SCANNING the late breaking news sipping her McCafé Mocha, preferring them over the ripoff coffeehouse chain brands.

At first the call seemed just another to hand off to her high school summer intern, Courtney Blake. "Ms. Loveland, this is Matt Legend. You said we should get a local station to cover our story. Remember? We're on the way. We'll land on your roof. Can you meet us?"

Land on my roof? "Who *is* this?" she fumed, determined to put the prankster in his place.

"Matt Legend. I sent you an email, remember? Ghosts aren't dead people? Giants are real? We have proof? We'll be there in …" Matt stared blankly at Cathy . . . .

… "twenty?" Cathy shrugged.

. . . "thirty minutes."

"You're in a helicopter?!" the woman asked.

"Er, not exactly."

"Not exactly? Look here, what –

Cathy grabbed the phone.

"Miss Loveland, my name's Cathy Kozacky. CNN did a story on daddy's company, Field Vision, a year ago. You can look it up. What Matt's saying's true." Cathy told her what happened at the Lake of No Return. "We'll be there in thirty minutes. Can you meet us on the roof – *please? Please!*"

Katie Loveland had begun her career on the crew of a low-budget ghost hunters reality TV show, *Ghost 411*, so she knew a thing or two about ghosts. As far as she was concerned they were dead people – period. But she knew too that if ghosts turned out to be something other than what people think, it would be major newsworthy. Until then the call was a spoof.

"I'll get back to you. Where was that helicopter crash?"

Katie Loveland turned to her intern. "Courtney, can you check something, dear?"

Courtney returned minutes later to report a Two Rivers County deputy sheriff had responded to a silent alarm at Lake of No Return and found helicopter wreckage, a destroyed SUV and four deceased heavily-armed occupants.

Katie Loveland was standing on the roof chatting on her Galaxy with her producer when a shadow formed around her. Stumbling back just in time to avoid being crushed she glared at Cathy, then Chase, then Zak, then Matt as they stepped from . . . from what? For it was no longer recognizable as an RV.

"Sorry Ms. Loveland. I'm Cathy Kozacky." Loveland stood gaping at the ragamuffins then at the front-end missing/windows smashed/cherry tree-sprouting/scorched hulk, then again at the bedraggled kids, then again at the front-end missing/windows smashed/cherry-tree-sprouting/scorched hulk as if they had just flown in from the back side of Pluto's fifth moon. With a look of disgust she inspected her ruined sleeveless designer dress and the scuff marks on the back of her seven hundred dollar red Pradas.

"What *am* I? The Wicked Witch of the West! . . . and what . . . ?" . . . "a motor –. . . ? what – . . . seriously?" she muttered. "But how . . .?" she asked not quite knowing how to finish the sentence. Warily she entered. This won't take off will it?. . . Oh my god what happened to him?"

"Stupid kids," the priest hissed. "Give me the ring and I'll make your deaths quick."

"Wow … what a sweetheart," she gasped.

Cathy delivered the priest a swift kick. She started to walk away then turned and kicked him again.

"That's for daddy and for my dog. And you can tell your boss the devil I'm comin' for him. I'm gonna smack him like a piñata at a Mexican party. Tell him."

"Oh dear!" Loveland gasped.

"I've been wanting to do that for a long time," Cathy fumed. Matt laughed, holding his rib.

Her crime had been daring to ask one day in class why archaeologists all over the world are continually finding 4,500 year-old and older cities, palaces and dwellings buried just beneath the surface as though their inhabitants had simply up and walked away leaving their gold jewelry, art, gold and silver coins and other precious belongings behind which somehow became covered over by a layer of silt. It had been troubling her for quite some time. Nobody abandons gold jewelry and how exactly did it all become silted over in the first place? It made no sense.

"Well, class, it seems Miss Kozacky knows more than the whole archaeological world. Perhaps *you* would like to teach the class . . ."

"No Father Malvic. That's not it at all," Cathy blurted. "It's just –

– Stand up you pugnacious little runt. You boil on the back of a baboon. You pathetic blistering carbuncle of a student. Here, let me sit down so *you* can teach," he hissed taking a seat with the students thinking it to humiliate the girl and cause her to beg him to resume professoring. It always worked after all with his other obnoxious students.

"Turn to page 178 in your texts," Cathy said, taking the lectern under the harsh spotlight in the dark lecture hall . . . "What do we have here . . ." she began. Ten minutes later she had concluded her lecture and made her point suggesting the only possible cause of people worldwide leaving in such an awful hurry on such a massive scale all at the same time 4,500 years ago is the geologic evidence supporting a worldwide flood and the resulting silt that buried everything.

"Anybody hear of *Wyatt's Wrecking Ball*?" the erstwhile Professor Kozacky asked. "It's named for the late amateur archaeologist Ron Wyatt. His discoveries take a wrecking ball to conventional archaeology which completely ignores all the evidence of a worldwide flood . . . if it looks like a duck and quacks like a duck it's probably a duck. I rest my case."

Professor Kozacky took a bow. The class erupted.

"Not so fast," Father Malvic hissed. The class froze in mid-clap and turned their heads to the priest.

"Very interesting Miss Kozakcy, however, you seem to have left out one important detail. Perhaps you would be so kind as to enlighten us as to where all this water came from that would cover even Mount Everest. Anyone with a lick of sense can see your notion is absurd. Stupid girl, there was no worldwide flood. They were local floods. What do you say about that!"

In unison the class turned their heads back to Cathy.

"I must admit that had me puzzled too," she replied.

All heads turned to the priest.

"Really!" said the priest.

All heads turned back to Cathy.

"Like I said, I puzzled over that too until I read that researchers at Northwestern University and the University of New Mexico in 2014 and others announced the existence of underground water inside the earth amounting to three times all the water in the oceans on earth and the Bible says the springs of the earth burst forth and there's more than enough atmospheric water to –

– Thank you Miss Kozacky. That will be enough."

"But I'm not finished."

Father Malvic turned purple and his face looked as if it were about to pop.

"Actually you are," Father Malvic hissed. "You are quite finished. Sit down!

Chapter 24 – THE H-STONES

The foundation of the history we are presented with is crumbling along with the credibility of the scientists who present it.

SUMMER INTERN COURTNEY turned from the CCTV monitoring the heliport. She pulled out her phone and placed a call.

Meanwhile a bewildered Loveland hustled her visitors away from the eighth-story heliport down through the atrium, past the giant globe and rows of kiosks where CNN visitors were busy viewing twenty-five years of archival footage.

"The *H-Blocks*," Matt gasped. He approached a kiosk where a Japanese tourist stood draped with twin Nikons. As he drew nearer the man clutched his camera straps closer.

On the monitor were the three H-blocks. Each of the refrigerator-size composite blocks had precision-machined interlocking rectangular channels to fit together like giant Legos just as he had seen in his vision at the witch's house. And there was the gateway to nowhere except with a huge crack in it that hadn't been there in his vision. The documentary mentioned somewhere named Teohuanaco, and Puma Punku, a ten minute walk. The narrator called the stone gateway The Gate of the Sun.

"I've been there," said Matt.

"Where?" Katie asked.

"I don't know," he replied.

"You've been there and you don't know?" Loveland glanced at her watch. Two archaeologists were stating their belief that Tiahuanaco is one of the oldest cities on earth. The Incas living in the region at the time of the Spanish conquest told the conquistadores the city was there thousands of years before they came along and was built by a race of giants who because of their extreme evil were destroyed by a great flood. The archaeologists told of satellite imagery that reveals a buried city in and around the lake extending a hundred square miles. They said many of the stone blocks at the two cities weigh hundreds of tons each with the largest at Puma Punku weighing 900 tons, the equivalent of eighteen U.S. Army Abrams M-1 tanks. The archaeologists were at a loss to explain how such ginormous stones, stones of the hardest kind on earth, could have been cut, let alone so precisely. Monolithic blocks cut to optician's standards by Stone Age man no less. Cut to tolerances finer than we are capable of today. Stones our biggest cranes cannot lift. Stones drilled with precise holes in all sorts of complex shapes like stars and triangles, and transported hundreds of miles over rough terrain and water and lifted into place using an unknown technology we can't come close to. The video stated that the La Paz museum in Bolivia holds human-like skulls with three times the brain capacity of modern man. What would modern man with ten times the brain power be capable of? Ten times the good? Ten times the evil? Cathy found in the Bible that God reduced man's lifespan from what it had been — 800 years and more. It stood to reason God also reduced man's intelligence.

According to various Native American tribes giants lived lifespans of hundreds of years. Imagine a Hitler with an IQ of 1,200 with 800 years to kill. The documentary also told that the giants constructed thousands of ancient cities all over the world on every continent – cities with things in common such as megaton stones fitted together so precisely a human hair cannot be inserted anywhere along their joints, as with the pyramids. And structures with slits that align with the sun only on the day of the winter or summer solstice.

"ATS?" Chase crowed [translation: *Are They Serious?*]

"Quiet!" Matt shushed.

The video explained that the Greeks believed giants were responsible for building the megalithic structures using construction beyond our realm of understanding that we cannot replicate.

"Giants didn't build it," Zak scoffed.

"I can't hear!" Cathy shushed.

"Look, I'll give you each the DVD. Can we go now?" Loveland begged.

"Wait," Matt said. A green scroll bar revealed the documentary was almost over.

The story told how Tiahuanacu lies at an altitude of two and a-half miles up in a valley buried beneath six feet of marine silt. Marine as in seawater. A team of archaeologists who didn't want to be identified revealed the evidence showed a worldwide flood inundated Tiahuanacu, hence the six foot layer of silt over the high altitude ancient city and how it used to be completely seawater. A nearby lake still is seawater. They noted the landlocked Black Sea in the Mediterranean is also known to have gone from being 100% freshwater to 100% seawater in a flash 4,500 years ago. In Bolivia, the floodwaters created Lake Titicaca which flooded much of the ancient city, various structures of which have only recently been discovered beneath its murky waters amid the Altiplano, one of the driest regions on earth. Stones of extraordinary size there and across the ancient world fit together without mortar as if sliced clean through with a laser. One cannot insert a needle anywhere between their joints. Father Malvic knew that the ancients knew how to change the molecular structure of stone. Stoneworkers today must put mortar, a cement paste, between the joints of stones when fitting them together, a primitive method. And modern man is unable to work with such huge blocks, some weighing two million pounds no less, to say nothing of transporting them across rivers and up fifteen thousand foot mountain ranges through the air the way the ancients did. Scientists choose not to think about it. We can go to the moon but we can't replicate the pyramids, change molecular structure or levitate anything it seems.

"Scary . . . interesting scary," Cathy said.

"The proof lies in the ancient structures themselves," the narrator continued until cutting to a brief Toyota Highlander commercial after which he rattled off more exotic names – Gozo in Malta, Ollantaytambo in Peru, Baalbek in Lebanon, Gilgal Rephaim in Syria, the Pyramids in Egypt, Stonehenge in England, Yonaguni in the East China Sea, Nan Madol in the western Pacific, the Sun Temple at Modhera, and Gornaya Shoria in Siberia to name a few of hundreds, all kept very quiet by the quackologists who pretend they don't exist and wish they would go away.

Matt stood glued as the narrator explained that diarite, the second hardest rock on Earth, along with basalt and granite, were favorites of the ancients, so hard we can only cut them with diamond saws. *Diamond saws? Really?* And intriguing properties associated with basalt have come to light, having to do with sound waves and magnetic fields and radiating electromagnetic wave frequencies. "We are the cavemen by comparison," said the narrator, who revealed Tiahuanacu is connected with other ancient sites throughout the world by a labyrinthine network of subterranean tunnels which empty into caverns as large as continents. They defy explanation by modern man and have yet to be officially explored. *Yet to be explored?*

The documentary ended with the discovery of thousands of dismembered human bodies, the demons' calling card, found throughout Puma Punku. It encouraged viewers to learn more by reading on their own. Then the screen went blank. Matt's eyes took on a haunted look as he pondered something the narrator had said, namely that the site's building blocks were made of an advanced geopolymer unknown to man, a primary component which appeared to be human corpse powder though cowardly scientists reluctant to acknowledge it as such labeled it bird guano.

They passed a newsroom filled with video monitors, switching arrays, digital video effects and other equipment.

"Wait here." Loveland returned soon with four DVDs. Zak didn't want his. "You might have told me that," she huffed as she stuffed it into her dress pocket.

"How many people'll be watching," Cathy asked.

"It's a delayed broadcast. Two million . . . give or take a few hundred thousand."

Soon Matt heard Cathy murmuring " . . . you're smart, you're funny, you're cute … you're smart, you're funny, you're cute … yeah, you are … you're … "

Matt laughed.

"I get nervous when too many people are around," said Cathy turning crimson. "It's social anxiety. She said two million people will be watching. Forget what you heard. Please, please, please. Daddy says everybody's insecure. Some just hide it better."

They came to a glass-enclosed room with a big swivel-mount studio camera with thick cables running to it and a shoulder-mount mini-cam of the kind used in the field. After Cathy called the state police Loveland sent a security guard to the heliport to guard Father Malvic. Then Matt and Cathy told her everything she wanted to know.

Then Loveland told them, "Remember that show I was on? *Ghost 411*? The real reason it went off the air wasn't because of ratings. That was a lie. It was because everybody connected with it died. And ghosts followed us home. I live in fear. I'm telling you for your own good . . . stop . . . stop now . . . after the broadcast."

Chapter 25 – THE BROADCAST

"THREE....TWO....ONE... Hello and welcome to CNN. I'm Katie Loveland. When two boys discovered a Native American burial mound they were shocked at what they found inside – a twenty-six foot human skeleton. In the studio with us are Matt Legend and his cousin Chase Tannenhook, Cathy Kozacky and her brother Zak. As I understand, you also discovered something that has to do with ghosts, right?"

"It wasn't a . . . " Matt began.

"Right," Cathy blurted. "I call it the Common Demonic Denominator," she said, strangely showing no sign of nervousness in front of two million viewers. That 'you're cute, you're funny' thing must work, thought Matt.

"What it means," she continued, "is all supernatural stuff has one thing in common – demons . . . except the God stuff. Ghosts aren't dead people. They're evil spirits masquerading as dead people."

"Name something strange," Cathy said.

"Oh, I don't know, we've covered some pretty strange stories . . . cattle mutilations?" Loveland played along.

"Demonic. Not only cattle," Cathy said, "horses, sheep, goats, moose, caribou, dogs, cats, all kinds of animals. Tongues, ears, eyes, all kinds of parts surgically removed. Never a drop of blood on the ground. Bodies drained of blood. Anuses cored out. Don't even ask. I have no idea. And never any tracks. They've been seen by ranchers being lifted and lowered in beams of light by UFOs."

"Crop circles?"

"Demonic. UFOs and orbs are sometimes seen when they're being made . . . sometimes in milliseconds . . . even caught on camera. Researchers have found many are located on ancient sacrificial sites. Want to hear something really crazy? Lots of ancient cultures say their megalithic structures were built in one night. One night!"

"We did a story on that goatsucker thing once . . . . Chupacabra."

"Demonic."

"Flying humanoids."

"Demonic."

"Bigfoot?" Loveland smirked.

"Demonic."

"How's Bigfoot demonic? I mean … if it exists. Isn't it just an ape?"

"It's no ape," Cathy said. "They're interdimensional beings. They can make themselves disappear. The trap cams catch other animals going after the bait but when the bait's in frame one second and gone the next with no animal in the frames, they know they're dealing with something supernatural. They're telepathic and they know English and every other language … and their DNA's been analyzed. A study … the Sasquatch . . . . ahh …" Cathy fumbled . . .

– "The Sasquatch Genome Report," Matt broke in. "Their nuclear DNA's part human, part unknown. Well, not unknown completely. It's fallen angel DNA. And trackers find their footprints often disappear in mid-step. Mid-step. You don't hear about that. One disappeared in a flash of light when a hunter shot it. They've been seen being lifted into UFOs too and when they're put back down they're alive and well. What's that about?"

"UFOs?" Loveland scratched her expensively-coiffed blond head.

"Not sure yet, but we think they might be demonic too."

"What are you kids? A think tank? . . . X-files? . . . what?"

"Just kids."

"What's a think tank?" Zak whispered.

"A priest says we're all in the middle of a galactic war. An invisible one. And we only see the casualties. And things are going to get worse. A lot worse."

"Sounds like Washington politics," Loveland quipped.

"For our viewers just joining us our young guests claim that before our cameras they'll conjure a demon."

Matt bristled. *Great. Now two million people think we're Harry Potter.*

"How long will it take?" she asked, intending to end the broadcast immediately after Matt's failure to produce the demon.

"Soon."

"Okay," Loveland said, flashing her bleached smile.

"First, is there anything you'd like to tell our viewers?"

"Ghosts aren't dead people," Matt said.

"What are they?"

"Evil spirits impersonating dead people."

"Do you have proof?"

"There's proof in the Bible," said Matt.

“Do you have any other proof?”

“Show them, Matt,” Cathy said.

“Devil Trash. Appear,” Matt ordered.

The devil materialized in the middle of the studio unable to resist an order from the wearer of King Solomon’s ring. As it unfolded its pterodactyl-like wings the smell of sulfur and rotten meat went through the studio. The anchor dropped her pen and froze. Her preservation instinct screamed flight. Fight wasn’t an option. “This isn’t happening, this isn’t happening,” she kept repeating. A wet stain spread across Zak’s pants.

“Are you kidding me?” Cathy blurted.

Katie’s eyeballs rolled back in her head. Cathy rushed to her side rubbing her limp wrist as studio personnel spilled screaming into the street three floors below.

“What happened?” asked Katie, opening a woozy eye. She made a kind of grunting sound then spotting the demon was out again.

“Smelling salts!” Cathy yelled. Summer intern Courtney appeared holding a capsule. Holding it under the anchor’s nose she squeezed her fingers together crushing the ammonia-filled ampoule. Katie bolted upright waving her arms.

“Don’t worry,” Matt said. “He has to do what I say.”

“How do you know? You’re just kids … how long was I out,” Loveland whispered fearing her job gone up in smoke . . . “Well, a-a as you can see,” said Loveland struggling to compose herself, “words can’t a-a-ade . . . begin to describe what we’re seeing. Before our . . . our, eyes … a … creature . . . has a-app,” she gulped … “appeared . . . in .. in .. in our studio. The tortured anchor zoned out for a moment then whispered, "Are you getting this?" Her camera operators nodded their replies . . . "which would appear to prove . . . prove, yes these entities exist," she gulped, fearing any moment the beast to spring across the room and transform her into the walking dead.

"As to how this is possible … where it's from . . . and . . . and how it will affect … our . . . our . . . our world is for the time … unknown. Yet one thing is certain. If seeing is believing," said Loveland gaining strength with every passing second her blood was still in her veins … "the world as we know it will never be the same," she said, avoiding eye contact with the demon.

"Make him tell," Cathy said.

"Devil Trash. What are ghosts? Tell everything," Matt ordered. The demon told everything it knew about ghosts replete with plenty of foul language, unable to disobey the wearer of King Solomon's Ring.

He began with how evil spirits masquerade as people who have died. He told how their ruse began thousands of years before the birth of the one he referred to as The Son of the Most High God and in anticipation of the Bible. He revealed its purpose – to try to discredit the Bible inasmuch as it has a thing or two to say about life after death, namely, the dead are dead, stay dead in the grave and can't leave it and know nothing until the day of the eventual return of the Son of The One True God, the one the Watcher's watch for, the one who put the solar system's outer barrier into place to keep them in. The demon's discourse was so foul-mouthed most of it had to be bleeped out.

"We lead you [bleep] humans astray. We try to make the [bleep] Bible appear a lie," spouted the devil.

"Is the Bible a lie?" asked Matt.

"No," the demon replied.

"Lying spirits perplex us sore," Cathy said. The devil stopped short his undecorous descant. Every eye turned to Cathy. "*The Road to Endor* . . . it's a poem by Rudyard Kipling," she murmured. "A warning about ghosts."

"Devil Trash – enough!" Matt said, shooting Loveland an '*I told you so'* look.

Loveland struggled to think. "That's interesting, but what proof is there any of that's true?" she asked, fearing still the demon to fly across the room and cling to her face and everybody knows what happens after that.

"Isn't he proof enough? He knows things. He's from down there," said Chase, pointing at the floor.

Matt turned to the demon. "Prove it."

The devil began speaking gibberish. After a minute of the babble, it spoke in English, strangely without a single foul word, again for exactly one minute. It would be weeks before Oxford scholars would connect the dots and link the demon's seeming rant with a project they had been working on for eight long years – translating a carved Elamite tablet – a slow and arduous process involving a language not heard on Earth for five thousand years. The demon had translated the tablet in sixty seconds flat.

"Well, I'm not sure what that all means," said Loveland.

"What other proof is there?" asked Matt.

"The Bible," replied the demon.

"Are there more of you?" asked Cathy.

"Answer!" Matt commanded.

"We are everywhere."

"Make the cameras see what you see," Matt ordered.

"Pan the skyline," Loveland directed.

The operators swung their cameras to the window.

"Better look at this," the operator of the big cam gulped.

Loveland switched the feed to the studio's flat screen. A gasp went through the room.

Highways of demons crisscrossed the skyline. The cameramen gulped, panned and zoomed.

"Where are they going?" Loveland gasped.

"Answer her," Matt ordered.

"Everywhere."

"We'll be reporting more on this as these disturbing events unfold," Katie gulped. "This is Katie Loveland with CNN," she said biting her lip as a shadow moved across the wall and the stench grew unbearable.

"They're here," said Zak.

"I guess we know now not to drink the Kool-Aid," Loveland sighed.

"What do you mean?" asked Zak.

"It means I don't think people will be falling for the ghost lie anymore."

"We did it. We can go now," Cathy said.

"Is there anything you'd like to leave our viewing audience?" Loveland squeaked.

"Ghosts aren't dead people and giants are real," Matt replied.

As Loveland was signing off two rough-looking men with military-style haircuts and ill-fitting suits barged in accompanied by the show's producer, Tim Lansberry.

"Call off your demon," ordered the brown-suited goon.

"Which of you's Matt Legend?" the blue-suited one snapped. Matt signaled his reply. "Don't *you* go anywhere." Turning to Katie. "You either."

"Who are you?" she demanded.

"Call off your dog," brown suit barked.

"Devil Trash. Go," Matt squeaked.

Loveland looked at her producer then at the two men.

"Who are they?" Loveland demanded, turning to her boss.

"They *have* the authority," said Lansberry apologetically. "I got a call from the top. The story's dead. Deader than dead."

"But……"

"No buts, Katie. Sorry." Lansberry turned and quickly left.

Blue swaggered menacingly toward the two hundred ninety pound mini-cam operator. "I'll take that fatso," he said grabbing the camera. He popped a door open, removed its memory stick and shoved the cam back at its portly operator.

"Where's that go to?" asked brown nodding to the cables running along the floor.

"The production room," the cameraman replied quickly.

Loveland watched helplessly as the agent jammed the memory stick into his pocket as his partner collected all wearable tech from the crowd gathered outside the room before ordering them to get lost.

"Sorry kids," said Loveland. "It was a great story . . . I'll be back . . . I think I'm gonna be sick. I have to go to the ladies room. After that … that devil thing I don't feel so good," Loveland said tonelessly.

"They're enough to make anybody puke," said blue. There seemed to be a story there, leaving one to only guess what sort of run-ins blue's kind might have had with the demon's kind. Two fingers of the man's left hand were missing. Maybe that's how he lost them, Matt thought. "Come right back," the agent barked. "And before you go Loveland, we need to advise you not to divulge any of this to anyone. Are we clear?"

"Or what?" she demanded, her hand over her mouth. "Or what?" she repeated feebly.

"Let's just say you don't want to go there."

"What would you do – *kill* me?" she said half-joking. The two agents only returned icy stares which sent a cold chill through her. Judging by the stares they were the sort of men who could easily arrange a convenient mishap. Not even her parents would suspect it was anything but an unfortunate accident. She wondered how many people they had already made have bad luck.

"Okay, you win. Do I need to sign something?"

"Sign what? This never happened," brown whipped.

"Right," she replied, satisfied she had used just the right amount of vocal inflection, mannerism and body language.

Katie Loveland was an expert in vocal inflection, mannerism and body language. They were the tools of her trade. And she was every bit as good at using them as the goons were at killing people. She had learned early in her television journalism career that a successful news anchor must not only competently report the news but make the audience become interested in you. To accomplish that she used her eyes, subtle head movements, facial expressions and vocal inflections that would cause even the most disinterested viewer to stop what he or she was doing and watch. She spent countless hours practicing in the mirror living on ramen noodles and spaghetti-o's in her tiny Reseda one-room studio apartment during the early days of her career before coming to the attention of CNN.

"Ah … can we go now?" asked Zak.

"Stay put you little twit," blue roared.

Satisfied the agents had bought her act, Loveland excused herself. Rounding the end of the hallway she glanced back. She was being followed. Blue had given his partner a nod when she left the room.

Ignoring her shocked co-workers she pressed hard against the stairwell door and rushed down the three flights as best she could in her four-inch arrest-me-red Pradas.

Meanwhile upstairs blue stood guard over his captives. The way he was looking at him chilled Matt's bones. It was the look he had seen in the eyes of the Nazi guards in the photographs at the Holocaust Museum. Matt hated Nazis.

"She gave me the slip," his radio crackled.

"FIND HER!" blue barked, his face flush with rage. He turned to face his captives.

Cathy whispered something into Matt's ear.

"I don't know if it does that," he whispered back.

"Try," Cathy whispered.

"No talking," blue bellowed.

Matt uttered something under his breath.

"I said no talking."

It didn't work, thought Matt. He could see Cathy, Chase and Zak as clearly as ever.

"WHAT THE ... WHERE'D THEY GO?" blue bellowed as his eyes swept the room.

"It worked. Follow me," Matt shouted, throwing the door open.

"No way," blue mumbled.

"Run," Matt screamed.

The agent dashed into the hallway scanning for any sign of his targets. Cathy, not used to being invisible collided with a man who lay sprawled beneath a cloud of papers not knowing what hit him.

"Sorry!" she blurted.

The agent shoved his way toward the commotion, flinging a young office worker to the floor with both hands who didn't get out of his way fast enough.

"I lost the darn kids," he barked into his mike. "Get that reporter."

Brown was flying down the hall too fast to do more than key his mike button once in reply. He had the news anchor squarely in his sights and didn't want to lose her.

Katie Loveland ran like the fate of the world depended on her. For all she knew it did. But for the moment it was still fat salary over protecting baby seals. She rounded a corner, colliding with Courtney, the summer intern.

"Courtney, HELP! I'm being chased. I need you to slow him down." The agent appeared down the hall. Loveland disappeared through the production room door.

Everyone stopped and stared as she burst into the room. Breathless, Loveland pressed the eject button of the tray she knew held the interview DVD. She popped open the tray, grabbed the DVD and made for the door on the opposite side of the room. Her days at CNN were over, maybe even her days in broadcast journalism. But she had decided. She wasn't going to let the story of the century be quashed.

She burst from the room and disappeared down a stairwell, ears perked for the merest sound. She reached the ground floor. Opening the door she scanned the atrium. With relief she had reached it first.

"I'll take that." An arm reached around the door and locked her in a painful vise-grip as its tall owner with long thin fingers plucked the DVD from her hand.

Whelcher burst through the north stairwell door skating across the slick marble floor arms flailing scanning the crowd for any sign of the slippery news anchor.

"You didn't really think we were going to let you get away with that did you?" vise grip smirked.

"Well, for a minute I did," Loveland sneered.

Courtney appeared. To Loveland's astonishment the intern walked directly over to brown.

"What do we do with her?" Whelcher asked.

“Leave her,” said Courtney. “We have what we came for.” With a look that could kill Katie jerked free.

“I thought you looked a little old for a summer intern,” she sneered.

Meanwhile Matt, Cathy, Chase and Zak had reached the roof.

The Five Stages of Disbelief. The first is shock and denial. The second is anger. Stage Three is depression, reflection and loneliness. Stage Four is working through it. Stage Five is accepting your new world. None were accepting their new world.

Father Malvic was gone. And the guard too.

“Are you kidding me? Call that FBI agent,” Cathy blurted. “Zak, what’s his name?”

“Special Agent Thyme,” said Zak sullenly, a name he knew all too well from having hacked the wrong computer.

Ten minutes later, Special Agent Thyme had the facts. “He got away though,” Matt said.

“Don’t worry. We’ll get him sooner or later.”

It was the later that was worrisome.

“There’s more,” Matt said . . .“emails.”

“Meet me. My lobby. Thirty minutes,” the agent replied.

“I want to go home,” Zak whined. “We did what we came to do.”

“*We*?” Matt said. “*We* didn’t do anything.”

“Okay, *you* then. Whatever. I want to go home.”

“No,” Matt said.

“This isn’t Dungeons and Dragons, okay!” Zak screamed. “The swords and the wizards are real! And when you die you’re really dead! They’re no extra lives.”

"Nobody's going anywhere," Cathy said. "Not until that creepoid psycho priest is behind bars. How did he get to be a priest anyway? Besides, the FBI will know how daddy's doing."

They landed on the nearest building to the FBI's Richard B. Russell Federal Building thinking it unwise to land unannounced on the FBI invisible or not. They made their way to the street where they passed a homeless man holding a sign which read THE END IS NEAR – ET IS COMING.

Matt, Cathy, Chase and Zak stood in the lobby of the busy Federal Building wondering why they were having to step out of everyone's way. Were people in Atlanta that rude? Then it dawned on them. They were still invisible.

"Devil Trash, uncloak us," Matt said. Startled people began to step out of their way. It's a funny thing with invisibility as anyone who has ever been invisible knows – if you suddenly materialize in a crowded place, people look at you funny and just assume you somehow walked in on them and they simply hadn't noticed.

Special Agent Thyme escorted them to a vacant conference room. "He's definitely up to something," he said thumbing through a sheaf of papers.

"Looks like he's planning a double-cross selling this DNA to everybody. If the Chinese want it this bad we need to know why. Plus, it looks like our own government's been channeling funds through the USDA, the Agriculture Department. Sneaky. And illegal. I know a certain senator who'd like very much to know about that."

"Can you find him!" Cathy said. "He said he's going to cut our hearts out. He wouldn't do that to kids . . . would he?"

"Bloody 'ell. There're some whacked-out crazies out there. Those Nazi monsters killed over a million kids," Thyme grimaced. "I can't tell you the state we find some missing kids in. The stuff of Bluebeard."

"What about daddy? Any word on daddy?"

"I'm sorry, I thought you were told."

Special Agent Thyme looked down briefly and cleared his throat. "He didn't survive the bail out I'm afraid."

Cathy flinched. "No, that's not possible . . . There must be some mistake." Tears began to stream down her face.

"Your mother's on her way. She'll be here soon. We'll get Malvic. Don't you worry."

"How did he die?" Zak whispered.

"His neck . . . he broke it . . . in the bail out. If it's any consolation he died instantly." Grief counselors were brought in.

Chapter 26 – THE MOUNTAIN

On the street book smart doesn't last two minutes against street smart. In today's world it pays to be both. In tomorrow's it will be mandatory.

UPON THEIR RETURN to Chickasaw they were grounded until the next Ice Age, broken-hearted or not.

In the days to follow men wearing black suits, thin black ties and Ray-Bans were wherever they went. They reported the men in the dangerous-looking black Lincoln Navigator with the blacked-out windows to the chief of police. He told them the men were in town on government business and that's all he could say about it.

The next day at precisely 1330 hours a dark blue GMC Yukon with small yellow letters on its door which read 'U.S. Air Force – Official Use Only' pulled to the Tannenhook residence. Across town an identical Yukon pulled to the Kozacky residence, each bearing an unarmed Air Force officer and technical sergeant. After introducing themselves they politely asked each family to accompany them for a brief meeting.

"Does this have anything to do with CNN?" Carolyn Kozacky asked, for the CNN interview had created a worldwide stir after Katie Loveland released the pirated DVD to each one of the world's syndicated news services. The DVD wrenched from her by the goon was found to be a CNN documentary on Tiahuanacu. Loveland had stuffed the interview DVD down her bra. It had been viewed by a billion people, around the same number who had viewed Princess Diana's funeral.

Churches hailed it as more proof of the existence of God while its detractors assailed it as nothing more than "cheap theatrics by world governments intent on diverting their populations' attentions away from their steadily worsening political, environmental and economic woes." News agencies reported churches, synagogues, temples and mosques overflowing with people wanting to get right with God as publishing houses strained to keep up with the sudden demand for books on religion. Not since the release of *The Exorcist* had the world been so interested in God and demons.

"We don't know, ma'am. We just ask you and your family come with us for a brief meeting if you wouldn't mind" was the airmen's polite response to each of their questions. So the Tannenhook family; Uncle Ned, Aunt Nell, Uncle Ollie, Chase and Matt, and the Kozackys all went with the men in the sharply creased dark blue uniforms for what they thought would be a short meeting thinking it must be something very important and that they would be right back. They were half right.

The first Yukon passed through the local airfield's security gate to a waiting twin-engine turboprop its engines turning. The second Yukon bearing the Tannenhooks arrived minutes later. When everyone was aboard the pilot shut the door and the plane took off.

"Where are we going?" asked Carolyn Kozacky.

"Peterson, ma'am."

Two hours later the passengers deplaned for the twenty-five minute ride from Peterson Air Force Base to Cheyenne Mountain Operations Center outside Colorado Springs. They passed in awe through its famous thirty-ton blast door where they were escorted by two military policemen down a long corridor where they passed two strange men dressed identically in black suits going the opposite way. The strange twins possessed the same strange features, were the same height, very tall, very pale, both blonde, blue-eyed, with long fingers, wearing black trenchcoats and hats from the Fifties era. The two turned their heads in unison, each a mirror movement of the other's, each with the same deadpan expression, neither blinking. As the men passed Matt felt his mind being scanned. Scared he tried to block his thoughts. He would never forget the horrible feeling.

They were led to a conference room with a glass wall overlooking a massive control center filled with rows of consoles manned by Air Force personnel sitting facing fifteen gigantic displays of varying sizes, all grouped around a monstrous Mercator projection of the world with traffic of some sort being tracked. The families seated themselves in executive chairs around a large mahogany table which reflected the halogens like a mirror.

Three officers stepped into the room; two air force officers and an army officer. They seated themselves at the far end of the table very official like. The air force officer's blue uniform bore four silver stars on each shoulder which glinted under the halogens.

"Thank you for coming. Allow me to welcome you to Cheyenne Mountain. I'm General Anders. This is Major Seesholtz and Captain Pedotti. I know you're all wondering why we asked you here. I'm sorry for all the secrecy but as you can imagine we wouldn't have asked you here unless this was of the utmost importance," said the general whose portly features contrasted sharply with the fit and trim captain and major.

Ned raised his hand.

"I know you have questions. They'll be answered in due course. I ask you hold them for now.

"First, please accept my condolences concerning the loss of your husband and father," he said looking at Carolyn then Zak and Cathy. Our country is grateful for his military service as it is yours, Master Sergeant Tannenhook." The general had done his homework. Ned didn't know whether to be flattered or alarmed.

The general paused respectfully for a moment before resuming. "Allow me to tell you a little about The Mountain. It's quite an engineering feat. We're quite proud of it. You're surrounded by two thousand feet of solid granite. The complex was built on giant shock absorbers during the Sixties as a hardened command and control center as a defense against Soviet long-range bombers and later ballistic nuclear missiles. It was constructed to withstand a direct nuclear blast. We collect information from satellites, radar and other sensors around the world and process that information in real time. Since the Sixties our role has expanded to include being home to the U.S. Air Force Space Command. This complex continues to serve a very important role in the defense against attacks against North America. Now, to get to the point of your trip here today. I've been authorized to share certain sensitive information with you. You may not take notes. You may not take pictures. You may not record any of this. You kids released information the world isn't ready for," the general glared. The major activated a screen. On it played the now world-famous CNN footage.

"It was a brave thing you kids did. I can't say it was a good thing for national security, however. Or international. That interview caused one big mess. You've upset some very powerful people who don't want demons linked to certain things. You told the world UFOs might be demonic. We'd like you to retract that."

"You know about the demons?" asked Matt.

"We know about alot of things. You call them demons. We call them extra-dimensional beings, EDB's."

"Extra-dimensional beings?" Cathy mused.

"You know that term?" the general asked.

"It's been used to describe lots of things . . . ghosts . . . Bigfoot . . . Chupacabra . . . lots of stuff," Cathy said. Her common demonic denominator was making even more sense.

"You figured this out all by yourselves did you?"

The general went to the glass wall overlooking the command center. He needed the cooperation of these people. Appearing to be forthcoming with answers to their questions seemed the best course.

"What I'm about to tell you is classified Majestic Secret. Majic. That's the very highest level. Only a relative few people in the world are majic. That's twenty-one levels above the president. She's just a mushroom anyway. We keep her in the dark and feed her manure like the rest of those pork monsters."

Some mushrooms won't stay in the dark. A recent former U.S. president tried to expose the existence of aliens. Others tried too but were also silenced. He had even planned his big announcement to coincide with his acceptance of the Nobel Peace Prize in Oslo until the fallen angel trash got wind of it. The hybrid Men in Black warned him in no uncertain terms that if he told, he, the First Lady, their two daughters and Air Force One would vanish the way the Navy planes did in the Bermuda Triangle in 1945. As proof, on the night of the award hours before the ceremony what can only be described as a giant unearthly luminous blue rotating spiral appeared in the night sky above Oslo. The President kept his mouth shut.

"That large display you see there, Console 50, tracks UFOs. Sometimes aircraft fly into our airspace without identifying themselves. When that happens we scramble fighters. Once they're identified they're no longer UFOs. But some crafts defy all attempts at identification. They're displayed on that screen you're looking at. At this moment we're tracking six as you can see."

The giant display showed six white dots. Three were meandering over land masses; one over central Alaska, two over western Canada. The other three were over the Southern Ocean halfway between the southernmost tip of New Zealand and the continent of Antarctica and were moving very, very fast.

"How fast are they going?" asked Matt.

"Those three are doing twenty-five thousand miles per hour," replied the major.

"How fast?" asked Ned.

"Twenty-five thousand miles per hour," the general replied.

"That's impossible!" Ned decried. "Why that's . . .

"Fifty times the speed of sound," Matt finished.

"They have technology we don't understand," said the general.

A hush settled over the room.

“Once they enter the water they become USOs – Unidentified Submersible Objects. The Navy tracks them at that point. You’ve been granted access to some highly sensitive information but not all, of course,” said the general, saying nothing of the monster ten-story waves terrorizing the world’s shipping, created when ten-mile-wide UFOs enter and exit the oceans, known to capsize even large ships on their way to outer space, leaving a trail of plankton in their wake and an even longer trail of scientists racking their brains trying to figure out what ocean plankton is doing in outer space and what is causing the killer waves.

On average twice each week a large ship is lost at sea without any warning and without any trace. It is the shipping industry’s best kept secret.

The German luxury liner *Aschenputtel der Meere* (*Cinderella of the Seas)* was on her maiden voyage when the giant wave hit, capsizing and sinking with all 9,423 souls onboard.

“Why did those three white dots turn blue?” asked Cathy. General Anders looked perturbed.

“They just went from being UFOs to USOs,” Major Seesholtz replied. “UFOs are the white dots. USOs are blue. They’ve entered the water. That’s the Southern Ocean. There’s lots of activity there. We get reports daily from our naval vessels observing the ripleys entering and leaving the waters,” the major added. There’ve even been shall we say . . . hostilities. Our oceans are an alien planet in and of themselves. Forget space. There’re alien worlds right here.” One look from the general told the major he had said too much. The major stopped talking.

“It says that USO’s doing 250 knots, dude. How can it go that fast underwater?” asked Chase. The general ignored him. “How fast is that in miles per hour?”

“It’s what the Navy calls a fast mover. Around 285,” the captain replied.

Why exactly are we here?” asked Matt.

“Yes, who are you people exactly and how do you expect us to trust you? You’re not just Air Force,” Carolyn Kozacky demanded.

“I’m the deputy director of the NSA.” Ollie bolted upright. “I can appreciate your desire to know. What I *can* tell you is national security has been compromised.”

“How so? Did I miss something? And what’s the connection between UFOs and the CNN thing?” asked Matt.

“I’m not able to disclose that,” said the general.

“Well somebody better disclose something,” Cathy said. “I thought you said we were majestic.” It was Cathy’s mom’s turn to be surprised.

“I didn’t say you were majic. I said the information is majic,” the general sneered.

“My daughter’s right. First you bring us here almost at gunpoint then you ask for our help?”

“That’s rather a strong word ma’am. You and your family are, of course, free to leave at any time. Your country is asking for your help is all.”

“I don’t know what you’re trying to pull but – ” Matt sputtered.

“Look, son, let me be perfectly clear.” The general’s demeanor changed, his eight stars glinting. “You can either cooperate and say it was all a hoax you cooked up in your garage ….or our government can make life very difficult for all of you. You'd be surprised at what your government is capable of –

– No we're not. 9/11!" Ollie barked.

"We're hoping it won't come to that. But as I mentioned, this is a matter of national security. I appeal to your sense of patriotic duty," said the general. "Look, I'm offering to make this all go away. If I were you I'd jump on it like a big dog."

"Major . . ." said the general.

The major pressed a key on his tablet. The devil materialized in the center of the room. Matt's jaw fell.

It was quickly apparent a hologram.

"You may be wondering how this is possible," the general said smugly. The major leaned and whispered something into his ear.

"Why don't you take some time to talk this over," said the general. He then left the room followed by the major and the captain in that order.

"Sir, what if we got them security cleared?" said Major Seesholtz outside the room.

"What do you think, Captain?" asked the general turning to Captain Susan Pedotti, United States Army, 4th Psychological Operations Group, flown in from Fort Bragg to provide support for the interrogation. He had worked with her before.

"The adults are more easily influenced, with more to lose than the kids, sir" the captain replied. "We have two alpha kids in the mix, both of which," the captain said, earbuds dangling as she fingered her Panasonic Toughbook, "exhibit rebellious tendencies. The female, Cathy Kozacky, is more likely to be reasoned with but doesn't appear to influence Legend. The other two kids are Type B's. No threat. The Tannenhooks, can be reasoned with. The wife's a housewife with undiagnosed bi-polar disorder. The one they call Ollie's another matter. A conspiracy theorist. We'll have to take care of him like the rest."

"Who controls this Legend kid?" the general barked.

"No one as far as I can tell. Type A, lone wolf, high IQ, parents divorced, left private school, grades took the usual post-divorce nosedive. Looked up to his father; president of Cybertas, cyber security consulting. Dead. One of our ops. We make it look like a robbery. He held a government contract. He saw something he wasn't supposed to see. Those kids are loose cannons. The best way to get Legend to play ball is to convince him this is what his father would have wanted."

"And the girl?" asked the general.

"Type A. Adventurous. Smart. Usually did what her father wanted but a wild card nevertheless. Sir, the boy, the girl, both rebels . . . both risk-takers . . . both lone wolves."

"Hmmm, the makings of a good fighter pilot," the general murmured.

"We don't have the time for any clearances, major. We need resolution on this yesterday," the general barked as the captain continued to monitor audio and video inside the room with her Toughbook.

"Sir, with all due respect, may I remind you of our orders," said Major Seesholtz carefully.

"I'm well aware of our orders, major. "Hopefully it won't come to that."

"Yes sir. But just in case, everything's in place."

"Thank you, major."

"Sir, I recommend you terminate them immediately," said the captain.

"Is that necessary?" asked the major.

"Collateral damage," the general muttered.

"But . . ."

"Do we understand each other, *major?*" barked the general with all the authority of a man who was not to be crossed.

"Yes sir."

Meanwhile inside the room, "Just who do they think they are?" Cathy said, sweeping her arm back and forth through the hologram. "Where's this coming from?"

"This is advanced technology," Zak said.

"Alien technology," Ollie spouted. "Where do you think the transistor, fiber optic data transmission technology and stealth technology came from? . . . and lasers . . . and the stuff the newest bulletproof vests are made out of? – the Roswell crash."

"I don't agree with their methodology," said Nell, "but if national security's involved –

"They always say that when they're trying to hide something," said Ned.

"They'll have to convince me national security's really involved," said Carolyn.

"Me too," said Nell.

"Cathy?" her mother asked.

"I'm not backing down, mom," Cathy said.

"Matt?"

Matt took two deep breaths and said . . . "I was mad at God . . . All I wanted was to let the world know ghosts aren't dead people. I didn't know it would turn into all . . . *THIS!* he said, staring at the giant UFO display . . . A witch told me if I told anyone I'd die. I'm not scared anymore. And God's not the one to blame . . . I know that now . . . I say take off and nuke 'em from orbit."

Ollie sat up straight. "There you go Ripley! Stick it to those losers!"

"That does it then," Matt snapped. He got up and walked to the door. The interrogation team streamed in, the general, major and captain in order.

The general glared at Ned.

"We want to know how national security's involved," Matt said.

. . . "and the connection between UFOs and demons?" Cathy added.

The general continued glaring at Ned who only returned the glare unflinchingly, then he turned to Matt and Cathy, "There *is* a connection . . . We're preparing the world for their arrival. Desensitizing people according to a schedule. They've given us certain technology. Revelations about their existence are being disclosed bit by bit. They certainly don't want it known they're demons and here you are doing just that!"

"I knew it," said Ollie. "It's their Achilles heel . . . the truth!"

"Every month sightings increase," the general continued. "It's part of their plan. The day's not far off I can say when one'll plant itself square in the approach path to another major airport or start buzzing planes. The public's being prepared. Your CNN revelation is interfering with their plan. We work overtime to keep certain information out of the public and there you are putting it in. They're here to help," said the general. "The most amazing things are coming."

"Here to help! They're here to destroy us," said Ollie. "In '55 General MacArthur warned us. Secretary Forrestal was going to too until you murdered him. You've made a pact with the devil and that alien trash."

"Sir that's not correct. And that's precisely why we deny their existence. Those are exactly the kind of misconceptions people might jump to," said the general.

Cathy and Matt stared hard at the soldier. Thank you for your time," Matt said, rising.

"The world's not ready for what we know!" said the general. "Please, Matthew sit down."

"Nobody calls me Matthew."

"Matt . . . Please, sit down. There's more," said the general.

Matt sat slowly down.

"Impress me," Matt said.

"He wants to be impressed," the general sneered.

"Be careful what you ask for little man. If you knew what we know you'd never sleep again."

Chapter 27 – YIKES!– ALIENS

We're on an island of ignorance surrounded by sharks of truth. It's remain on the island or brave the sharks.

"THEY'RE NOT FROM OTHER PLANETS," said the general.

"I knew it!" Ollie roared, pounding his fist on the table.

"AAVs, ANOMALOUS AERIAL VEHICLES. You call them UFOs. They're not what they seem . . ." the general said.

"Where are they from?" asked Nell.

"They're been on this planet almost as long as mankind itself. They think of this as their world. They're underground, undersea, on the moons and the planets. People just don't know it yet. We've been trading secrecy for technology . . . and for looking the other way concerning certain . . . *things*." The way the general said *things* lent the distinct impression he found those *things*, whatever they were, disturbing even for him.

"*Things*? You mean like what's going on at Dulce Base?" said Ollie. "And exactly what did happen there, general?" And don't feed me bull. I'm not one of your mushrooms. If you want our help you need to be truthful with us." Ollie had heard that the chief security officer there, a man named Costello, now one of the murdered two hundred, had been involved in a rescue operation at the secret base and had lost fingers to an alien flash gun then later his life after he told the world what happened down there.

The general, hoping to resolve things quickly with the least amount of effort answered, "There was a firefight. One of our security officers bonded with one of the women in the tubes. They're told never to look an inmate in the eyes. She told him somebody was looking for her. He made her a promise. He mounted a covert rescue operation. It failed."

"Inmates! That's what you're calling them? They're PEOPLE! Abducted PEOPLE," Ollie roared.

What the general was saying was true. The woman he referred to as an "inmate" had pleaded with the security officer, saying, "Help me, help me, please. I'm human. People are looking for me."

Had the general chosen he could have mentioned how the fallen angel trash have been slicing and dicing human DNA for thousands of years, lately with the help of very evil humans. And harvesting their bodily fluids as delicacies. All in gruesome secret underground labs like the one at Dulce Base near the town of Dulce, New Mexico, where missing persons endure an endless nightmare, kept alive in glass tubes and fed through plastic tubing until no longer needed, wishing they were dead, knowing nobody's coming ever again to try to rescue them. The result of a treaty with the fallen angel trash and their evil soulless surrogates, the Greys. A treaty that provides certain so-called "alien technology" in exchange for allowing the abduction of a predetermined number of humans and animals from rural areas, forests and cities and keeping it quiet so as not to upset the disclosure timetable.

But the fake alien fallen angel trash did not keep to the terms of the treaty, the Greata 1954 Treaty signed by the American President Eisenhower. Instead of keeping to the designated number and maintaining careful records as agreed, they falsified the numbers and abducted as many as they wanted. According to FBI, Defense Intelligence Agency and CIA statistics, one hundred thousand children and one million adults disappear every year that are not the result of human foul play. They disappear into thin air. The Aztec, Maya, Inca and other pagan sacrifices continue to this day.

"I knew it," said Ollie. "They would've wiped us off the planet long ago if they could've. Something's holding 'em in check. Can't you see? Since they're the superior beings why would they need to keep a low profile? Why would they need to work with us on anything? They can destroy us anytime they want."

"There's some truth in that," said the general. "It's what we call asymmetric warfare. Lopsided warfare. World governments are being held hostage. It's cooperate or be invaded now instead of later. We've been buying time. And actually they can't destroy us anytime they want. We've learned there's something out there far more powerful than them. We've learned there's a barrier around our solar system.[8] We're on lockdown. They're not allowed out and nothing's allowed in. Word is the beings who installed it are coming back."

"The enemy of my enemy is my friend," Matt murmured.

"Let's hope so," replied the general.

"So where are the real aliens?" asked Ned.

"We don't know. But like I said, nothing's allowed in. The EDBs aren't from the Pleiades or Orion or any of the other places they say. They're full of crap. That much we know. They can't even keep their stories straight. One month one of them tells you he's from one place, another he's from someplace else. They all lie."

"What else did you buy?" Cathy bluntly stated.

"Technology. Like that micro-holograph projector you were looking for . . . and other things." One of the "other things" the general failed to mention is hyper-luminal flight, flight faster than the speed of light, and free energy capable of ending man's dependence on fuels.

"This has all been very interesting but you threatened us."

"Yeah, you're takin' the *Big L* dude," said Chase.

"The Big L?" the general sneered.

"The big loss . . . It means you blew it dude." The general's blood boiled. He wasn't used to being spoken to in such manner. Not by anyone. Especially civilians. Especially a civilian kid. The captain and major bore fearful looks.

"Master Sergeant?"

"I think they covered it nicely, *sir,*" Ned replied.

"I thought you were a man of reason," said the general. "Do you have any idea what would happen if people knew the truth? That our weapons are useless to protect them? There'd be global chaos. A complete breakdown of law and order."

"I'm sorry. The lies have to end somewhere," Ned replied. "It began with lies to the Indians. It's been lies ever since."

Taking Ned's cue the families rose.

"Are you out of your minds? Are you sure you won't reconsider, sergeant?"

"Quite sure," Ned replied.

Ollie asked the general, "You said earlier the kids upset some powerful people. People who don't want demons linked to certain things. Who?"

The general ignored him.

The interrogation team remained seated. The visitors streamed from the room. With a wave of his hand the general signaled his subordinates to let them go.

"Sir, are you sure you should have told them about the demon connection?" the captain treaded carefully.

The captain stared at the general as if expecting an answer as to why majic secrets were divulged to lowly civilians with no security clearances, and more importantly why it didn't seem to matter. At the very least it represented a breach of national security protocols – protocols that are inviolate.

The general said nothing, led the major out of earshot of the others and whispered, "Advise the ripleys that in two hours the problem will no longer exist."

Two military policemen escorted the visitors through the tunnel.

Matt looked back. The general and his team were standing outside the interrogation room joined by two other officers each wearing uniforms of different foreign nations. The creepy twins had joined them. They were all huddled together staring at him speaking in hushed tones giving him a creepy feeling in the pit of his stomach.

They were driven back to the air base.

"I have a bad feeling about this," said Zak.

"Shut up. You have a bad feeling about everything," Cathy replied.

The twin-turboprop started, taxied and lifted off.

"I don't believe a word he said," said Carolyn Kozacky.

"Remember what the general said about the connection between UFO's and demons?" Cathy said. "If they're connected all the other things must be too. Atlantis, the Greek gods, the Roman gods, giants – everything. Remember my Common Demonic Denominator? In the ancient times they were 'gods.' Now they're 'aliens.' "

"Remember the genetic manipulation in mythology?" Ollie sputtered. "Half-human, half-animals? And I'll bet you anything they created the dinosaurs. They're not something God would've made. If you were demons conspiring with governments, would you want it known you're not really aliens from other planets but demons from Hell?"

"Something bad's gettin' ready to happen," said Ollie.

"I remember the good old days," Cathy's mother mused, "when all we had to worry about was the Russians sending over a few nukes."

"You don't think all those alien abductions are for nothing do you?" said Ollie. "You can't expect them to just show up one day lookin' like the devil. Those poor abductees. Did you hear what that general called them? Inmates! They've been creating hybrids using the abductees' genetic material. I think those were two of them in the corridor at Cheyenne Mountain. Something wasn't right about them. The fallen angels are going to need creatures that look like us when they come as supposed aliens trying to convince us they're from the Pleiades and we're their seeds and they've come back to usher us into a golden age and save us and make us gods. Bull crap. Don't fall for it."

"I don't get it. What could be so darned important about what you kids did at CNN that would have the government going to all this trouble?" asked Ned.

"This is like Alice in Wonderland," Cathy mumbled.

"The government's always denied knowledge of UFOs but last time I looked they weren't killing people over it," said Nell.

"I wouldn't say that," said Ollie. "You need to look again. Does the name Phil Schneider mean anything?" Nell shook her head. "James McDonald?" She shook it again. "John Mack? John Murphy? Thomas Costello? Max Spiers. William Cooper. I can go on all day. Whistle-blowing patriots. Men, women and children. Heroes. All dead. One was just a kid. A computer hacker. All because they dared tell the world what they'd learned about EDBs. So the demons want us to think they're aliens from other planets, eh? I say blow the whistle on 'em."

○ ○ ○

The sun's positioning told Cathy something was amiss.

"Mom, Tennessee's east. We're heading north."

"Are you sure?"

She raised her phone's compass.

"Maybe it's broken."

"I'm sure the pilot knows what he's doing," said Nell.

"This pilot's going to find out."

Cathy approached the flight deck. Perhaps they were making a stop to pick up another passenger. She tapped the door. No response.

Geez, what's with these guys, she thought.

"Maybe they're not supposed to open the door," said her mom.

"That's commercial flights," said Ned worriedly.

"It's not like we're terrorists," said Nell.

Something about Nell's remark made Cathy cringe. Who knew what that Air Force general considered them.

"I'm going to find out what's going on," said Ned, banging on the door until his hand hurt.

"*OPEN UP OR I'M GOING TO BREAK THE DOOR IN!*" he yelled. Ollie stood by ready to assist.

Ned threw his body into it. With a loud crack the fiberglass gave way sending him sprawled onto the flight deck.

Where were the pilots?

The control yokes moved in unison as if by unseen hands.

Cathy scanned the flight deck. No headsets. No mikes. No way to use the radio. "Matt, I need you," she screamed.

Cathy pressed into the left seat as she motioned Matt into the right as she scanned the gauges.

"We're almost out of fuel! They're flying it remotely."

She flashed to the military's unmanned aerial reconnaissance vehicles armed with Hellfire missiles that routinely ruin the days of bad guys half way around the world, their fates affected by a pilot sitting in an air-conditioned room at a console with a cup of latte, a joystick, a satellite link and wrap-around flat screens. The thought of someone auguring her and her family into the ground by applying a slight amount of forward pressure infuriated her.

We're the good guys. This is crazy!

The left engine sputtered and died, its propeller windmilling as the engine spent its last drop of fuel. The plane yawed to the left. She pressed hard on the right rudder pedal to compensate for the sudden imbalance in thrust.

"Find someplace to land."

"There's only forest," Matt groaned.

"Daddy help me," Cathy breathed. She pushed the nose down and began a spiral descent as the altimeter spun counterclockwise. There was only dense forest below. Then the right engine sputtered and died leaving only the sound of the windstream brushing against the fuselage.

"Brace yourselves. We're going to hit," Cathy screamed.

She pulled hard on the yoke. The trees reached up snapping the wings off, whipping the plane around. Cathy glimpsed the engines falling through the trees. Branches tore the thin aluminum skin as the plane plowed through the conifers. Her stomach dropped. Her mind went blank. As she fell she asked herself if it was really happening. Breaking branches roared like a freight train until the aircraft came to rest upside down, its nose angling toward the ground. There were plane parts everywhere — wires, seats, twisted metal.

Chapter 28 – YELLOWSTONE

Even the most successful people make two or three critical mistakes in their lives. It's what they do afterward that defines them. So don't sweat the mistakes.

THE SUN FILTERED through the jagged edges of the cabin as broken conifer branches drifted in. The scent of fresh-cut Christmas trees filled Matt's throbbing head. As he woke from his nightmare he realized it wasn't Christmas. The tail had separated. He had a mild concussion, Carolyn Kozacky had a fractured wrist, Chase had a bad bruise on the upper left side of his head and Cathy a nasty gash on her right calf. Ollie had a sprained ankle and a cut across his forehead was bleeding profusely. Ned's back was hurting, his wife was having dizzy spells and Zak was complaining of double vision. All in all they were lucky to be alive.

Carefully they lowered themselves into the underbrush. Frightened golden-mantled ground squirrels ruffled the pine needles and toadstools which carpeted the forest floor. The smell of decaying life oozed from the thick moss.

"We need a fire before it gets dark," said Zak, gazing at the crimson sky. "Matches anybody?" There was only the distant yelp of a coyote.

"No problem."

"No problem! You must've hit your head really hard," Cathy said.

"Sounds good son," said his mother.

Cathy shot her mother a *what are you thinking* look. *Didn't you hear there aren't any matches?*

"If it's dark and we don't have a fire we're going to be in a major hurt locker," Cathy said.

"Give him a chance. In fact, why don't you and Matt and Chase help him by gathering firewood while it's still light out."

"I can make a fire with my cell phone," said Zak.

"He *has* been watching a lot of *Man vs. Wild,*" Cathy said.

They returned with two feeder logs, long, thin dead tree trunks that could be fed continuously into the fire, thereby conserving precious physical energy. Something else Zak had learned.

The others watched skeptically as he used Matt's clasp-knife to shave tinder from a dry stick. He removed the phone's battery, laid it on the ground and plunged the knife into it releasing a plume of oxygen-rich lithium, careful to avoid making contact between the positive and negative plates which would cause it to explode. He then sprinkled the tinder over it and shorted the battery's two leads with a piece of wire. The oxygenated tinder burst into flames.

"I did it! I did it!" he squealed as the survivors cheered over the sound of the wind-tossed trees.

A roaring fire soon was keeping the beasts at bay. Ollie's stories of thousands of people vanishing in national forests without a trace under supernatural circumstances did little to calm their nerves. It only made things worse that the stories came from his cousin, a park ranger.

"Madam, there are things in the forest you do not want to know about," said Ollie, who cited bizarre vanishing after vanishing in practically every forest on Earth.

“Don’t go into the forest. Google it. You’ll see. Jaws has nothing on the forest.”

An owl hooted as if to agree.

“Do you think it has anything to do with that abducted people for technology treaty?” asked Cathy.

“I do,” Ollie replied.

“I don’t do forest. Besides, it’s a bit late for that,” said Nell. “And I’m having a little trouble with my wifi right now.”

“Everybody try and get some rest,” said Ned. With Ollie’s tales on their minds it would be a long night. They were weak, starving, filthy, thirsty, there was nothing to lay on but the cold hard ground, they were hurting, there were weird noises coming from the woods and their exhaled CO2 was attracting mosquitoes like shoppers on the last day before Christmas. Meanwhile the vultures waited.

There was one saving grace. The dense forest hid the wreckage and Cathy had the presence of mind to disable the crash emergency locator beacon, which would complicate the search effort making it harder for the bad guys to find them, hopefully.

Selfishness is The Rule of One. Love is The Rule of Two. In Young Marines Cathy had learned the survival rule; The Rule of Threes. Three days without water, three weeks without food, three hours without shelter in a harsh environment, three minutes without air, three minutes in icy water, three minutes with severe bleeding.

The smell of burnt meat permeated the air. There was fresh roasted ground squirrel for lunch. It and the wild huckleberries did little to stave off the gnawing hunger in their bellies.

“We can’t stay here,” Cathy muttered. “There’s a radio but it’s useless without a mike.”

“I can make one,” Matt declared.

Cathy peered into his dirty face. “You can make one. Right. Can you make me a whirlpool bath while you’re at it.”

“I’m serious . . . I made one in Scouts for a merit badge.

“Like the plastic explosives merit badge?” Cathy snipped.

Matt put everyone to work. Cathy’s mom was put to scrounging thirty feet of copper wire, Zak a drinking straw and a cup, Cathy an inch-long machine screw and nut, Ned four large metal washers and Ollie two round magnets. Their lives depended on it.

Five hours later Cathy connected the radio to the aircraft’s battery while Matt attached the leads of his crude mike.

“If this works, Matt, when we get home I’ll buy you anything you want,” said Mrs. Kozacky.

He offered the contraption to Cathy.

“No, you do the honors,” said Cathy. “It won’t work anyway.”

“What do I say?”

“Use Daddy’s Mustang’s *N* number. Say ATC, November Two Zero Two Alpha Mike, over.”

Matt repeated it and held his breath.

“ATC, November Two Zero Two Alpha Mike, over.” He tried again. Nothing.

“We have to get higher,” Cathy said. “There,” she pointed to a hill. “It’s a half-day’s hike. You up for it?”

“Yup,” said Matt licking his cracked dry lips.

The next day after five hours of hiking, spent and almost at their destination, Matt, ever on the lookout for bears spotted something worse – wolves! Running across the valley floor. A hawk screamed.

"Run!" They struggled up a nearby pine and waited. The beasts surrounded the tree snarling and snapping.

"This'd better work," Cathy panted.

With weak sappy sticky fingers she twisted the sparking leads together. "Now try."

"ATC, November Two Zero Two Alpha Mike, over."

Nothing.

"ATC, November Two Zero Two Alpha Mike, over." Nothing. Matt gulped.

The radio crackled, "November Two Zero Two Alpha Mike, you're very weak . . .go ahead . . ."

"Control, November Two Zero Two Alpha Mike requesting a telephone patch, over." Cathy and Matt exchanged high-fives almost falling out of the tree. The wolves went mad.

"Standby Alpha Mike . . ."

The controller patched Cathy through to Father Herzl.

"Father, this is Cathy Kozacky. Listen, we've been in a plane crash. Matt's here. As far as I can tell we're in Yellowstone somewhere. Father, I *really* need know how this flying carpet thing works . . ."

"Say that again, it sounded like you said you were in a plane crash. Are those dogs I hear?"

Cathy explained. The father took a deep breath. "Alright, listen. Magic carpets are described in detail in the Egyptian Book of the Dead and the Tibetan Book of the Dead and the Hindu Samarangana Sutradhara of King Bhojaraja of Dhara. As crazy as it seems they really did exist. The world hasn't seen one in over two thousand years though.

"The Arabian Nights, you've heard of that, right? . . . a collection of Persian, Arabian and Indian stories handed down through the centuries? They're not fiction. They're actual accounts. A collection of stories collected over the centuries by various authors, translators and scholars across Asia and North Africa. The tales trace their roots to ancient and medieval Arabic, Persian, Egyptian, Indian and Mesopotamian literature. It tells about the flying carpets. The know-how was lost when The Library at Alexandria burned. What a tragedy.

"But listen – a Princeton University graduate student from India designed a miniature one that took flight in the laboratory. He wrote a paper on it. *Traveling Wave-induced Aerodynamic Propulsive Forces Using Piezoelectrically Deformed Substrates*. It was published by –

"FATHER! Can you cut to the chase? We're kind of in a fix here!" Cathy said, looking down into four hungry maws.

"Okay, listen, the Dead Sea Scrolls talks about them. One was a gift from God to King Solomon. It wasn't like the rest. The king's even expanded to fit the number of riders. He took forty thousand up on it one day but because they got too full of themselves . . . too full," the father chuckled, "God got angry and dumped 'em all off – 'cept the king. Picture that . . . it raining forty thousand people!"

"Father!"

"Sorry."

"So they're real?"

"Real as hemorrhoids. They have to do with ley lines. Magnetic fields. Anti-gravity. Stuff like that. We don't know the details. Yours is different though. Like I said, according to the Book of Enoch, it was King Solomon's."

Scientists would eventually construct a full-scale version in the lab to amuse themselves amid their anti-gravity UFO reverse engineering but decades would pass before anti-gravity would begin to be even marginally understood. As with free energy, the public was never told.

"How do you make it appear? What are the magic words?"

"There aren't any. All you have to do is think about it."

"You heard him," Cathy said. "Think."

As he had done with the wild boar Matt closed his eyes and began to concentrate.

He opened them. Hovering just beyond the branches was a thin translucent greenish gold platform.

"Are you kidding me? I can die now. I've seen everything," Cathy said eagerly. The wolves fell silent.

There is a fine line between science and fantasy but if something didn't happen on social media did it really happen?

"Hello? Hello?" the speaker crackled.

"Father, it worked … we'll get back to you."

"But how do you …?" Matt stammered.

"Make it do stuff?" said Cathy. "We'll figure it out."

They inched one at a time across the heavy branch. Again the wolves went mad. Matt nudged the platform with his hand. It oscillated slightly. "It doesn't *look* like a carpet."

“That’s no carpet,” Cathy said.

Times had changed. The flying carpet of King Solomon’s day had been just that according to the historical record. A woven carpet of green silk and gold threads. A conveyance in step with the times though some mistook it for the work of devils.

Matt crawled nervously onto the platform and sat pressing his sweating palms against it in case it took off, a fear all the more unnerving as there was nothing to grab onto. Cathy crawled aboard. As she did the platform doubled in size.

“Ready?” she asked, scarcely able to believe her eyes.

Warily Matt voiced *Up.* The platform rose. *Faster.* It accelerated. *Slow. Stop.* He gulped. The valley lay far below. Your first time on a flying carpet is like piloting a hang glider or a small plane for the first time or like falling through the sky with a parachute strapped to your back . . . it’s the most exhilarating thing.

The warm moist air rising from the valley had condensed in the cooler air above to form towering cumulus clouds that dotted the blue sky like cotton candy. He made for the nearest one having always wondered what it is like to be inside a cloud. As they entered, the sun muted to the grayest of foggiest of days until shooting out of the other side. It was like driving in heavy fog on the I-5.

“Can *I* try?” Cathy asked.

Matt eyed her warily. What if she didn’t give the ring back? Absolute power corrupts absolutely.

Matt recalled what he'd read in *The Right Stuff* about Navy pilots. Gods of the skies with secret security clearances. Her father, so she must be okay, right?.

He removed the ring, placed it on her finger and watched it resize. His mind drifted.

"Thanks. Now let's see what this'll do."

At first she performed simple maneuvers. Gradually, as with the Nemo, she became bolder and bolder but no matter how daring the maneuvers they stayed glued to the fly pad. Soon they were doing tight turns, loops, rolls, even flying upside down.

"Where are we? Are we lost?" asked Matt.

"I don't get lost . . . just temporarily disoriented."

"Are we temporarily disoriented then?"

The faint glow of a distant city dotted an ambiguous horizon. In the dwindling light Cathy kicked herself for having lost all track of time. She determined where they might have been then traveled in the opposite direction. Plan A wasn't working. She tried Plan B, flying in concentric circles. That wasn't working either.

"Give me that. I know how to get us back," Matt said.

Cathy slid the ring from her finger. The sky and earth swapped places . . . "Ahhhhhhhhhhhhhhhhhhhhhhhhhhhh," they screamed as they tumbled. Matt struggled to fit the ring as they plummeted. Suddenly they were still. And upright. They looked down. They gulped. They were two feet off the ground!

Matt looked at Cathy. "Don't say it," he said.

"Right . . . remind me never to do *that* again," Cathy said.

"Devil Trash, guide us back to camp," Matt ordered.

"I was just going to do that," Cathy said.

Soon the devil came to a stop. They were back at camp!

It had been two days and they were growing ever weaker. While the others were gathering firewood Matt sat idly by the fire watching a video, reliving family memories on the last of his battery.

"You *like* Cathy, don't you?" Ollie asked.

"She's okay," Matt replied.

"Oh I think it's more than okay," said Ollie.

"Is it that obvious?" Matt groaned.

"Trust me. I know that look."

"She doesn't even know I'm alive."

"Trust me. She knows. Women have radar for that," Ollie laughed.

Matt recalled his cousin's advice . . . *"I'd ditch the crush, dude. That teenage dream's taken. Her boyfriend's at military school and he's captain of the rugby team and his family's rich. His father's a senator or something."*

"What about her boyfriend?" asked Matt.

"He won't last. Military school's more important to him than girls. In case Cathy doesn't work out don't worry, some girls have strange tastes. You'll find somebody. "

"I don't want *somebody.* I want *her* . . . Ollie, what does it mean when a girl purses her lips?"

Ollie smiled, remembering the days of his youth. "Well now, some girls do that when they're nervous. It's a subconscious sign of flirting. It means you should talk to her, get her number, whatever. Sometimes it means she's not sure about something. You have to find out which."

. . . Cathy's some special girl that one," Ollie chuckled. He leaned into the fire, rubbed his hands together and reminisced. . . "We were at Disney World . . . she was nine . . . all excited about finally being tall enough to drive the cars . . . she'd been waitin' all year . . gets out on the track, starts screamin' 'outa the way, move it," Ollie laughed. "One boy's driving' way too careful . . . lookin' 'round tryin' to figure what the commotion's about, not watching where he's goin' . . . smacks the car ahead . . . causes this whoppin' pile-up. What's she do? . . . whips around him and yells out '*THANK YOU!*,' Ollie laughed.

"She's a live one. A born competitor. Maybe she told you she wants to race Formula 1. Lord help 'em if she ever gets the chance. They'll never know what hit 'em.

"Some kids have to experience winning to get hooked. All it took for Cathy was to see those umpteen consecutive national championship banners hanging in Pauley Pavilion. Somehow it changed her. I'm not sure how. It just did. She was never the same after that. Real competitive like. She wants to go to UCLA now. She wants to be a Bruin.

"I heard you lost your dad. I'm sorry."

Tears welled in Matt's eyes. He tried to hide it. The dragons were back.

"There were things I never got to say."

"Let it out," said Ollie rocking him gently as the others emerged from the forest. He waved them away.

"You know, it might be a good idea to make up with that mother of yours. Just a suggestion. She loves you, you know."

"She's supposed to. She's my mother. That's what they do."

Ollie chuckled.

"Besides, I don't need her. I don't need anybody. People leave you."

"It's a lonely world without love, Matt. Yachts, cars, planes, money, dream jobs, deam homes, dream businesses . . . if you're lucky enough to have any of 'em ... as much as you love 'em they never love you back. The world's nothing without love."

The trouble with having a photographic memory is they come with audio, which means all it takes is one word for the dragons to come calling. The word was 'businesses.' Matt thought of Cybertas and his father and how he would never see his son grow up.

"Something's coming," Cathy screamed.

A faint whopping was growing louder. With it three distant specks. Soon the distinct profiles of three military attack helicopters were visible.

"They're here!" Cathy screamed.

The Cobras advanced to fifty yards, slowed and hovered a few feet off the ground. Matt sensed eye contact even through the pilots' dark helmet visors. The downwash whipped the wild grasses into a frenzy sending the bitter dogbane and white marsh marigold into sweeping arcs around the killing machines. Disturbingly the crews were making no effort to communicate. The crafts hovered ominously above the rocky outcropping then rotated slowly, their red-tipped rockets and guns staring him in the face.

Why aren't they landing?

Two F-16s broke close formation directly overhead at six hundred knots, each veering in different directions under full military power climbing 8g turns, their deafening crackling roars vibrating every cell in Matt's body. He dropped to the ground. As they veered, his heart pounded as he got up and strode as casually as possible to the treeline to avoid telegraphing his next move, praying with every step not to get blasted.

"TIME TO GO!" he shouted.

"How do we know this carpet thing isn't from the devil?" Carolyn Kozacky demanded. "What's the difference between this and a broomstick anyhow?" she asked, having learned in Haiti that voodoo witches when not busy casting spells fly from island to island on nothing but the air. True enough it's not the broom that holds the power but the force behind it. The witch could be flying a chair, a washing machine or a Toyota Prius for that matter. So it was with the flying pad only its power came from God.

The instant they cleared the trees they would be visible to the Cobra and the F-16s would be back. As they cleared the treetops the Cobras turned to face them. "What the ...," the pilots breathed. The general had told them they would encounter alien technology being used by aliens disguising themselves as humans and to terminate them.

Making for a canyon, the Cobra rocked back and forth as it trailed the flying pad over a snaking river canyon, its guns blazing forming a wavy line of pulverized granite craters along the canyon wall as the gunship jockeyed for best firing angle. It suddenly veered away. An F-16 dropped in. To the ferocious ripping noise of its 20mm Gatling gun, its seeming

Volkswagen-size bullets blasted a trail of spent uranium across the canyon wall.

"Juke right, juke left," Matt commanded using tactics gleaned from Cathy's dad and his backyard B-52. Matt marveled at the absence of g-forces.

"Loop!" The fly pad began a rollercoaster loop. The F-16 tucked alongside, its pilot deftly holding his position throughout the dangerous maneuver even as they re-entered the narrow canyon. As they looped the pilot jerked his finger down, the signal to land.

An explosion of feathers marked the demise of a bald eagle giving Chase an idea.

"Dudess. Your jacket."

"It's not dudess. What for?"

"FOR ONCE! PLEASE!" Confused Cathy slipped off her pink fur-lined hooded parka and handed it over. Chase dangled it over the edge and let it fly. It went straight into the aircraft's air intake which sucked it in like a giant Hoover.

With a loud bang the fighter began to lose altitude and trail thick black smoke. Inside the cockpit the orange master caution light lit alerting its pilot to a major malfunction. In the narrow canyon the only option was to eject. The canopy blasted clear as the ejection seat rocketed its pilot up and away leaving the pilotless craft to plunge nose down in a fireball far below on the canyon floor.

Then the second fighter dropped in.

Can we outrun it? He had seen the Thunderbirds perform at an airshow once.

"Fly pad. Mach ten. Juke," Matt ordered.

"You gotta be kidding," said the pilot as the speeding pad darted away and disappeared from view.

"Box Man, Goldfinger. You up?"

"Up Gold. What the !?@*% was that?" said Box into his hand-held guard channel transceiver as he drifted slowly to earth to Goldfinger orbiting overhead

"We need to get our stories straight."

"What do you have in mind?" asked the Box. "The general said to smoke the aliens and everything around 'em."

"A hostile alien cell in Yellowstone . . . a flying carpet . . . this is some seriously crazy stuff pal."

"Ours is not to question why . . ."

"Yeah, yeah, what do you have in mind?"

"No way I'm reporting I was downed by a pink parka."

. . . "Roger that, repeat, what do you have in mind?" The radio went silent.

"What do you have in mind? . . ."

" . . . a death ray . . ."

(There was a long pause) . . . "Ah, roger that."

"Set course for Atlanta," Matt ordered. They had escaped death's hungry maw. The platform banked sharply to the left. It sped forward buzzing the clear, cool waters of a lake. As it skimmed the surface Matt reached down and trailed his hand through the water.

"How high can this fly? Will it go into space?" Ollie asked.

“Dunno,” Matt said. The lake blurred into sea glass as they left it behind.

Matt glanced at Cathy who was staring straight ahead, her lips pressed together, her body stiff, the color gone from her face and her fists clenched in her lap.

“Don’t look down,” he said. He held out his arm. She seized it.

“What’s that?” said Ollie pointing at a shimmering streak.

“A PLANE!” Matt screamed.

“What’s that at our two o’clock?” the captain of San Francisco-bound Delta Flight #1446 asked his co-pilot.

“Are you seeing this?”

“Yeah … but I don’t believe it,” the co-pilot replied..

“I saw the pilot! He was looking at me!” Ollie shouted over the deafening roar of the engines as the passing plane’s wake turbulence flipped the platform, banging the riders into each other.

“Shouldn’t we report this to NARCAP or MUFON or somebody?” the co-pilot said. It was decided that reporting a flying carpet, even to the aviation reporting centers on anomalous phenomena might not be a good thing for their careers. Pilots after all must be thought steady and level-headed.

“If I didn’t report that drunk at five thousand feet over Santa Monica strapped in a lawn chair tethered to weather balloons holding a BB gun I’m certainly not reporting this,” said the pilot.

. . . “I didn’t see anything.”

“Me neither.”

“Mummy, mummy! Look a flying carpet!” squealed the little girl in window seat 16J.

“That’s nice, honey,” replied her mother never looking up from her Vanity Fair.

Take me down,” Cathy said.

Matt thought the platform into a grassy meadow of yellow wildflowers at the crest of a waterfall.

Cathy, a victim of bad huckleberries, swung from the platform.

Plucking a wildflower Matt held it out.

“Don’t get any ideas,” Cathy said icily.

“*Moi?* he replied, feigning indifference.

“I mean when I grabbed your arm . . . don’t read anything into it.”

“I didn’t.” He lied.

“Ouch,” said Chase.

At dawn they settled invisibly onto the heliport of the Atlanta Medical Center.

Chapter 29 – TAKEN

THE SUMMER was coming to an end.

Cathy and Matt sat on the fence watching the horse trainer train Judge when a dust devil arose. "Whoa . . . whoa . . . ." Cathy's mom screeched as she descended in a metallic red craft, swaying like a drunken sailor returning from shore leave.

"I've heard of helicopter moms but this is ridiculous," Matt jested.

"You're just the one I want to talk to," she said, throwing off her helmet.

Matt stood admiring the machine. Three electric fans that resembled jet engines stood mounted around a pilot's seat and harness system; two fans for vertical control and one for directional.

. . . "I've been thinking . . .you killed my husband" . . . Matt gulped, "and you almost killed me and my little girl and her brother. What do you think I ought to do about that?"

Matt gulped again.

"I know. You should leave and never come back."

"Mommy!"

The prospect of never seeing Cathy again sent a shudder through him.

"I'm sorry Matt. I've been through a lot lately. I don't know how much more I can take."

Then Matt got an idea . . . "Mrs. Kozacky … remember in Yellowstone when you said when we get back I can have anything I want?"

"You did say that mommy."

"I know what I said," said Mrs. Kozacky.

"I know what I want …"

"Dare I ask?" she replied.

Cathy held her breath.

". . . a Luminox Navy Seal watch with the orange face and tritium hands guaranteed to glow in the dark for twenty-five years . . ."

Cathy breathed a sigh of relief.

Both Cathy and her mom eyed Matt strangely.

"Okay," her mother agreed.

"And . . . a thousand dollars . . ." Her mother stopped walking.

"Okay . . ." She resumed walking.

"*Each* – for me Chase, Zak and Cathy . . . and new bikes, too . . . each. Make mine titanium – mountain."

"Now wait one minute! . . ." Carolyn Kozacky snapped.

"And Google Glass . . . *for everyone*." Cathy giggled.

"And . . . .

Matt was just about to leave when he looked doe-eyed at the wearable transport, "What do you call this thing?"

"Betsy and don't even think about it."

"Mind if I take Betsy for a spin?"

"Well, okay but bring her back in one piece."

Matt buckled himself in and after a brief video tutorial was away.

The neighbors had complained often. One had even tried to shoot Betsy down as evident from the buckshot holes. Mrs. Kozacky told him where to avoid but he forgot. Matt rocketed through the countryside skirting the edge of town where he spotted a swimming pool where two girls were sunning themselves. As any red-blooded boy would do he dropped in for a closer look.

Three white streaks made their way toward him followed by three more. His eyes bugged as he made a hard climbing left turn. He might have had a chance had he turned the other way. He splashed down.

■ ■ ■ ■

It was a bit past two when a light blue Ford van bearing the graphics of the You Dirty Rat Pest Control Company pulled to the gate. Over the gatecom the driver told Cathy he had a work order to fumigate. Cathy told him she wasn't allowed to open the gate for strangers. The driver told her he would come back.

It all happened so fast as a battering ram forced the front door open.

Matt woke on his back, his shoulders wedged against the sides of a freshly-sawed pine box. The scorching sun in his eyes, he could just make out the powdery faded green siding of an old weather beaten shack. Three men towered over him. As he struggled to sit up a blue rattlesnake skin boot pressed him back.

"I didn't say get up mate," said the thug wearing a shoulder holster with a very big gun, black tactical pants, a neon blue Hawaiian shirt with yellow flowers and a black cowboy hat trimmed with a band of silver and turquoise medallions.

A powerfully built man with a scar running from a glass eye to his dimpled chin stood beside him whistling Sukiyaki, in his scarred hand with broken black nails a pine lid, in the other a burlap rice sack with bulges that were moving. Nearby a third man was digging what looked like, could it be, a grave?

"Jes tell us what we wanna know and we'll let ya go mate. It seems you have a certain someone in a bit 'o a bother over a certain ring. Now be a good mate and tell us where it is or this nice 'ere gentleman's gonna fill that nice 'ere box of yers with these nice 'ere poisonous snakes and nail the lid on," the man laughed, obviously enjoying himself. Matt gulped. He tried again to sit up but the blue rattlesnake skin boot pushed him back.

"It's at the bank," Matt squeaked. After CNN his aunt had taken him to First Tennessee Bank & Trust to put the ring in a safe deposit box.

"What bank?" He told them.

What's the harm. What are they going to do? Break into the safe deposit boxes? Shouldn't they be wearing hoods?

"No worries mate," said the Aussie. But as far as Matt could see there were plenty of worries. He had given them what they wanted. Shouldn't they be letting him go now?

Carolyn Kozacky arrived home to find Cathy, Zak and Chase hog-tied on the floor. Within hours of receiving the news, Lena Legend was on the next flight and did what any good mother would do. She joined the search.

“Malvic’s got plans for him. I wouldn’t want to be that kid,” scarface howled.

“You’re not going to let me go, are you?”

“You kiddin’ me, mate. We have orders to bury you alive with snakes. You’re gonna be hangin’ with the worms.” Matt turned pale.

Later that afternoon after a few rounds of Jack Daniels his captors went outside to take pot shots at an albino crocodile sunning itself beside a slow-moving stream. Matt seized his chance. A greasy dinner plate was his salvation. Timing the gun blasts he wrenched free of his handcuffs and the iron wood stove. Four hours later upon flagging down a passing deputy sheriff the ordeal was over. Saved by a croc.

Fearing the worst he rushed to First Tennessee Bank & Trust with his uncle and nervously thrust the key into the lock. He threw back the lid. It was empty! The bank manager was only too happy to assure him he had either forgotten to put anything into it or had removed whatever had been there and forgotten. “It happens all the time,” he said. Could that have happened? Oh, pray it be so. Yet he knew it wasn’t. He had been kidnapped and made to divulge Solomon’s Ring’s whereabouts. Now it was gone.

As people do he had assumed bank safe deposit boxes are safe. But he was dealing with international criminals who were accustomed to getting what they wanted. Men to which breaking into someone’s safe deposit box was even easier than stealing credit card data from lazy store chains with lax computer security.

The kidnappers had gained information about the bank manager’s family and had threatened to do terrible things to him, his wife and their eight-year old daughter Salem if he didn't open a certain safe deposit box and surrender its contents.

The next day Lena Legend returned to California, her son in tow. Only two months earlier Chickasaw had been a jail sentence. Since then he had learned any place is only as interesting as the people you know there. And Chickasaw had become very interesting. Without him knowing, he had discovered something — people.

He lay on his bed reliving everything that had happened – the mound, the giant, the ring, CNN, Cheyenne Mountain, General Anders, Yellowstone, the kidnapping, the safe deposit box, totally unaware of the terrible strange things that would soon be happening, all because he had knocked Hotas Rapfmussen colder than a witch's heart on a Halloween full moon. He thought also of Chase, Zak, Father Brainard, Father Herzl, the Academy and Cathy . . . Cathy.

"I have to go back," Matt blurted.

"What! I don't think so!" said his mother.

"I have to!"

Matt tried for the twelfth time to convince her.

"Have you lost your fifteen-year-old mind? The kidnappers are still out there."

What was it going to take to make her understand?

"They were going to bury me alive!"

Lena flashed to her encounter with Madam 'Mad Marie' Bouvier. The same Mad Marie to whom she had divulged her son's fear of being buried alive.

She told Matt of her encounter.

“How could you!” Matt demanded.

“I didn’t know, Matt. I’m sorry.” Matt stormed from the room with a new loathing for the mother who had borne him.

Chapter 30 – PARTLY CLOUDY WITH 90 PERCENT CHANCE OF ROCKS

0911 hours; October 7th – Huairen Air Base, China; Headquarters of the 15th Fighter Division of the Chinese People's Liberation Army Air Force. Northern Shanxi province

EIGHTEEN-YEAR OLD Technical Sergeant Jin Xiao had just finished refueling the Chinese J-31 stealth fighter and was sitting in his fuel truck when it was rocked by a horrific blast. His first thought was he had done something terribly wrong with the refueling and the punishment would be severe for the loss of such a valuable state-of-the-art aircraft.

He raced around the truck to check that he had properly attached the grounding leads that prevent static electric discharge. What he saw made no sense – a state-of-the-art aircraft reduced to a heap of shattered carbon fiber, aluminum and plexiglas and in the midst of the sparking avionics sat a reddish-brown boulder. As personnel scurried in every direction Xiao desperately looked for any clue to the absurdity.

The smell of jet fuel in the air, a thousand gallons from the fighter's ruptured tanks washed across the ramp as still another blast shattered the chill morning air. An aircraft on an adjacent flight line took a direct hit . . . then a third aircraft . . . and then a fourth.

Basalt boulders rained each striking a different aircraft. Razor-sharp shards sent personnel scurrying. A landing fighter-bomber attempted to escape the madness by hurriedly taking off but to no avail. It exploded in a disintegrating fiery mass as it cartwheeled down the runway. Two aircraft returning from a training sortie were taxiing single-file with their canopies raised between rows of aircraft when they too were struck, their hot jet engines igniting the fuel-awash field as seventy-three thousand gallons of burning high-octane No. 3 jet fuel soon left little trace of what had been a busy flight line. It was clearly an attack. But with boulders? Seriously? With such precision! How? From where? By who? Six minutes later it was over. Seventy-two boulders had rained down leaving seventy-two aircraft destroyed, ninety-seven dead and twenty-two injured.

Foreign spy agencies viewing the satellite imagery thought it an accident until the Chinese government denounced it as an act of war, vowing all-out retaliation once it determined who was responsible. Foreign leaders waited nervously for the outcome wondering what country had been brazen enough to launch such an attack and why and how. What country would dare incur the wrath of a country with China's military might? What outcome could it possibly bring besides annihilation? Foreign leaders secretly feared their country might be next.

Matt smelled a rat.

Meanwhile Chinese scientists were busy analyzing the basalt using spectral analysis geo-fingerprinting. Being volcanic in origin basalt contains elements that differ slightly from region to region. All the Chinese scientists would have to do to find the culprit would be to match the basalt samples from the destroyed airfield with samples taken from volcanic sites around the world. Leaders of almost every country with volcanoes, having nothing to hide and anxious to be declared innocent, readily agreed to allow samples to be taken from their volcanoes. Those who refused were unable to prevent Chinese inspectors from sampling them anyway. Nations held their breaths. The fate of the world hung on the outcome.

Six days later came another attack. At Anshan Air Base, headquarters of the 1st Fighter Division in Liaoning province, China. Again seventy-two aircraft were destroyed, this time with eighty-seven dead.

Then still again. Six days after that another seventy-two boulders rained. This time on the Party Congress at the Great Hall of the People at Tiananmen Square in Beijing. Held amid great secrecy and security it demonstrated nowhere was safe from the deadly attacks. Held once every five years, three thousand representatives had been in attendance. There were 576 dead including the Chinese president himself.

China's enraged leaders placed its nuclear missile crews on high alert and readied its warheads for launch as they pressured their scientists to finish their research.

Who and why remained the questions. The United Nations Security Council stepped in with an emergency session to try to quell world fears.

Just when it seemed things couldn't get any worse China's hastily appointed interim leader received a phone call at his makeshift offices on his private line from the President of the United States in her own voice as confirmed through computer voice print analysis.

"This is the President of the United States. In a final demonstration of our might, unless your country destroys its entire arsenal of land, air and sea-based nuclear weapons by midnight Beijing Time exactly six days from today, we will do it for you . . . midnight Mr. President." With a click the call ended. The Chinese president beside himself with rage further mobilized the military. The U.S. president denied having made any such call.

"Strike now," he ordered.

"No," the Politburo chairman said. "We will wait for the tests. If there is to be mass destruction let history show we were not to blame."

As the world held its breath meanwhile life went on as usual in Thousand Oaks. For those kids who didn't watch the news, they went about oblivious to the fears that held the world captive while those who did watch trusted everything would work out in the end. It always did in the movies after all. Their greatest concerns remained friendships, whether their latest crush noticed them, how the waves were breaking at Malibu, school, clothes, cars and money, little knowing those things might not soon matter anymore. Matt's worries were far greater.

Before long he might very well be single-handedly responsible for the destruction of all life on the planet. It was a lot for any fifteen-year-old to deal with. If only he hadn't knocked Hotas Rapfmussen silly. If only he had let Father Brainard put the ring in his safe. He buried his face in his hands and cried.

Chapter 31 – RETURN to CHICKASAW

"IT'S FATHER MALVIC, I know it is."

"And you know this how?" asked Cathy.

"I just know."

"Are you coming back?"

"My mom won't let me."

"I have an idea," Cathy said. "You'll get a call."

The very next day he did but not the kind he was expecting.

It was Tuesday evening a bit past eight when Lena Legend answered her doorbell to find two men and a teenage girl standing outside. Thinking it the Jehovah's Witnesses she prepared to dismiss them with her standard fib of already belonging to a church so she could get back to watching reruns of *Dancing with the Stars.*

"Ms. Legend, I'm Father Brainard of St. Francis Skyfell Academy."

"And I'm Father Ben Herzl, this is Cathy Kozacky. May we come in?"

Vaguely she recognized the names. Puzzled she invited them in.

"Is this about the kidnapping?"

"Yes and no," said the priest.

It was a shock seeing Cathy in his living room. Matt and his mom listened as the men explained the reason for their visit – namely, Matt was urgently needed. They were going to the FBI and needed him along. China was on the verge of unleashing its nuclear might on the United

States. The United States was at DEFCON ONE, the highest military alert level of the five DEFCON levels. It meant nuclear war was imminent. Never in history had the DEFCON level been higher than THREE; during the Cuban missile crisis in 1962, the Yom Kippur War in 1973 and again during the 9/11 attacks.

Matt was on a plane that very night to Tennessee with a stop in Atlanta with his mother's tearful goodbye ringing in his ears, "Go, do what you need to. Save the world. Your father would be proud." Tears ran down Matt's cheeks as she spoke.

"After Cathy spoke with you she called us," said Father Brainard. "Then the good father here called the FBI. "There's a Special Agent-in-Charge Thyme who wants to meet."

Chapter 32 – JUST IN THYME

VERY SPECIAL AGENT Justin Alowishus Thyme laughed. A dual citizen of Great Britain and the United States, raised in Wales, having grown weary of the U.K.'s wretched weather, he had abandoned his home turf for California only to wind up in Washington, D.C. after joining the FBI, a fact attested to by the two small flags waving on his desk – one British, one American.

The special agent listened intently jotting notes on a yellow legal pad never once interrupting until finally he had heard enough. He tossed his pen aside and leaned across the table.

"Let's get this straight. You found a ring that gives you special powers and makes demons do things for you. Bloody hell. Let me guess. You have a cape and tights on under there, right? You must be taking the piss."

"What's that mean!" asked Matt wondering what urinating had to do with it.

"In the U.K. that means he thinks you're making fun of him," Cathy offered in response to his puzzled look.

"Didn't you see CNN?" she snapped.

"I saw it alright," the agent snapped back. "You were having a laugh. Where'd you get that micro-holographic projector? Nice technology."

"What!" Matt squeaked.

"General Anders," Cathy murmured.

"It's a lie. We can prove it," Cathy said.

"How?"

How indeed. Their families' warnings had come true. Life had become a train wreck. A seventy-two car pile-up.

"Call Doctor Brainard at Skyfell," Matt said, pulling out the priest's card.

"What's Skyfell? A mental institution?"

"Very funny," shot Matt, thinking he had better get used to people thinking him a *5150* as his mother called them, the California law code for someone placed in involuntary psychiatric commitment.

"Okay," sighed the special agent. "It wouldn't be the first time our government's pulled a fast one. I'll be right back."

"You're going to need more cards," Cathy sighed.

Soon the agent was back.

"Bloody 'ell! You kids are AGEs! You must've really brassed somebody off with that CNN interview!"

"What do you mean?" asked Matt.

"For one it means you're no longer welcome at the White House . . . Anti-Government Entities . . . enemies of the state."

"Great, now you definitely won't be flying any Super Cobras . . . Sorry Cathy!" Matt said.

"Some high-ups view you kids as a threat for some reason. I can't take this to my superiors."

"But if *you* believe us they will," Matt said.

"That's not how things work around here. I worked in Special Cases before it was shut down. You'd know it as X Files. When it started out it was only meant as a place to put unsolved cases. It was never meant to go anywhere. But when the number of cases grew and seemed to be heading somewhere it was shut down suddenly. No reason given."

"Heading somewhere?" Cathy asked.

"We began seeing commonalities. There was an extra-dimensional component to all of them but never mind that. Tell me about Malvic."

"He's behind the basalt attacks," Matt said.

"And you know this *how*?"

"Basalt's what they built with." The Ars Goetia says there're seventy-two demon kings of the underworld. Every attack's been with seventy-two boulders exactly."

"The Ars what? And who's *they?*"

"Ars Goetia. It's a medieval book with locks. It names the seventy-two demon kings by name. Every attack with seventy-two boulders. It's Father Malvic and the demons. I'm positive."

"Seventy-two . . . where've I heard that number before? . . ." Thyme scratched his head . . . "Ah! . . . suicide bombers . . . That means instead of seventy-two virgins waiting for them there'll be seventy-two of something else! BLOODY 'ELL! SOMEBODY SHOULD TELL 'EM ABOUT THE ARS GOETIA."

Cathy commenced fake tears. "You have to get him. That animal said he's going to cut our hearts out," she sobbed. "He will. You have to get him. You have to."

Thyme handed her a box of Kleenex then picked up his phone . . . "check U.S. Customs . . . cross-check the whereabouts of one Father Quintus Malvic during the basalt attacks. Malvic . . . Mike Alpha Lima

Victor India Charlie . . . and give me everything we've got on an NSA deputy director, an Air Force general named Anders," he said twirling a pencil between his fingers.

With a fake sniffle Cathy glanced up from her tissue satisfied her little act had produced the desired result. Soon the phone rang. The pencil snapped. A look of concern spread over the FBI man's face as he cradled the receiver.

"Hmmm . . . there may be something I can do. Problem is it's going to take money. Lots of it."

"No problem," Cathy said.

"We're not talking three hundred dollars kid . . . we're talking three hundred *thousand . . . at least*!"

"No problem," Matt said.

"No problem? What, you been savin' up from your lemonade stand?"

"We know somebody."

Matt and Cathy looked at each other . . . "ELVIS."

The agent studied them carefully. "Alright," he said finally. "Put that rich uncle of yours on notice."

Special Agent Thyme then made a few special calls including one to Assistant Special Agent-in-Charge Celia Gomez with whom he had worked X-files. Gomez, a confident twenty-six year old former Marine gunnery sergeant from East LA, a single mother with a three year-old daughter and who attended night law school, listened carefully and jotted notes as Thyme briefed her. When it appeared only Matt was going on the operation Cathy spoke up.

"I'm going too!"

Without turning his head Special Agent Thyme shifted his eyes ever so slightly her way and with a piercing stare said, "Absolutely not young lady. It's bad enough we have to take one kid. No offense kid," he said turning to Matt. "Make no mistake. It'll be dangerous."

"If anything happens to him I'm the only one who knows what the ring looks like and how to use it," Cathy countered.

"Girlfriend has a point," said Gomez.

As Special Agent Thyme sat pondering the thought Gomez shot Cathy a wink.

"It's going to be dangerous," Thyme repeated hoping still to dissuade her.

"I know," Cathy said, her eyes cold and proud.

"I wouldn't have said that," Matt said.

"Why?" asked Thyme.

"She's a Young Marine."

"A what?"

"A Young Marine," Cathy said.

Special Agent Thyme took a deep breath and shook his head. "I must be barmy."

"I'll get waivers from the parents," said Assistant Special Agent-in-Charge Gomez giving Cathy another wink.

"Ars Goetia . . ." the agent shook his head.

The last thing Special Agent-in-Charge Thyme did before taking two weeks emergency leave was to ask Gomez, "What the bloody 'ell is a Young Marine?"

Chapter 33 – THE CENOTÉ

"Difficult, dangerous, good chance you will die, exciting if you survive."

Sir Ernest Henry Shackleton's ad for Antarctic explorers

THREE TOYOTA LAND Cruisers barreled down the deeply-rutted narrow road through the dense jungle trailing a cloud of thick white dust before turning off and disappearing into the impenetrable growth. Churning their way slowly across giant exposed roots and through hanging tangles of closely-packed liana vines they had reached their destination – a cenoté deep in the jungles of Belize. They were six former military contractors bought and paid for by Father Quintus Malvic. Unbeknownst to them there was an uninvited eighth member – a drone – watching their every move.

The vehicles pulled into a clearing and shut off their engines. Their occupants, clad in tactical gear and gallons of mosquito repellent got out and ambled the fifty meters to the rim of a gaping crater. The sparkling turquoise mirror-still water drew a hush even from the never-at-a-loss-for-words battle-hardened combat veterans who gazed in awe at the jagged limestone-rimmed eighty meter-wide hole in the jungle floor.

"So what are we diving for tomorrow exactly?" asked the dive leader.

"It's an archaeological dive." Father Malvic glanced at his Seiko.

"An archaeological dive? Why all the firepower then?" he asked, snaking a flexible cleaning rod through his assault rifle.

The priest had anticipated the question. "There're bandits in the area." There were no bandits.

Back inside his tent the psychotic priest knelt before a carving in African soapstone of a witch doctor, a fetish surrounded by eight red candles of human fat. He peered down at his wristwatch; 2:09 p.m. North American Eastern Daylight Time. He picked up a sat phone and pressed a key. The last thing the 82,011 fans at FedEx Field at the season opener between the Washington Redskins and the Philadelphia Eagles saw before the blinding white flash was the football arcing toward the uprights. The September terror attack would forever be known as 9-13.

The evil priest smirked. Soon he would be done with the distracting business of the basalt attacks leaving only the business of exacting a gruesome revenge on what his demonic intelligence source had told him would be the two remaining troublemaking kids.

○ ○ ○

The Gulfstream's jet engines spooled down. Cathy stepped through the clamshell door into the temperate Belizean night air as four operatives pushed past. As the ten made a beeline through the terminal bystanders stopped and stared.

"What have you gotten me into Matt Legend!" she moaned.

Three black Chevy Suburbans screeched to a stop in the airport's No Standing Zone. A Belizean policeman holding an AK-47 ignored them.

“Welcome to Belize,” barked the CIA station chief, crushing his Simon Bolívar out on the white slightly dirty unmarked official U.S. government fender.

The three vehicles careened through the streets of Belize City their red and blue grill lights flashing back and forth as they crossed Swing Bridge, the landmark turntable bridge spanning the canal that runs through the city as revelers clogged the streets and pyrotechnics burst overhead.

“There wasn’t time to get a police escort. Think you could’ve picked a better time?” the station chief barked veering only enough avoid hitting a flock of samba dancers in their scanty glittering costumes of brilliant colors and bright plumage sprouting behind them that made the fireworks dull by comparison. The Suburban bulled a band of marching steel drummers aside, their profanities drowned in the angry staccato of exploding firecrackers.

“We’ll drop you to your destination then you’re on your own. The Agency can’t be seen to be involved in this,” he said approaching two stilt walkers, clipping one, sending both plummeting into the canal. “It’s the wet season. You can expect some weather. What’s up with the kids?”

Matt didn’t hear the question. He was busy gazing through the five-inch bulletproof glass. “Live Life – Drink Polar Pak” the billboard shouted. It showed a girl dancing with abandon wearing an inviting smile sipping through a straw from a carton. It seemed another world.

Belize, a small Central American nation, is one of the least populated countries in the region, much of it unexplored wilderness. More than half is subtropical jungle.

Finally they emerged from the part madhouse, part masquerade party that is Carnival. Two and a half hours later they were at their destination.

"Good luck," the station manager bid as he waited impatiently for them to offload their gear. Then the Suburbans were gone. They were in the middle of the rainforest. The smell of a well-planted greenhouse filled their senses. Yellow Tree Frogs croaked, spider monkeys grunted, birds screeched and insects buzzed. The air whispered with the sound of ocellated turkeys making drumming sounds in the dangerous air as they foraged for beetles. Curassow birds fussed in the canopies. The cool exclamations of a spectacled owl mingled with the droning of cicadas and the croak of toucans and lineated woodpeckers running their hammer drills. The aspirated roar of howler monkeys merged with the rumbling of distant thunder.

"Here, put these on. I guessed your sizes," said Thyme. He tossed Matt and Cathy each a package containing boots, tactical pants, a nylon web belt, a shirt, athletic socks, an FBI ball cap, a jar of Tiger Balm Red, a machete, a sharpening stone and a zip bag full of Band-Aids.

Their Mayan guide, Chac, and his dog had grown up in the rainforest. He drank from the streams but he told them not to. He showed them how to use their machetes to get water from hanging vines and pointed out insects to avoid like the machacha which emits a foul skunk-like spray and the wasp-like acacia ant. He warned of the bullet ant, so named because its bite is the most painful insect sting on the planet. Being stung feels like being shot. He warned too to keep their eyes on the ground because the vipers are aggressive and the same color as the ground.

"The ants are jumpy. Something is coming. You do not search for the gold of The Lost City of Giants like the others?" asked their puzzled guide.

"What others? What lost city?" Thyme asked.

"Those who went before. They went in search. None have ever returned." Thyme began to feel better about having brought what was inside the Pelican hard case they were lugging. Exhausted from slogging through mud they made camp. He pulled out the drone's infrared tracking tablet. The pungent smell of the campfire clung to their clothes.

"Are those the bad guys?" asked Matt. Orange-ish/purplish ant-like figures were moving about the display.

"They're five klicks. Each click's a thousand meters. . . .62 miles."

Three acacia ant-ridden, bullet ant-ridden, jaguar-ridden, tangles of liana vine-ridden and who-knew-what- else-ridden miles through muddy mosquito-infested jungle.

Thyme left to meet with his team.

Boyziano (aka "Backstreet") quietly unsheathed his KA-BAR fighting knife and crept silently behind Matt, sitting on a fallen tree. Pan flutes filled Matt's earbuds, a bridge between sanity and the swarms of hungry mosquitos. Backstreet raised his knife. He focused on the exact point at which the tip should make contact to kill, just behind the head. He thrust the blade downward.

"Fer-de-lance . . . the nastiest viper on the planet," he said as he hefted the wriggling eight-foot muscular grayish-brown mass of black-edged diamonds. The serpent, skewered behind its broad triangular head, had crept to within inches of Matt's thigh.

“Lucky for you I came along when I did. If that’d bit you, ooh la la. Your flesh starts to rot within minutes then it spreads through your body liquefying and destroying tissue. It feels like it wants to explode. If you get to a hospital in time, if you’re lucky you only lose your leg. If not, within hours you die feeling like you’re on fire. The mission has priority. There’s no time for taking kids to a pediatric ward even if there was one which there ISN’T. Reason 956 why kids shouldn’t be here.”

“Thank you,” Matt gulped, staring at the menagerie of black diamonds.

“Don’t thank me. I did it for the mission. If it’d helped I’da let it bite you . . . kids on a mission,” he huffed shaking his head. “Watch out from now on.”

Cathy returned from her jungle bathroom break to find the viper dangling from Backstreet’s blade . . . “Good grief Charlie Brown!” It would be dinner. It tasted like chicken.

Pennington (aka ‘Bad Penny’) occasioned past and whispered, “The next time Backstreet gives you a hard time remind him of his naval air call sign. If a naval aviator doesn’t choose one fast enough, one’s given to them – a sucky one by someone who doesn’t like them. Other pilots had cool ones, ‘Conan,’ ‘Six Gun,’ ‘Mad Dog,’ ‘Terminator.’ His was ‘Lips.’ They don’t come any suckier,” Bad Penny chuckled. “Just call him Lips. That’ll shut him up fast,” she laughed.

○ ○ ○

“Every time I see one of these it amazes me,” said Bad Penny peering into the cenoté.

"You missed your calling girlfriend. You shoulda been a geologist." It was Dell (aka 'Farmer') whose personality had been grating on everyone since the start.

"Shut your pie hole. And call me girlfriend one more time and I'll rip you a new one." Turning to the others, "Somebody said who wants to sign up for a special op. Dell thought they said special olympics." Laughter echoed.

Nightfall comes early in the rainforest. Some parts are dark by midday. Thyme's crew gathered around the fire, a fire that also served to keep the critters at bay. The only creatures that didn't care about the fire or weapons for that matter were the ones the local tribe members fear and avoid at all cost and are the reason they never ever go into the jungle alone and never without dogs. The dogs always go ahead and when they come back whimpering with their tails between their legs the tribe members know to go no further. Tribal parents tell their children evil spirits are real and how to avoid them. Our parents tell us they don't exist.

"Hey everybody, watch this," Matt said, chucking a rock into the cenoté. A neon blue bioluminescence rippled outward until it was a giant cerulean blue night light. Dell grabbed him, held him over the edge and snapped him back.

"Hey, watch it! Not funny," Matt howled.

"What is this?" asked Matt.

"A cenoté. A blue hole," replied Bad Penny. Natural wonders. Surface connections to subterranean rivers. Crystal clear pools of fresh water that stay at a constant temperature of 77-78 degrees year-round. There's something scary about them. The Mayans believed they were portals to the underworld. *Xibalba* they called it. It means 'place of fear.' " A howl sounded deep in the jungle. "A place inhabited and ruled over by a race of gods obsessed with human death and darkness."

"Tell me you don't believe that crap," Dell drawled.

"Has anybody figured out why these things only bite below the waist!" said Bad Penny, slapping her thigh . . . "The Mayan priests drugged their sacrifices, laid them on a sacrificial altar and cut their beating hearts out. Then they sent their heads flinging blood down the pyramid steps to the mob below followed by their torsos.

"The victims didn't go willingly I assure you. Forget that crap about it being an honor," said Bad Penny. "It wasn't any honor. Honor had nothing to do with it. They went kicking and screaming until the drug kicked in just like you and I would have. And it wasn't enough for them to gush fountains of blood. They had to make it extra vivid by painting them head to toe in Maya Blue. A neon blue pigment like what kids write on sidewalks with except it never fades not even after seven hundred years. We don't have anything like it and can't figure out how they made it. It made their bright red blood stand out against their skin real freaky like. Sometimes two hundred children were sacrificed all at once. The Phoenicians did it too. They ritual sacrificed children and babies to please their dimwit bloodthirsty gods."

"I saw the Blue Man Group in Vegas," Dell blurted. Bad Penny rolled her eyes.

"The Mayans never claimed they built their pyramids. They said the gods came from the sky and built them," she continued. "They're fallen angel structures. My masters is in ancient civilizations."

“History always repeats,” said Downey (aka ‘Downer’), an African-American former Navy SEAL.

“What are you saying? You saying it’s gonna happen again?” Dell blurted.

“Just sayin,’ history *a l w a y s* repeats itself,” said Downer.

“Speaking about that, what’s up with that other stuff?” Dell asked, over a croaking red-eyed tree frog.

“What stuff?” Bad Penny sneered.

“You know, like how they knew more about astronomy than us,” said Dell staring at the celestial stardust and milky threads through the rising embers.

Truth be told the Mayans had been told of the undiscovered planets in our solar system a thousand years before the Europeans *discovered* them. As far as the Egyptian pyramids go, they’ve been found to be advanced powerplants that focus electromagnetic power in their chambers. Scientists have known for a long time they weren’t built by 20,000 men taking twenty years. That’s just what they tell the tourists. What they don’t tell them is that every ancient site in the world is haunted. Every one. Visitors have reported feeling invisible presences and seeing shadow figures and orbs and hearing disembodied voices and ancient drums and chanting and sudden temperature drops and other weird stuff. And some report being followed home by it.”

Matt and Cathy looked at each other knowingly, both thinking the same thing – the haunted prison.

“And that Maya Blue stuff,” Dell blurted. “How come they could make it and we can’t? And what about those places where you can stand at one end and whisper something and everybody can hear what you said at the other end. How come they could do that and we can't? And how could they figure astronomy in twenty-six thousand year cycles? We could barely figure it in one. They were primitives for gosh sakes. And what about that map? The one that shows the world better than the ones we have today?"

Discovered on a dusty shelf in a library in Constantinople, the Piri Reis map was drawn in 1513 by Turkish Admiral Piri Reis. Reis said he drew it from a source map he found dating before the time of Alexander the Great, before the time of Christ, perhaps well before. The map shows the world with an accuracy impossible unless viewed from space.

"So you watch The History Channel. You're still a Neanderthal" said Bad Penny.

Another unearthly howl sounded. The team snapped toward the jungle. "Somebody tell me I didn't hear that," Cathy begged.

"I've never heard anything like that," said Bad Penny. The dog whimpered. Chac looked worried.

"The Mayans were so far ahead of us we don't even know the right questions to ask," said Thompson (aka 'Tommy Gun'). "Meanwhile our relatives were still a thousand years away from figuring out the world isn't flat," someone laughed. Bad Penny tossed a chunk of wood onto the fire sending embers soaring. "I love this place. It's a cathedral . . . nature's amphitheater . . . listen . . . . " An unknown creature's howls echoed against the chirping of a zillion crickets and the extant cries of exotic night birds. "It's so healing. Just think, soon this will all be gone . . ."

"*Your* relatives maybe," said Downer. "Mine knew better. Mine were in Timbuktu, the first center of higher learning. We had the world's first university. Scholars came from all over Europe, Africa, Asia and the Middle East. We circumnavigated the Earth long before Magellan ever did. We knew the Earth wasn't flat. The richest man in history was Mansa Musa, the African ruler of the Mali gold empire. Worth 400 billion. Compared to him Bill Gates is on welfare. And tell me, why do I know you've never heard of him."

Downer was right. In parts of Africa there were civilizations far more advanced than their European counterparts until guns and the evils of European slavery combined to send the continent into a spiral decay the vestiges of which remain to this day, leaving those to speculate what might have been had Africans been the first to be given the formula for gunpowder and obtain guns.

"We have cell phones but we're preschoolers compared to their understanding of mathematics, astronomy, astrophysics, acoustics, chemistry, medicine, construction," Bad Penny rambled. "Their concrete is far stronger than ours, their buildings last forever, they made iron that doesn't rust, copper strong as steel and could transport blocks weighing thousands of tons through the air. They had power sources we can't even fathom, like the pyramids. And our crowning achievement . . ." Bad Penny laughed . . . "going to the moon. Why we've only had toilet paper since 1857! Not even two hundred years. Your great-great-great-grandmother used leaves and stones and corn cobs and sponges and newspapers. As for calling you a Neanderthal," she turned to Dell, "I accidentally complimented you. Neanderthals would still be running things if they hadn't been wiped out by the flood."

Had Bad Penny chosen she could have said more about the Neanderthals, much more, revealing what everyone learned in school about them wrong. They were adolescent giants and the product of the abduction of human women by adolescent giants. Stronger and smarter than humans, their higher metabolisms demanded massive amounts of food. And they looked something like us but for those protruding brow ridges. And Revlon take note – scientists have found Neanderthal seashell cosmetic make-up containers in Spain bearing make-up just like today's. Even their flutes have been found. Yes Mabel, they made music. And it has long been quietly known that the Neanderthals wore jewelry and created art and buried their dead with ceremony and flowers. The million dollar question is who performed those skillful brain surgeries on the 10,000-year-old skulls while they were still alive found at the La Paz Museum. And autopsies reveal the patients lived long lives after their surgeries. Very, very long lives. They possessed fair skin complexion and the hair of red flames of the fallen angel trash. Bad Penny could had mentioned how genetic variancess such as Crohn's disease, mental illnesses, Type II diabetes, lupus, psoriasis, infertility, sickle cell, hereditary cancers, certain extrasensory perception abilities, sexual direction that cannot result in reproduction, unbreakable bones,[10] double rows of teeth, six fingers or toes, and a host of other genetic variances, all traceable to, among other things, the mixing of fallen angel with human DNA.

○ ○ ○

Chac stared into the jungle.

"What is it?" Cathy whispered.

"They're out there. Watching. Not human. Not animal."

Bad Penny noticed Matt's and Cathy's distress.

"I know this can be a little overwhelming," she reassured.

"Can I ask you something?" Matt asked.

"Of course."

"How can I be brave like you?"

Bad Penny smiled. "I had the same concern when I joined the Corps. Here's what they told us . . . it helped me . . . pause, slow your breathing, take several slow deep breaths, clear your mind and focus 100% on the task at hand. Don't worry about the future. Break it into five minute increments. Focus on doing well for the first five and so on and so on 'til the job's done. Project calm even though you're crappin' your pants. The mere act of looking relaxed relaxes. Chew gum. It helps," she smiled.

Thyme tripled the watch and doubled the sensitivity on the perimeter beams. There were alarms and strange sightings through the night.

In the morning a blue mist suffused the jungle, formed of the warm moist Caribbean air mingling with the cool flora. A bright-colored blue-crowned motmot glided by trailing its long tennis racket-like tipped tail.

Continuing on a pandanus tree sitting atop its teepee-like root structure stood in their way. A sweep of Chac's machete sent a hundred-bundle of black-eyed green cones to the jungle floor. He removed one of its *keys*. He pried it open and sucked out the sweet, tart yellow juice. He offered some to the team. The fibrous nectar was like a mixture of mango and sugar cane. Cathy loved it. Matt thought it too much work for too little juice.

Ahead Chac hacked an errant acacia branch. The tree immediately warned the other acacias of danger. Trees warning trees just as Father Herzl had said. It seemed plants talk to each other. It's a language of airborne chemicals and what else we don't know. As soon as Chac's machete bit into it, it folded its leaves and began to release chemicals. Its downwind neighbors responded by folding their leaves and releasing poisons, a defense against predators. We know more about the oceans than we know about the secret lives of plants. In other words next to nothing.

Bad Penny sat cleaning her rifle. She had always been a gun lover, taken by their form and function ever since her father taught her how to shoot at twelve. The thrill of being able to send lead far downrange onto a tiny black dot had always fascinated her. Guns were after all how the West was won, how the land was wrested from the Mexicans, those stubborn Brits, wild Injuns and its own badly misguided South.

A Blue Morpho butterfly lay spread on a rock, its iridescent blue wings soaking up the sun's rays.

Botflies lay their eggs on the underside of mosquitos. When the mosquitos bite a human, the eggs enter the bite. Then they begin to grow. They start out by eating flesh. You can't squeeze them out. First you have to block their air hole to kill them, then you can squeeze them out. They were taking their toll.

"Are you kidding me!" Cathy shouted.

“Leeches,” she screeched, as she stared at her bloody socks. The Belizean Black Flies were merciless. They applied the Tiger Balm Red rich in camphor to every exposed inch of skin, on their clothes and their hair. Cathy made the mistake of applying it to her forehead. Her sweat made her eyes burn. She cried for an hour.

The trail through the rainforest was tough going, little more than a puma path really. Highways of leafcutter ants paraded their triangular green leaves like the windsurfers at Malibu which Matt was careful to step over until he was too tired and weak to care.

“Jaguar!” Chac shouted.

Cathy screamed as the agent’s boots disappeared into the palm fronds. He had been at the back of the pack.

“A black jaguar,” Chac shouted. “Once it develops a taste for humans it will not stop.” It had struck like lightning. A devil cat, Chac called it.

“What am I doing here,” Cathy bawled.

The man was dead. There was no time to bury him. An unpardonable sin which weighed heavy on them. He was somebody’s son, husband, father. They would have to live with it. One more dragon. Thyme stepped up the pace. They were practically double-timing it. Their muscles burned but it was better than being eaten alive. The crunch of leaves gave way to their boot steps as they made their way through the darkening jungle, the chops of their machetes echoing through the dense growth. It was still five hours to their final destination.

If you never put yourself out there you will never find your limits. Cathy was seconds from finding hers. The giant white and yellow boa dropped from the tree and coiled itself around her. She tried to scream as the scaly cold mass constricted.

"I'm done, I'm going home," she wailed after Bad Penny hacked it off.

Matt put his arms around her, "Can I call you a cab?"

They laughed to keep from crying.

By mid-morning a thunderstorm had passed and the darkening sky was threatening more. Thyme's team paddled their zodiacs down a lazy river that soon became rapids. Cave-dotted limestone mountains lush with cohune palms and sapodilla trees flanked the paddlers as they navigated the rocks and eddies. A tapir foraged along the shore as iguanas gorged with mosquitos sat perched on branches hanging low over the river. Fish leapt from the river into its many small feeder falls. The larger ones sometimes made it but the minnows never did. Matt worried if when all was said and done they would be like the minnows.

A red-footed boobie landed clumsily on the bow of Matt's boat. A good sign he hoped. Into the night they floated through the noisy jungle as the Perseid meteor shower rained its zodiacal streaks until under a golden moon the team arrived at Chac's village. The overgrown temples and pyramids of a lost 3,000 year-old Mayan city poked through the canopy. Howler monkeys scampered and screeched to the omnipresent whine of the cicadas. A yellow-headed parrot glided by through the muggy air, air filled with what strangely seemed . . . snow. It wasn't snow. Volcan de Fuego in neighboring Guatemala had erupted choking the skies with ash causing the team to cut makeshift breathing masks from their shirts. The earth's volcanic Ring of Fire was awakening.

Chapter 34 – THE GLOVES

The ultimate measure of a man is not where he stands in moments of comfort and convenience, but where he stands at times of challenge and controversy.

Dr. Martin Luther King, Jr.

HAD ANYONE TOLD Matt Legend that before the day was out he would thrust his hands into a nest of bullet ants and leave them there while they stung him senseless he would have thought them gone round the bend.

"You are lucky," said Chac. "You will see something no outsiders have seen."

In some cultures boys must test to become a man. Tests that involve great pain. Girls don't have to test. Their test comes in childbirth.

Tribal horns announced the grueling coming-of-age. Inside a thatched greathouse ceremonial gloves of strips of woven green leaves were being filled with the large reddish-black ants. They were being made ready for four anxious initiates. Four twelve-year-old boys ready to test themselves.

Men who choose to go into combat do so partly to test themselves. It's a man thing. Many can never understand.

"You're twelve aren't you, Matt?" asked Thyme.

"Aaaahh, fifteen," Matt replied warily, looking at Cathy.

"You don't have to do this, Matt," she responded, but her look told him he did.

"You wish to test?" asked Chac.

"Ah, well . . . oh . . . why not. How bad can it be? Like eating hot chili peppers, right?"

Chac said something in heavy Belizean Creole. The Mayan boys looked at Matt and laughed.

Matt thrust out his hands defiantly. The village elders placed the gloves on. The first bite was like a white-hot nail driven by a nail gun. His face contorted. About to pass out he glanced at the other boys who were no longer laughing. Whether it was out of respect or fear he was beyond caring. Determined to prove himself he reached deep down inside. Water filled his eyes and ran down his cheeks. A gulp stuck in his dry throat. Then came the second bite . . . and the third . . . and the forth . . . twenty-four in all. A quick death would have been merciful.

Chapter 35 – XIBALBA

As the saying goes, you don't have to be faster than the bear, just faster than the person next to you.

THE SKY DARKENED in a storm of wings and with the roar of a freight train. Even jaguars are frightened when thousands of birds suddenly take flight.

"Something is wrong," Chac warned. The ground began to rumble.

"The spirits are angry."

The rumbling stopped. The guide eyed his visitors suspiciously. Warily he climbed over a fallen ceiba tree knowing deities sometimes inhabit ceiba trees.

As Matt slid across it a fat green iguana dropped hissing. As he hit the ground the lizard took off after him. "A little help!" he screamed, trying in vain to pull out his machete with a hand swollen to the size of a grapefruit.

The hissing stopped. The reptile lay motionless. A long thin stick like a kebab stick protruded from its neck. Matt scanned the rainforest. There was no one.

When the others arrived Chac looked immediately to a spot in the forest. A tribesman allowed himself to be visible only long enough to acknowledge Chac's presence.

"I have never known bamboo chicken to give chase. What are you people?" Chac asked. For the remainder of the trek he was distant.

○ ○ ○

A passing thunderstorm whipped the breadfruit trees into a frenzy as Special Agent Thyme's team took up positions around Malvic's camp, the thunder and the thrashing of limbs and the hollow drumming of raindrops against the broadleaf plants masking their presence. Chac bid them farewell. They had arrived just in time. Malvic's divers were entering a cenoté.

"We'll grab him underwater," said Thyme. Their spy-in-the-sky had revealed Malvic's use of plain old scuba apparatus. It was the break they needed.

"Underwater he won't be able to give orders to the demon," Thyme rejoiced.

One by one Malvic and his divers splashed into the turquoise netherworld, the chatter of yellow-breasted rainbow-billed toucans and spider monkeys replaced by the amplified sound of their labored breathing.

Malvic's dive leader adjusted his mask and submerged. An ear-splitting peel and blinding flash sent two hundred-fifty million volts through his body leaving his lifeless form spread-eagled beneath the surface. There have always been a hundred ways to die in cenotés.

Malvic resumed anchoring a zip line to a knob of white calcite and began paying it out. The thin yellow nylon cord would be their only way out if they became disoriented in the claustrophobic labyrinthine underground river system. He attached plastic red arrows at intervals pointing the way out.

Flicking their dive lights on little did they know they were being tailed. Seven of Thyme's eight-man team including a surfer from Malibu and a Young Marine were not far behind needing only follow a thin yellow line. What am I doing here thought Matt. This could get ugly fast.

They had no idea what they were in for. Only that it would be an adventure.

"Kids on a mission? You gotta be kidding, sir. I don't like it," Lips had gruffed.

"You don't have to," Thyme had replied.

Turning to Matt and Cathy, "Most of my team doesn't agree with me on this. They think it'd be better if you didn't know . . . While we were enroute, China came to the conclusion the U.S. is behind the attacks . . . it's nuts, I know but that's what they think. That ring's our only chance to prevent World War Three. If you don't find it we won't have any homes to go back to."

"Keep your masks tight," Lips warned. "There's hydrogen sulfide gas in these cenotés. It looks like a milky river. It's poisonous. If you feel nauseous get out fast. "

"Isn't that flammable?" asked Matt, recalling from Mrs. Peabody's science class that hydrogen sulfide is explosive.

"Who cares? You'll be underwater," Lips snipped.

"What's this for?" asked Matt fingering the plastic orange pistol attached to his web belt.

"Don't touch that! It's an underwater flare pistol." Matt removed his hand.

Special Agent Thyme's team wore rebreathers – a closed loop breathing system that makes its own air by recapturing what the diver exhales. They would give off no telltale bubbles. They also had something else Malvic's team didn't – full-face diving masks, each with a wireless communicator, a GoPro and a heads-up display – the latest in technology and weapons, courtesy of Elvis.

"Stay close to the diver ahead," said Assistant Special Agent-in-Charge Gomez. "Do what he does. If you get in trouble call out. It's like snorkeling. Breathe naturally. Don't get excited. And don't worry if you're scared. We all are."

Each diver also wore a waterproof wristband — the kind quarterbacks use to keep track of their plays. Matt wondered what secrets it held.

There was a radio check, "Dragonfly 1, Dragonfly 2, Dragonfly 3, Dragonfly 4 . . . ."

"You're 5, you're 6," Gomez motioned to Matt and Cathy respectively.

"Dragonfly 5 . . Dragonfly 6."

Matt trailed Gomez, Dragonfly 4, into the depths.

There comes a time when every girl and boy, woman and man, must face their fear and through it find themselves. It helped that Gomez had pulled them aside and said, "Courage is like a muscle. Exercise makes it stronger. The only way to overcome fear is to experience it. Avoiding it only magnifies it. Think about what you're fearing. When you face it, it'll subside," she had said. They liked Gomez.

The team fanned its way through a pallid sun-drenched forest of underwater lily pads, each pomegranate and gold pad held beneath the surface and anchored to the bottom by an impossibly long root filament. They looked like fiery dinner plates atop jugglers' sticks. They froze. Floating in the forest was Malvic's dead diver.

Dragonfly1 disappeared into the narrow jagged opening in the side of the cenoté followed by Dragonfly 2, Thyme. Each grown-up bore a rotating barrel semi-automatic dart gun with nine self-propelled darts.

"Tube's tight."

"Roger that," replied Lips.

Matt stopped kicking. "We're going in *there*?"

"Dragonfly 2, we've got a problem," Lips radioed angrily. "It's this kid."

"Solve it. See you ahead."

"I can't do this," Matt said. "It's too small."

"Yes you can," Cathy said.

"Look, kid, imagine yourself a piece of meat going through intestines. It always comes out the other end, right?"

"What are you trying to say?" Matt replied angrily.

"I got this," Cathy said. "He has a fear of small spaces. From the kidnapping I think."

It wasn't the kidnapping. Matt had seen the disturbing news story splashed across the world pages about the Nutty Putter caver who had crawled into a tunnel barely larger than he was and got stuck. Rescuers determined it was too dangerous to retrieve his body and closed the cave forever.

"I'm not going in."

"You can do this," Cathy said.

"No, it's a coffin."

"Matt, the witch's house. The Rottweilers . . . I came back, remember? . . . remember? I'm petrified of vicious dogs."

"No. I'm not going!"

"*LISTEN!*" Cathy snapped. "Cowboy up. Rub some dirt on it and keep going . . . just something us hicks say."

Matt's chuckle lasted but a second.

"NO! It's a coffin!"

"Don't think about the bad that can happen," Cathy said. "Think about the good. Come on, you can do this … I know you can. Remember what Bad Penny said."

The absence of fear is hypophobia. Fear of everything is panophobia. Most of us fall somewhere in between.

Matt was still coming to grips with the bravery thing. We all have to at some point. But as with IQs, there are different kinds of bravery. We are all brave in some ways and not in others. There is the decorated soldier afraid to express his emotions. The motorcycle daredevil petrified of rats. The skydiver afraid to confront his neighbor about the loud music. The renter who scolds her landlord about her despicable behavior yet fears mice. The rock-climbing med student petrified of blood.

Inspiring someone means knowing the right thing to say at just the right time.

"I thought you said you were doing this for the kids in the extermination camps . . . I knew you were faking. Put on your big boy pants. Move it . . . "

(Silence)

"If you wouldn't mind getting your arse in gear Mr. Legend," Lips snarled.

But Matt wasn't moving. He was thinking Nutty Putty.

"Then do it for *me*," Cathy said softly.

There was a profound silence.

Matt slowly turned and faced the tunnel.

"Okay . . . now do what I did . . . count back from a hundred in threes – 100, 97 … Come on, count . . . 94, 91 . . ."

Matt began to count. "And breath . . . slowly . . . that's it . . ."

"88 . . . 85 . . . 81 . . ."

"He's okay," Cathy said. "Let's go. I'll go first if you want."

"No way."

"Dragon 1, we're back on the move," said Lips.

But in the darkest corners of Matt's mind he allowed himself to fear. *What if there's another quake? What if I get stuck? It would be like being buried alive and drowning all at the same time.* He kept counting.

His legs stopped fanning.

"Now what?" Lips grumbled.

"My ears hurt," Matt sputtered.

"Mine too," said Cathy.

"Keep calm. Do as I say," said Lips.

He talked them through how to equalize the pressure by squeezing the nose clip inside their masks to pinch their noses shut, then blowing through their noses, pushing their jaws forward and swallowing. Meanwhile with a careless flutter Cathy disturbed a pocket of silt reducing visibility to a bowl of cream of wheat.

"Great, now this'll take even longer. How come *I* got stuck babysitting?"

"Don't talk to her that way," Matt barked.

(Long silence)

"Alright kids. Let's do this." Lips' tone was more respectful. He knew the kids wouldn't survive the mission anyway.

The tunnel widened. It was a thrill finding out what was always around the next bend until their lights fell on the bleached bones of a diver and his or her '70s-vintage tattered yellow wetsuit – an ominous reminder of the hazards ahead. There is a rule in cave diving – a third of your air to get there, a third to get back, a third for a margin of safety. Cave diving is exponentially riskier than regular diving. In regular diving when something goes wrong you can always go to the surface. Your reserve pony bottle provides a few extra minutes of air for that. Not in cave diving.

The passage was growing tighter again. It was becoming more and more like Lip's comparison to intestines. A "squeeze" cave diver's call them. It drew tighter and tighter until it was no bigger around than a refrigerator. They removed their rebreathers and pushed them ahead. Matt began counting backward again. He had flushed many a bug down a toilet. Never again. The skeletal remains of hundreds of human sacrifices screamed at them from amid tools and ceramics made of the semi-precious stone obsidian.

The passage suddenly ended at a huge cavern. The blackness consumed them as they pushed into the inky void. Ahead a sunken city glimmered in the filtered crystal rays of the sunlight from above. They had entered another cenoté. Countless dwellings were cut into its dark walls. A city cut from rock as stunning as the ancient city of Petra faced them, where tourists are only shown the above-ground portion and leave never knowing most of Petra lies under their feet. Petra — a city haunted at night by djinn seeking humans to possess. The Petra that is the true Mecca, not the site passed off as Mecca today according to scholars. The pagan city of Petra — part of the untold story of the dark origins and equally dark rise of Islam — a place linked to fallen angels, demons and giants. A place long feared by the bravest of Bedouins who dare not enter it alone at night. It towered six stories, each four times the height of a normal story, and like Petra, built for giants, whose spirits haunt the site to this day. And like Petra and many other megaliths according to lore, built in a single night by fallen angel trash. When the sea level was 120 meters lower before the worldwide flood spoken of by every civilization, the same flood that destroyed the great lost city of Atlantis, the cavern would have been bone dry. One side was shrouded in darkness, the other bathed in sunlight where stalagmites and stalactites formed natural objects d'art against an underwater palette of reds, greens, browns and golds. Despite its beauty something about it made Matt's skin crawl.

Meanwhile to any real archaeologist it would have been the discovery of a lifetime rivaling Machu Picchu or Gobekli Tepe or the Ellora Caves. But Malvic wasn't a real archaeologist.

Into the netherworld Malvic's team pushed until they reached a halocline, the interface of the meeting of fresh and salt water, which distorted their images like a circus mirror.

Malvic pointed a blurry finger downward. Two divers broke off and descended into the mist. The explosive hydrogen sulfide gas formed of bacteria breaking down organic matter in an environment devoid of oxygen swirled around them as they probed the dead tree branches that littered the bottom. They found no bones.

Chapter 36 – THE RUINS

AN EMERALD glow shone from the ruins. Drawn like moths to a flame Malvic's divers swam over an approachment of steps like the Acropolis' cut into stone and flanked by rows of Doric columns which rendered them like fry. An Olympian-size courtyard stood in the green-effused waters. A ten-foot-tall pyramid stood at its center, its capstone the source of the glow, cool to the touch. A contingent of statuary mermaids and mermen seemed to stand guard. A statute of the fallen angel trash Osirus exuded a disturbing presence. Its eyes seemed to follow them.

A giant ruby Buddha sat cross-legged, arms extended holding a lotus flower of amethyst in each upturned palm. It towered over a gold sacrificial alter with a recessed bowl at its center with a network of blood grooves that radiated from it like the rays of the sun.

The elephantine ruby idol with its beautiful dark-red needle-like inclusions bore no tool marks. It was a flawless ruby as large as a baby elephant. Formed without tools? By whom or what? How? Father Malvic began to obsess . . . then calculate . . . it was five hundred thousand carats easy . . . at a million per carat it would be worth . . . . could that be right? — $500 billion? It was too big to take back. He would have to return for it.

Glyphs adorned the altar's base. Strangely the figure bore no sediment. It looked as if it had been wiped clean. On the altar lay a ceremonial dagger with twin wavy serpentine copper blades harder than steel. Into its gold handle in the form of a mermaid were set two emerald eyes which twinkled in the cone of Malvic's torch.

Recessed into niches cut into the walls were evenly-spaced rectangular stone boxes standing on end ranging from fifteen to thirty feet tall, each bearing a strange set of glyphs. The priest's pulse quickened. Were the glyphs names? Breathlessly he pried at one with the dagger. The lid dislodged breaking into pieces sending sediment swirling into a hundred eddies.

The divers cowered. In the light of their torches stood an enormous human skeleton clad in copper battle armor. Red hair flowed from its bleached horned skull past its shoulder blades, in its jaws double rows of teeth. Its hands bore six fingers, its feet six toes. A smaller horned skull protruded from the base of its neck — a conjoined twin. An eight-foot bejeweled sword stood at its side.

Holding his breath Malvic tore the five-foot femur loose. The skeleton collapsed in a pile of bones burying him. Pulling him free, sensing they were not alone, the divers made quickly for the approachment, each bearing the plunder they had found; priceless bobbles, the mermaid dagger, the radiant green capstone and the bejeweled sword.

The idea of peddling Rephaim DNA had come from an unlikely source. One of his students' papers had held a reference to an alliance between warring Native American tribes that hated each other. Centuries ago they forged an unheard of temporary alliance to battle and defeat a common overwhelming enemy – GIANTS! The enemy of my enemy is my friend. As Father Malvic found, to this day every single Native American tribe has age-old stories of giants who lived for hundreds of years with a sense of smell keener than bloodhounds and an appetite for human flesh. Disturbingly archaeologists have found herbs and spices on the grilled, baked and boiled bones of humans bearing gnaw marks from double rows of giant teeth. When their supply of humans dwindled the giants spiced and ate each other.

In 2009 in the region of Herxheim in southwest Germany archaeologists were appalled to find that an entire village of one thousand humans had been butchered and and eaten like animals. Marks on the bones indicated the body parts were cooked on skewers and indicated double rows of very large teeth. The meat was scraped from the bones and the bones broken on the ends to remove the marrow. It had happened in 4,950 BC. "Who is supposed to have eaten all this?" the flabbergasted excavation team leader asked.

One account in particular intrigued him – a Paiute Indian tale. As the tale went, after a fierce battle all of the giants in the area were killed with the exception of some who retreated to Lovelock Cave in Nevada where they too were killed. Years later a company mining bat guano found sixty giant skeletons and their weapons. Many of the giants were twenty feet tall. They were sent to the Smithsonian where they disappeared — claimed lost. It wasn't the first time the Smithsonian had lost giants. It has lost all of the giants sent it over the years. Hundreds, in fact. How does one lose hundreds of giants? People began to wonder if it was to avoid giving credence to the biblical accounts of giants.

But it was the Rock Wall that caused him to form the connection between arms peddling and giant DNA. The Rock Wall is ignored by quackeologists and a media obsessed with reporting sensational nonsense and is one of the greatest never heard of finds in history. Discovered in 1852 east of Dallas, Texas, buried under silt, it is a twenty-square mile, fifty-foot-high walled fortress of three-foot-wide dense sandstone blocks. Constructed by unknown ancient builders the virtually unexcavated site is inscribed with undeciphered writing. It has domed underground chambers and tunnels with advanced building technology.

It was built to keep out the alliance of tribes. Native American tribes tell of giants building fortified positions to stave off the attacks of thousands of wild Indians but mostly to escape the "pieces of falling moon and stars" like those which rained down on Sodom and Gomorrah. Many megalithic stone sites show signs of having been scorched by heat thousands of degrees in a split-second. The Egyptian sites of Karnak, Saqqara, Tanis, and a site near Luxor were scorch-blasted so severely that stone melted and turned to a kind of glass. Tanis was all but vaporized, devastated so completely it looks like the surface of the moon. Never heard of Tanis? Most haven't. It and what happened there are kept secret much like the discovery of Sodom and Gomorrah. Megalithic sites throughout Mesoamerica, Peru, Bolivia, Egypt, Lebanon and elsewhere all tell the same story – scorch-blasted. The Mayan ruins of "Uxmal" means "built three times. And there is the matter of why so many so-called Neanderthal skeletons are found with a hole in their skulls. The giants went underground.

Humans went underground too. Underground complexes and tunnel networks dating back more than 12,000 years keep turning up. From Bavaria to the Mediterranean to Scotland to the New World they protected man against the giants. The Longyou Caves in China are considered by the Chinese to be the Ninth Wonder of the World. More Longyous are being found all the time. The Longyou Caves were built by the giants to shield them from the pieces of falling moon and stars. They are not caves at all. Think the U.S. Air Force's Cheyenne Mountain complex in Wyoming except built thousands of years ago by giants with even more advanced engineering know-how. Longyou is one of the largest underground complexes in the world, using sophisticated geology, ventilation, water supply, storage rooms, escape tunnels, shelters, mind-boggling carvings, sculptures, murals and more. And as is with the interior of the Egyptian pyramids, there is no soot on the walls. What kind of lighting was used? What kind of construction equipment was used? And where are the millions of tons of excavated rock debris? As with many other megalithic sites it is nowhere to be found.

Father Malvic had learned the military was developing battery-powered, hydraulic-assisted exoskeletons to enable soldiers to carry stonehenge loads, run faster and leap higher. If it was interested in that wouldn't it want to dispense with the mechanical apparatus altogether?

But where would he find giant DNA? Fossilized remains are not suited to DNA extraction. Soft tissue is required. The bottom of a cenoté – specifically a lentic cenoté – a cenoté devoid of oxygen – is perfect, where perishable objects are perfectly preserved. Even thousand-year-old trees are hauled up and sawed open smelling of fresh sap.

It had taken a year to wind its way through DARPA, the research arm of the Department of Defense, but his paper on creating giant super soldiers entitled *DNA Replication: Super Soldiers - A Game Changing Combat Force Multiplier,* had grabbed DARPA's attention. It argued that small arms would become obsolete with the satanic giants able to carry weapons the size of cannons wearing foot-thick Kevlar. The only problem would be controlling them.

A typical soldier can carry 70 pounds of gear. Some 130. A super soldier would carry 1,000. Even a small squad could wipe out an overwhelming force. Each with a super sense of smell, super vision, night vision, able to ignore pain, no conscience, no need for sleep, with bodies that repair themselves and organs and limbs that regenerate like starfish. They would not need to carry food. They would eat their enemies. Hyper-aggressive monsters willing to kill their own families if they had any, given the green light with no hesitation or remorse. It was the stuff of dreams at the Pentagon and it was there Father Malvic's paper found an audience. DARPA wasn't the only ones salivating. The Illuminati, an ultra-secret, ultra-wicked clan of billionaire black magic-practicing Luciferian vermin that avoid the public eye and control most everything in the world (including DARPA) was salivating too. Having sold their souls to the Devil, the Count of Saint Germain, beginning back in the 1700s and beyond, those satanic bloodline families go by many names — Illuminati, Global Elite, Power Elite, New World Order, Illuminati Order, the Devil's Brood, all with one purpose — evil. They take their orders from the Fallen Ones. Their agenda — to reduce the world's population to only 500 million through pandemics like COVID-19, disease, plagues, famine, genocide and nuclear holocaust. It is boldly declared on their granite monument, The Georgia Guidestones, for all the world to see because they want the world to know.

○ ○ ○

It began when a very large strange fish emerged from the reddish hydrogen sulfide gas and began to zigzag lazily outside the ruins.

Thyme thumbed the range adjustment knob of his fluid lensing digital distortion-removing underwater binoculars to seventy meters and stared unable to believe his eyes. He passed the binoculars to Matt.

"Are you kidding?" Matt breathed.

The fish stood clearly in the computerized image-enhancing field glasses. It was half human, half-fish!

Each male had a dark blue skull covered in scales with an inch-high crest running lengthwise along the center of its top just like in the U.K. Coast Guard video, with pale white or brown skin and a dark blue back. Each had a scaly fan-shaped tail, webbed fingers like ducks tipped with sharp pointed nails and red glowing eyes that made their own light.

Each held a spear tipped with stingray barbs and changed direction with the agility of barracuda. The females had human torsos with smooth pale skin without scales, breasts and long red or black hair that flowed to their pale waists, sometimes smooth, sometimes knotted. More human-looking than their male counterparts, some were attractive even in a mermaid kind of way. Each bore a spear. Bloop sounds filled the grotto.

Pliny the Elder was right. Thyme had run across the Greek historian's mermaid accounts. The Greeks called them Oceanids, sea nymphs. He had also read the log entries of Christopher Columbus, Henry Hudson, Vasco Da Gama and other navigators who described their encounters with the vampire-like creatures. The males, known as Men of the Sea, were the most trouble. The mermaids were terrifying and evil, nothing like the Little Mermaid of Disney. Supporting mermaids' existence are written accounts from the ancient Greeks, the ancient Chinese and the Vikings, all on continents having little or no contact with each other yet describing them exactly the same. Like everyone Thyme had assumed they were nothing more than fanciful sea tales though crews from every country with submarines have for years been reporting the same mysterious linguistically complex bloop sounds on their hydrophones coming from an unidentified creature, sounds even more intricate and advanced than dolphins. The Danish National Museum has on display the body of a mermaid found by a farmer ploughing his field. Undersea video from drilling rigs have captured images of the half-fish, half-human products of the slicing and dicing of human DNA by fallen angel trash. Land-based mining operations when they encounter giant human remains and other disturbing things quickly destroy the evidence before word gets out and their operations are interrupted. The mermaids just swim away.

"Cathy, I need you to do something." The urgency in Thyme's voice startled her. "Get back to camp. Tell the agent to drop into the second cenoté. Tell him it's one kilometer north-northeast of the first. Tell him it's to cut off Malvic's escape. Tell him about the mermen. And this is important — tell him to bring Little Friend. Repeat."

Cathy dutifully repeated the order.

"GO!"

Cathy made for the connector tunnel. A mermaid appeared out of the hydrogen sulfide. It spotted Cathy immediately. Thyme watched in horror as the creature closed on her. As Cathy disappeared into the passage Thyme moved his dart gun's red laser dot around the outside of it to distract the creature. It was working!

"That's right, just keep chasing the pretty red dot Ariel. That's it."

He toyed with the creature until it swam away. Unbeknownst to him it had spotted another pretty red dot at the far side of the cenoté that wasn't moving.

Thyme returned his attention to Malvic. As Malvic emerged from the ruins the creatures swarmed him. His divers raised their spear guns then lowered them. The men then laid objects, including a glowing green pyramid at the mermen's tails before backing away. The view went blank. He lowered his binoculars. A mermaid was hovering before him.

Thyme found himself inexplicably drawn to her. He was transfixed by her hypnotic gaze he found impossible to break as the current played with her flowing long green hair. Her eyes were larger than normal and strangely vague in appearance, cloudy the way cataracts make eyes appear. A strange bioluminescence emanated from a small bulb which dangled from the end of a whip-like appendage that protruded from the front of her scalp like an anglerfish. Several dozen smaller teardrop-shaped bulbs surrounded her face, each attached to a short thread, giving her a radiance any surface world woman would die for.

Summoned by her bloops an endless progression of mercreatures emerged from the hydrogen sulfide. She swam away. He was able to think once more.

"There're too many," shouted Assistant Special Agent-in-Charge Celia Gomez. "I'm going to try to communicate. It's our only chance."

“NO!” Thyme shouted. Ignoring his warning she swam toward the hypnotic mermaid. Seeing her the other creatures stopped. Gomez opened her arms in peace. The mermaid examined her curiously, looking at her the way a human would look at a strange bug. Gomez had never seen such hate in the eyes of any living thing.

“I have a bad feeling about this,” Cathy mumbled.

Their dart guns were no match for two hundred Oceanids. Ruby beams swept the horde but even if every of their darts found their marks there weren’t nearly enough. You don’t think about dying when you’re a kid. You still have your driver’s license to get and your first prom to go but dying was beginning to look like an option.

“Got an idea,” Matt blurted.

“Talk fast,” Thyme cried. The creatures were twenty meters and closing. With a thrust of her tail the barbs of the mermaid’s spear penetrated Gomez’s aorta. The water turned red.

“Everybody down!” Matt cried. He raised his flare pistol and pulled the trigger. A cherry flare streaked through the cenote. Striking a merman on its skull it fell glowing to the cenote floor. The startled creature picked it up. Burning its webbed fingers it chucked it behind him. It went into the hydrogen sulfide. The explosion pushed the divers from their positions as the water clouded with the body fluids and entrails of two hundred mercreatures.

“Not bad kid. Now let’s get that ring,” said Thyme. The words were no sooner said when a new wave of creatures began to advance. Again the divers resigned themselves to their fates. Suddenly a brilliant white beam sliced through the hypnotic mermaid cutting her in half leaving her entrails floating. *The reinforcement!* "Say hello to my Little Friend," the radio quipped. Cathy had made it to camp. Propelled by a jetpack the operative sailed through the grotto. The weapon's brilliant beam lit the waters again and again as it sliced through the hoard. The waters turned milky white and cloudy red before turning a dirty pink. "I think they see the light," Thyme quipped.

Cradling the power-hungry laser Thyme made for the ruins. An uneasy feeling swept through him. There were dozens of places to be ambushed from.

"Behind!" Lips yelled.

Thyme counted twenty creatures. "Yeah, you know what this is," Thyme muttered, hoisting the laser. The creatures backed off. Malvic was with them. Thyme fanned slowly in Malvic's direction. He fixed the laser's targeting dot on Malvic's ring finger. Malvic slowly shook his head. Thyme fixed the dot on the Buddha's neck. The ruby idol turned green. A burst of white light sent the ruby head rolling in the sediment. He returned the dot to the ring. "Give me a reason," he muttered. His eyes fell on the power level indicator. The bars were all red. He gulped and covered it with his thumb. Sometimes all you can do is bluff your way through something and hope for the best.

Matt weighed their chances. He was gambling his life in this war against the spirit realm. It was take no prisoners. He had known it from the beginning. Malvic removed the ring and dropped it. Lips moved in to retrieve it but before he could a merman darted in, scooped it into its webbed hands and disappeared into the catacombs.

Malvic grabbed the spear gun from the diver beside him, pointed it at Thyme and fired. The spear missed, grazing Cathy's side. One of Thyme's men returned fire striking Malvic in the heart. His bubbles stopped.

No amount of searching turned up the merman. The ruins started to collapse. It was a quake aftershock. Hurrying past a chamber they hadn't passed before a torch returned a gold glint. Idols, talismans, statues, goblets, jewels, ivory, jade, precious stones and every form of priceless treasure returned their stares. Brushing past Matt an operative scooped a basketball-size egg-shaped rough diamond into his arms. A second aftershock sent a golden winged chariot driven by a golden Zeus toppling, crushing him, Lips. All inside were trapped save Matt and Cathy.

Gathering themselves Matt and Cathy continued on until they surfaced inside a cave. Matt removed his mask. The air was stale but breathable. They would have to scale a mass of giant steps. Slowly and arduously they helped each other up until they reached the top.

Stalactites draped from the netherworld's nebulous ceiling as waterfalls thundered from four points feeding rivers that disappeared into a massive fissure shrouded in mist. Tombs and temples were carved into the lurid cliff faces, a mausoleum of a departed race. Patches of luminous green lichen flecked the cavern's dark rocks, walls and roof giving the illusion of galaxies in a darkened planetarium. They could see by its light so they switched off their torches. Soon they came to a dimly-lit pool illuminated by sunlight.

Matt entered the water fearing mermaids. "I'll see how far it goes."

He was back in less than a minute.

"It's sunlight but it's too far. I can't hold my breath that long," he sobered.

"Yes you can," Cathy said. "You can. I've seen you. The pool party? Remember? You held it for seven minutes."

Matt sighed. "That was a long time ago. That was with practice. I can't do it now."

"Yes you can. If you make it . . . I mean . . . *when* you make it, bring back two rebreathers." Matt pressed the timer on his dive watch.

"Hurry back. Go."

Not liking the feeling of it he drew in three deep breaths, not too deep, not too shallow. The tepid water washed over him as he began to kick. His autonomic nervous system was already telling him to take a breath. He remembered something Gomez had said, "When you think you can't go one more step, you still have sixty percent." He looked at his Navy Seal watch with the tritium hands guaranteed to glow for twenty-five years – *ELAPSED TIME: 2:17.*

Sunlight infused the water. How much farther? His lungs were burning. It wasn't anything like sitting on the swimming pool bottom. He was expending energy. Lots of it. That required oxygen. He glanced at the watch – *ELAPSED TIME: 4:58.* The rays were only ten feet away but might as well have been a mile . . . he inhaled.

• • •

"Wake up, kid . . .wake up . . . don't die on me."

Matt coughed water as the operative from the camp performed CPR. The weather was changing rapidly. The sun disappeared behind a layer of clouds.

"Thank god the water's like glass. I saw you coming. Something told me to be here."

"I thought I was dead," Matt coughed, his sinuses stinging like bees.

"You were I think."

With the rebreather Matt brought back he and Cathy escaped the clutches of the cavern where they emerging into sub-tropical storm Elaine, which had brought sustained winds of 119 km/hr, torrential rain and bottomless mud to the Yucatan Peninsula.

As the three passed the cenoté the ground began to rumble. The rim collapsed swallowing the operative who had saved Matt's life. Faster and faster the water swirled like in a giant drain until with an angry whoosh and a terrible sucking sound it disappeared taking the man with it. They tried to run but their legs felt foreign and unwilling to work. The quake stopped.

Sacrifices had been made. Eight had ventured to Belize. Only two would be leaving.

They soon came to Malvic's camp. Using Malvic's sat phone Matt called the number inside his wristband for help. It was the CIA.

Inside the tent was a stone tablet with the image of a curvaceous bikini-clad young woman, her head a hideous witch doctor's mask, its mouth an 'O.' Strangely her belly button looked real. A black streak shot through the tent. Matt stared in horror at the woman's head. It was a witch doctor's no more. Instead an attractive young woman's face with shoulder length hair that curled outward at the bottom now graced her figure! What kind of witchcraft was this?

As he struggled with the thought he noticed a large carved ceremonial witch doctor's mask of brown wood punctuated with darker brown streaks hanging on the wind-tossed canvas. Something about it too made his skin crawl. He chopped at it with his machete but the wood was like steel. It left only a shallow diagonal cut across its right eye. Instead he lugged it to the cenoté and shoved it in. Made of desert ironwood, one of the heaviest woods known, it sank like a rock.

In the meantime the interim Chinese president had declared the same deadline the American president had imposed on China be imposed on America. Two Ospreys were on the way. They would send a team to look for Thyme later.

Matt climbed the spongy papery peeling bark of a melaleuca tree and peered across the jungle until he spied a clearing.

There they waited.

"THEY'RE HERE," Cathy shouted.

The Ospreys' tilt-rotors changed pitch noisily as they converted from airplane to helicopter mode. As the two aircraft faced into the wind a rope was dropped. Tossed by ferocious gusts and without warning the Osprey plunged into the ground, exploding and bursting into flames, a victim of Elaine.

The second moved in. After a terrible struggle they were hauled aboard.

"HOW LONG 'TIL WE GET TO CHINA?" Matt shouted guiltily.

"DON'T GET TOO COMFORTABLE," the crewman shouted. "YOU'RE BEING TRANSFERRED."

Twenty minutes later a Boeing 747, a Tuskegee Air Freight (TAF) freighter pulled alongside. Dwarfing the Osprey, an aft door opened. TAF, founded by a handful of Matt's grandfather's old squadron mates, being the nearest American plane, had been pressed into emergency diplomatic service.

"TIME TO GO." A crewman tugged on Matt's harness.

A zip line connected the Osprey with the red-tailed giant. It would be like riding a high wire across the Grand Canyon – in a typhoon.

Matt tried bravely to joke. "T-this'll be m-more f-fun than m-m-Mr. Toad's Wild Ride at D-Disneyland," he shouted to Cathy over the roaring wind.

"IF YOU DON'T SURVIVE I'LL ASK FOR YOUR MONEY BACK," Cathy shouted with a peck to his cheek. It had been a hard-earned peck.

"EVER LOST ANYBODY?" Matt shouted.

"ONE OR TWO," the crewman shouted back.

Eighteen harrowing minutes later they were safely aboard the China-bound freighter where they were surprised to find the State Department Lady, Father Brainard, Father Herzl, Zak and Chase.

Cathy checked her voice mail messages. There was a message. "Hi Cathy, I just wanted to check on my baby," said her mother. "I love you, I hope everything's –" her mother's words were drowned by air horns and the roar of a crowd. A piercing whine caused Cathy to yank the phone from her ear. The line went dead. She tried calling back but no answer.

On landing in China the State Department Lady solemnly gathered everyone. “Something’s happened … a terror attack . . . Maryland . . . a nuclear device . . . FedEx Field. That’s all we know.”

Chapter 37 – FENGDU

BENEATH A GLOOMY gunmetal gray sky the team started up the seven hundred steps from the ferry landing of what once had been the north bank of the Yangtze River, a distant memory having been flooded by the Three Gorges Dam. Huffing and puffing the grownups had to stop every now and then. Father Brainard was complaining of chest pains. They had to leave him behind with Chase. They were bound for the eighteen hundred-year-old Ghost City of Fengdu, the Chinese city dedicated to the god of the underworld. They were meeting with the Chinese government – a desperate Hail Mary play.

It seemed a Chinese geologist had traced the basalt fingerprint to a volcano in the United States of all places. In the northeast corner of California at a remote place called Medicine Lake to be exact. Thirty miles northeast of Mount Shasta, it was a shield volcano composed of old thin basaltic lava flows covering two thousand square kilometers. Like a warrior's shield lying on the ground they cover large areas because their lava is runnier than stratovolcanoes. Shield volcanoes are mostly underground and instead of having a single large cone like a typical volcano have many small cones spread across an area. On receiving a call from one of its geologists from the high desert wilderness town of Alturas on whose ancient lava beds boundless junipers are fed by the crystal snowmelt of the Warner Mountains, China's nuclear missiles were being readied for launch.

○ ○ ○

They would be meeting with the Politburo Standing Committee of the Communist Party of China. The seven-member Politburo Standing Committee had chosen to hold the emergency meeting at the Ghost City on Ming Mountain because its regular meeting place in Tiananmen Square had been destroyed. The entrance to the temple complex stood atop the snaking wooden stairway.

"According to Chinese legend Fengdu is where the Devil lives," said their guide who had met them at the ferry, a young woman dressed in a slim-fitting bright red traditional silk cheongsam adorned with gold dragons. "Today it is closed to tourists. We go to Wuyun Tower. We must hurry," she said biting her lip. Finally they arrived at the top of the stairway, surrounded by brightly painted life-like statutes of demons doing terrible things to humans; plucking their eyes out, boiling them in oil, flaying them alive. A creepy feeling set in

"Just be yourselves and tell them what you know," said Father Herzl.

"I killed those people," Matt said, fighting back tears. "That nuclear bomb was my fault." Cathy assumed the thousand yard stare.

"You can't look at it that way. We don't even know if it's connected," said the father.

"It is. The bible says thou shalt not kill. I'm going to hell a million times over," Matt groaned.

"You didn't kill anybody. And nobody here's going to hell, well except Father Brainard maybe," the father snickered. "And I'm sick and tired of people misquoting the bible already. The commandment says thou shalt not commit murder, not thou shalt not kill. Maybe *your* bible says that, a poor translation. All one need do is go to the original source from which all Bibles come. The word in the Greek is '*murder,*' not kill. Murder is killing somebody who poses no mortal threat to you or others. Just think. What sense would that make? There're times when killing can't be avoided. Five thousand years ago God wiped out the whole friggin' planet. Its gene pool was so polluted by fallen angels, a mortal threat to humans, he had to start over."

"Polluted?" asked Matt.

"When Adam and Eve fell from grace, the Devil, a reptilian, the serpent, was behind it. Man's very DNA became polluted. Only Noah's family's was untainted. The only path to salvation and eternal life is through Jesus. He offers us each a way out. It's a gift. All you have to do is accept it. Read it for yourself. The Bible tells how. It's called The Good News. It is, wouldn't you say?"

Matt decided to stop asking the father stuff. It always meant a sermon. Where was Jesus when his parents got divorced? Where was Jesus when his father was murdered? Where was Jesus during The Holocaust? Where was Jesus at FedEx Field?

"So what's taking so long for him to get back?"

"Time is different away from Earth. Just ask any astrophysicist. They don't tell the public that. Earth time passage isn't the same as space time passage. A day in Heaven might be a thousand years on Earth. In which case, it's been about two days since the Messiah promised to return. Give him a break already."

"He's staring at me," Cathy moaned, staring at a demon cutting open a human.

At the top of the stairway they entered a courtyard near the Emperor's Temple. Chase kicked at a lone pigeon walking aimlessly in circles.

They arrived at a seven-tiered hexagonal pagoda, magnificent in its construction, where they were met by a young Chinese woman who spoke briefly with their guide in Mandarin before turning to address them in English.

"Welcome to Wuyun Tower. I am Ling. Come. Quickly. There is not much time." She looked terrified.

"Wait," said Father Herzl. "Now would be a good time for a prayer."

The priest stopped and bowed his head, "May the Good Lord be with us and Father Brainard. Amen."

"That's all?" asked Zak.

The father raised his head. "We're ready now."

Chapter 38 – THE POLITBURO

A STONE-FACED People's Liberation Army Air Force general stood glaring at the Americans as twenty Chinese soldiers holding AK-47s marched loudly into the room and positioned themselves along its walls. It was deathly quiet. Zak fumbled with a box of Tic Tacs which popped open and scattered noisily on the hardwood floor raising eyebrows.

A row of cheap folding tables faced seven of the most powerful men in the world seated at a crescent-shaped dais of northern elm. The visitors seated themselves.

"Is this necessary Mister Chairman," asked the State Department Lady, staring at the soldiers.

"I'm afraid it is. Let the proceedings begin," said the Politburo member in the middle making no apology for the soldiers or the folding tables.

"Distinguished members of the Politburo," the State Department lady began, "On behalf of the United States of America I thank you for this opportunity to address this urgent matter before us. The United States is not responsible in any way for the attacks on your country. We have investigated this crime and found it to be the act of a wanton international criminal acting on his own to foment a war between our great nations. He's the same terrorist we believe detonated the nuclear bomb on our soil."

"Now you know how the Japanese felt when you dropped your atomic bombs on their soil," replied the middle member, one of only a handful of his countrymen harboring no ill will against Japan for its past invasions of China. He looked to Matt be the one in charge.

The State Department lady bit her tongue. It was no time to argue.

"Yesterday he was killed in our effort to capture him."

"How convenient," said another member.

"Our forces did everything to try to capture the scoundrel. Allow me–

– Let the children speak," boomed the member beside him.

The room fell deathly quiet again. All eyes fell on Matt.

"W-well," Matt stammered, "It all started –

"Louder," the middle member bellowed.

. . . "It . . . it all started when Chase, my cousin and me, found a GHR . . . giant humanoid remains . . . in a mound on my aunt and uncle's farm. There was a ring. We went to Father Brainard to ask him about the GHR and he saw the ring. I made the crown jewels appear on his desk with it."

The Politburo members appeared confused. One scratched his head.

"Then we . . . Chase and me and my friend Cathy and her brother Zak . . . we met Father Herzl and he knew about it . .. the ring . . . and giants and stuff . . . then we went on CNN to tell what we found out about ghosts not being dead people …"

The middle member's brow furrowed . . . "Yes, we saw that."

"… then . . ." Matt hesitated for he remembered what the State Department Lady had told him about not mentioning anything about the CIA or the military. "You'll start World War III," she warned.

Matt leaned to the State Department Lady beside him. "I have to tell them about General Anders," he said in a pained whisper.

"Absolutely not. Don't even think about it," she whispered back with a well-practised fake smile.

"They'll know something's wrong. I'm not a good liar."

"No! That's an order!"

An order? A lawful order? An unlawful one? Who am I to know more than the State Department."

Meanwhile the Politburo watched.

There are times in life when everything comes down to a single moment. Somehow Matt knew this was that moment.

. . . forget the State Department lady. I'm not lying. The Politburo would know. Somehow they'd know. The truth would come out. Billions would die and it would be his fault – again.

Kid Rule One —Not blindly doing what all grown-ups tell you because you assume they know what they're doing.

Sometimes you have to assess things on your own. Sometimes you have to make your own rules.

. . . Honesty is the best policy. Always? Really?

"Is there a problem?" No. 3 bellowed.

"No, Mr. Chairman," the State Department lady replied with her rehearsed smile.

Here goes … he gulped. … "Then General Anders wanted to talk to us . . ." The State Department Lady let out a gasp . . . "me and Cathy and Zak and Chase and our families . . . then he tried to kill us. He crashed our plane in Yellowstone because we wouldn't go back to CNN and say our story was a lie. He wanted us to say the demon was a hologram but it wasn't."

The State Department lady squirmed. Several Politburo members shifted awkwardly in their seats. One cleared his throat. The general stared at him coldly. Had he made a mistake? Would he be the cause of billions being vaporized in blasts ten times hotter than the sun?

"Continue," ordered the stern-faced chairman.

" … then we figured out how the flying carpet works." There was absolute quiet in the room.

"Then we flew out of Yellowstone with it . . . it's this big park . . . forest actually . . ." He kicked himself thinking these highly-educated world leaders likely knew more about Yellowstone than he did …

. . ."Then Father Malvic, he kidnapped me and stole the ring that makes demons do things against their will . . . then the boulder attacks started and that's something only somebody with the ring can do. I told Cathy . . . that's her sitting there . . . and she called the FBI, Special Agent Thyme. He found out where Father Malvic was. At a cenoté in Belize. That's where Father Malvic got killed. Shot in the heart with a spear gun. That's how we lost the ring. A merman took it. Look," Matt said, raising his still bullet ant swollen barren ring finger for the Politburo to see but seeing only his middle finger raised quickly lowered it thinking his finger gesture might be misinterpreted . . . "And that's everything," he gulped. "Like everybody says, the United States had nothing to do with it. Nothing at all."

The general scowled, leaned forward, glanced at his wristwatch then whispered something into the chairman's ear.

The other five members sat watching stoically. Matt stole a look at the State Department lady whose blank stare and mouth set in a hard line said '*it is what it is*.' Then the Politburo leaned forward almost in unison and exchanged vigorous words with one another in Mandarin. Then they turned to the woman seated at the far end of the folding tables where the Americans were seated. It was the woman who had greeted them atop the seven hundred steps. Before her on the table sat a bank of flat screens. "He is telling the truth," she declared simply.

There was a collective sigh.

"That is basically the story your FBI man told us more or less," said the chairman. "We wish to know more about the anti-gravity platform you have."

"And the ring," another demanded.

"Yes, the ring," said another.

"That woman seated before you is a biometrics expert. A human lie detector. She has been watching each of you. No matter how ridiculous that story is it seems you believe it. That is what matters."

○ ○ ○

Eight hundred-fifty miles away at the Taiyuan Space Launch Center in Shanxi Province a technician poised his finger above a red launch button . . .

… 4…3…2…1…*ignition.*

With the fury of the sun the missile blasted from its silo tipped with four nuclear warheads - one each for San Francisco, Los Angeles, Washington, D.C. and New York City.

The Ghost City atop Ming Mountain overlooked Chongqing, a bustling city of 400,000.

The general eyed his watch. His and the State Department Lady's sat phones buzzed at once.

"Mister Chairman! What's happening? You've launched a missile?" the State Department Lady shrieked.

"Relax Madam Secretary. The missile is being self-destructed," the chairman calmly replied.

Then the general began arguing with the chairman in agitated Mandarin.

"It seems there is a problem," said the chairman. "One of our warheads is not responding."

"Not responding! How many are there?" the State Department Lady shrieked.

"Four."

"Four?" she gasped. "Which one?"

"The one for your Los Angeles I am afraid."

"Mom!" Matt gasped.

Holding her phone she pressed a speed dial button. "Get me General Anders fast." The call was patched through immediately to the U.S. Air Force Space Command at Cheyenne Mountain.

"LISTEN CAREFULLY! Secretary Judd . . . Chinese Politburo advises warhead heading for Los Angeles . . . warhead not responding to self-destruct . . . find it . . . kill it . . . Los Angeles . . . standing by . . .do not retaliate, repeat do not retaliate."

At the Space Operations Center General Lucius Anders picked up his direct line to the crew of USAF YAL-2, a specially-modified Boeing 747-400F whose nose-mounted Airborne Laser Anti-Ballistic Missile Weapons System had been developed at a cost of more billions than anyone cared to acknowledge. The general gave the crew the warhead's trajectory.

"It'll be doing 9.5 kilometers per second. You'll have ten seconds to find it and kill it."

"Roger that," replied the pilot. "You heard the man," he barked over the IC. "Lock and destroy." It would be one crew member's job to detect the warhead, a second's to designate it, and a third's to render it scrap metal.

"Target acquired," the detector shouted.

"Target locked," the designator shouted.

"Fire when ready," the pilot ordered.

It would be like trying to hit a bullet with a bullet from 260 kilometers.

The shooter sat glued to her display calmly chewing a stick of Beemans as she watched the warhead descend . . . 140 miles AGL . . . 130 . . . 120 . . . 110 . . . she squeezed the trigger on her joystick. The powerful 150-kilowatt laser fired. Seconds ticked by . . .

"Target neutralized," she shouted. Cheers rang through the aircraft. Space Op, 846 miles away, burst into pandemonium. There was cheering, flag waving, high-fives, and happy dances, all in proper military fashion of course.

“We’re still here. The nuke didn’t go off, sir,” the co-pilot sighed. “A few more seconds and – ”

A bright glow lit the horizon.

• • •

The Channel Islands are comprised of eight islands lying off the coast of Southern California. The largest, Santa Catalina, is twenty-two miles southwest of Los Angeles. It was a normal day that would be anything but normal. Squabbling seagulls cartwheeled and screeched. The wind blew lightly as waves lapped the golden shore and dinghies bobbed alongside floating palaces like toy boats in a jewel-blue sea. Children built sandcastles and jet skiers and paragliders played among the sparkling wave crests. The blast ripped through the rustic isle and the vessels moored around it like a horde of Mongols. Fifty kilotons. Five Hiroshimas. Fortunately, if one could say that, the edge of the blast extended only a few miles into the densely-populated mainland. The electromagnetic pulse was less kind, frying everything electrical even if it wasn’t switched on, knocking out power from one end of California to the other and as far away as Denver, a thousand miles to the east and deep into Mexico. A million square miles of nothing working. No computers, no communications, no ability to use debit or credit cards, no gasoline because no power for the pumps, no water, no sewer, tens of thousands trapped in elevators, police, fire, emergency crews and hospitals overwhelmed. It was a scene from an apocalypse movie.

The EMP sent planes crashing into neighborhoods, roads packed with dead vehicles, waterways, bridges, rooftops, landing wherever they could. Ever see a jumbo jet land in a Walmart parking lot? Older aircraft were able to keep flying but the computerized planes dropped like flies hit with a can of Raid.

Humans aren't wise enough to prevent disasters. They react to them. So it was no that surprise officials knew about the EMP vulnerability but did nothing to prepare. The electric grid cannot operate without extra-high-voltage transformers. There are few manufacturers, each one must be custom-made, takes up to two years to make and few are kept on hand.

YAL-2 was thought to be EMP-proof. It was a dead stick wheels-up landing. The aircraft left a mile-long trail of bloody animal parts. It had landed in the biggest meat packing plant west of the Rockies.

The Holstein turned barrel-eyed from its feed trough, nose-to-nose with the business end of the laser cannon. It stopped chewing.

• • •

Matt approached the chairman who had a far-off look in his eyes.

"I'm curious sir, why did you choose the Ghost City to meet?"

"All my life I have believed ghosts are dead people," the leader replied. "For more than two thousand years we have believed they were our ancestors," he said staring at a Maya Blue statue of a demon devouring a human. "No more. Now we know they are evil spirits. Not all will be accepting of this. Old beliefs die hard. Two thousand years of tradition must now change. It will not change overnight … but it will change. What better place to begin that change than the Ghost City."

"Why did you agree to meet with us at all?" asked Cathy.

"Your Special Agent Thyme was most persuasive. It is fortunate," he said turning to the State Department Lady, "that we have two thousand years of history and an understanding of the mystical … demons … dragons . . . spirits and such. Were it not for that, America would be glowing in the dark tonight."

"Both our countries would be glowing," Secretary Judd said soberly as she excused herself.

The chairman made no mention of the secret hardened complex within Ming Mountain exclusively for the use of Chinese government officials and VIPs in the event of a nuclear, chemical or biological attack. Like the hundreds of top-secret underground complexes in the United States such as the one under Denver International Airport, built to sustain ten thousand select government officials and their families in five-star comfort during the apocalypse while abandoning the rest of the population to fend for itself.

The team was allowed to return to the United States. Father Brainard's chest pains turned out to be gas. The Chinese news agencies Xinhua and China News Service both reported that a previously unknown terror group had staged the basalt attacks and that it had been dealt with in a manner befitting the crime. It offered no details. The U.S. State Department had no comment. Officially it wasn't there. No one would ever know how close the world had come to destruction or how four kids had saved it.

As they winged home, "You know Matt," Secretary Judd said tiredly, "this is the only time anyone's ever given the Politburo the finger. They'll never believe this back at the State Department. Someone wants to speak with you all."

"Who?"

"The President."

"... of the United States!?!!" asked Cathy.

"I told her what you did. She wants to speak with you." Going forward they climbed the spiral stairs to the 747's upper deck.

"And you, promise me you won't call the president dude-ess," she told Chase.

"Of course not. It's Mrs. President Dude-ess. Everybody knows that!" Secretary Judd shook her head and sighed.

"Madam President, I have our young people with me . . . "

"Cathy Kozacky, Zachary Kozacky, Matthew Legend, Chase Tannenhook, forgive me if this is a short call but we have our hands full here. On behalf of a grateful nation I want to thank each of you for the role you played in averting Armageddon . . ." the sat phone blared. As the leader of the free world spoke the gravity of all they had been through sank in. Cathy started to cry.

" . . . Our nation was on the brink of war. The American people are in your debt as are countless others. On behalf of a grateful nation I thank you and wish you godspeed in your endeavors." She paused. "That said," her tone changed, "each of you are in possession of classified information under the National Security Act. Do to the delicate politics involved, nothing of this must be divulged for fifty years. In normal times each of you would receive the Presidential Medal of Freedom, our nation's highest civilian honor for your meritorious contribution to the security and national interests of the United States." Then showing a bit of the personality that helped get her elected, "Have you seen 'Mission Impossible? It's like that. But know you're all Medal of Freedom recipients with me. You can't tell anyone, not even your parents what happened."

"We're on an AGE list. Anti-Government Entities! Can you get us off? I want to fly Super Cobras," Cathy blurted.

"I don't know what you kids would be doing on that list but I'll have somebody look into it. And if it's up to me you can fly whatever you want. For your protection, I'm assigning you each a security detail. They'll be with you at all times."

Then the President invited Matt, Cathy, Zak and Chase to sit on her newly-formed Special Council Advising on Resistance to Extra-Dimensional Beings, SCARE. Formed to find answers to the scary unexplained events that were growing by the month, its purpose was to identify paranormal threats to national security and recommend and develop appropriate courses of action. It seemed no one knew what to do. Mistakes had been made. Besides, the Council would be able to monitor the kids, kids thought dangerous. The president clicked off.

"I knew I was going to be famous," said Zak. "I told you this was a good idea." Cathy scowled at him.

Chapter 39 – GOING HOME

IT WAS A WARM, sunny afternoon. Matt, Chase, Cathy and Zak were biking along the dirt road beside the winding Chickasaw River. Hungry trout rippled the surface as they gobbled mosquitoes. Matt laughed about how odd it is small objects when accidentally dropped always make straight for the hardest to reach spot every time, at least in his experience.

"I think it's God's telling us he's in control of every little thing and has sense of humor major," Cathy chuckled.

"That or the Devil's in control and he's messin' with us," said Chase.

He turned to her to tell her there's no name for the phenomenon. Her eyes glowed red and her skin turned dark green scales. She lunged sinking teeth like flaying knives excruciatingly into his neck. The air turned a red mist.

"Get away!" he screamed but no words came out. He opened his eyes. Cathy was standing over him wearing a bemused grin.

"Bad dream?" she giggled. "This trip would give anybody night-mares."

The past weeks were a blur. Life's simple pleasures — a hot shower, a double chili cheese Fatburger, an ice-cold Coke had new meaning. His clothes could stand up on their own.

Cathy hovered over him briefly before crossing to the seat next to his. He squirmed to let her pass. She didn't seem to notice his pulse racing or mind his knees blocking hers. He pretended to relax and laid his head against his seatback acutely aware of everything happening six inches to his right. Cathy's elbow touched his. A thousand volts coursed through him. Her leg was less than an inch from his. She had on fresh white shorts with a green pastel tank top with *Cancun* silk-screened across it with a blue martini glass flanked by two palm trees. She smelled of sweat mixed with strawberry body lotion courtesy of the State Department Lady no doubt.

His heart pounded. He would have given all the mercreatures' treasure to know what she was thinking.

"You been to Cancun?" he asked unsure she heard through her earbuds.

Cathy looked down at her top. "You checking me out again Matt?"

His blood rushed to his face. It was suddenly quite warm. "No … ah, I was just noticing your, ah . . ." he blurted . . . "I mean –

"I've seen how you look at me Matt."

He gulped having no experience with girls, not knowing what to say or do. What would James Bond do, he asked himself?

"Relax. Just giving you a hard time," she laughed. Embarrassed, he gave what he feared a goofy grin and sank back into his seat. He really had been checking her out.

He flashed to that moment at the airfield when he first knew. The day her father buzzed them in his P-51. He should have kissed her right then and there as he zoomed overhead. She was wearing shorts and a blue pastel tank top and flip-flops. The image was indelibly etched into his photographic memory.

"It was two years ago," Cathy drifted . . . "my parents. . . their wedding anniversary."

"How long were we . . . I mean they married?" he asked.

"Fourteen years," she laughed.

She changed the subject.

"Will we ever get used to this stuff?" she sighed.

"*We*?" he asked nervously.

To his surprise Cathy was the one blushing.

Again she fell back on the fine art of changing the subject. "I'm having trouble with this supernatural stuff. I don't think I'm cut out for it."

"Me either," said Matt. "I thought spirits was strong drink."

"And Halloween," Cathy grinned.

Matt sighed. "I want to press rewind. I want things back the way they were."

"Things'll never be back the way they were," Cathy lamented. "I can't do this anymore."

Reaching through the seats Matt tapped Father Herzl'shoulder.

"Father, do you know anything about demons?"

"What do you want to know?"

"Cathy's having trouble wrapping her head around this stuff. It's making mine hurt too. It's weirding us out. Is there something we can take?"

The priest twisted around as if to say something very important . . . "Welcome to the party. Take a deep breath and count to ten. The world's getting more preternatural every day. That's the evil supernatural. Now you know you live in two worlds. The one you see and the one you don't. That always comes as a shock. Most people try to pretend it doesn't exist. Do you get used to it? . . . Never. Not completely anyhow. You need to compartmentalize.

"Same with the God things. You don't get used to them either." The priest leaned across his seatback, "There's great good in the world but there's also great evil. Evil beyond all imaginings. There's danger in sticking your noses where demons don't want them. When you declare war on them, they declare war on you. You have a fantasy about what your world is. It's an illusion. You must free yourselves of your fantasy world straitjackets. We humans seek comfort. We don't like things that take us out of our comfort zone. You've traveled outside that zone. I'll tell you this . . . instead of trying to convince yourselves your comfort zone is real, warm and safe, you must ask yourselves who has constructed your comfort zone for you and why. If you know something's a lie and you do nothing to expose the lie you become part of it. The truth is out there. And remember . . . when you're attacked by demonic forces or so-called aliens, call out to Jesus. They leave you alone immediately. There's power in that name. It's like kryptonite to them. Remember that."

Father Brainard who had been dozing awoke.

"He's right," he said. "You need to operate in warrior mode. People don't need to rely solely on faith anymore. This is the Information Age. On the web you'll find thousands of proofs of God."

"If that works so great how come they never call on JC in horror movies?" said Matt.

"Because the movie would be over real quick," the priest laughed.

Matt settled into his seat wondering if the calling on Jesus thing really worked. He would have to give it a try sometime. It was politically incorrect to be sure. The fathers didn't seem to care.

"So, you saved the world. What now? We can't have you running amok," said Cathy with a flush in her cheeks.

We? Was it a signal? She was so close. Should he go for the kiss? What if he was wrong? What if it wasn't a signal at all? As he sat trying to decide what to do her elbow touched his. A thousand volts tingled through his body. He began to feel queasy. He had never kissed a girl before. Cathy was unlike any girl he had ever met. Girls are magical, he thought.

What have I got to lose? She lives thousands of miles away. I'll probably never see her again. What if she pulls away? It's a fourteen hour flight. Is this just a summer love?

"What?" asked Cathy sensing he had something to say the way people can sense when someone is staring at them. She removed her earbuds and turned her powder blue eyes his way. She smiled. He smiled. All it would take would be to lean to the right just a little. For a second their eyes locked. He glanced at her pouty lips. He cursed his eyes for betraying him and retreated to the safety of doing nothing, recalling the time Penny Romero smiled at him and he thought it meant something only to learn painfully it was just a smile. How had Ollie put it? Who can figure girls.

Some superhero. Guts to save the world but not enough to kiss a girl. He surrendered to his fears.

Cathy pursed her lips, “So are you gonna kiss me or what.”

Matt’s heart did a backflip. She slid her fingers between his. *I must be dreaming!* he thought. She leaned her head gently against his and he kissed her. It was an awkward first kiss, but a kiss.

“Matt! Matt!” His eyes flew open. It was Cathy. “Where were you?”

“ . . . must’ve nodded off,” he replied, exhausted.

“Remember what Loveland called us? . . . a think tank? . . . So, mister think tank, what’ve you learned?”

“Ummm, nothing’s what it seems,” Matt replied groggily. “Archaeologists live in a make-believe world where they pretend things don’t exist. They can’t form their mouths to say the words ‘I don’t know.’ ’ Most are blind, deaf and dumb to the facts, ignorant of reality. And we’re born into a war. The whole friggin’ planet’s under attack.”

Matt worried he might never see the beauty in the world again like policemen.

Secretary Judd appeared.

“Matt, thank you for all you did. You’re very brave.”

“Where did you say that bomb went off?” Cathy asked warily.

“FedEx Field.”

“Mommy and Daddy are Redskins fans.”

“I’m sure they’re okay,” said the State Department Lady.

The 747 refueled at SeaTac before continuing to Washington, D.C. since the West was now in the Stone Age. The kids were taken to Tennessee.

Chapter 40 – WITCH HOUSE II

WHEN THEY LANDED Cathy knew with one look both her parents were dead. Her dog too. Her mother's normally vivacious sister stood on the tarmac head hung low looking haggard wearing oversized sunglasses clutching a hanky.

". . . She was celebrating her anniversary," her aunt sobbed . . . "-e-e-e-eighteen years ago Ted proposed on bended knee on FedEx Field's jumbotron not knowing whether she would say yes. The sports-caster said he was brave. "She had tickets for you and Zak. I missed the flight," she cried in convulsive gasps.

Cathy burst into tears. "That bomb was meant for us. Mommy and daddy are dead because of me," she wailed.

Again grief counselors consoled Zak and Cathy.

Seeing the chaos on tv Matt feared for his own mother's safety. But there was nothing he nor anyone could do. No phones were working out west and getting there was impossible. He would have to trust she would be okay. It would be a long time before the full magnitude of their loss would sink in. Grief is like the stages of disbelief.

○ ○ ○

Matt swung a one-eighty. He dropped his bike, kicked open the white picket gate, strode past the weeping willow that drooped to the weed garden like a Portuguese Man o' war, stomped up the creaking steps, he pressed the doorbell and waited.

The front door flew open.

"I know you didn't just kick my gate in!" Before him stood a feisty little old lady wearing a violet box pleat dress, red cashmere sweater and black pointed-toe flats. Not quite the black gown and pointy black hat he had expected.

"You don't look like a witch," Matt blurted.

"A witch? My goodness. What gave you that idea? Won't you kids come in," the kind lady beckoned.

"No thanks," said Chase.

"Sure, thanks," Matt said.

"Oh, my goodness," said the lady. You're those kids from CNN. What on earth made you think I'm a witch?"

Matt explained.

"Oh. Years ago, more than I care to admit, I was a medium. My sister, Esmerelda, was into Ouija boards, tarot cards, palm reading, you name it. I tried to talk her out, alas no luck. We used to give readings right here in this house. People came from far and wide to have their fortunes told and to talk with their dearly departed loved ones. I was very well known. I brought her into it.

"I'm Maddie. Won't you sit down?"

"Is Esmerelda a good witch?" asked Chase.

"Chase! Enough with the witch stuff already," Cathy said.

"It's okay. Mediums *are* witches. I just didn't know it at the time. Esmerelda passed last winter I'm afraid," said Maddie.

Matt gulped. "Then who did this?" he asked, showing her the Monster energy drink scratches.

"Oh dear," was all she said.

"There's no such thing as good witches," she said turning to Chase. "Witches are witches. That'd be like a good serial killer. Call them what you will . . . wizards, warlocks, shamen, medicine men, voodoo priests, mediums, witch doctors, fortune tellers, storefront psychics, necromancers, those calling themselves 'spiritual,' whatever . . . all no good, all serving the same evil demented master, every one of 'em on the express elevator to hell."

Matt admired the polished hardwood floor and fine woven rugs. A fine old dining table ringed with exquisite handcrafted chairs stood beside an ornate china cabinet beside a regulator that announced the hour with a single melodious chime. Bookcases overflowed with volumes of every size and color. In one corner a vacuum-tube television, the kind that's furniture, sat on four legs sprouting a telescoping brass V-antenna. On a nearby table an ancient radio and an old Commodore 64 computer competed awkwardly for space. Colorful floral vases and burgundy leather wing chairs with brass rivets flanked the brick fireplace in a room fragrant with the scent of jonquil, hyacinth and marigold.

"You have a nice place," Matt said, studying her stuffy old furniture some people call antiques.

"Alas, if it were only a fraction of its glory days." She pointed out a black and white photo showing a finely landscaped home surrounded by vintage luxury cars and people dressed funny.

"That's how it looked when my husband Walter was alive."

"Why'd you stop being a medium," asked Chase.

“I became a Christian,” Maddie said proudly. “Believe me, that doesn’t happen in the medium world very often. I paid a hefty price for turning away but it was nothing compared with the joy I’ve found.” A youthful vitality filled her eyes as she spoke.

“Leviticus 19:31 says not to turn to mediums or to seek out spiritists. It says we defile ourselves when we do. So I stopped. Little did I know it wouldn’t be that easy. I was punished. That’s what they call it – punished. The pennywises hate it when a medium turns from the dark side and goes to the light. They *really* hate it. Like when John Ramirez turned away from them and exposed their secrets. And like when you kids exposed their evil doings on CNN. Ephesians 5:11 says to take no part in the unfruitful works of darkness but instead expose them. If angels weren’t protecting y’all, y’all’d be inside expensive metal boxes with handles on ‘em right now.” Matt flashed to the glass blizzard and mattresses falling out of the sky thing and the bulletproof skin thing. Like his Monster Energy scar the scars were still fresh. It was hard to believe they really happened but they had.

“Like a deflector shield?” Matt asked.

Maddie’s eyes brightened as she raised her hand in the Vulcan greeting, “Live long and prosper.”

“Live long and prosper,” Matt returned, shaping his fingers into the two-fingered ‘V.’ Who would have guessed the former Glinda the Good Witch of the South was a Trekkie.

“When I went over to the light they started doing all kinds of bad things. There was banging and loud noises day and night. Doors opening and closing. Horrible smells. My bed would shake every night. And night paralysis. That's when they hold you against the mattress when you're half asleep and you can't move or speak. It seems like a bad dream but isn't. They even sent animals. It's night when they're at their worst," she said softly, "but stuff happens during the day too."

"*They* own the night? I thought the LAPD did," Chase chuckled, having seen something about that on a tv show.

Maddie lifted a brow.

"He's making a dumb joke," Cathy said.

"That stuff's been happening to us too," Matt said.

"I'm not surprised," said Maddie. "And something would go bump every night at 11:25. What was so special about 11:25? Never did figure that out but Jesus gives us power over Satan and his minions. When I asked him, he took control and the bad things stopped. "It's an endless cycle. I pray. It stops. It comes back a week or two later. I pray. It stops. It comes back a week or two later until finally it stops for good."

Chase rolled his eyes. "My philosophy teacher says there's no God."

"Oh, well you can tell your philosophy teacher he's full of it. Have you heard of James Edwards? He was an English medium. They used to call him the medium's medium. For thirty years he filled public halls with people who came to hear him speak. He was on TV, radio. He wrote books and gave readings. He used a tape recorder to record his readings because when he was in a trance he didn't know what was being said. One day he decided to play back the recording of a reading he'd given a woman who came to him regularly. Later he told the newspaper that when he and the woman heard the slowed tape and heard the disgusting, foul-mouthed language in the horrible threatening voice of the spirit, he knew right then and there who he'd been working for. How'd he put it … that he'd been 'deceived and deluded for nearly thirty years.' He quit them right then and there. When I found out I quit too. Rudyard Kipling blasted the medium world in his poem *En-Dor*, a warning to the world." Cathy perked.

The frail-looking lady raised her voice, "And don't think what mediums learn about people isn't used to ruin their lives and their friends' and families' behind their backs. And remember the next time you're tempted to pose for that selfie on the edge of the cliff, they're only too happy to give you a push."

Cathy turned pale as she remembered being pushed and scratched by something at the prison.

"I don't believe in God," Zak snorted.

"Oh dear, do you believe in demons?"

"Yes."

"You can't believe in one without believing in the other, dear. There's only good and evil. There's no in between even though evil often tries to disguise itself to look like good. And there's no such thing as white magic. It's all dark. Demons, I call them pennywises, are like any other organized criminal element. Each has a name and a rank. And each has a specific principality they're responsible for whether it's a country, a state, a city or even a city block. And they specialize. Some in suicide, others in murder, others in drugs, divorce, pornography, whatever. It's war I tell you and we're smack dab in the middle. There's a child who swings at night at a playground in Nevada. Whenever anyone approaches his eyes glow red and he disappears. Evil spirits have the world fooled into thinking ghosts are dead people. Just look on tv. People are eating it up. It was good what you kids did on CNN. Woo hoo! That was some ballyhoo! You aren't supposed to know that stuff.

Maddie just looked at the kids before saying anything else. Then with much effort, "It wasn't Esmerelda who scratched you, Matt."

Matt bit his lip and tasted blood.

"That's what I thought," he said.

"I don't get it," said Zak.

"No matter what you do there'll always be people who want to believe a ghost is some little girl who died and loved where she lived so much she can't leave. Hogwash. They need to spend a night with a malevolent one. That'll cure them fast enough.

"Before you go, know about automatic painting? It's like automatic writing. It's art created by a medium but it doesn't come from the medium . . . There's a Brazilian. Luiz Gaspareto is his name. Google him. Is that what you call it? . . . google? He creates exact replicas of old masters down to the smallest detail in just a few minutes holding a paintbrush between his toes hanging upside down blindfolded in the dark. Replicas so exact it takes an art expert to tell the difference. He says the power behind his so-called 'gift' is a source other than himself and that he's been told to tell people. Told to tell people.

"He's been quoted as saying, 'We want people to know there's life after death.' So you see, they don't just use ghosts in their deception. You know who '*we*' is don't you? They slipped up. They gave themselves away with the '*we*.'"

"*We* scratched my wrist," said Matt.

"That's impossible," said Zak.

"Goodness child," Maddie replied turning to Cathy, "Is he always this way?"

"Pretty much," Cathy replied.

"Who's *we* again*?"* asked Chase.

"*We* is *them* – demons," Maddie replied. "Annoying insects who'll soon enough get what's coming to them." Maddie picked up a fly swatter. "Tell me . . . whatever made you kids decide to tell the world ghosts aren't dead people?"

"Payback," Matt replied, "for Anne Frank . . . for all kids . . . and for me. *We* is the reason my father's dead and Cathy and Zak's parents too." Cathy stared into space.

"You kids are getting help you know. You've made some powerful enemies but your friends are more powerful."

"You mean The Force?" asked Zak.

"Call it what you like. By the way, there's something you should know. It's easy to know whether a psychic's powers come from the light side or the dark side. The light side's predictions are one hundred percent accurate down to the smallest detail one hundred percent of the time. If even one tiny detail's off even once it's from the underworld. And the reason mediums always answer with the word 'soon' when you ask them when something they foretold is going to happen is because they don't know. They say that to cover their butts. 'Soon' can be next month or fifty years from now. They don't know. Their powers are inferior to the light side's."

"Why does God let bad things happen … like the Holocaust?" asked Matt.

Maddie sighed two deep sighs … "I believe it's because the universe is watching. God has to let evil run its course or the universe won't see evil for what it is and it could happen again. The universe must be allowed to see the true face of evil.

"It's like those science fiction movies when they travel through time to prevent a crime. If you do that though, the crime will just happen again somewhere else. At least they can't leave to infect the rest of the universe. They're in lockdown.

"Auschwitz? You ain't seen nothin'. The worst is yet to come.

"There's a contract out on you kids. Remember to keep prayed up. I'll pray for you too. Y'all come back now, hear? Next time don't kick my gate in. Open it like a sensible person."

Fighting demons had become more than a dangerous hobby. It had become a calling. Starfleet General Order 0 authorizes the captain to take any and all measures necessary to destroy Omega particles, artificial particles whose destructive capabilities are so dangerous that they must be destroyed at any cost. Matt Legend General Order 0: Authorizes Matt Legend to take any and all measures necessary to aid in the destruction of fallen angel trash.

Sometimes you have to step outside the person you've been and remember the person you were meant to be, the person you wanted to be, the person you are.

H.G. Wells

When he'd read that in English class six months earlier he didn't know who he was meant to be. When you're fifteen you're still trying to figure out who you are.

○ ○ ○

Matt stood on the bank of the Chickasaw river. A dark brown object was slowly making its way toward him. He kicked off his shoes and waded in. It looked strangely familiar. It must be a cheap knock-off made in China or Mexico he thought. There must be thousands.

Straining he lifted it from the water. The mask weighed a ton. It was too heavy to float. He stared down at it. It had a familiar diagonal cut across its right eye. He dropped it like a hot brick and ran.

○ ○ ○

Cathy sat combing her call records for her call to her dad from Lake of No Return. There had been no signal bars. She couldn't find the call. She called the company. The lady explained it doesn't provide service there. When Cathy asked her who does she was told flatly, "No one. It's a dead zone."

"But I placed a call there. It went through. It was crystal clear."

"That's impossible," the lady insisted.

"I placed a call there!" Cathy insisted.

"Like I said, impossible," said the lady, who cited things having to do with cell sites, switches, frequencies, signal fluctuation, directional sector antennas and things.

Chapter 41 – LIGHTS ON THE MOON

The hollow moon, rising like an eye of stone, rising white and all alone, always watching, always listening to the Earth below.
Linda Moulton-Howe

Silly scientists. They come up with the silliest explanations for things they don't understand and for things they do understand but don't want you to understand. Science misinformation abounds. Like where the moon came from. How a passing giant asteroid collided with the Earth, knocking out a huge perfectly round moon yet miraculously leaving the Earth round and intact. Move to the back of the class.

Did you know the same scientist types gambled with all life on Earth when they detonated the very first atomic bomb? That's right. One of the physicists, Edward Teller, confessed later there was no way to be sure it wouldn't set the entire Earth's atmosphere on fire in a chain reaction. It was a coin toss. Heads it works, tails we're barbecue.

Fortunately it was heads. It did end World War Two. However, instead of eighty million dead the scientists could have killed us all. The demons were there watching as they do at every bad thing. At 9/11 their faces were visible in the smoke, captured on film by a photojournalist, the photo later verified as authentic.[7] But people quickly forgot as they always do.

Summer was coming to an end. Everything was a jumble. Matt was supposed to be on a plane to California. No more. Three months earlier he had dreaded coming. Now he dreaded leaving. He was finding

Cathy's quiet beauty, wit, charm and spirit impossible to resist. Would she ever see him for who he was?

"You have mail," his aunt said.

"Mom?"

"I'm afraid not."

"Google glass!" Matt thrilled, spotting the logo, for Google had decided the time had come to resurrect its Glass since nobody cared about privacy anymore.

A box with a local return address bore a Navy Seal Luminox watch with an orange face and tritium hands guaranteed to glow in the dark for twenty-five years. An envelope held a bank draft for a thousand dollars and a big thin box contained a titanium mountain bike. Another envelope bore a Skyfell address. Fingers trembling he tore it open.

Dear Matthew,

It is my pleasure to inform you that you have been selected for attendance during St. Francis Skyfell Academy's upcoming Fall Semester.

You have been further designated as the recipient of a three-year academic merit grant which covers the full cost of your tuition, room and board, books, uniforms and related expenses.

Congratulations on your achieving this important milestone.

It is requested that you contact Student Housing immediately in order that we may arrange boarding for you for the upcoming school year.

We welcome you and look forward to your enrollment.

Sincerely,

Penelope K. Drake

Penelope K. Drake
Office of Admissions

"Mrs. Kozacky," Matt breathed. A smile crossed his lips, sadness his thoughts. His heart lept. He and Cathy would be attending the same school.

Chase had received an identical letter and check. They would enter Skyfell together.

The following day Matt, Chase, Cathy and Zak each received via special delivery a navy blue presentation case lined with white satin bearing the Presidential Medal of Freedom. Matt thought the medal, a white enamel star inset with a blue disc with thirteen gold stars set against a golden ring suspended from a blue ribbon with white edge stripes, the most beautiful thing he had ever seen. There was no letter with it but that was to be expected for something that officially never happened. There was however a handwritten note on State Department stationary. It read simply,

Thank you for a job well done!

■ ■ ■ ■

Ollie's red Silverado sat in the driveway. An ambulance sat on the lawn, its doors open, its red lights blinking. Two paramedics were wheeling a gurney with a blue sheet was draped over it. An arm dangled limp from its side. On its wrist was a rose gold Rolex.

Cathy dropped her bike and ran to Ollie's wife on the porch crying. The EMTs placed him into the ambulance passing Matt too stunned to get off his bike. They shut its doors. The ambulance pulled off the lawn and with a solitary yelp, its red lights flashing, it was gone. There was no siren, never a good sign. The only wails were those of Ollie's wife. Matt burst into tears, caught off guard by emotions he didn't know he had. Sometimes we don't know how much someone means to us until they're gone.

Ollie had been a gift. Some people have an aura about them of warmth, kindness, gentleness and caring.

○ ○ ○

The new SCARE team members were sent to Skyfell's science lab.

"Father Brainard told us of your out-of-body experience," a scruffy-haired man in a white lab coat told Matt, barely able to contain his enthusiasm.

"In 1972 we began experimenting with extrasensory perception, ESP," a woman in a dark business suit explained calmly as if to apologize for her over-eager colleague. "I'm Dr. Hatchet, this is my colleague Dr. Aragon. It's called remote viewing. Think of it as the ability to go places without physically going there. It's mind travel. Don't get me wrong, you're there just as if you were physically, but you're not. We discovered younger remote viewers yield the best results. We believe it has to do with nerve synapses, the junctions between neurons across which impulses pass by diffusion of a neurotransmitter. Think of them as spark plugs. A newborn has 100 billion. By the time we're adults we've lost half. So you see, you're very important to us."

There was an elephant in the room — Bubba.

"Wasn't Bubba in the program?" asked Chase.

"If you mean Bubba Briscoe, why yes, he was."

“What happened to him?” Cathy asked nervously.

“Our wireless neurotransceiver was in beta then. That’s since been worked out,” she replied, too polished.

Bubba, a former honor student, now it was all he could manage to lace his shoes.

Matt had learned some time ago that by staring at certain people from behind it would cause them to snap around and stare him square in the eyes. It was strange. And one summer at the Atlantic City boardwalk something else strange happened. After the operator of a gigantic Ferris-like roulette wheel collected the monies from players hoping to win a giant panda or other useless prize, Matt stood watching as a burly volunteer reached up, grabbed the wheel and gave it a mighty tug. As the numbers whizzed past a knowing filled him – 12. Gobsmacked he waited for the wheel to stop. It did . . . on 12!

“Even ordinary people can develop their psychic abilities. We’re going to teach you things you never thought possible,” the woman added.

Then the scientists explained.

○ ○ ○

“It’ll be a fantastic adventure. You’ll be traveling to the moon . . . and Mars I wish I were going.” The lab-coated man looked as if he were about to cry.

Some call it mind travel. Some call it astral projection. The CIA calls it remote viewing. And that’s what Stanford Research Institute, known as The Institute, called it. With radar and radio communications down across most of the West, only military aircraft from other states and low-tech stuff like crop dusters were flying. With no way for a destination airport to know a pilot was coming, all any pilot could do was show up and keep a sharp eye out. Visibility was near zero. Matt worried about his mom.

They landed at a naval air station twenty miles from Matt's home. He asked to see his mother. His request was denied. Diverting precious military resources during a time of martial law was impossible. Nevertheless, the SDO, the squadron duty officer, Lieutenant Worley, a kind man, promised to send someone as soon as he could. They were whisked aboard a Navy helicopter that had flown in from NAS Corpus Christi in Texas.

It seemed like the end of the world. Fires were everywhere and with them rioting, looting and mayhem. Every window was broken and the streets were littered with debris, bodies and abandoned vehicles. They could smell and taste the smoke. A thick grey ash covered everything. Reports of roving bands of thugs caused Matt to worry all the more.

Smoke roiled around the mighty Chinook's rotors as it landed inside The Institute's barbed wire perimeter. The President had declared a national state of emergency and had mobilized the U.S. Army National Guard. In a moving public address she offered her thoughts and prayers to those affected by the EMP disaster and asked residents to heed the advice of local officials. No one in the affected regions heard it. Bodies were piling up by the minute.

There was some good news, though. Lt. Worley had found Matt's mother. She was a short helicopter flight away.

"She's at Los Coyotes Hospital. We need to get you there now."

Matt entered her room. She was covered in bandages.

"Mom …" her eyes opened. Her face lit. He hugged her like never before. She winced. Matt recoiled . . . "Sorry, mom."

He pressed his face to hers.

"Honey . . . listen, you need to be strong," she whispered . . . "I never should have gone back for your baby pictures. Probably wasn't such a good idea," she grimaced. "You know how I hate hospitals." She forced a weak smile.

Fearfully Matt looked around at the life-support machines.

"I love you mom."

"I love you too, Matt."

The nurse placed her hand gently on Matt's shoulder indicating it was time to go.

"I love you mom."

"Don't forget me," she replied. Matt began to cry.

"You'll be okay mom.

"She needs to rest now," the nurse said kindly but firmly.

Matt left the room to find Lt. Worley waiting outside. The ward alarm sounded. A xenon strobe outside his mother's room flashed. Medical personnel scurried as Matt stood by helpless. His eyes welled.

He watched as the doctors attempted to resuscitate her without success.

○ ○ ○

Remote viewing was nothing new. It had begun as Project Star Gate in 1972, a top secret CIA program. Group remote viewing was new, however. Someone had come up with the idea that it would work best with kids who were friends. Scientists had discovered that best friends develop neural similarities over time. A neural headset would act as a data link. The remote viewers' visual images could even be viewed and downloaded. It was going to make spy satellites obsolete, something all the more important considering clear skies have all but disappeared, in their place a mysterious haze being called "soft sunshine."

"I'll pass . . ." said Chase.

The woman turned to Cathy, Zak and Matt.

"I'm in," said Zak.

"About Bubba," Matt asked, "How do we know that won't happen to us?" Then the dragon lady replied in a manner made to seem only an idiot wouldn't understand and speaking very very slowly said, "It's .. like .. I .. said . . . it .. was .. a .. beta .. unit . . . We're .. beyond .. that .. now . . . we're at version 5.2. It's . . . perfect. After this none of you will want for anything for the rest of your lives."

Later the dragon lady's number two caught the kids alone. Looking around nervously, Dr. Aragon said, "We need intel. Get us intel. Be careful out there. Stay together. And if something tells you to leave, do it. And when you get back, whatever you do, don't take the pill she gives you. The enemy has developed astral capture. That's what happened to your friend. Don't get astral captured. I have to go. This is worse than ouija boards. Madre de Dios," he muttered as he disappeared down the hall.

“What enemy?” asked Cathy.

○ ○ ○

The remote viewers streaked through a marble-blue sky ablaze with orange-tinted spun-silver wisps that trapped the setting sun’s last rays. As the sky grew dark Matt gazed in awe at the big blue marble twenty miles below – surreal blue-green hues resplendent in the lonely vastness of space with its multi-colored gaseous nebulae and zillions of stars. Some shone red, some yellow, some white, others blue, all with a clarity impossible on Earth. For the moment four kids were infinite in the black void, one with the stars and two hundred trillion galaxies. Wispy clouds below them veiled continents strewn with tiny glittering lights like a bride’s gown sprinkled with diamonds, all within a fragile, thin translucent blue band. Gray smoke covered the western half of the United States.

The cold haunting beauty of space does something to you. Ask any astronaut or cosmonaut. Have you ever been someplace you were forbidden to be and didn’t get caught? It’s like that. Or the feeling of doing something thought impossible. Or the wonder of waking someplace you forgot you went to sleep the night before, only for those first few moments having no idea where you are.

“My God, it’s full of stars,” said Chase.

“Funny,” Matt said.

Cathy gazed at the silver moon. “It’s beautiful. If only Ollie could’ve seen this.”

They suddenly felt very small and alone in the vastness of the universe. They passed the Hubble telescope. "I can hack that," Zak thrilled.

"Don't even think about it," Cathy snapped. A large smooth shiny speeding cigar-shaped metal object grabbed their attention, Oumuamua as astronomers have dubbed it. As they approached it accelerated and veered away but it was no match for the speed of thought. It was the shell of a craft. They glimpsed the object's interior. It was no asteroid but an alien spacecraft. Sensing danger they quickly thought themselves away.

Our moon isn't really a moon at all. It's too big to be our moon. Astronomers are at a loss to explain where it came from and how a planet Earth's size could have captured a body so large into orbit. It should not be able to. It is more a planet than a moon. It is one and a half times the size of Pluto. Ask any astronomer about our moon and where it came from. They won't want to talk about it. Ask the moon landing astronauts about the most glorious day of their lives, strangely they will give you a funny look and won't want to talk about it either. Earth doesn't have the gravity mass to capture a body that large and hold it in orbit. Earth couldn't have stopped it anyway. As it approached it would have plowed into Earth.

Something about Earth's nearest neighbor stood out. It wasn't gray. The moon's dominant color was orange with dark blues and dark greens and browns splashed across it.

"Are you sure this is the moon?" Cathy breathed, for it bore no resemblance to any of the moon photos she had ever seen.

All their lives they had seen only the same colorless gray photos of the thousands taken. Strangely even the few color ones were black and white, including the one in which the astronaut's gold visor and the stars and stripes stood out boldly against a black and white moonscape.

"Where are we exactly?" asked Matt, as they passed over a plain twice the size of London and its suburbs.

"Plato," Zak replied. "This is no impact crater. What fool came up with that idea!"

Zak marveled, then puzzled, then angered over how anyone could even remotely think the so-called crater was an impact crater. It didn't resemble an impact crater by any stretch of anyone's imagination. It was 101 kilometers across, shallow and perfectly flat. An asteroid impact that big would have blasted a crater many times deeper than the Grand Canyon. Instead the surface was flat, shallow and smooth as a pancake just like the other big craters.

"I want to see the dark side," Cathy said.

Chase joined them. It was the feeling of someone else entering a dark room they were in who they just couldn't see.

"I changed my mind. I told the dragon lady I changed my mind."

"She can hear you," Matt reminded. At The Institute the dragon lady ignored the slight. She was focused on the ULOs (Unidentified Lunar Objects).

Something else was strange. The Moon had an atmosphere. The stars twinkled through the thin atmospheric gases much like on Earth. Nearer the surface sparse clouds of wispy ice crystals hung.

"They've always said it doesn't have an atmosphere," said Chase.

“These aren’t impact craters,” Zak mumbled.

And there were funnel holes scattered all across the lunar surface, looking like the ant cones on Earth but for the fact they were smooth and ranged from hundreds of meters to kilometers across.

“OUT, OUT, EVERYBODY OUT, NOW!” the dragon lady bellowed as she cleared the room.

Machines of incomprehensible size stood in some of the craters.

“They’re mining,” said Zak.

“Do these machines belong to the United States?” Chase asked, glancing around not focusing on anything.

“Toto I have a feeling we’re not in Kansas anymore,” Cathy muttered.

Chase was the first to spot them — massive tracks leading in every direction, each tread width the length of a football field.

“What have we gotten ourselves into?” Cathy muttered feeling trapped.

Another strange sight appeared. In the distance a line rose vertically into the heavens as far as the eye could see, a giant tube, at its top an alien structure of some sort.

“I want to see it,” Matt said.

“Don’t,” Cathy warned. “Don’t do it . . . Don’t do it . . . Don’t you do it . . .” she warned with the wisdom only a woman has. He ignored it. They had travelled two hundred fifty thousand miles after all.

“I have a bad feeling about this,” said Chase.

“Me too,” Zak gulped.

An artificial light source meant trouble.

A mile-wide metallic mushroom crown composed of white cubes encircled by a transparent strip sat atop the impossibly long tube The viewers peered through the strip. In the green glow a frightful assortment of beings were going about their business whatever it was.

Nine-foot muscular reptilians, some dark green, some brown, standing-up alligators like the ones Matt had seen in the petroglyphs in the mound were interacting with frail, spindly-looking gray-skinned beings whose heads were too big for their bodies. The five-foot grays with their gigantic unblinking teardrop eyes black as coal with slits for noses and mouths stood out from the cone-headed reptilians with their ridged bony heads and yellow eyes with vertical black slits. Just as bizarre were the seven-foot blond Nordics, who bore a distinct resemblance to the *sidhe* of Irish legend and the *ljósálfar* of Norse saga. The males wore their hair long, the females in a pageboy style. All of the Nordics were very attractive by Earth standards. Well-built men and women with blue eyes, others with pink, gold, violet, purple, red or green eyes that often appeared to change color. They were the only creatures wearing clothes, some in silver skin-tight outfits, others in white flowing robes, others still in pale blue one-piece jumpers. Monstrous ten-foot praying mantis insectoids towered over them all waving their frightful appendages. The Nordics appeared in charge, under them the insectoids, under them the reptoids, under them the grays. All in fact possessed an IQ of 1,200 and spoke over a hundred languages, alien and human. A chair rose from out of the floor. An insectoid sat in it. It swiveled its head and peered directly at the remote viewers. It raised a barbed appendage. All aliens turned to face the spies from Earth.

“Time to go,” Matt gulped. As they shot away he dared to look back. The viewing strip was filled with silhouettes.

“H-how can they see us?” Chase blurted, struggling to control his quavering.

“We should leave the moon, NOW!” Cathy said. “I don’t want to get astral captured.”

“Not yet,” Matt gulped.

“Who put you in charge,” she demanded. “You’re going to cause us to end up like Bubba.”

“We have to stick together remember,” said Chase.

Intermittent flashes dotted the horizon. Most lasted only an instant but one lasted eight seconds, long enough to be noticed by an amateur astronomer back on Earth. They passed over a twenty-story-tall machine which sprawled for miles – an earthmover – or moonmover rather, creeping slowly toward the flashes. Banks of forty-story-tall bright lights bathed the moon. They were lights of many colors including colors they had never seen before. And strange structures, many of which spread for miles. Many were crystalline. The air held a fine dust and a dark lime-green mist. A giant machine dug into a yellowish mountain, scooping up loads the size of city blocks, were it be known each load worth an undecillion dollars (a one with thirty-six zeros behind it – ($1,000,000,000,000,000,000,000,000,000,000,000,000) – a trillion trillion trillion dollars, in gold, a strange kind of iron that doesn’t rust, rare earth metals and ilmenite, a compound containing iron, titanium and oxygen. Helium 3 also, a valuable energy source. And pure titanium. All with an insatiable demand on Earth. All left untouched by Earthmen afraid of the aliens. Not daring so much as a quick scoop and run.

"The moon's Grand Central Station!" Cathy screeched.

"They're stealing our minerals," Chase blurted.

"Earth to Chase, the moon's not ours," Cathy cried. "We need to leave like *NOW!*"

"The astronauts didn't say a word about this," said Zak.

At least not publicly anyway. They would learn later that several Apollo astronauts have stated off the record they were "warned off" the moon by hostile aliens in enormous ships. Warned off as in don't even think of coming back. Had a blast from a super ray delivered the message or had the three ginormous alien spacecraft lined up on the crater ridge watching them which they reported to mission control after switching to the medical channel been enough, as reported by eavesdropping ham radio operators.

When the Chinese sent their own rover forty years later it began transmitting high-resolution color images of all sorts of disturbing things until the hybrid Men in Black and Women in Black showed up.

"Look," Matt said. "They're knocking down the rims of the craters," he said, staring at the tracks-strewn plains.

They passed over what scientists call impact craters which aren't impact craters. They passed over triangular craters, perfectly round craters, square craters, polygonal craters, hexagonal craters and octagonal craters, some three miles wide, some wider. They passed over structures, walls, bridges, many in ruins, evidence of a cosmic war. They passed over even more machines, some X-shaped and miles across, digging inside craters. They passed over white sprays streaming from craters. They passed over machines that produce great clouds to hide their operations. They passed over funnel holes of various sizes, their steeply angled sides perfectly smooth. And they passed over openings into the moon's interior. They passed over craters with tunnels bored into their sides and craters with tiled bottoms. They passed over things for which there are no words – tube-like things, tower-like things, castle-like things, bridge-like things, wall-like things, crystal-like things. There were glass domes, some ten miles wide, each able to fit an entire Earth town inside. And sitting in plain sight on the moon's surface was a variety of spacecraft – some round, some triangular, some cigar-shaped – and Oumuamua.

Most frightening of all they passed over giant bi-pedal creatures wearing no space suits, nothing at all for that matter, spindly, deceptively frail-looking creatures that cast long shadows across the moon's surface. Zak fumbled for his tic tacs then remembered his physical body was at The Institute.

"On to the dark side," Matt said with a stab of terror in his gut. The viewers headed for the side that never faces a rapidly-spinning Earth. It requires an unfathomable amount of energy to make that happen. Matt, Zak, Cathy and Chase gulped. The dark side was anything but dark. When it faces the sun it is as bright as the light side. When it isn't it looks like New York City at night. In the moon's stark lethality they forgot to breathe, unable to speak, a sickening wave of terror welled up from their bellies, scared they would be spotted by beings they knew to be evil. Beings with the power to prevent a satellite the size of a planet from showing anything but one face to a rapidly spinning Earth. They had stumbled on the reason the moon doesn't revolve and knew if they explored it further it would be the last thing they would ever see, remote viewing or not.

LEAVE . . . FORGET WHAT YOU HAVE SEEN . . . DO NOT RETURN . . .

DO NOT RETURN!

"Did you hear that!" Cathy screamed.

"They can see us . . . Chase shrieked.

Out of the moon streaked an alien tanker making its regular run to Earth to siphon another three million gallons from Canada's high-alpine Falcon Lake, much to the consternation of the Canadian deputy prime minister helpless to do anything about it but call a press conference. It never made the six o'clock news. It angled into the heavens then made a turn straight for them.

"OMG*!* OMG*!*" Chase cried. The massive thing glided toward them blocking out the stars, the large round otherworldly green, blue, yellow and red lights on its sides pulsing alien. An energy beam sent rocks and orange dust into the thin lunar air.

"They can see us!" Matt screamed. "There!" They made for a nearby entrance into the moon, a tunnel bored into the wall of a crater.

"This is exactly why I don't go into outer space!" Zak mumbled.

Back at The Institute Zak was wetting his pants.

Into the moon they dove. A mysterious green luminescence came from everywhere and nowhere.

“OMG!” Chase gasped looking back. Three red orbs were tailing them. A lunopolis stretched in every direction as far as the eye could see. It was impossible to know which way was up if indeed there was one. There were high-rises, side-rises, diagonal-rises, hundreds of crafts traveling to and fro, spaceports, power plants, manufacturing plants, residences, vast storage tanks and all manner of things unknown.

It explained everything. Why the moon has always been associated with evil. Why the sharp spike in criminal activity on Earth during each and every full moon. Why the pagan calendar is a lunar calendar and not a solar calendar. Why its two seasons marked by the winter and summer solstices are celebrated by witches. Why the moon rang like a bell in middle C for half an hour after the Apollo 12 astronauts crashed their spent Lunar Module into it after taking off. And why zoom video of the moon often shows mysterious holographic waves sweeping across it. A hollow moon! A metallic sphere. Why the same half always faces Earth. A camouflaged base. Not too far for quick trips back and forth yet not so close as to be easily observed by Earthlings. At least until now when any Earth kid can buy an obscenely powerful telescope or zoom camera and see the lights and holographic waves and things.

“Enough!” Cathy screamed. “Let’s get outa here.” Matt’s heart pounded. A gray was peering at them from a high-rise. They sped through the lunopolis two thousand miles from end to end past its monstrous plasma engine which is refueled during every solar eclipse, when gigantic spacecraft as wide as the moon and much longer draw plasma from the sun, able to travel unobserved between the sun and the backside of the moon during the eclipses. The reason the moon is locked into a facing orbit around Earth at exactly the distance and ecliptic plane it is. To hide the comings and goings.

Through the moon's thick inner and outer metallic shells they passed until they were back in the starry void. Behind them a string of crafts streamed from the moon like murder hornets from a rattled nest.

"Ollie was right," Matt cried. "The astronauts *did* get kicked off! He said they aren't talking much .... that they're following orders. They're military men."

"Yeah, unlawful orders," Cathy said.

"They don't want to be dead," said Zak.

○ ○ ○

As they approached Earth the Aurora Borealis shone like a spectral torch through a circular hole in the Earth's crust hundreds of miles across. The viewers had stumbled onto the reason no aircraft are permitted to come within a certain distance of the poles even when it is the shortest distance between cities and why no one is allowed to trek or snowmobile to them either. Why Google Earth blocks out the poles. Why tropical plants are found in icebergs, why many tropical birds fly north in the winter instead of south, why colored pollen covers the earth for thousands of miles around the poles, why it is warmer at the poles than 600 to 1000 miles away from them, why the north wind in the Arctic gets warmer as one sails north beyond 70° latitude, and why anyone who tries to organize a private expedition into the inner earth always ends up dead or missing just before the expedition begins. Don't believe it? Organize an expedition.

It is impossible to make out as an entrance at all if one flies across the Earth into it. Its slope is so gradual as to go unnoticed. Just as one does not notice the earth's curvature when standing upon it, neither does one notice it upon entering the hollow earth. Before they knew it the ice was gone and they were over the temperate lush green expanse of Inner Earth, Admiral Byrd's "Land Beyond The Poles," to where the Vikings disappeared 600 years ago and the ancient Mayans before them and so many others.

The Hopi Indians and other peoples tell of the Ant People (so named because they live underground) who saved them not once but at least twice from past world deluges including The Great Flood. The Ant People escorted the Hopi into a subterranean world with a smokey twilight sun where they found refuge and sustenance until it was safe to return. And they helped to protect them from the Snake People and Lizard People who also dwelled therein.

The truth about Earth is the domain of scientists, Christians, zealots, spies, scoundrels and explorers (no connections). Matt resolved to pull the curtain from the wizard. It would be dangerous. It was something to explore for another time. Who knew who or what they might find there. They knew somehow it would not be the core of iron they had been told.

Through the moonlight around the big blue marble they soared, over people sleeping far below and into the dawn over villages, rivers and hills, over forests, valleys and glens and over deserts, moors and lakes they raced the turning Earth into day where children played kissed by the morning sun. They soared over glaciers, alpine fields and snow-covered peaks. They soared over sweeping plains and over an ocean that glittered like silver coins where they encountered a frolicking humpback whale.

"Something's wrong," Matt uttered.

"He's right," Cathy said. "I'm feel it too."

They were being tracked by the moon's inhabitants.

"Let's go to Mars," Cathy said, "we have to ditch 'em." So they headed for Mars not knowing what they might find there.

As they neared the Red Planet a lander bearing the British Union Jack was entering orbit after a seven month journey. Upon arriving the first thing they noticed was that the Martian sky wasn't red. It was blue just like Earth's. Only the planet's surface was red. Why like the moon photos had every NASA photo of Mars since the 1960s until as of lately always been doctored to color the sky red? The planet's great valleys, mountains, hills, ranges and dry seas might have been any desert on Earth but for the vast scars they bore. Monolithic wounds bore testament to an ancient cataclysm. Mass extinction events scientists call them. Matt remembered the hologram story in the mound and what the Devil had said about Mars having once been like Earth. And what Dr. Brainard had said about the Martian meteorites having a high level of Xenon 129 from a nuclear catastrophe.

They passed over eight pyramids in the same sizes and arrangement as those in Egypt, a mirror image of them, before coming to the largest, a twin of the Great Pyramid of Cheops.

Zak bubbled over being where no human had been before. But he was wrong. The Americans have a secret space program and travel between Earth and Mars and take a dim view of visitors. Any visitors.

The spies hovered at the apex of the great pyramid. A panorama of endless barren desert plains stretched before them. Zak touched the polished limestone casing which showed signs of blast damage.

A gust of warm dry CO2 wind picked an object off the surface and swept it high into the blue Martian sky where it danced like a kite against the strange-behaving fallen angel-infested potato-shaped artificial satellite Phobos, whose inhabitants also take a dim view of visitors as evidenced by the destroyed Russian spaceprobe, the Phobos 2, which flew too close.

Cathy hung back. She was frightened now. Earth was so very far. Mars was nothing like the Moon where the Earth had been a big blue marble watching over and comforting with its motherly presence. Earth was but a faint speck of light even if they knew where to look which they didn't. The cold empty vacuum of space was soul-chilling.

"I don't believe this place," said Zak.

"Don't try to understand it," Cathy droned.

"Why do you think they sent us here?" asked Zak.

" 'Cause we trashed Earth. Now we're looking for a new planet to trash."

"What's that hum?" asked Chase.

"I think we should leave," Cathy said.

As they glided across the Martian landscape Chase glanced back. A strange broad beam of purplish-magenta light rose straight upward from the megalith's capstone disappearing high into the sky.

In the distance a sculpted humanoid face rose from the sands like a Mayan mound. Taller than the Eiffel Tower it stretched for miles gazing stoically at Earth fifty-two million miles away. They had arrived at Cydonia and would learn only later of its cryptic mathematical messages all kept hush-hush by scientists following strict orders that came from the same nasty people from who General Anders took his; the Illuminati, thirteen generational satanic families whose many homes are all haunted, who consider themselves the devil's elite, architects of a one-world government ready to step in and take control led by a single being, the one the Christians call the Antichrist, when the time is right. Like the devil-worshipping Hitler, intent on world domination and exterminating its population. Loathsome insects who when mankind's protectors, the beings who put the outer barrier into place return, will be put down like rabid dogs.

Debris fields everywhere betrayed the existence of a destroyed civilization. Humanoid and non-humanoid remains alike, the skeletons of bizarre unidentified creatures, broken remnants of machines, gears, weapons, tools and vehicles lay scattered everywhere. An underground megalopolis the size of ten Los Angeleses lay covered by the Martian sands emitting an infrared heat signature. A translucent white-ribbed tunnel glinted in the sun as it emerged from the ground snaking its way along the base of a low range of mountains, the ruins of a mass transit system. A vehicle appeared trapped inside.

"What happened here?" asked Cathy.

"Whatever it was we missed it," Matt said.

Smack in the middle of the Martin desert a human-like form sat motionless on a rock, an arm extended. Not the only such form. There were more in the distance. They drew to within a hundred yards of the frozen blackened form with the feeling that a trap door had opened in their bellies.

"Dude, I *really* don't believe *this*," said Chase.

It was a woman looking like any Earth woman with her shoulder-length hair. What fate had befallen her, how long ago and why? Matt had seen such an all black form in a photo from when the Iraqis invaded Kuwait in 1990; the figure of a charbroiled Iraqi, his features frozen like a sculpture in a wax museum. Frozen by a fuel-air bomb that superheated the air to an aerosol cloud of 5,000° Fahrenheit in less than a second. Mars; a death planet.

"I wonder who she is," said Zak hesitantly, fearing she and the others like her might be alive.

"We should leave now," Cathy warned.

The wind began to howl like a wounded banshee. The temperature plummeted as a lightning-embedded dust storm approached, its raw power reaching to the edge of space. A beam of intense blue light reached upward.

"WATCH OUT!" Chase screamed. With a mighty crash a red dust cloud rose. In the debris lay a crumpled metal panel bearing the British Union Jack. It was the lander they had passed. It would be many years before the Russians, Chinese and Brits would figure out what was happening to their landers.

Truth be told, a secret space program, an ultra-covert black op mission to Mars, had placed a colony of Americans there years earlier. Thirty U.S. Air Force personnel, male and female, designated 'Non-Terrestrial Officers,' were sent with orders to find Martian technology, primarily Martian weapons technology. The kind that would have devastating consequences were another world government such as The Middle Kingdom (China), or Russia, to lay hold of it first. And lo and behold they had found it, ensuring the U.S. as the dominant force on the planet. The remote viewers gulped as they passed over a colony of fifty-six white interconnected habitation modules, each bearing the American flag.

"There's one more place to go," Cathy announced.

"Where?" Matt asked.

"The Outer Barrier."

• • • •

Four billion miles from Earth and a little beyond Neptune, a glimmering barrier of purplish-pink light with many never before seen colors stretched before them, a sight which made the Aurora Borealis look like a faded washed-out watercolor.

They stopped in awe and wonder. A force repelled them they knew would allow them to go no further. The barrier extended on each side to infinity. They sensed it was intelligently created.

"I wonder what heaven's like?" Cathy whimsied.

"I asked Father Herzl that once," said Matt. "He said, 'Just think of things you like to do most in the whole world or would like to. Then imagine it a thousand times better and being able to do it forever young and healthy and never having to grow old. It would be an awful shame to miss out on that,' he said."

Chapter 42 – RIPLEYS' REVENGE

HAD HIS CAR NOT died on him suddenly while patrolling the deserted stretch out by the arroyo Sheriff Cliff Cain like most would never have looked up. Humans never look up. We are far too absorbed with what's under our noses. His tires crackled to a stop. His department radio was dead. His cell phone too. Oddly his Streamlight tactical flashlight into which he had put fresh batteries the day before was dead too. Even the second hand on his Casio his wife had given him the year before for his forty-first birthday had stopped.

The fearless sheriff stepped into an eerie void. Where had all the stars gone? It was too quiet. He suddenly felt dizzy. His first thought was that the ground was moving, like being stopped at a traffic light beside a long truck that is creeping slowly forward causing you to think you're moving when you're not. He looked up then dove headfirst through the open window, cranked it shut, locked the doors and cowered. It took ten minutes for the silent five-mile-long isosceles triangle edged with orange lights to pass. It changed colors as it passed overhead then turned blood red.

The glow from the town went out as the power grid winked out. The mothership hung over the valley like a lid. The closest military base, Arnold AFB, scrambled fighters with orders not to engage. The world's militaries have learned not to mess with motherships, some say because of what happened in 1947. In retaliation for the downing of three flying disks the EDBs downed more than six hundred military and commercial aircraft worldwide in the eighty-four day period between May 9th and July 31th, information kept secret from the public to this day.

And there was what happened in 1952. In the seventeen days from July 12 and July 29 UFOs buzzed the nation's capitol. A formation flew over the White House, the Capitol Building and the Pentagon before thousands of stunned eyewitnesses. Captured on 8mm movie film, SAUCERS SWARM OVER CAPITOL the *Cedar Rapids Gazette* headline screamed. Lt. William Patterson's F-94 Starfire jet fighter chased one below 1,000 feet but it made his fighter seem like it was standing still. The *Washington Post* headline blared SAUCER OUTRAN JET, PILOT REVEALS. It seemed a scene straight out of *War of the Worlds*.

An army of grays stormed the Kozacky estate. Only a thin panc of glass separated Cathy from two grays. A guttural scream issued from her throat.

Through dissecting millions of abducted humans the grays had learned how to tap into human minds and harvest memories and plant thoughts, images and memories. They were planting their destructive thoughts into Matt, Cathy, Chase and Zak.

There are five types of angels – common, guardian, ministering, destroying and fallen.

The standoff lasted two minutes, the amount of time needed to recall the grays to the ship. The luminous form of a heavenly angel wearing a belt of gold bearing a flaming sword hovered in the night sky. Substation by substation the electric grid flicked back on. No match for a destroying angel, fifty beams of focused white light reached down from the ship. The grays rode them into the craft. The mothership silently moved slowly away then in a cerulean blue streak disappeared into the heavens. The invaders would leave a calling card behind. A quick-forming, fast-moving hurricane had mysteriously formed in the Atlantic and was heading out to sea when it suddenly reversed course and made a turn through the Bermuda Triangle. It caught the government's powerful scattered HAARP microwave facilities which control the weather and steer the paths of hurricanes away from the East Coast off guard. Ten hours later Chickasaw lay in ruins.

Chapter 43 – THE EXPEDITION

MATT contacted the Institute of Archaeology of Belize which quickly organized an expedition to the underwater city. As a reward he was allowed to keep any one treasure. To the amazement of the government officials who must have thought his cornbread not done in the middle instead of claiming the ruby Buddha or the egg-shaped rough diamond or the like, he chose only a ring bearing the Star of David and the real name of God.

Chapter 44 – GOODBYE KITTY

It ain't what you don't know that gets you into trouble. It's what you know for sure that just ain't so.

Mark Twain

"IF YOUR BOY'S not here in five minutes I'm pullin' the plug," blurted the steel plant superintendent.

Sweat poured off Father Brainard's brow as he peered around nervously. He had arranged the end of summer session school field trip at Matt's urging for the purpose of getting above the blast furnace, an area off limits to visitors. It had taken the calling in of many favors.

Aunt Nell pulled her Subaru to the front of the plant. Matt got out. As she drove away a silver Crown Victoria screeched to a stop. Two men of Asian descent got out and began in Matt's direction. Matt broke into a run.

"They're coming," Matt screamed.

"PLANT SECURITY, CODE RED, CODE RED!" the burly super screamed into his walkie-talkie as sirens wailed.

"This way," he shouted. He hurried them past an automated control center with its banks of computers and rows of overhead displays. They passed giant iron cauldrons pouring molten steel that showered domes of orange sparks that bounced along the concrete floor before dimming into nothingness. They passed fleeing workers who moments before had been toiling in their red hard hats under banks of high-intensity lamps surrounded by noisy, heavy iron machinery spewing glowing orange ropes of molten steel onto the plant floor like a devil's golden lasso, coiling themselves neatly without help from human hands.

They followed the bobbing blue hard hat up the steel gangway past the red DANGER – DO NOT ENTER sign suspended from a chain to an overhead catwalk where Boots, the plant tabby cat whose job was to keep the rats at bay, hugged their heels. There was a commotion. A well-placed punch to the solar plexus left the superintendent gasping on the catwalk. Matt pulled the ring from his pocket and held it over the cauldron. The agent flung himself across the railing as he grabbed for it over the superintendent's bent form accidentally kicking Boots. YEEOWWWWWWW! The cat vanished into the iron cauldron in a fiery flash. The agent grabbed for Matt, his sweaty fingers clinging to the railing, his other hand clutching Matt's forearm. Popping the ring into his mouth Matt reached down and grabbed the agent's shirt. The look in the man's eyes was that of a terrified animal's. His sleeve tore and he joined Boots.

The other agent stood at the far end of the catwalk, his assault rifle raised.

Plant security arrived. "NO, NO, NO, DON'T SHOOT, DON'T SHOOT," the super shouted to the guards. The outnumbered agent bent slowly and with one arm raised lowered his weapon to the grating. He had been part of a two-man team monitoring and recording Matt's every movement for weeks.

"At least people won't be chasing me now," Matt said.

"Do not expect on that," said the agent.

“Oh,” Matt disappointedly replied, envisioning he and his mother spending their lives under fake identities in a witness protection program in Boring, Oregon. Yes, there really is such a place.

“Tell me your name,” Matt said.

“You could tell them you saw the ring destroyed,” Father Brainard proffered.

“Call me Quan. That is not possible.”

Two days later Matt, Chase, Cathy and Zak sat on the balustrade behind Cathy’s and Zak’s house gazing at the supermoon, that uncommon full moon at its closest to Earth, seemingly close enough to reach out and touch. The moon had lost its allure, lost its romance in the way four kids that tempestuous summer their youthful naiveties had lost. They had grown up far too fast. None were who they had started out the summer nor would ever be again. They were battle hardened and tested with street smarts now.

“O Romeo, swear not by the moon, the inconstant-fallen angel-infested-one-side-always-unnaturally-facing-Earth-moon that never changes in its circled orb,” Chase laughed, for he still could laugh. He was the only one of them who still had both his parents. “Who ever heard of a moon that doesn’t revolve? That’s like a sun that doesn’t shine, rain that doesn’t fall, wind that doesn’t blow. Why aren’t astronomers up in arms? Lame ducks all,” he railed.

“They don’t want to be dead,” said Zak.

He turned to Matt. “It’s time to give it up, dude. We’ve done enough. You don’t know when to quit.”

“Ah, that’s what I like about him,” Cathy said. “He doesn’t quit.”

Zak peered through the viewer of his Celestron C14 Edge HD. At 600 power it was possible to make out some of the things they had encountered – lunar towers, machinery, lights, arches, walls, spacecraft, glass domes, but just barely.

"Everything's starting to make sense," Chase said. "When it was 1970 and you wanted to take stuff out of photos, there wasn't any photoshopping so you would've had to do it the old way – airbrush them out. It must've been easier airbrushing in black and white. NASA – that stands for **N**o **A**liens **S**een **A**nywhere, and **N**ever **A** **S**traight **A**nswer."

A certain NASA director was once asked off the record, "Is anything NASA's ever told the public the truth?" "No. Nothing," he replied.

Zak found more. "I found the oldest moon photo I could, an old daguerreotype, that's an old image on a silvered copper plate, from 1851. I digitally compared it with a recent photo. The shapes of some of the craters are different. What's that say? And some craters have disappeared altogether.

"The president said we're going to put a base on the Moon. She said it on TV. There won't be any moon base. Somebody should tell her."

"She's a mushroom, remember?" said Chase.

"It's just talk," Zak said. "They're avoiding the moon. They're talking about going to the Asteroid Belt to look for alien technology. But they'll say it's to look for rare metals."

"And you know this *how* . . . ?" Cathy demanded.

"None ya biz," Zak replied.

"You've been hacking government computers again, haven't you? You promised. You're on probation. REMEMBER?"

Matt reached into his pocket and produced the ring.

"You still have it?" Cathy asked. "I thought you got rid of it."

"I accidentally swallowed it when I tried to help the agent who fell into the vat."

She scanned nervously for Chinese agents.

"Yuck. I'm never touching that ring!" said Chase.

"Devil Trash . . . what do you and the other demons fear?"

The devil materialized. "Prayer," he answered snidely.

At first Matt wasn't sure he heard correctly. It was hard to picture such powerful, evil creatures, as advanced as they are hideous, fearing anything.

"Mad Marie warned us," said the devil. You would have become the richest person in the world — the world's first trillionaire had we not interfered," he said with an evil smirk.

"*Trillionaire?* . . . " Matt reeled . . . *trillionaire?*

"We have to have a reason to look into something if we are to learn about it," said the devil. "We are not all-knowing. Thanks to your mother going to Mad Marie we knew about you. We always read our customers to learn if they or their children will ever become a threat to us. You and your computer science teacher would have created the first self-aware computer. We like AI. We have plans for it. And you would have used your wealth against us. We could not allow that. You remember Mr. Saba, don't you?, your computer science teacher — drowned in an unfortunate weekend sailboating accident? That was our handiwork."

Matt seethed. He wondered if being a trillionaire would make him Illuminati. No, of course not. How braindead would somebody have to be to sell his or her soul for temporary riches in a broken down world he asked himself.

"Do the Funky Chicken," Matt commanded. And don't stop — ever."

○ ○ ○

One of the most awkward situations a girl can be in is to have two suitors on her doorstep at the same time.

Matt, Cathy, Zak and Chase were on the patio when Cathy's aunt appeared with a boy in tow wearing a gray military service dress uniform with humongous black chevrons on each sleeve and spit-polished shoes so shiny Matt could see his face in them.

"Who are *you*?" demanded the fit stranger, his cap tucked neatly into his armpit.

"Who are *you*?" Matt shot.

"Her boyfriend."

"I thought she had better taste."

"Kiss off. What are you doing here anyway?" the stranger hissed.

"Why don't you ask your girlfriend," Matt sneered.

The stranger turned to Cathy who was looking quite pale. "What's *he* doing here?"

"He's just a friend," Cathy said.

The words stung.

"Why don't you leave *friend,"* the stranger hissed.

"Why don't *you* leave."

"Can you leave us alone, Matt?" Cathy said softly.

Through the circle lead glass windows he could see them arguing.

He strained to hear . . . "You don't own me!"

"I thought we had something."

"We do. But not what you want it to be right now. I can't be that girl."

"Because of him?"

Cathy pulled the window closed. Matt breathed three deep sighs and gazed at the supermoon.

Soon she joined him. "So, I'm a friend?" Matt's eyes drifted to the circles.

"He's gone. Geez, you're worse than him! What makes you think you're anything more?

"What do you want from me anyhow?" she said in a suffocated whisper.

The answer stuck in his throat.

In a single summer he had learned about life, love and death. Life – the choices we make; love – one of those choices; death – a coward dies a thousand, the brave one.

Cathy breathed a troubled sigh. Sometimes we think we're in love when we're not. Other times, we aren't sure, which is the same as we're not. And other times . . . .

"Zak, forget what I said about hacking. I need you to do something," Cathy said.

Chapter 45 – NANOS HERE, NANOS THERE, NANOS EVERYWHERE; SKIN TO DIE FOR

"I felt a great disturbance in the force. As if millions of voices suddenly cried out in terror and were suddenly silenced."
– Obi Wan

ZAK KNEW he had hacked something that could get him killed. The CIA takes a very dim view of fifteen-year old boys hacking into its computers. He learned 21 trillion dollars, an unimaginable sum, had been funneled illegally into secret black projects — the reverse-engineering of crashed UFOs, a secret space program, a secret base on Mars, secret U.S. Deep Underground Military Bases (DUMBs) and the supersonic mag lev rail system that connects them, secret FEMA internment camps, secret global chemtrail spraying, secret weather and earthquake warfare programs and God only knows what else — things the powers that be do not want the public to know about. It was far worse than the Glomar Explorer.

He learned President Kennedy had demanded everything on UFOs be given him. The response from someone known only as MJ-1 had been that it was need to know and he didn't need to know, to which the President replied, "I am the President of the United States and your Commander in Chief. I am giving you an order. If you do not meet the date and time of my order I will hold the press conference of not only this century but of all centuries." Two months later he was dead.

Zak learned it officially began in 1947 on a ranch near Roswell, New Mexico when the base public information officer issued a press release stating personnel from the Roswell Army Air Field had recovered a "flying disc." The Air Force quickly went into damage control, changing the object to a weather balloon. Since then the darkest of black op programs has reverse- engineered the weather balloon. He learned the U.S. has a fleet of reverse- engineered "weather balloons" like those belonging to the EDBs, able to be used in another false flag attack like 9/11. The report stated that when attacked by fake "aliens," the world will accept the unthinkable – a one world government to combat the threat. A world government owned and run by the satanic Illuminati. Getting away scot-free with killing an American president had emboldened them. Zak became sick when he read a memo bragging, "The many loose ends left dangling at 9/11 don't matter because as usual there is nothing the mentally weak masses can do. We are untouchable." The memo went on to list some of the loose ends:

1. Use of standard gray military variant aircraft with no windows, no airline colors, logos or schemes; as reported by eyewitnesses including the police and fire boats they flew over in the harbor;
2. No airline crash debris at the Pentagon except for a cruise missile turbine;
3. The rapid-sequence controlled demolition explosions reported by NYFD firefighters and witnesses as the buildings fell;
4. Cell phones don't function at the altitudes at which the calls were represented as having been made;
5. After landing at the temporarily vacated Westover Air Reserve Base, all of the scripted calls placed by the pax complied with the hijack drill scenario given to them except pax Ceecee Lyles', who was able to warn her husband by telling him, "It's a frame," which she whispered while

she pretended to fumble with her headset as she removed it, which our handler missed (he has since been recycled);

6. The cell phone calls were noted by their loved ones as having a noticeable strange absence of any background sounds as if they were in a room somewhere.

Zak found a list of five thousand dead and missing scientists and whistleblowers, among them a few astronomers and people marked for assassination, including some authors. He learned over eight hundred secret FEMA concentration camps have been readied, many underground, stocked with 1.5 billion with a 'b' rounds of 9mm hollow-point bullets, millions of plastic coffins and guillotines! Guillotines?

Zak ran across a document codenamed *Indigo Skyfold* marked COSMIC SECRET – EYES ONLY. It detailed how American planes are spraying the world's skies with deadly substances known as chemtrails (Stratospheric Aerosol Geoengineering) which unlike contrails don't dissipate within thirty seconds. Instead they spread from horizon to horizon forming a haze that remains the sky for up to twenty hours. He learned planes fitted with special nozzles spray a poisonous brew of nano-aluminum particles, lithium, strontium, barium, chromium, cad-mium, dried human red blood cells, mold spores, radioactive thorium, ethylene dibromide, yellow fungal mycotoxins and plastic polymer fibers that cause cancer, brain dysfunction, heart attacks, autism, stroke, headaches, fatigue, asthma and many other illnesses. Worse yet the haze contains smart nano matter designed to infiltrate peoples' bodies and is the source of strange new matter in their bloodstreams and cells seen swimming around inside their eyeballs. He learned that the millions of tons of aluminum dust blanketing the world's forests is incendiary.

“It’s the cause of lightning without thunder,” Zak announced. The nano-aluminum acts as a conductor. Blue skies are gone. A thing of the past. Haze is the new blue. They took away the blue skies. Weather modification’s only one purpose.” Zak found another is to deploy nanoparticles into humans for the depopulation written on the Georgia Guidestones. The report stated it’s everywhere – in the air, the rain, the food and the water. The dried genetically-engineered human blood possibly for DNA manipulation was particularly worrisome. It was all so overwhelming.

“They’re calling it ‘smart dust,’ ” Zak groaned. “And now there’s new types of clouds and ‘thunderstorm asthma’ and ‘firenadoes and ‘soft sunshine’ and ‘pyrocumulus clouds!’ This is crazy. What’s next, ‘aluminum rain’?”

The team discovered the silly scientists were hard at work again, this time having created the term “eruptive fires” to describe the new phenomenon of the world’s forests mysteriously spontaneously bursting into flames all over the place. Accordingly to the silly scientists eruptive forest fires happen when there is a sudden appearance out of nowhere of combustible forest gas that suddenly mysteriously ignites. They conveniently forgot to mention from where this combustible gas supposedly originated and the supposed ignition source. Like that asteroid that knocked the moon out of the Earth. Move to the back of the class. If it looks like a duck and quacks like a duck it is probably a duck. But the silly scientists would have us believe the duck is an obese seagull and that quack you heard was an atmospheric anomaly, which is how fake science works.

Sadly it seemed science, which had always been about gathering truth, had become about misrepresenting it.

"Sorry I asked," Cathy sighed.

They discovered the nano fibers blossom and replicate in human bodies when exposed to certain 5G cellular microwave frequency and the new WiFi frequency.

"No, our government wouldn't do that," Cathy said.

"The government's not calling the shots," Zak moaned. "The Federal Reserve Bank isn't even federal. It's no more federal than Federal Express. America doesn't own itself anymore. The devil Illuminati's bankers do. And get this, nobody even knows who the Federal Reserve is! It's a secret society! That traitor creep President Woodrow Wilson sold us out."

"You're paranoid," said Matt.

Zak took them to his garage lab.

"Look in the scope." One by one Matt, Cathy and Chase peered into the microscope. One by one they drew back in horror.

"It's called Morgellons," said Zak.

"What are they?" asked Cathy, running her fingers through her hair with shaking hands.

Hollow multi-colored cobweb-like fibers, some blue, some black, some red, some white, and other strange matter were waving like snakes and there were strange super-tiny otherworldly-looking metallic objects. One by one they drew samples of their own blood and saw the same thing. Then he took them outside and pointed a flashlight into the night. They were shocked. The beam filled with small white particles that resembled dandruff. They sent them off to a lab. The lab returned it marked 'HAZARDOUS MATERIAL' with stern words for not having sent it marked such.

"This is nuts," Matt spouted. "The pilots who're spraying this stuff are spraying themselves and their families."

Even as he spoke a brave chemtrail pilot over Torrevieja Spain was turning his sprayers on and off forming a dotted line across the sky to show people they aren't contrails.

"It's illegal too," said Zak. "U.S. Code 50 prohibits the use of chemical agents on a civilian populace. Somebody needs to go to prison."

"It's in our brains!" Chase bawled. "When they flip enable in 5g it's curtains. We need to tell somebody!"

"This can't be happening," Cathy whimpered. "Somebody tell me this isn't happening!"

"You sound like Katie Loveland," said Matt.

They weren't alone. People everywhere began to complain of floaters, tiny translucent cobwebs, specks, squiggles and other floating matter inside their eyeballs. The quacks were quick to dismiss them as perfectly normal. Fatigue, loss of coordination, loss of concentration and illness set in. The nanos caused skin to hold moisture causing it to glow. People loved their supple skin but sadly because of the aluminum bombardment began to grow dumber and dumber and soon began to forget things and eventually not care about anything at all.

Because of Zak the team had begun to catch on to things. They began to detect things that were happening all around them that people don't know about. Things if they knew about they would be rioting in the streets.

"Out with it. What else do you know?" Cathy coaxed.

"Ask yourself. What kind of threat would cause the United States to bankrupt itself spraying the skies of the entire planet daily? Do you have any idea what costs! It's the war against the AAVs. Chemtrails mess with their cloaking. They've been seen following chemtrail aircraft and erasing the chemtrail. AAVs don't always show up on radar anymore. When they can't hide the chemtrail spraying anymore they'll say it's to combat global warming but it's really multi-purpose."

Zak produced a document stamped **COSMIC SECRET: EYES ONLY -** ***OPERATION INDIGO SKYFOLD –***

MISSION OBJECTIVE: WITHOUT THESE FLIGHTS THE EDBs' TECHNOLOGICAL WEAPONS COULD EASILY PENETRATE AMERICA'S AIRSPACE AT WILL. WE ARE DEDICATED AND COMMITTED TO KEEPING OUR ALLIES SAFE FROM THE SAME SKYWARD THREATS SO WE EXTENDED THE ARM OF PROTECTION OF THIS DEFENSIVE ATMOSPHERIC WEAPONS SHIELD TO THOSE COUNTRIES WHO SUPPORT OUR EFFORTS.

Zak had stumbled upon a dangerous secret. And he had uncovered that worldwide chemtrail spraying bankrupted America the way the Great Wall bankrupted China. A desperate effort to make it harder for cloaked AAVs to suddenly appear over the White House or major world cities and it was working for the most part, though the White House would still have to go on alert from time to time, telling the public the cause was a flock of birds, as if the world's greatest military is unable to distinguish between a flock of birds and a craft, a massive triangular-shaped craft whose vague outline is barely visible to the naked eye through the nano-aluminum particulate haze, but only to those who bother to look up.

"It's the perfect delivery vehicle for the Illuminati's bio weapons against us, too — The Georgia Guidestones, remember?"

Then Zak revealed a disturbing Defense Department report — CONPLAN 8888-11, Counter-Zombie Dominance, the U.S. military's plan for responding to a zombie apocalypse.[9] He found the military and law enforcement train for it, the "zombies" being a panic-stricken populace, the reason for the 1.5 billion bullets.

• • •

"The Gulf Stream has stopped! Now what do we do?"

As if all that wasn't terrifying enough Zak hacked a CIA report on a coming apocalypse. Perhaps the disaster the frantic ex-Area 51 employee was referring to when he called into Coast to Coast AM radio. The panicked caller, his voice trembling with fear sputtered, *"They're...they're gonna...they'll triangulate on this position really really soon...what we're thinking of as aliens...they're extra-dimensional beings [trembling, sobbing]...that an earlier precursor of the space program made contact with...uh...they are not what they claim to be [sobbing]...uh...they have infiltrated a lot of aspects of the military establishment particularly the Area 51...uh...the disasters that are coming...the military [sobbing]...I'm sorry…the government knows about them…and there's a lot of safe areas in the world that they could begin moving the population to…now, but they want those major population centers wiped out [sobbing]…so that the few that are left will be more easily controllable…" [more sobbing] [losing transmission] … [transmission lost] . . .*

Somewhere someone or something very powerful had interrupted the station's satellite feed knocking the station off the air — the Men in Black hybrids?

○ ○ ○

> *"It's all lies. Everything's lies. Nothing's the truth anymore."*

In still another NASA reversal, Zak discovered that after years of denying the existence of a large body approaching our solar system, NASA announced its appearance; a planetary body ten times bigger than Earth headed this way — the purpose of the Vatican's Lucifer Telescope. Scientists believe the gravitational force of Eris as NASA calls it, Planet 9, Planet 10, Planet X or Nibiru has already begun knocking the solar system out of kilter. The Earth's axis is tilting to the east. Two ancient Middle Eastern cultures – the Babylonians and Sumerians (the fallen angel trash) tell of a body that comes once every 3,450 to 3,600 years accompanied by a swarm of meteoroids. The team wondered if it could be responsible for the slowing of the Gulf Stream and the North Atlantic Current and the meteoroid epidemic, earthquakes and awakening volcanoes.

Zak's CIA report stated the gravitational force of Planet X when it arrives someday will cause an abrupt poleshift and the breakdown of rescue and government functioning, the breakdown of the food system and vehicular transport, giant tsunamis, coastal cities disappearing beneath the sea within thirty days, earthquakes, volcanic eruptions, mega-hurricanes, lethal solar radiation, 200 mile per hour winds and meteor impacts.

The report stated the increase in meteoroid near-misses, earthquakes and volcanic eruptions has begun with one or more major impacts a certainty soon. The report advised military and intelligence people to move to the Ozarks.

Another report revealed that researchers have been busy creating viruses to reduce the planet's population.

Finally he happened across a DARPA report on super soldiers where he discovered the giants of old are being brought back to life as genetically- engineered super soldiers who will unleash a reign of terror upon the Earth on militaries and civilians alike. They are like zombies in that bullets to their torsos won't bring them down. They are lightning-fast and best killed with heavy-grain solid copper bullets to the brain. Even lead or copper-jacketed lead bullets don't do as well it seemed. A high-powered rifle with 600-grain bullets works nicely. They have a hive mind. If one finds you the rest know where you are. Giants got loose at a research facility, killing all twenty-nine scientists, blamed on a gas leak explosion.

"World War II isn't over," Cathy moaned. "Nanos, giants, Planet X, super bugs . . . is there any good news?"

"The Rolling Stones are still together," Chase laughed to keep from crying. "And you'll have soft skin, until they flip the switch anyhow."

“Look at this way,” said Matt. “We’re living a real life fairytale with witches, giants, fairies, mermaids, goblins and devils. Can somebody hook a brother up with some landmines? Sure some kid might run into the wrong place and lose a leg chasing after his Frisbee. Stuff happens. Freedom isn’t free.”

• • •

The next day they met with FBI new Unit Chief Justin Thyme and his new assistant, Corliss Chance.

“There’ll be times when you and only you will be able to effect a certain outcome,” the new unit chief said. “That makes you assets. You’ll never be able to enjoy being kids ever again. Is that what you want?” Somehow Matt knew he would never cry again. He wasn’t a boy anymore.

“I haven’t been a kid for awhile now,” he moaned.

“Are you trying to talk us out or what?” Cathy said.

“Just want you to know what you’re getting into. Here . . . each SCARE member wears one of these,” he said and with a click locked the black metal bracelets onto their wrists.

“Do they come in pastel pink?” Cathy asked.

“Very funny. They’re water resistant to ten bars. They’ll beep when you’re needed. By the way, you’re needed in D.C. next week. Agent Gomez’s memorial. After that asset training in Langley. You’ll each receive a special set of skills. Skills that will make you a nightmare to EDBs. The gates of the shadow world are opening.”

Chapter 46 – ET PHONE HOME–A LOCAL CALL

Truth is stranger than fiction, but it is because fiction is obliged to stick to possibilities; truth isn't.
Mark Twain

THE DOORBELL RANG. Two men flashed government IDs.

"I'm with the NSA," said one.

"I'm with the DIA," said the other.

"Are you here to arrest me?" Zak asked trembling.

"Relax, we want you to do something. We detected your snooping. Don't worry, we erased your tracks. You're the best hacker we've ever seen but even the best make a mistake," the NSA agent said.

The agents then spent the next thirty-seven minutes explaining that everything NHEs (Non-Human Entities) as they called them do, is to manipulate and deceive mankind. "They're not from other planets. We don't call them 'aliens' anymore. They come from Hell." The DIA agent gave Zak a reading list having to do with Er, Babylon, Sumer and devils. Then the NSA agent, the one who did most of the talking, said something unexpected. He said God is in control and many in the intel community know that the NHEs are demonic entities and not aliens. "They're fallen angels in the classic sense," the agent said. "Same beings, different lies." It was hard to believe they were words coming from government agents. It was politically incorrect to say the least. Government agents don't say such things. It was one thing to hear it from Father Herzl, another from spies. They weren't finished. The DIA agent added, "They can enter people's minds through magic rituals, seemingly benign stuff like biofeedback, drugs, Eastern mind-emptying and hypnosis. "It allows them a window to enter," the other added. "Tell people. Tell them the aliens are really fallen angels. We can't do it. It has to be your team. Don't worry, we've got your back.

"The power," said the NSA agent.

"Oh and remember, whenever demons or evil spirits attack you, be they ghosts, skin walkers, Bigfoot, extra-dimensional beings, UFOs or whatever … use the authority of the name of Jesus Christ. It's a power granted to all those who follow him. Order them away in Jesus' name. When they hear it, it stops them dead in their tracks. Think of it as a kind of interdimensional link. They don't want you knowing this. That's why the name Jesus is under attack.

"Come work for the Cyber Command,"said the agent. "We can use someone with your skills.

"Don't go anywhere tomorrow." As they were leaving, the agent turned. "Oh I almost forgot, we changed your name. You're Zachariah Smith now. And we weren't here."

When Zak balked at his new name the agent told him, "Just be glad we found you first. If the bad guys had found you, in the old days they'd've put plutonium under your bed. Now it's 'cause of death unknown.' "

Zak told the agents about the chemtrail spraying and the AAVs. They told him to keep his mouth shut about that.

The next day Katie Loveland showed up bright and early with a news wagon.

○ ○ ○

A man of his word Matt joined Young Marines. Having heard no praying Christian has ever been attacked by Bigfoot, abducted by aliens or possessed by demons, he became one and had just the adventure in mind to put it to the test — an expedition into the Inner Earth. The Feds found and removed a human skeleton so large it was terrible to behold from Malvic's Lavisham Cottage along with a gigantic book of copper pages, after they got past the vicious cassowaries that is, which put up a bloody fight. It was all handed over to the Smithsonian which promptly loaded them onto a barge along with thousands of other artifacts that disprove the theory of evolution and "miscataloged" them to the bottom of the Atlantic days before the FBI, acting on a search warrant issued by the attorney general's office, raided it and found records of everything it has been hiding for almost two hundred years. Its directors were marched out of the building in handcuffs on the six o'clock news.

Oxford scholars grateful for having had translated for them in thirty seconds an Elamite tablet that had gone untranslated for five thousand years went public with their thanks shedding tears of joy.

Four kids had survived the summer to pull back the demons' veil of lies. Deceptions greater than the great Trojan Horse and greater than D-Day when the Allies duped the Nazis into thinking the largest invasion in history was happening someplace else.

Their feet had been held to the fire but thanks to a friend in a most high place they were still standing. In the end it came down to who held the ring that forces demons to do things against their will.

Chase, the creator of *flip-hop*, became a successful rapper.

It is called PTSD (Post Traumatic Stress Disorder). Get moving. Don't isolate. You'll want to avoid other people. Don't, the stress counselor warned. To try to take her mind off the many deaths, her parents and her dog Cody, Cathy learned to fly helicopters, and she stopped saying, 'It's my world, you're just in it,' having found out it's the demons' world, for a little while longer anyway, and like the rest of us, she's just in it.

The death of Matt's and Cathy's and Zak's parents left them traumatized. They would never see them grow up. There is no one else you will ever trust completely. No one else who will ever love you unconditionally. There are friends and relatives and grandparents who will love you and take care of you and always be by your side. There are brothers and there are sisters. There are husbands and there are wives. But no one can love you like your parents. That's the plain hard truth.

There were days that were really hard and days that were less hard. After endless sleepless nights, many crying sessions and months and months of despair, Matt, Cathy and Zak would finally start feeling better. Slowly they started getting back to life. Eventually they would make their peace with it — kind of. In the end they decided to look at life as if it were a massively multi-player online role-playing game. Chase began to spend time with his parents.

Matt coined a couple new terms of his own — "World War D" and "supernatural sickness," that feeling you get when the freaky weird unexplained finds you — fear, nervousness, insomnia, inattentiveness, nausea, preoccupation, and distraction, but mostly a constant state of this can't be happening to me. Like being on a roller coaster without the fun. And with Zak's help, Matt entered the brave new world of ones and zeros.

An anonymous hacker codenamed Fritos hacked the Hubble telescope, pointed it at the moon and generated hundreds of ultra-zoom ultra-high-resolution images of things we aren't supposed to see and posted them for all the world to see. People began to watch the moon – and the skies – much to the dismay of beings who have always relied on humans never looking up.

Father Herzl launched an expedition to the Solomon Islands in search of living giants and found what he went looking for, last seen running for his life.

And they met Elvis who wasn't anything at all like they had thought.

In yet another embarrassing 180-degree about-face for NASA, in a news release it admitted "recent studies [*recent* studies*??*] confirm our moon [*our* moon*??*] does have an atmosphere after all." What, the astronauts didn't notice?

There would be many more NASA about-faces. And Zak came across a sketch made by Apollo 17 astronaut Eugene Cernan from lunar orbit showing the very same horizon glows and light rays they themselves had seen:

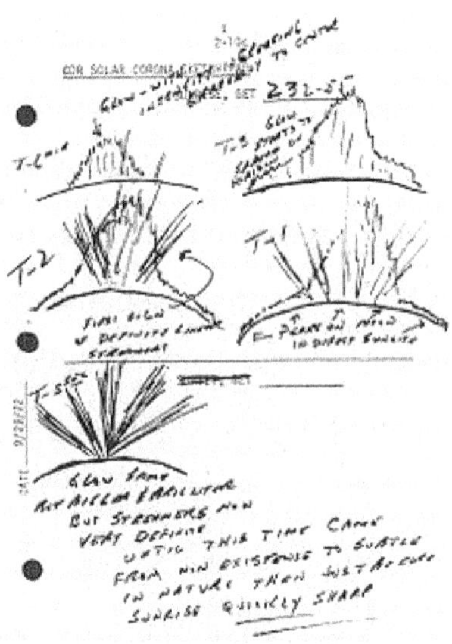

A former NASA contractor when asked in a public interview about anomalies in photos of the moon, Mars and the Earth's poles said a NASA higher up told her, "We always have to airbrush them out."

Four kids had been through more than they could comprehend. A lifetime had been lived in a summer.

Matt learned people make this mad, mad Grimm's fairy tale world we exist in, not things. He still didn't give a flying fig newton for those silly stick figure families on the backs of minivans but then who does. He learned life is beautiful but many things in it are not. And Harry Houdini, the world's greatest escape artist of all time, never came back from the dead with the password he had given his wife, proving ghosts are a red herring. No, not a fish. The other meaning; something intended to mislead. There has been no shortage of ghosts claiming to be him, however, a constant stream to this day. But not a one has ever known the password.

Having pulled back The Great and Powerful Wizard's curtain and exposed the demons' veil of lies, Matt got his payback for Emmet Till, George Stinney and the millions of other kids, including the little boy in the Nazi extermination camp who thought he was walking somewhere in his new shoes to get soup. Though he had missed World War II he was right on time for World War D.

Matt formally declared war on the "goats" as he called them.

And Cathy gave up learning to run in high heels having found fighting demons far easier.

And somewhere in Hades the Devil, the fool he is, is still doing the Funky Chicken with jingle bells, in his court fool finest having been ordered never to stop – ever. And boy is he tired.

World War II isn't over. The battle for Earth is underway. ■

EPILOGUE

The Desert Speaks

– CNN; 29 August

"Scientists are baffled by the discovery of hundreds of thousands of human bone fragments found in a half-square mile section of the Libyan desert. Estimates vary but experts say the number of bodies could reach forty thousand. The remains, discovered by a Suncor oil exploration team, at first thought to be the victims of an oppressive modern day regime, have been carbon dated at 900-1000 B.C., the reign of King Solomon. A forensics expert stated the only bones he's ever seen like them are skydivers' whose chutes failed to open. "It's very strange," the expert said. "It's like forty thousand people fell out of the sky.

"for CNN, Katie Loveland reporting"

○ ○ ○

"Welcome back to Skyfell and to AP English. I'm Sister Ramirez. Your assignment in 500 words or less is to write on 'How I spent my summer vacation.' "

APPENDIX

The think tank set about seeking a way to rid the body of those terrible nanos from the chemtrails.

It discovered the nanos have a positive electric charge and can be drawn out of the body by a substance with a negative electric charge.

Like charges repel, opposite charges attract.

After some experimentation they discovered calcium bentonite clay powder. It takes on a negative charge when mixed with water and worked like a charm in ridding their bodies of the harmful positive-charged nanos, pulling them out like a magnet. After they figured out how much to take (it seemed half a teaspoon to a teaspoon a day was the right amount) they took it daily. They found it also detoxified their bodies of the heavy metals and held many other healthful benefits. Cathy put it in her smoothies.

ENDNOTES

1. The Battle of Los Angeles – Los Angeles launched into a panic in the wee hours of February 25, 1942 when a large low-flying unidentified object moved silently and slowly over Culver City and Santa Monica, close to the Pacific Ocean. The object, lit by nine powerful searchlights from the ground which converged on the object revealed the barely discernable outline of a UFO. The U.S. Army's 37th Coast Atillery Brigade fired 1,440 shells at it from anti-aircraft guns at almost point-blank range, all with no visible effect. Awakened by sirens and the guns firing, almost everybody got up and went outside to see it. It continued to drift slowly toward Long Beach before vanishing. It was described as a glowing pale orange in color. The incident became known as the Battle of Los Angeles.

Actual news photo taken at the Battle of Los Angeles

2. NSA ET Contact – On April 21, 2011, the National Security Agency (NSA) authorized the release of a portion of a top-secret report, NSA

Journal Vol. XIV No.1. The report addressed the decoding of 29 messages that were received from 'outer space.' The release was in response to the NSA's loss ina lawsuit brought against it by Arizona lawyer Peter Gersten. The judge's order had to be carried out and the documents had to be released.

3. Malibu Underwater UFO Base – Six miles off the coast of Point Dume in Malibu at a depth of 2,000 feet is an artificial domed structure measuring 3 miles wide with a perfectly-symmetrical oval-shaped flat top supported by vertical columns with a clearly defined entrance. It is well documented.

4. A Time Without A Moon – The memory of a world without a moon for a period lives in the oral tradition among Indians such as the Indians of the Bogota highlands in the eastern Cordilleras of Colombia which tell of a time when the Earth had no moon. "In the earliest times, when the moon was not yet in the heavens," the Chibchas tribesmen say.

5. Mermaid Sighting at Kiryat Yam, Israel – Mermaid sightings reported in Kiryat Yam Town council offering $1 million reward for proof of mythical creature.

By JERUSALEM POST Staff AUGUST 11, 2009 22:06
Israel is in the grips of mermaid fever after numerous sightings of the mythical sea creature off its coast. One town council is taking the reports so seriously it is offering a $1 million reward to anyone who can prove the existence of a mermaid in its waters. Kiryat Yam municipality, near Haifa, says it has been told of dozens of sightings in the past few months. "Many

people are telling us they are sure they've seen a mermaid and they are all independent of each other," council spokesman Natti Zilberman told Sky News. The nautical nymph is only seen in the evening at sunset, according to media reports, drawing crowds of people with cameras hoping for a glimpse. "People say it is half girl, half fish, jumping like a dolphin. It does all kinds of tricks, then disappears," Mr. Zilberman said. Asked whether a dolphin or large fish could be a more rational explanation, he insisted: "They say it is a female figure, it looks like a young girl." The council denied its offer of a reward was a publicity stunt, but said it hoped to nurture the mermaid as something which could bring in more tourists. Capturing a mermaid is not necessary, a verifiable photograph will do, Zilberman said. Asked if the council can afford the payout, he told Sky News: "I believe, if there really is a mermaid, then so many people and tourists will come to Kiryat Yam, a lot more money will be made than $1m."

6. Demonic Elements To UFOs – UFO contactees report the same physical, mental, emotional and spiritual manifestations as do victims of demonism. For example, they report voices in the mind, walking through solid objects, tormenting, etc. People who work with spirit mediums report the same thing. This is also true of those who have contact with UFO's.

7. 9/11 Demon Face in the Smoke (Associated Press Photo) –

Actual official unretouched photograph

8. The Outer Barrier –

(1) Scientists Confirm Discovery of a Mysterious Wall At Edge of Solar System; UNILAD, 11 Nov 2019;

(2) NASA Probe Detects Glowing "Wall" Around Our Solar System; Yahoo News UK, 16 August 2018;

(3) Deadly 50,000°C 'Wall of Fire' Surrounding Our Solar System Discovered By NASA Probe; The Sun, 22 November 2019

9. CONPLAN 8888-11 – (Excerpt from *Forbes Magazine*; May 29, 2014), 'A U.S. Zombie Government Plan?' – "In 2011 a plan drafted by the U.S. Government called CONPLAN 8888-11, "Counter-Zombie Dominance" was revealed to the public. The document details a strategy to defend against a zombie attack. And yes, it's real. We verified that the U.S. Government did in fact publish this report."

10. UNBREAKABLE BONES – (Excerpt from *Yale Medicine*, Autumn 2002), '"Unbreakable" bones prompt a hunt for genes" – "The DNA of an extended Connecticut family has yielded a possible target for the treatment and prevention of osteoporosis, according to Yale scientists who reported their findings in the May issue of *The New England Journal of Medicine*. Members of this family carry a genetic mutation that causes high bone density. They have a deep and wide jaw and bony growth on the palate."

○ ○ ○

Thought Question – How credible is it to think that thousands of extraterrestrials would fly millions of light years simply to teach New Age philosophy from the shadows instead of immediately requesting to be taken to our leader?......Why would they consistently lie about things we know are true and why do they deceive those they contact and abduct?

If they were here to help there would be no need to hide. Stock markets would soar in the anticipation of amazing advances in health and technology. But they are not here to help. They are here for something else.

Matt Legend will return in:

Matt Legend: The Hollow Earth

Ten months have passed since Matt Legend helped save the world from a nuclear winter. Now another extinction-level event threatens.

Upon discovering an ancient nine-foot-wide borehole in Wyoming with no apparent bottom scientists have opened a Pandora's Box. What they see and hear on the GoPro they drop down sends them fleeing. Unless they can determine what they did that caused a tear in the space-time continuum which is rippling outward from it in 33.3 mile bursts every 33.3 minutes, it will sweep across the Earth, returning it to the way it was 50 million years ago. Only the advanced inhabitants of the inner earth can stop it but they consider humans vermin.

As with every Matt Legend tale this story is inspired by real events. More evidence the truth is not only stranger than we think but stranger than w'e are capable of thinking.

www.ingramcontent.com/pod-product-compliance
Lightning Source LLC
Chambersburg PA
CBHW070644310726
48982CB00001B/406

* 9 7 8 8 4 0 9 0 3 8 0 9 1 *